Alfred Frederic Falloux

Life and Letters of Madame Swetchine

Alfred Frederic Falloux

Life and Letters of Madame Swetchine

ISBN/EAN: 9783337015961

Printed in Europe, USA, Canada, Australia, Japan

Cover: Foto ©Raphael Reischuk / pixelio.de

More available books at **www.hansebooks.com**

LIFE AND LETTERS

OF

MADAME SWETCHINE.

MADAME SWETCHINE.

BY

COUNT DE FALLOUX,
OF THE FRENCH ACADEMY.

TRANSLATED BY H. W. PRESTON.

BOSTON:
ROBERTS BROTHERS.
1867.

CAMBRIDGE:

STEREOTYPED AND PRINTED BY JOHN WILSON AND SON.

INTRODUCTORY NOTICE.

THE conscientious pains taken by the translator to make the present volume a clear and correct English representation of the French original have, it is hoped, been crowned with marked success. Whether this has been achieved, is left to the decision of the critics. But as to the substantial interest and value of the work itself, there can be no question.

The outer life of Mme. Swetchine was laid amidst scenes combining, in a high degree, almost all the elements of power and splendor and romantic vicissitude adapted to awaken and gratify curiosity.

The record of her inner life is richer still in attractiveness and instruction. She was an acute and unwearied student of herself and of others. In the course of her mental career, she ran through the whole scale of human experience, either directly or by a moral mastery of the secrets of society. Few women have lived so deep and wide and crowded a life as she, or with such a profound appreciation of its contents. Nothing which combined energy, wisdom and innocence can fathom, was unknown to her.

As a character, Mme. Swetchine must henceforth hold a front place among the most powerful, original, pure and fascinating, revealed in all history. The combination in her of natural force, intense passion, acquired knowledge, resignation, and repose, is truly wonderful. The picture of her steady progress from the perturbations of earthly and personal desires, towards the perfection of saintly virtue and peace, is charming in its portrayal, and divine in its significance.

During the largest part of her long and rich life, Mme. Swetchine stood in intimate relations with a large number of the noblest, most interesting, and commanding characters of her century. These are described by M. de Falloux, and their mutual relations set forth, with great precision and skill. The history of the central personage forms a glorious, spiritual epic. The accounts of her friends make a portrait-gallery of exalted characters.

It may seem strange, that a work so eminently Catholic in its quality as this biography should be introduced to a Protestant people by a Protestant translator and Protestant publishers. But, on further consideration, will not this be found especially fit and serviceable? In this country, a traditional antipathy or bigoted repugnance to the Catholic Church prevails in an unjustifiable extreme. Whatever is repulsive in the Catholic dogmas or rule is fastened on with unwarrantable acrimony and exclusiveness. The interests alike of justice and of good feeling demand that the attention of Protestants shall, at least occasionally, be given to the best ingredients and workings of the Catholic system. In the present work, we have the forensic doctrine and authority of Catholicity in the background, its purest inner aims and life in the foreground. We here have a beautiful specimen of the style of character and experience which the most imposing organic Symbol of Christendom tends to produce, and has, in all the ages of its mighty reign, largely produced. If every bigoted disliker of the Roman Catholic Church within the English-speaking race could read this book, and, as a consequence, have his prejudices lessened, his sympathies enlarged, the result, so far from being deprecated, should be warmly welcomed. This is written by one who, while enthusiastically admiring the spiritual wealth of the Catholic Church, the ineffable tenderness and beauty of its moral and religious ministrations, is, as to its dogmatic fabric and secular sway, even more than a Protestant of the Protestants.

Finally, this book is especially commended to women as a work of inestimable worth. The character and life of Mme. Swetchine, her lonely studies and aspirations, her sublime personal attainments, her philanthropic labors, her literary productions, her sweet social charm and vast influence, her thrice-royal friendships with kings and geniuses and saints, the sober raptures of her religious faith and fruition, form an example whose exciting and edifying interest and value are scarcely surpassed in the annals of her sex.

WILLIAM ROUNSEVILLE ALGER.

AUTHOR'S PREFACE.

WHAT Mme. Swetchine was, others have told, and others will yet tell, better than I. No one will tell it better than herself in this volume, which contains at once her thoughts and her example.

Yet I owe the public a word. I feel bound to explain by what means, and under what circumstances, I became the depositary of the treasure which is soon to pass from my hands into those of the public.

Mme. Swetchine herself — and I can support the assertion by a thousand irrefragable proofs — never conceived the ambition of posthumous fame. Her constant and much-to-be-lamented anxiety was to keep a veil between her private life and the world, and never allow it to be raised. In this respect, her humility took every precaution which a haughty reserve could have suggested; and she was always humble.

After the death of General Swetchine, Mme. Swetchine made known her purpose to appoint me the executor of her will. She had mentioned the subject

to me ; speaking, however, from a purely legal point
of view, and without allowing me the slightest
glimpse of her intentions concerning her memoir.
I was so profoundly sure that she would shroud in
inviolable obscurity all which concerned herself personally, that I never felt at liberty to question her,
or to obtain information which would have been
exceedingly precious to me as her biographer.

Mme. Swetchine did not suppose it possible for
her life to be written, or her works published.
Never, for an instant, did she either hope or fear
that her papers would be examined with the minute-
ness necessary for the discovery and restoration of
their connected order. Nevertheless, when she honored me with this legacy, I believe she did it delib-
erately, and not without the affectionate and discerning
thought which she exercised in other matters.

During her lifetime, she had no desire either to
hoard her thoughts, or to make them public. Neither
did she wish arbitrarily to condemn aught, save that
which she destroyed, out of prudence or delicacy for
others. Many of her books of notes, extracts, and
pious meditations, were sources of pleasure and
profit to herself; and for her own use she preserved
them till the day of her death. She left to Providence the care of determining the value and the
destiny of these scattered fragments ; but, with all
her discretion, she was not forgetful. She would
never have deprived her friends of a source of consolation and support ; still less would she have

arranged and prescribed the execution of any wish
of her own. By withholding all confidential communications and indications, by the absence, as it
were, of any conducting wire, she caused all the
chances to lean to the side which she preferred, —
that is, the side of silence. After that, she closed
her eyes to the future, accepting whatever resolution her friends might take, as a decision in which
it had sufficed her to have no voice.

The judgment and the wish of the friends consulted have been unanimous. I will venture to add,
that she herself justified us in advance, when she
wrote as follows, on the death of her friend, the
Princess Alexis Galitzin : —

"If I might make a suggestion, I would entreat you to com-
mit to paper a few dates, a few words, some slight sketch, for
the sake of preserving the memory of that holy woman. I know
well that she needs it not, and that all which concerns her now
is, that her name be inscribed in the book of life ; but for us, and
those who are to come after us, it is a great consolation to know
something of our elders in the faith. As long as we are ignorant of their character, their vocation, and the acts of their lives,
they live for us in an abstract state ; and abstractions, as you
well know, do not touch the heart."

These lines alone would have sufficed for the security of my conscience, and the inspiration of my
work.

CONTENTS.

CHAPTER I.

CHAPTER II.

CHAPTER III.

CHAPTER IV.

CHAPTER V.

CHAPTER VI.

CHAPTER VII.

CHAPTER VIII.

CHAPTER IX.

CHAPTER X.

CHAPTER XI.

CHAPTER XII.

CHAPTER XIII.

CHAPTER XIV.

CHAPTER XV.

CHAPTER XVI.

CHAPTER XVII.

LIFE OF MADAME SWETCHINE.

CHAPTER I.

A glance at the court of Russia in the eighteenth century. — Birth of Madame Swetchine. — Her education. — Her marriage.

MADAME SWETCHINE was born at Moscow, on the 22d of November, 1782. Her father, M. Soymonof, was descended from an ancient Muscovite family, occupied an important post in the internal administration of the empire, and was one of the founders of the Academy of Sciences at Moscow. Her mother belonged to an equally distinguished race, remarkable alike for literary taste and military ability. She was the daughter of Major-General Jean Boltine, a native of the environs of Kasan; and one of her ancestors had been Russian ambassador to Denmark. General Boltine kept up a protracted controversy with Prince Sherebatof on the subject of the Russian annals, — several pages of which he helped to elucidate; and he carried the translation of the French Encyclopedia into Russian up to the nineteenth volume.

At that period, even more than at present, Moscow was the real national capital of Russia; and the most illustrious of her country's memories mingled naturally with Mme. Swetchine's earliest impressions. It will be necessary to pass in rapid review the events, the contrasts, the spectacles, which were the first teachers of her young

.

1

mind, and long continued to influence her, if we would not
neglect the principal feature of a rare predestination, and
make light of that love of country which she so faithfully
cherished.   In her biography there are facts which cannot
be adequately appreciated till one has become penetrated
with the true spirit of the Russian mind and manners at
that epoch, and till the reader has first transported himself into a realm of history differing widely from our own
time in its habits of thought and action.

Russia — although the rude interruption of her history
by the will of a single man has utterly changed its tendency, its theatre, and its aspect — is not merely a powerful empire: she is an original and mighty nationality.
A survey of the Kremlin at Moscow is equivalent to a
rapid review of the surviving traces of the old Russian
dynasties, and leaves a profound impression upon the
memory.

The common notion in France is, that the Kremlin is
a citadel, and that there is no other kremlin except that
of Moscow.   Both these ideas are erroneous.   Every
ancient and important Russian town has a fortified enclo-
sure containing a church, which is the object of peculiar
reverence, — often several of them, — a convent, a maga-
zine for artillery, and some munitions of war.   This *ensemble* they call a kremlin.   It is, in effect, a fortress where
the people concentrates all which constitutes its strength;
its religion, namely, its archives, and its arms.   Treasures
of the most important and interesting nature have accumulated at Moscow in this triple connection.

In the centre of the Kremlin stands the cathedral; beyond are the old manor of the Czars, the senatorial palace,
and, lastly, the arsenal.   Here are collected relics of all
the ages, from the sceptre and globe sent by Alexis Com-

menes to Vladimir Monomachus, to the litter of Charles XII., a trophy of the battle of Pultowa. The crowns worn by the successive Russian sovereigns are arranged in their historical order. A single glance comprehends them all: the first, simple fur caps, adorned with some cheap emblems; afterwards, velvet skull-caps, enriched with precious stones; lastly, the modern diadem of gold and diamonds. Then come the thrones: the ivory one of Iwan III. Wasiliewitch, carved in the Byzantine style; that of Boris Godounof, a wooden seat plated with gold, a present to the Czar from a shah of Persia. Alone on a platform at the back of a gallery, there is a double-seated throne of silver gilt, which attracts the attention less by the magnificence of its workmanship and its profusion of turquoises than by the singular arrangement of a movable curtain behind it, which falls from a spacious daïs, and served to associate in the royal scene a third invisible personage. This is supposed to have been the Princess Sophia, who used to dictate to her two brothers, Iwan and Peter, the words which she dared not trust to their infantine or intractable memories. But the younger of the two brothers soon grew weary of this tutelage; the prompter was relegated to a monastery, Iwan was reduced to silence, and Peter the Great was left the sole occupant of this throne, which he found none too large.

The revolt of the Strelitz, which had rendered his accession bloody and terrible, had left on his mind an ineffaceable impression of the barbarous violence of his subjects. His education, necessarily confided to strangers of different nationalities, had developed this germ; and the Prince grew up with a determination to implant European civilization by main force in the heart of Russia. Every thing was sacrificed to this dominant idea, — his repose, his

dignity, the life of his own son, the old ancestral residence of his predecessors. Peter knew well that he could
not accomplish single-handed the regeneration of which
he dreamed. He wished to open to strangers a door into
his realm, and to his subjects a window with a view of
Europe. St. Petersburg was improvised in the midst
of sands and surge. Was this enterprise, undertaken in
defiance of the soil and the traditions of a people, a success? It is still an open question. To this very day, the
traveller meets, as he would have met two centuries ago,
with Russians who are smitten with love of the young
Prince Alexis, who leagued with the long-beards to resist
the impetuous innovations of his father, and who fell a
victim to his fidelity to the old Russian instinct. Whatever may yet result from the rival destinies of St. Petersburg and Moscow, an undeniable revolution took place in
the lifetime of Peter the Great, and survived him. Progress in the mechanic arts, and even in the sciences; the
improvement of mines; a stronger military organization;
the creation of a navy; acquisitions of territory; and constant and deliberate invasions of other lands, — date from
his reign. But unlimited power was at the same time
inaugurated, in lieu of the laws and customs with which
authority had hitherto been clothed. The supreme power
destroyed at one blow its useful auxiliaries and its inconvenient opponents. Attendance at the court and residence on the great estates having become incompatible,
lord and peasant lost sight of one another to their mutual
disadvantage; serfdom, far from being expunged from the
annals, was perpetuated and aggravated; the remnants
of religious liberty were swept away; the Czar became
absolute pontiff of the Church, as well as sole head of
the State; confiscation accompanied the administration

of justice, and corrupted it; even the rules of the royal succession were abolished; and forty years afterwards, at the close of a reign of crude and fantastic grandeur, Peter departed this life, leaving behind him only a huge rough sketch, and as many ruins as monuments. His successors inherited an irresponsible despotism, chastised but unmitigated by plots and assassinations. Paul I. soon became possible, and Alexander necessary.

Catharine I., the second wife of Peter the Great, succeeded him, with no better title than the ascendency of the favorite Menchikoff at the head of a soldiery which he had carried away, won over, or intimidated. The wife of a Swedish corporal, taken prisoner by the Russians; rendered conspicuous, first by her beauty, afterwards by her courage and presence of mind, — Catharine I., in the field and upon the throne, is the representative of one of Fortune's caprices. She died two years after the Czar, worn out by the abuse of intoxicating liquors; a vice which had first stimulated and then conquered her, by imbruting the very intelligence which had paved her way to supreme power.

Peter II., son of the unfortunate Alexis, who was proclaimed emperor at the age of fifteen, but succumbed almost immediately to an attack of small-pox, is scarcely to be counted in the chronology of the Russian monarchs.

The Empress Anne, Duchess of Courland, was the next occupant of this formidable throne. She made use of the new attributes which the sovereign authority had arrogated to itself, and named as her heir an infant in the cradle, a son of Prince Anton of Brunswick, who was connected on his mother's side with the imperial family. The Duchess of Brunswick was angry at finding herself balked of the prerogatives of the regency in the interest of the Duke of Courland; and the field-marshal, Munich, promised to avenge her. Followed by forty grenadiers, he went, one night, and seized the Duke of Courland in his bed, and exiled him to Siberia. A daughter of Peter the Great, Elizabeth, who had beheld with the seeming calm of passive indifference the accomplishment of these ambitious revolutions, suddenly takes a new turn, or is relieved from her abnegation. Woronzof is summoned; the imperial palace is once more invaded at night by three hundred grenadiers; the Duke and Duchess of Courland are confined at Riga; and the infant Emperor Iwan is shut up in the fortified monastery of Waldaï, and afterwards transferred to the citadel of Schlusselburg.

The movement which had placed Elizabeth upon the throne was not confined to the narrow circle of the conspirators. It appeased the national dissatisfaction, which was everywhere manifesting itself against the interference of foreigners in the government of Russia. A single day saw the principal personages in the empire led to punishment, — Munich, Osterman, Mengden, and some others. Chancellor Osterman, who had presided for several reigns over the conduct of foreign affairs, was carried down in an arm-chair while suffering from an attack of the gout, and enveloped in a dressing-gown. The executioner placed the Chancellor's head upon the block, bared his neck, and raised the axe. At that moment, an officer came up, and announced that the Empress had granted Osterman his life, but condemned him to perpetual exile. The old minister merely bowed his head in acknowledgment of the favor, and said, without the slightest trace of emotion in his countenance, "I would thank you for my cap and perruque." The other victims, who were assembled at the foot of the same scaffold, then received commutation of their sentence. Munich and Osterman were sent to Siberia, while the Duke of Courland was recalled thence. The old regent, and he who had ousted him from power, met at a relay station in a suburb of Kasan. They regarded one another with astonishment, exchanged a courteous but silent salute, and continued their opposite routes.

For a long time, Elizabeth divided her confidence between two simultaneous favorites. Razoumofski and Schouvalof vied with one another without jealousy, and behaved less like rivals than colleagues. The conflicts of Europe had not yet shaken the Russian government; and the employment of its mighty resources was confined to neighborhood quarrels with Sweden, Poland, and the Ottoman Porte. Elizabeth, however, interfered actively between Prussia, Austria, and Hungary. The cabinets of St. James and Versailles maintained at her court accredited diplomatic agents of a distinguished rank; and Frederic wrote as follows in his military memoirs: "Of all the neighbors of Prussia, the Russian Empire is the most dangerous, and deserves the most attention. It is powerful, and it is near. The future rulers of Prussia will be under an equal necessity of cultivating the friendship of these barbarians."

Count Schouvalof was a lover of the fine arts, and did much to cultivate a taste for them at the Russian court. He founded the University of Moscow, the eldest and foremost of the Russian universities, and opened with the French philosophers that correspondence which attracted to St. Petersburg the attention and the respect of the eighteenth century. He conceived the idea of intrusting to Voltaire the mission of writing the history of Peter the Great, and transmitted to him those mutilated and sycophantic memoirs on which the popular judgment of this prince is based. Finally, he introduced the French language into the official documents, and founded a French theatre at St. Petersburg.

Civilization continued to spread in Russia; but the improvement was superficial, not thorough. Immorality made its way into high places, along with polish of manner. The lower classes were taught dissimulation rather than probity, privileged abuses claimed the right to walk abroad without disguise, and no thoughtful or careful study was bestowed upon the tumults and oppressions of the people. Costumes were changed rather than manners; and a people, than which there is none more richly gifted with intelligence and vigor, was made a spectacle of by its masters, rather than conscientiously prepared for the accomplishment of its true destiny.

Elizabeth died in 1761. Her chosen successor was her nephew, Ulric of Holstein Gottorp, whose mother was a daughter of Peter the Great. He took the title of Peter III. The wife who was to share his throne was Sophia of Anhalt-Zerbst. On embracing the Greek religion, she took the name of Catharine, which was given her by the Empress Elizabeth. An avowed misunderstanding already existed between the married pair at the time when they assumed the crown. Peter III. offended the Russians by the sternness of his manners, and by his extravagant fondness for the Prussian discipline. The young officers passed rapidly from discontent to conspiracy. Peter III. was attacked at Peterhof, while the Empress continued to reside at St. Petersburg. The abdication and death of Peter were the mysterious business of a few hours, and the Empress was proclaimed under the name of Catharine II.

Such an advent necessitated the hushing of many rumors, and the flattery of many hopes. Having been crowned with great pomp at Moscow in 1762, Catharine summoned to her presence the deputies from all parts of her empire, with the purpose of submitting to them her plans for reform and new institutions. An assembly of something like two hundred members, representing hostile interests, and speaking different languages, fatigued and frightened her.. The deputations were dismissed, and pleasure once more took precedence of business.

But Catharine never lost sight of her double purpose of winning the hearts of her subjects, and securing the suffrages of those who dispense European fame. M. de Breteuil, the ambassador of Louis XV., wrote from St. Petersburg to Versailles: "The Czarina has taken pains to ascertain whether or no I am acquainted with M. de Voltaire, in order to insure the rectification of his ideas about the melancholy tragedy of Peterhof." The education of her only son, the Grand-duke Paul, was offered to D'Alembert: Grimm and Diderot were summoned to St. Petersburg. Baron Grimm, who had left Bavaria for Russia, soon established himself at Paris in the character of diplomatic historian and literary *chargé d'affaires.* Diderot wrote to his Parisian friends: "I am treated here as the representative of the honorable and able portion of my countrymen." He was, however, opposed to maintaining the seat of government at St. Petersburg, and often repeated that " to have the capital at the extremity of the kingdom was like having the heart at the fingers' ends: it rendered the circulation difficult, and the least wound mortal." Before returning to France, Diderot imparted to the Empress a number of plans for the education of her people, all of which she promptly forgot. Other selections were more fortunate. Prussia saw herself deprived of the laborious and celebrated naturalist Pallas, of whom Cuvier said, "He just missed of changing the whole aspect of zoölogy: he actually did change that of the theory of the earth." In short, a just appreciation of the difficulties, if not of the duties, of her situation; an ambition cherished and ripened in her youth; frivolity of taste joined with grandeur of imagination; a constant pre-occupation with schemes of fascination and seduction, — all these suggested to Catharine incessant enterprises, often less important than they appeared, but always gorgeous and imposing.

Nevertheless, this height of prosperity was not exempt from trouble and menace. A simple Cossack, Pugatchef, conceived the bold project of passing himself off for Peter III., raised regiments in the provinces, and was vanquished only at the gates of Moscow. The imperial captive at Schlusselburg, young Iwan VI., was poniarded by his guards, who had their orders beforehand, at the very moment when an attempt which had been crowned with an initial success was about to place him at the head of an armed insurrection.

These storms allayed, the court continued to ring with the feuds of the favorites, Gregory and Alexis Orlof, and Potemkin, who took turns in stirring up cabals which assumed dangerous proportions. All the ambassadors entertained their sovereigns with them, as with events which exercised an immediate influence upon Russian politics.

One day, the Empress sent for Count Alexis Orlof, and addressed him as follows: "Make friends with Potemkin. See that this extraordinary man is more circumspect in his conduct, more careful in the fulfilment of the duties

her travels in the Crimea, where she had seen so many make-believe villages, and ephemeral foundations, wittily characterized by the Emperor Joseph II. when he said, "The Empress and I did a great thing this morning: she laid the first stone of a city, and I the last!"

The fairy pantomimes performed at the Hermitage were the first to strike the imagination of the child, who, as yet, relished neither the tragedies of Voltaire, nor those of Count de Segur, — then ambassador of Louis XVI., — nor the dramas of the Empress herself. The little girl took it into her head to compose a ballet, which she entitled "The Faithful Shepherdess and the Fickle Shepherdess." She danced and played all its scenes to her father; and he imparted to his friends the extreme pleasure it had given him, — a success which made so deep an impression upon her childish memory, that it woke a smile in advanced age.

The palace was resplendent with gilding, and brightly lighted every evening; and the slightest pretext was seized upon for a sumptuous illumination. These also little Sophia repeated in her play. A long gallery led to the saloon of M. Soymonof, where she often abandoned herself to the enjoyment of her great dolls, and her ingenious inventions. She had passed her sixtieth year, when she wrote as follows: "One of the liveliest pleasures of my childhood was to compose festive decorations, which I loved to light up, and arrange upon the white-marble chimney-piece of my schoolroom. The ardor which I threw into designing, cutting out, and painting transparencies, and finding emblems and mottoes for them, was something incredible. My heart beat high while the preparations were in progress; but, the moment my illumination began to fade, an ineffable, devouring melancholy seized me.   God, the world, all Christianity, were revealed to the soul of a child; and never has the 'sic transit gloria mundi' saddened me more than then."

One evening in the autumn of 1789, M. Soymonof, when he returned to his rooms, was astonished to find his gallery studded and sparkling with an innumerable quantity of little candles. Being interrogated as to the occasion of so grand a festival, his daughter replied, "O papa! shall we not celebrate the taking of the Bastile, and the release of those poor French prisoners?" One may judge by this of the habitual tenor of the conversations in which, at that early age, the child felt an interest, and bore a part. In short, the reigning fashion in the north of Europe, at Berlin, at Vienna, and, above all, at St. Petersburg, was to resent the abuses of power, to speak warmly of the redress of all wrongs, of human liberty and dignity, and of the general emancipation of nations and of mind. In a moment of truly royal inspiration, Peter the Great let fall this avowal: "Ah me! I have toiled to reform my subjects, but I know not how to reform myself."   This noble word was yet to be the motto of Catharine and her court, and of the majority of the reformers of the eighteenth century.

M. Soymonof, who had all the accomplishments of his time, had also all its illusions.   He was generous, liberal, interested in any prospect of social amelioration, but oblivious of experience, Utopian in his schemes, and utterly led astray by his irreligious prejudices.   Under these circumstances, the education of his daughter was finished, and nothing neglected save the idea of a divine law.

No better teaching had the Empress Catharine herself received from her father, the Prince of Anhalt.   A low-born governess had scarcely taught her to read when she was taken to Russia, where the first work which fell into her hands was Bayle's Dictionary, which she read with avidity three times in succession in the course of a few months.

At the age of fourteen, Sophia Soymonof was acquainted with the Russian language, of which most of her compatriots were ignorant, spoke English and Italian with as much ease and purity as French, and the German correctly, and was studying Latin, Greek, and Hebrew. But she knew no religious exercises save the pompous spectacles of the imperial chapel, and had never called upon God to bless the beginning or end of the day. Her heart's instinct, the love which she bore her father, and the almost maternal cares which she lavished upon her young sister, born in 1792, — these had been her sole guides, and had sustained her in well-doing.

The attention with which the French Revolution was regarded at St. Petersburg was as profound as its catastrophes had been unexpected. The Empress assumed at first an angry and threatening attitude, but soon foresaw the cue which covetousness and ambition might take from the Revolution. In 1794, Poland was invaded anew; and Catharine was preparing an expedition against the English dominion in Bengal, when death overtook her. She was seized with terrible apoplexy, on the morning of the 9th of November, 1796, in the midst of the pleasures and projects which age had neither interrupted nor abated.

The Prince who ascended the throne under the name of Paul I. had been kept, until the age of forty-two, under frigid and severe restraint. His mother had given him no proofs of affection or confidence. The favorites, who in turn disputed one another's pre-eminence, found it advantageous to keep him out of the way. His youth wore away in ennui and constraint, and he sometimes even feared for his own life. The Empress, we are assured, cherished the design of disinheriting her son, and substituting her grandson Alexander. The young Grandduke had been proclaimed Czarowitch; and Potemkin, at the same time, King of Tauride. But the horror which Catharine experienced at the thought of death; her unwillingness to contemplate the future of her kingdom; and the sudden death of Potemkin, who expired by the wayside, at the foot of a tree, while travelling in the Chersonese, — prevented the Empress from realizing her plan, and bequeathing him to Russia in her will.

In vain had Paul pleaded with his mother for the honor of commanding an army. Catharine could not forget after what fashion the way to the throne had more than once been opened. On one occasion only, she associated him with her policy. · It was when she despatched him to Austria, Italy, and France, to strengthen and draw closer the bonds of alliance with those countries. When war was declared against the Turks in 1788, Paul insisted on taking part in it. "All Europe," he said to his mother, "knows how I desire to fight the Ottomans. What will they think when they hear that I cannot do it?" — "They will think," replied the Empress coldly, "that the Grand-duke is a dutiful son."

Paul was in the habit of living at some distance from St. Petersburg, at Gatschin, a country-seat which he had by degrees converted into a kind of stronghold, flanked by towers, and surrounded by moats and drawbridges. His face was harsh, and almost deformed; the cartilage of his nose being pressed down into his cheeks in consequence of a surgical operation. After a first marriage, which lasted but a year, he contracted a second with the Princess Mary of Wurtemberg. The change of rulers re-acted immediately upon the life of Sophia Soymonof, who was just entering upon her sixteenth year, and was appointed maid of honor to the new sovereign.

The Empress Mary, under whose auspices young Sophia was now to grow up, was in all respects an illustrious example of amiability and high principle. Gifted with rare beauty, and encompassed by seduction, she did not give occasion for a single calumny. She was the mother of six children, and their education was the business of her life. The accession of Paul and Mary at first belied the unfavorable auguries which some sagacious minds had drawn from the imperious and gloomy character of the Grand-duke. He displayed a touching — some said an ostentatious — anxiety to reclaim the dishonored memory of the unhappy Peter III. The Baron Ungern-Sternberg, an old man of eighty, formerly aide-de-camp to his father, was living in retirement and oblivion. Paul created him general-in-chief, summoned him to the palace, and, turning to a portrait of Peter III., whose image saw the light for the first time in forty years, "I wish," he said to the old man, who was affected to tears, "that your former master should be witness to my remembrance of his faithful friends."

The body of Peter III. had been obscurely buried in the convent of St. Alexander Newski. Paul repaired thither. The astonished monks conducted him to that forsaken tomb; the coffin was opened; the Emperor kneeled down, and seizing the glove, which still covered the withered hand, he kissed it with emotion and respect. Solemn obsequies were ordained; and all who might feel their presence at the funeral ceremonies as a just and memorable reproof were constrained to take part in them.

But formidable symptoms soon gained the ascendency in Paul's character. His reprisals on his mother's reign were pushed to an injurious and puerile extreme. Rings which bore upon an enamel shield the date of Catharine's death, had been distributed to the court so long under her sway. Her son was jealous of these rings; and, not content with proscribing them, he gave out others, on which was engraved, "Paul is my consolation." His arrogance was as alert as his jealousy. General Dumouriez, having on one occasion missed the hour appointed for an interview, excused himself by laying the blame upon a person of considerable importance in the empire, whom he had met. "Understand, monsieur," replied Paul, "that there is no considerable personage in my house, save he with whom I am conversing for the time being."

The Empress Mary controlled his fits of passion, but only by dint of sweetness, humility, and patience. Capricious exactions, excessive fatigue, distasteful exercise, she underwent with a smile. Neither prostrating heat nor freezing snow interrupted their horseback rides. The Emperor delighted to station her on some elevated point, to serve as an aim or a landmark for military manœuvres. It was a rare thing for her to be released from this painful situation short of some hours, and occasionally she was forgotten for a whole day. The serenity of her spirit was never visibly altered by these things; but Mlle. Soymonof, who, at a subsequent period, was to appreciate, anticipate, and console so many sorrows, began even then to guess the secret of deceitful prosperity and silent tears.

Under this wholesome guardianship, Sophia Soymonof attained her seventeenth year. Residence at court had not rendered her idle, and emulation had stimulated her in her accomplishments. Crayon drawings of hers are still in existence, which would do honor to a professional artist. Her voice — rich, sonorous, flexible, and of extraordinary compass — was trained in the scientific and affecting harmonies of the North, as well as in the brilliant melodies of Italy. She sang music at sight, and accompanied herself upon the piano.

Her personal appearance was not remarkable; but her face, her gestures, and the accents of her voice, were endowed with an indefinable sympathetic charm. Her blue eyes were small, and slightly irregular, but lively and kind. She had a piquant, Calmuck nose, and a brilliantly fresh complexion. Her height was medium, her gait graceful and easy, her lightest word and movement stamped alike with refinement and distinction.

At an early age, she had numerous and ardent suitors. M. Soymonof could not see falling around him the men whom Catharine had invested with the highest offices, without a fear that he, in his turn, might fall into disgrace. He therefore made haste to insure his daughter a brilliant lot in life, and, at all events, a protector. His eye fell upon General Swetchine, a man who enjoyed a high reputation, whose career had been illustrious, and who was already his own personal friend. He was forty-two years of age; a tall man, of imposing presence, with a firm, upright character, and a calm and kindly spirit. Sophia acquiesced in this choice, as in all which emanated from her father, with loving deference. She had lost her mother several years before; and what specially attracted her in this union was the certainty that she would not be separated from her little sister, but might continue to lavish her care upon her, and supply to her a mother's place.

Among the Russian noblemen whose wishes this marriage frustrated, there was a young man whose birth, fortune, and rare qualities of mind, opened to him a great destiny, — the Baron, afterwards Count, Strogonof. He made no secret either of his preference or his disappointment. The wife herself could not ignore them, but she forbade their expression; and, when young Strogonof had resigned himself to another marriage, Mme. Swetchine became the truest and most faithful friend of his wife.

M. Soymonof's keen enjoyment of a union which promised such security and consolation to his declining years was of short duration. The harsh mandate of the Emperor suspended him, before his daughter or his son-in-law had time to intercede in his behalf. He must leave St. Petersburg immediately. Moscow offered him a natural and honorable asylum, and thither he went. But his bitter sense of disgrace, the separation from his darling daughter, and his freezing reception by a friend on whom he had specially relied, plunged him in unconquerable melancholy. A severe stroke of apoplexy snatched him away at a moment when those who loved him were thinking only of facilitating his return.

A sorrow so profound overthrew Mme. Swetchine, and forced her to her knees. That first solitude of the soul; that need of a support which had never failed her, and whose loss she had never faced, — lifted her eyes at once to heaven. Her first prayer sprang from her first trial; and, when she could no longer say "My father," she cried, "My God!"

CHAPTER II.

The French *emigrés* in Russia. — Their connection with Mme. Swetchine.
— Reign of the Emperor Paul. — Courageous generosity of General
Swetchine. — His high position at court. — His disgrace. — Extracts
from Mme. Swetchine's letters.

THE military position of General Swetchine necessitated his presence at St. Petersburg. He was soon to be promoted to an active and important post. Mme. Swetchine was therefore obliged to remain in the world; and she became mistress of a great mansion at a time of absorbing personal sorrow. Constraint, subordination of all her own impulses to the convenience of others, and submission to a multitude of duties morally unimportant, but from a worldly point of view imperative, dated, for this young woman, from the first day of her so-called independence. Thus her mind, naturally inclined to precocious maturity, became more and more meditative. God was the constant object of her unquiet thought. She sought him, appealed to him, questioned him. He was already her favorite subject of study, but not, as yet, the sole treasure of her heart.

The society in which she occupied, from her first appearance, a distinguished rank, was, at that time, one of the most brilliant in Europe. The French Revolution had introduced into it an element rather new than foreign, which appealed to the mind of Mme. Swetchine in the liveliest manner. The most distinguished guests from Paris and Versailles, when they sought the protection of the most intrinsically despotic of governments, became sometimes, unconsciously to themselves, a warning of the futility and peril of many an illusion. The *emigrés* who undertook the far journey to Russia were, in general, those whom the proscription had not utterly impoverished, and whom Paul had known personally, when, under the name of Count du Nord, he had paid a visit to France, — happy and proud, as yet, of the new reign of Louis XVI. and Marie Antoinette.

Paul had ascended the throne between the Reign of Terror and the Consulate, and considered himself bound in honor to accept the challenge of the French Revolution. He had offered to Louis XVIII. a royal residence in his dominions. He had desired to sign the marriage contract of the Duke d'Angoulême and the orphan of the Temple; and, by his orders, a copy of the act was deposited in the senatorial archives. The Prince de Condé, who had entertained the Emperor at Chantilly, was established in the Hotel Tchernitchef, with a livery and table-service bearing his arms. During the few days of necessary preparation, the palace of the Tauride was placed at his disposal; and the grand-dukes and principal dignitaries of St. Petersburg repaired to the saloons of Potemkin to do homage to a French prince in their own country, before he had himself paid his respects to the sovereign of the land. The Empress had bestowed the office of *dame à portrait* upon the Princess de Tarente, with whom the Emperor had become acquainted in Paris, at the houses of her father, the Duke de Chatillon, and her grandfather, the Duke de la Vallière. The Duke de Richelieu and the Count de Langeron received places of trust in the empire. Young persons were eagerly welcomed, and placed in the army. The drawing-rooms of St. Petersburg, and especially those of General Swetchine, heard daily the announcement of names which had echoed in Versailles and Trianon, — Broglie, Crussol, Damas, D'Autichamp, Rastignac, Torcy, La Garde, La Maisonfort, Saint Priest. The Marquis de Ferté, and, subsequently, the Count de Blacas, were accredited as representatives of the King of France.

An ambassador of the Order of Malta had come to salute his new Grand Master in the person of the Emperor Paul. The Abbé Georgel, the old vicar-general of the Cardinal de Rohan, accompanied this ambassador; and one page of his memoirs is devoted to Mme. Swetchine. It will be interesting to those who knew the general; for they will recognize, after a lapse of fifty years, the same courtesy which distinguished him to extreme old age. The Maltese ambassador had encountered some police difficulties on his arrival, and had received an order to report himself at daybreak at the house of the military commandant. "The General," says the Abbé Georgel, " received us with infinite grace and frankness, and made a thousand apologies; adding, that the order to report to him so promptly regarded only Russian officers, and that so severe a regulation must give strangers a very unfavorable idea of Russian politeness. He took pains to inform us about the maladies prevalent at St. Petersburg, indicated the precautions necessary to secure one's self against them, and the remedies which had been used successfully in case of an attack. His reception and conversation indemnified us for our too early start."

The Revolution had also cast ashore at St. Petersburg several eminent members of the French clergy.

The Abbé Nicolle, already celebrated as a teacher, had accompanied from Constantinople to Russia the children of the Count de Choiseul-Gouffier, author of the " Voyage

Pittoresque en Grèce." He was permitted to found an educational institute; summoned to his side French assistants; and became, in the course of a few years, the master, counsellor, and friend of the young *élite* of St. Petersburg. The Galitzin, Lubomirski Narishkin, Gargarin, Menchikof, Orlof, were among his first pupils. The Duke Louis of Wurtemberg intrusted his son to his care. The Jesuits, whom the Empress Catharine had never consented to sacrifice to the demands of Paris or of Ferney, gathered together, at St. Petersburg, under the generalship of Father Grüber, the débris of their French houses. Father Rosaven, so long an object of veneration at Rome, was so at that time in Russia: and when, at the age of more than eighty years, he paid a last visit to his family in Brittany, his remembrance of Mme. Swetchine induced him to stop at Paris; and the tender-hearted old man lingered some days, on the journey from his birthplace to his tomb, with the early friend of his exile.

The merit of such acts of devotion entailing voluntary privations, the virtue of these brave examples came by degrees to act upon the society of St. Petersburg like an eloquent apostolate. One of these chivalrous apostles was a man unknown to fame, — M. d'Augard, an old officer of the French marine. He had devoted himself to the Christian life under the inspiration of Father Beauregard, at the close of a sermon preached in 1776, in which the preacher had declared, in prophetic words, that the axe was to be lifted above the head of the king, that a sacrilegious hammer would beat down the tabernacle of our altars, and a pagan divinity sit in the place of the living God under the consecrated vault of our temples. From that day forth, religion and science shared his life between them. Fifteen years later, having resolved to leave the country, he paid a final visit to Mme. Elizabeth, who had always shown him peculiar kindness; and that princess herself placed in his hands a prayer of her own composition, which she constantly addressed to God for the king and France.

The Chevalier d'Augard, recommended to the notice of the Empress Catharine by so lofty a suffrage, was appointed assistant director of the imperial libraries. At the same time, he became one of the most intimate and constant guests at the drawing-room of Mme. Swetchine. He had neither the superior mental endowments, nor the religious fervor, which afterwards distinguished Count de Maistre; and, in his humility, he did not aspire to ascendency: but the very simplicity and essentially French grace of his mind, his gayety in company, the sweet frankness with which he expressed his convictions in any serious controversy, exercised an influence all the more irresistible that people did not dream of being on their guard against it. He deserved, in short, that, after the lapse of thirty years, Mme. Swetchine should protest, in the following words, against the oblivion into which the memory of her modest friend had fallen. In reply to a letter announcing the conversion of a young Russian, she wrote:—

"Like you, I thought of Count de Maistre, and the fine solemnity of Chambéry. One ought to revive his memory at the accomplishment of every act like this; for he sowed much seed, though far from being the first in the field. The honor of the introduction of Catholicism among the Russians belongs to the Chevalier d'Augard, the old chevalier of St. Louis. Not even a beginning had been made; but when not merely the execution of such a work, but even the unexpressed desire for it, seemed absurd and impracticable, it was for the genius of faith to conceive and rely upon it. I never see a 'seventy-four' without rendering a more lively and appreciative homage to the canoe of the first navigator." [1]

---

[1] Letter to P. Gargarin, Sept. 19, 1844.

Paul did not confine himself to the personal consolation
of the proscribed and impoverished servants of the French
monarchy, — the eldest, and for so long a time the model,
of the European monarchies. He set on foot three armies.
One he threw forward into Holland, in aid of the English; the second he despatched to Switzerland; the third,
under the command of Souvarof, he opposed to McDonald
and Massena in Italy. It was this Souvarof, a genuine
Sarmatian soldier, who never slept in a bed. "I hate
laziness," he used to say. "I keep a cock in my tent,
that wakes me promptly; and, when I want to give myself
up to comfortable slumber, I take off one of my spurs;"
a saying often repeated in Russia, and whose application
Mme. Swetchine was soon to extend from military to
Christian heroism.

While Souvarof was conducting the Russian armies
into unfamiliar latitudes, and bearing away the palm of
victory from adversaries unaccustomed to defeat, Paul,
unhappily for himself and Russia, was yielding more and
more to the extravagant impulses of a tyrannical temper.
Punishment and reward were lavished in obedience to
the first promptings of unreflecting wrath or favoritism.
The places at court ordinarily reserved for the oldest
families in the empire were bestowed upon subalterns
selected from the house-servants, in whose presence he
felt under no restraint. At the memorable siege of
Bender, the Russians, urged to extreme measures by an
obstinate defence, had slaughtered the women and children. A young Tartar moved the heart of the victors
by his beauty, and his childlike grace turned aside the
mortal blow. Prince Repna paid his ransom, and made
a present of him to Catharine II.; and Catharine, in turn,
gave him to her son, under the name of Koutaïsof. Paul

took a fancy to him, made him his favorite *valet de chambre*, and the confidant, now of his pleasures, and now of his murmurs against his mother. When Paul finally ascended the throne, he bestowed upon him one title after another, until he had raised him to the position of a Narishkin. Koutaïsof flattered Paul, and everybody else flattered Koutaïsof. Thenceforward the imperial caprice knew no bounds. One day, ukases interdicted pantaloons and frock-coats; the next, the universities were forbidden to employ the word *revolution* in speaking of the courses of the stars. Police regulations were multiplied to infinity, entailing intolerable vexations. An order, posted in the public squares of the capital, enjoined, that, whenever the Emperor passed through the streets, whether on foot, — which was comparatively rare, — or on horseback or in a carriage, — which was happening continually, — every one should stop; descend from his carriage, if riding; uncover, take off his pelisse, and remain with bowed head while His Majesty passed. A young merchant, for an involuntary transgression, was sentenced to fifty blows of the knout, — a punishment all but mortal. A young lady, known and beloved at the court, saw her carriage seized by the police for the same offence, and fainted. Her indignant family hastened to appeal to the Emperor. Paul took grave cognizance of the facts, pardoned the coachman on condition of his joining the army, exempted the carriage and horses from confiscation, but sentenced the young lady to eight days of seclusion for her failure in decorum, and administered the same corrective to an aunt who had adopted her, for having taught her ill.[1]

The Emperor disciplined his own family no less severely. A single slip in etiquette, an irregularity in the manner

[1] Memoirs of the Abbé Georgel.

of kissing the hand, drew down upon the grand-dukes and grand-duchesses several days, and sometimes a week, of arrest. The grand-dukes were the victims of incessant military parades. Alexander excelled in the drill, and Constantine was unequalled as a drummer.[1]

An equally minute surveillance was exercised over all the different army corps far and near. Officers were seized without warning, thrown into sledges, and dragged breathless before courts-martial, sometimes into the very presence of the Emperor. Hesitancy or intimidation was considered equivalent to confession, and the most rigorous sentences were pronounced without appeal. One day the Emperor charged General Swetchine with the execution of a cruel arrest upon a certain colonel. The General repaired to the parade-ground; walked up to the victim, who was already stripped to the waist; and said, "Here is your sword. Now leave St. Petersburg instantly! The Emperor pardons you." Retracing his steps, the General goes up to the Emperor's apartment. "Sire, here is my head! I have not executed Your Majesty's orders. The Colonel is free, I have restored him to life and honor. Now let the blow fall on me instead!" The Emperor pressed the General's arm violently, hesitated, and said, "You have done well! I regretted not having spoken to the Grand-duke Alexander on the subject." And he added, "Let this, at least, never be known at St. Petersburg!"

The conduct of foreign affairs was as rash and inconsequent as the internal administration of the empire. Dissatisfied with the proceedings of Austria in Italy, and irritated against England on the subject of the Isle of Malta, Paul suddenly recalled his armies, tore up his

[1] Recollections of General Swetchine.

treaties, ordered the Bourbons to quit his dominions, and opened negotiations with the First Consul, in which he was pleased to display a chivalrous enthusiasm. There was a caricature circulated in Europe at that period, representing the Czar bearing upon one side of his face, Order; on the other, Counter-order; and on the forehead, Disorder.

In the midst of these sudden revolutions, from which no situation or order of ideas was exempt, General Swetchine maintained his position; and the Emperor even redoubled his favors. The General had received the post of military commandant; and subsequently he was intrusted with the functions of provisional governor of St. Petersburg. This last piece of preferment made him either a dangerous obstacle or a necessary accomplice in the case of those projects for a compulsory abdication which were hatching in the shade. The General himself has described one supreme event in his career, whose story no one else would have had the right to furnish us : —

"Of all the personages who came to congratulate me on my appointment as governor-general, the Admiral R. was the most flattering in his encomiums. He came to my wife's soirées, and succeeded in making himself conspicuous there. Count ———— also paid his respects to the new governor, contrary to his dignified rule of visiting no one. He invited me to call on him, and talk over some matters of business; and accordingly I repaired to his house at six o'clock in the evening. With the exception of the porter, the mansion was empty, — not a servant to be seen. The Count received me, candlestick in hand; apprised me that he was alone, and conducted me to a remote cabinet. 'General,' said he, 'I have to acquaint you, as military commandant, with a plot which has been formed against the Emperor. I am its president. Mindful of the glorious estate of Russia on the death of the Empress, mortified at seeing her isolated from Europe, and stripped of all her alliances, an assembly of the most distinguished individuals in the nation proposes, with the countenance of England, to overthrow the present violent and disgraceful government, and place upon the throne the heir presumptive, — the Grand-duke Alexander,—whose youth and well-known sentiments inspire us with high hopes. Our plan is matured; the means of execution may be relied on; the conspirators are numerous. It is proposed to invest the palace of Saint Michel as soon as the Emperor shall take possession, and demand his abdication in favor of his son. The Emperor will be treated as a state prisoner, confined in the fortress, and guarded with all the consideration due the father of the sovereign. We cannot, however, answer for the accidents which may attend the passage of the Neva when the ice is breaking up, and in the darkness of the night. What I wish to know now is the part you will take in this national crisis.'

" 'Monsieur le Comte, I do not share the opinion, that private individuals possess any right to change the order of a government to suit themselves. The sovereigns, or hereditary chiefs of nations, are, in my view, beings who cannot abdicate. A sick or imbecile king, such as we have seen in other countries, may properly be replaced by a council of regency; but the deaths of Charles I. and Louis XVI. were assassinations, crimes of high treason. That is my opinion. My intention is to play my proper part, and not change, like Harlequin in the play. For the rest, give yourself no uneasiness. I shall not abuse your confidence nor obtain emoluments for myself by a mean denunciation. The law gives me the right and the means of ferreting out this conspiracy for myself: I shall proceed to do so. Forget what I have said, Monsieur le Comte, and pray regard our interview as a dream.'

" A few days later, Admiral R. paid me a visit, and asked me this question: 'General, if the improbable contingency of an insurrection should occur, and you should be forced to decide one way or another, what part should you take?' — 'I should take counsel of my honor, and abide by my oath.' The Admiral threw his arms about my neck, embraced me cordially, and advised me to persevere in my fidelity. Two days afterwards I was appointed senator, and the same evening relieved of my command."[1]

Shortly after the sudden disgrace of General Swetchine, Count Palken was named governor, *ad interim*, of St. Petersburg. Paul took possession of the palace of Saint Michel, oppressed by strange visions and melancholy forebodings. On the 12th of March, 1801, he was no more.

---

[1] Recollections of General Swetchine.

The Grand-duke Alexander, proclaimed at midnight by the sombre gleam of torches and flambeaux, offered at first an energetic resistance; but the chief of the conspirators approached him, and whispered these words in his ear, " You are to reign, and you shall reign!" and the Grand-duke was lifted in the arms of soldiers, and hurried off to the cathedral, where the clergy and the people soon assembled.

General Swetchine and wife did not, on his quitting office, remove to a great distance from St. Petersburg. Their estates were very remote; and the Russian aristocracy does not affect country life. Moscow had no charms for them since the death of M. Soymonof; and they continued to reside in the midst of a large circle of friends whom they had chosen independently, and now retained. The interchange of philosophical and literary ideas occupied a place in their drawing-room, which was shared, but never usurped, by the politics of the day, so fruitful in catastrophes. Then were knit those ties whose strength was yearly attested in Paris, — attachments always tinged with reverence, and which time had no power to weaken. From that period also, Mme. Swetchine, whose health had long presented some very singular phenomena, became the victim of sufferings which must have broken a spirit less energetic than her own. The physicians had already declared that she could never know the happiness of maternity; and she sought to console herself under this severe sentence, by taking redoubled pains with the education of her young sister, by multiplying her affectionate and respectful attentions to General Swetchine, and last, but not least, by consecrating to industrious study the moments unclaimed by her heart, which she always consulted first.

Reading with her was never a simple relaxation. She had not done with a book until she had filled it with her notes and comments, and, in some cases, copied it entire. The earliest of these enormous masses of extracts bear date in 1801, — that is, in her nineteenth year, and the second of her marriage. These collections are no luxurious albums, not even volumes purposely prepared. They are common paper note-books, covered with fine and close writing, and afterwards bound up for the sake of preserving and keeping them in order, as we see from the lines being taken in with the binding at the back, and the absence of words cut away by the paring of the margins. There are thirty-five of these volumes in existence, besides some that have been lost. The smallest are in octavo; thirty are quarto.

Whatever of interest and emotion these books represent for Mme. Swetchine may, by a singular coincidence, be described in the words of Count de Maistre, at that time a wanderer in Switzerland, Italy, and Sardinia, who was to make her acquaintance only at the last stage of his protracted exile. "You see these immense volumes on my table," says Count de Maistre in his "Soirées de St. Petersburg." — "There, for thirty years, I have noted down all the most striking things I have encountered in my reading. Sometimes I confine myself to simple indications, and at others I transcribe important passages, word for word. Often I accompany them with comments, and often also I have jotted down here those instantaneous thoughts, those sudden flashes, which are extinguished without fruition, if their brilliancy be not fixed in writing. Swept by the storms of revolution through many of the countries of Europe, I have never parted with this collection; and, now, you would scarcely believe what enjoyment I have in reviewing it. Every passage awakens a throng of interesting ideas and plaintive memories, sweeter a thousand-fold than what we ordinarily call *pleasures*."

For Mme. Swetchine, as for M. de Maistre, these voluminous extracts represent the successive stages of her mind's journey; and, under this aspect, some fragments will be presented to the public.

The first volume commences with the year 1801; and the earlier pages are devoted to Barthélemy's "Traité de Morale." The precepts of Pythagoras also figure largely. Bernardin de Saint Pierre comes next in order; then follow long and dolorous pages from Young's "Night Thoughts."

Fénélon is represented in the first volume by a letter to Mme. de Maintenon.

Short fragments of Mme. de Genlis, and some letters of Micheau to the Abbé Delille, and translations from Horace, are intermingled with fragments from a poem of La Harpe on Woman.

A large space is devoted to Rousseau, but there is not a line from Voltaire. Even before she left Russia, Mme. Swetchine wrote to a young friend, "I have rarely been able to read Voltaire without being painfully affected, while Young's 'Night Thoughts' often leave me in an agreeable frame of mind." The quotations from the "Nouvelle Heloïse" are numerous. The candid mind of this young woman, which was offended by the levity and smartness of Voltaire, seems to have been dazzled by the pompous sentimentality of Rousseau. The Preface to the "Nouvelle Heloïse" is carefully analysed; and the apology for the moral romance, as then understood, is reproduced in perfect good faith.

" If romances offered to their readers only pictures of actual objects, duties which it is possible to fulfil, and pleasures suited to their condition, they would no longer make their readers fools, but wise," &c.

The most intense pages of St. Preux to Julie are not excluded.

" O Julie! what a fatal gift of heaven it is to have a sensitive soul," &c.

But it is the descriptions of nature, and the exhortations to virtue, simple manners, and study, which especially attract the sympathies of Mme. Swetchine to Rousseau.

" O my friend! what an argument against the sceptic is the life of the true Christian!" &c.

Side by side with Rousseau, we find Marmontel. "Bélisaire" had enjoyed a great popularity throughout Europe, but particularly in Russia. Speaking of some of the incidents which preceded the publication of his work, Marmontel says, in his "Memoirs," "I dreaded allusions, malicious applications, and the accusation of having had in my mind another than Justinian when I portrayed a weak and wicked monarch. The King of Prussia felt it so much, that, on the reception of the work, he wrote with his own hand, at the foot of a letter of his Secretary Lecat, 'I have just read the opening chapters of your "Bélisaire:" you are a bold man.' But," adds Marmontel, "while the Sorbonne condemned my book, letters reached me on all hands from the sovereigns of Europe, and her wisest and most illustrious men, full of encomiums on the volume, which they declared ought to become the breviary of kings. The Empress translated

it into Russian, and dedicated the translation to an archbishop of her own country." The "Bélisaire" of Marmontel, therefore, figures largely among Mme. Swetchine's
readings.

But there is no lack of satire; and we get glimpses
of the excesses and eccentricities of the eighteenth century. After that description of Maupertuis by himself,
"I am as pale as death, and as sad as life," we find the
following portrait of Fontenelle : —

"M. de Fontenelle took cognizance of nothing but mind.
He had no vices, and consequently no battle to fight. He never
laughed. One day I said to him, 'M. de Fontenelle, did you
ever laugh?' — 'No: I never executed an ah! ah! ah!' That
was his idea of laughter. He only smiled at fine things, and
never knew what it was to feel. He received no impressions
from others. He never interrupted anybody, but waited at-
tentively till his interlocutor had finished, and was in no hurry
about his reply. If you had brought an accusation against
him, he would have heard you all day without saying a word.
From his birth up, nothing had ever moved him. He resembled
some very delicate little machine which will last for ever, if
placed in a corner where it cannot be rubbed or jostled. It
is to his absolute apathy that his long life must be attributed.
His mother was like him. He speaks of both his parents with
the same indifference. He used to say, 'My father was a
brute, but my mother had mind. She was a quietist; a sweet
little woman, who used often to say to me, "My son, you will
be damned:" but it did not trouble her.' Fontenelle never
raised his voice on any occasion whatever, and did not speak in
a carriage, for fear he should be obliged to do so. He disliked
music, and did not care for painting or sculpture except in
their relations to the imagination. He loved no one. People
pleased him; but the word 'love' he never pronounced. 'Do
you esteem me?' Mme. Geoffrin once asked him. 'I think you
are very agreeable.' — 'But what if some one should come
and tell you that I had cut one of my children's throats, —
should you believe him?' — 'I should reserve my judgment.'"

"It was said of Diderot, that he often liked to converse
with the most commonplace people, because they would listen
to him. He was like a man playing ball against a wall,

who exclaims at each rebound, 'That wall plays remarkably
well!'"

"A correspondent of Ferney once said, 'I have just received a delightful letter from Voltaire. Let me read you
my reply!'"

"Mme. Deffaud, having made up her mind to reform,
wrote, 'As for rouge and President Hénault, I shall not do
them the honor of forsaking them.' The President, on the
other hand, said, just after his conversion, 'I am in process
of bringing all my sins to light for the purpose of getting rid of
them. We never know how rich we are till we break up
housekeeping!'"

"Mme. Geoffrin claimed that, having always been up with
the spirit of her age, her years and her tastes had kept pace,
like two perfectly matched horses."

"Voltaire cared very little for the country; and it was wittily
said of his 'Henriade,' that there was just grass enough in it
for the horses."

"Tallien once had the audacity to say to the Assembly,
'When we are alone with the people.' So artificial had life
become! One man met another, and asked him, 'Well, what
do you think of all this?'—'What do I think? I hardly dare
be silent!'"

"Somebody, struck with the change that the two first years
of the Revolution had wrought in the political opinions of
Alfieri, asked him to explain it. 'Ah!' said he, 'I knew the
great; but I did not know the little!'"

The last traces of the eighteenth century, under its
spirituelle and literary aspect, linger in the "Souvenirs"
of Mme. Necker. Mme. Swetchine borrows largely from
them:—

"M. Borda was a distinguished seaman and traveller, and
a great favorite in Mme. Necker's circle. The story was told
in his presence, that Streunsée, at his examination, had made
some admissions which compromised the Queen of Denmark.
M. Borda replied instantly, 'A Frenchman would have told
everybody of that, but he would have admitted it to nobody.'"

"M. Dubucq, who has left a brilliant record of his administration in our colonies, once said, 'The gibbet is a species of
flattery to the human race. Three or four persons are hung,
from time to time, for the sake of making the rest believe that
they are virtuous.'"

"'Those persons who never speak till they can make a hit are insufferable. They oblige you to fill up the embroidery of which they will only do the flowers.'"

"'The man who is most inferior to us as a whole is our superior in some one particular. In conversing with him, therefore, we must choose those subjects on which he has the advantage, that we may derive some benefit from our intercourse with him.'"

"'To receive a visit is always to run a risk. We are not obliged to please the persons whom we do see; but, when they are our guests, they must be treated with favor, consideration, and patience.'"

"'We must never assume an authoritative air in society, nor exhibit any change of countenance in disputing with those who are not of our mind. Conversation is an arena where a race is to be won, and that with the swiftness of Atalanta; but it is allowable to arrest our adversary only with apples of gold. Self-love will forgive weighty and even severe objections in a tête-à-tête; but it never overlooks a too serious face or expressions of disapproval in public.'"

"'M. Thomas said that an expressionless face is born deaf and dumb.'"

"''They blame you;' 'They accuse you;' 'They say of you'—last, but not least, 'They will say'—Who, then, is this King *They*, whose authority is thus proclaimed? It is a king without state, splendor, or visible throne; yet all obey his voice, and tremble before him. A remarkable king in this respect, that he is sovereign in small matters as well as in great.'"

This portrait of King *They* is from Mme. Necker's own hand. She had a perfect right to speak of him; for she had known him well.

Vers de Société were so fashionable at that epoch, that of course we find some traces of them in Mme. Swetchine's volumes. Very few deserve to survive the occasion which called them forth. Perhaps, however, we ought to except the following apologue of Count Elzéar de Sabran, whose charming old age is fresh in the memory of many, and who, in his turn, recalled the grace and refinement of the Chevalier de Boufflers, the second husband of his mother, Countess de Sabran: —

BONHEUR ET MALHEUR.

Bonheur et Malheur sont deux frères,
  Qui furent toujours ennemis.
Fortune et Hasard sont leurs pères,
  Que l'on vit toujours fort amis.
Malheur, à la mine pauvrette,
  Ne fut jamais trop bien traité;
Bonheur, d'une beauté parfaite,
  Fut de chacun l'enfant gâté.

        .   .   .   .   .

Bonheur veut un parti sortable,
  Riche dot, et bonne maison;
Malheur se sentait moins aimable,
  Il eut moins de prétention.
Bonheur, épousant l'Inconstance,
  Se trouva bientôt malheureux;
Malheur épousa l'Espérance,
  Et finit par se croire heureux.

The second volume of Mme. Swetchine's selections is dated on the 12th of December, 1803. Her reading, for the most part, embraces a more connected and lofty order of ideas. Duclos is occasionally found side by side with Pascal; but Pascal and Massillon have the preference.

Some one expressed surprise that she should read so carefully Mercier's "Tableau de Paris," and would have demonstrated to her the weakness of the work. Mme. Swetchine interrupted him with the remark: "Since I am to read every thing, what matters it where I begin?"

Religious questions, Mme. Swetchine already investigated thoroughly:—

"Other religions, as the pagan, are more popular than the Christian: they consist wholly in externals, but they are not for people of ability. A purely intellectual religion would answer for the gifted, but it would be useless to the mass of men. Christianity alone is adapted to all."—*Pascal.*

After a passage from Father Bridaine, we read:—

"St. Vincent de Paul was very drowsy on the day of his death; and, one of his friends having expressed some anxiety about his constant slumber, he replied, 'It is the brother coming before the sister.'"

La Harpe re-appears, — but La Harpe outraged by the excesses of the age whose enthusiasm he had shared : —

"Senseless destroyers! you shouted ' Victory,' and where is your victory now ? You were in a chronic rage at the wealth with which our temples abounded. They are rich no longer, but they are sacred still. They are stripped, but they are frequented. Pomp has vanished, but worship remains. They are no longer crowded with marbles and precious tapestries ; but men bow there, and weep over the ruin. Sacrifice is poorly apparelled ; but adoration is deep, and piety pure."

"Common sense enjoins on the irreligious, instead of thinking to interrogate God, to think how they will one day answer him."

"Our self-love can be resigned to the sacrifice of every thing but itself."

Then follow several pages consecrated to the preparation for, and acceptance of, death : —

"A friendship will be young after the lapse of a century. A passion is old at the end of three months." — *Vigee.*

"Plato once gave a sumptuous feast. Diogenes, when he entered the house, had to walk over a superb carpet. ' I am treading under foot the pride of Plato,' said he. ' Yes,' replied Plato, ' with the pride of Diogenes.' "

Over a fragment from "Zimmermann on Solitude," Mme. Swetchine has written, in pencil, "What a blunder in the translator to have put *fierté* for *orgueil!* "

The letters of Count de Valmont ; Barruel's "Histoire de Jacobinisme ; " "Paul and Virginia," Bourdaloue, M. Laya, the Marquise de Lambert ; some poems of Dueis, and the "Jour des Morts" of Lemière, — occupy the third volume, in which Bossuet appears for the first time. Italian sonnets abound. German and Russian have also a place. The third volume closes with a long analysis of the principles of the Lycurgean legislation.

The fourth volume bears the date of 1806. It is filled with the romances of Mme. Cottin, the sermons of the Abbé Poule, and English and Italian poems.

The fifth volume opens with long extracts from Mme. de Staël's "Delphine." And here, for the first time, Mme. Swetchine interrupts her citations, and speaks somewhat at length in her proper person: —

"If these extracts were destined for any other eye than mine, I should hesitate about copying any portion of this letter, in which 'Delphine' unfolds opinions so unlike my own. They might well scandalize the least devout, while those who are most indulgent to me would find them shockingly incongruous, and no one would appreciate my motive. But since I am collecting these scattered materials for my sole behoof, and consequently have no malicious interpretations to dread, I have thought it right to allow myself to insert a fragment which seems to me full of sensibility, warmth, and life; content to add, by way of forestalling any false judgment which the oblivion of the past might lead me to pronounce upon myself at the advanced age when I shall review this collection, that, since my eyes first opened to the light of truth, my convictions on this important point have never wavered."

And beneath these lines, which are written with ink, we find in pencil: —

"To-day, on the 5th of May, 1831, at the age of fifty-one years and five months, I bear witness, with a smile at my old scruples, that, in the twenty-eight years which have elapsed since then, my faith has been growing ever stronger and clearer; that the slightest doubt has never arisen within me; and that, firmly fixed on the great basis of Christianity, I have never wavered except to become, in the bosom of the Catholic Church, more of a Christian than ever."

After the fragment from "Delphine," we read: —

"Before God can deliver us from ourselves, we must undeceive ourselves." — *Saint Augustine*.

"Perfection easily endures the imperfection of others. God lets remain, in the most advanced souls, certain weaknesses disproportionate to their high estate, as they leave mounds of earth which they call landmarks (*témoins*) in a piece of ground which has been levelled, to show how deep the work of man's hands has gone. So God leaves, in great souls, landmarks or remnants of the wretchedness he has removed."

"The soul has no secret which the conduct does not reveal." — (*I think this is from the Chinese.*)

"The Frenchman is that naughty child whom the mother of Du Guesclin characterized as the one who is always beating the others."

"If I have made out a case for science, it gives me the right to demand silence when I speak of religion." — *Leibnitz.*

"When any one has offended me, I try to raise my soul so high that the offence cannot reach it." — *Descartes.*

"It is of no use to be angry with *things;* for our wrath cannot harm them in the least." — *Marcus Aurelius.*

"The celebrated Morgagni once let fall his scalpel in the midst of a dissection, and exclaimed, 'Oh, if I could only love God as well as I know him!'"

"My poor," said Boerhaave, "are my best patients. God pays for them."

CHAPTER III.

Accession of the Emperor Alexander. — Arrival of the Count de Maistre
at St. Petersburg. — Adoption of young Nadine Staeline. — Works of
charity, and correspondence with Alexander Tourguenief. — Marriage
of the Princess Gargarin. — Earliest letters to Mlle. Roxandra
Stourdza.

ECCENTRIC as was the reign of the Emperor Paul,
he left behind him one memorable and salutary enact-
ment, — the re-establishment of the direct and legitimate
order of succession to the throne, — which was promulgated
the day he took his oath.   His capricious and violent
measures were speedily forgotten, and the advent of Alexander I. was hailed with enthusiasm.

His grandmother, Catharine, whose partiality had been
undisguised, had married him, when he was barely twenty
years old, to the young and beautiful Princess Louise of
Baden, who, on embracing the Greek religion, assumed the
name of Elizabeth.

Imposing in stature and bearing, with a winning face,
sweet and gentle manners, and a degree of polish which
sometimes amounted to affectation, generous and enthusiastic, Alexander possessed, in about an equal degree,
the qualities which captivate the masses, and those which
attract earnest minds.   His tutor, Cesar de la Harpe, born
in the canton of Vaud, was a republican by persuasion, as
well as by birth, and began by inspiring Alexander with
an ardent desire to make terms with the French Revolution, whereof he himself was ever the open partisan.

One of Alexander's first acts, therefore, when he ascended the throne, at the age of twenty-seven, was to repair to Memel, and confer with William III., King of Prussia, with the hope of interesting him in some plan for a definite reconciliation with France. At Riga the inhabitants detached the horses from his carriage, and drew him through the streets; and a German naval captain burst through the crowd, shouting, "Let my eyes behold the Emperor of Peace!"

The aged Klopstock, who interpreted the sentiment of Germany, wrote an ode in honor of "the tutelary saint of humanity." As a trifling indication of the intellectual direction which he proposed to give his reign, Alexander showed himself less strenuous than his father about costumes and military drill. He conversed with the civil functionaries, and voluntarily adopted the manners of a simple private gentleman. On great review-days only, which were rare and solemn occasions, he appeared in a brilliant uniform, and surrounded by a numerous *cortége.* It used to be said of him, at this period, "He is the courtier who least frequents the court."

"Who would have guessed the nature of our disputes?" writes Napoleon, in the "Mémorial de Sainte-Hélène." "He used to maintain that hereditary power was an abuse in government; and I have had to employ all my logic and eloquence to convince him, that in this same hereditary power lay the peace and happiness of a people. Perhaps he was mystifying me, after all: for he is subtle, treacherous, and adroit. He is a man of ability."

Alexander shared the cares of empire with certain young persons of his own age, whom the malecontents of the new *régime* stigmatized as the coterie of "young men of mind." The individuals who incurred this odd re-

proach were Count Strogonof, whose name has already
been mentioned in connection with his early preference
for Sophia Soymonof; Prince Kotchoubei; Prince Adam
Czartoryski, a noble and faithful representative of Poland;
and M. Novossiltzof. The national writer, Karamzin, was
also intimate with the Emperor Alexander; but it was
in the character of an historiographer. The old annals
of Russia, her hopes, and her future, formed the subject of
their disinterested and high-minded intercourse. Finally,
Spéranski, the son of a priest in the Greek Church, and
the first example of an illustrious career in that class, a
learned lawyer, and a man of strong and systematic mind
and fascinating conversational gifts, exercised a daily increasing influence over the mind of Alexander in favor
of European ideas and institutions. Such a change of
régime appeared to the inhabitants of St. Petersburg like
a renewal of the atmosphere, we might almost say a
revolution in climate. No one enjoyed it more keenly
than Mme. Swetchine. From the time of Alexander's
accession, she was at ease, and breathed freely, at least
in the sphere of conversation and intimate intercourse;
yet neither General Swetchine nor herself endeavored to
regain place at court. The general's was naturally an
indifferent character; and he was, as one could see at a
glance, totally destitute of ambition. Mme. Swetchine
was full of ardor and power; but her energy was ex-
pended on moral activities, and she made no concessions
to the pomps or the slavery of human grandeur. Her
sole tie to the imperial court was a grateful devotion to
the Empress Mary. But the widow of Paul I. had made
haste to escape the theatre of politics, which had proved
so tragic a one for her. At Pawlowski she created for
herself an existence apart. A library rich in rare edi-

tions and new publications; mahogany tables loaded with drawings and medals; collections of cameos and precious stones, engraved by her own hands, — indicated at a glance the serious nature of her employments. Every year she shut herself up in the vicinity of her husband's tomb, to offer up prayers to God for him, and attest before men her religious remembrance. She kept with her, in the character of a friend, the Countess Liéven, who had had charge of the early instruction of her children. She also took pleasure in superintending the various benevolent institutions of St. Petersburg. The Baroness d'Adelberg, lady-superior of a convent similar to the celebrated foundation of Mme. Maintenon for young people of indigent families, having fallen ill on one occasion, the empress took her place, and fulfilled her duties until her recovery.

To these influences, which wrought so happily on Mme. Swetchine, was finally added another, — the most powerful and decisive of them all, — the arrival of Count de Maistre.

M. de Maistre was a man whose practice never contradicted his theory. His virtue had all the simplicity, purity, and elevation of his ideas. The ambassador of an unfortunate king, he thought only of concealing, by dint of personal privations and intrepid pride, the poverty which he shared with his master. The plenipotentiary's repast often consisted only of a piece of bread and a glass of water; but, even at this price, the carriage and footman, indispensable to the dignity of his mission, were always retained. The generous zeal of this "Caleb" of diplomacy could not escape Russian perspicacity; but, while the Emperor Alexander and his ministers were lavish of their attentions, he was exposed, at times, to offensive attacks from the second-rate men who surrounded the king. Mediocrity, totally unable to appre-

ciate an elevated range of view and purpose, unable even
to comprehend the language in which you answer it, lends
a ready ear to shabby intrigues and base suspicions. But
M. de Maistre was not of the number of those to whom
may be applied the words of Scripture, " Prophesy not
unto us right things: speak unto us smooth things;
prophesy deceits." Nothing could shake his devotion or
conquer his sincerity. With him frankness was the truest
measure of love. Addressing himself, alternately, aloud
to the people and in whispers to the king, he said to each,
not what he presumed might be agreeable, but what he
judged would be useful. Both were for a long time ungrateful. Justice is a plant of slow growth, but it grows;
and God, who, unlike men, despises nothing, has caused
even the malice of his enemies to redound to the glory of
Count de Maistre.[1]

The illustrious author of the " Soirées de St. Petersburg " was accredited at the court of Russia in the spring
of 1803. He was then forty-nine years old. His " Considérations sur la Revolution Française " had already
brought him into public notice; already his eagle eye had
pierced below the surface; already he had written, " Let

---

1 See the work recently published by M. Albert Blanc, under the title
of " Memoires Politiques et Correspondence Diplomatique de J. de
Maistre." This publication, evidently dictated by a spirit hostile to
Catholicism, and consequently to Count de Maistre, is, in the end, advantageous to both. If, in the *abandon* and presumed secrecy of a private
correspondence, the language sometimes transgresses the bounds of
propriety, the sentiment is always so thoroughly pious and so profoundly
intelligent, that, after the perusal, we honor M. de Maistre more than
ever, and feel an increased respect for ourselves in that we share with
him such large and strong convictions. I trust that the comparison with
Caleb will not seem disrespectful. Aside from his menial position, the
aged servitor of the Ravenswoods is certainly one of the most touching
and poetic of Walter Scott's creations.

us have the courage to avow it: we long failed to comprehend the Revolution, of which we are a standing proof. We took it for an event, but we were mistaken: it was an epoch." [1]

M. de Maistre and Mme. Swetchine, thus providentially brought together, were not long in divining, spite of the disparity in their ages and antecedents, the congeniality of their souls. Their connection began by a mutual attraction; but the woman's mind was in no respect subjugated. Slow to embrace the observances of a positive religion, Mme. Swetchine, at that period, professed Russian Orthodoxy. Nevertheless, her mind, familiar with the great intellects of all lands and ages, watched modern controversies keenly; and her researches were then tending in the direction of German philosophy. With Pascal, Descartes, and Leibnitz, it had been her desire to compare Kant, Fichte, and Hegel. A young German professor, Raupach, who had come to Russia for a private education, had established himself at St. Petersburg, and was developing, in his brilliant conversation, the philosophical principles and the wealth of imagination which were subsequently to render his name famous in Germany. Of him Mme. Swetchine saw much. Moreover, the innate independence of her nature revolted against what she then called the absolute dogmatism of Count de Maistre; and when, at last, she gave her friend the unspeakable joy of her conversion, it was by other methods than those which he had indicated that she came to touch the solid earth, and plant her foot upon truth.

However prominent the place that study and intellectual interests occupied in the daily life of Mme. Swet-

---

[1] Funeral Oration of Eugene de Costa.

4

chine, they never sufficed her.   The tender cares lavished
on her young sister stimulated without exhausting her
maternal instinct; and she soon resolved to undertake a
new charge.   General Swetchine had promised to act
a father's part to a child who bore the name of Nadine
Staeline.   Mme. Swetchine, so far from being disturbed
by this project, associated herself with it.   She welcomed
little Nadine, who knew no other home and no other care
than that of this second mother.

At the same time, her inexhaustible need of helping
and loving sustained itself by an active, constant, daily
supervision of the poor.   The Empress Elizabeth joined
the Empress Mary in works of benevolence; and educational and charitable institutions multiplied under their
patronage.   Mme. Swetchine contributed her share to this
movement, and was soon constrained to rise from the rank
of a simple co-adjutor to that of an authoritative directress.
Doubtless she was unconsciously rendering herself worthy
of the works of grace which were afterwards to take effect
in her: her character was developing, strengthening, and
gaining in solidity, where before she had been only brilliant.   At the age of twenty-five, she was invaluable to all
her friends, — and her friends were of all ages, — enthusiastic in study, modest in thought, gay and demonstrative
in intimate intercourse, grave and collected in her hours
of meditation.   Her natural level was high; but she was
sincerely condescending to shyness and humility, and tenderly affectionate with the poor, the afflicted, and the
penitent.   Her word was weighty, her advice sought;
and the best possible evidence of the beautiful unity of
all the phases of her existence may be found in a few careless, unimportant, undated notes of hers, addressed to one
of her fellow-laborers in good works.   What description

could equal, in fidelity of resemblance, these brief lines, written so hurriedly that they are scarcely legible, and in which she unconsciously portrays herself struggling with ill-health, and reconciling, without confusion or mutual encroachment, the laborious duties of her private life with the cares of her life of charity, — such, in a word, as we ourselves knew her in the exquisite perfection of her maturity and her old age!

This correspondence, small fragments of which are here introduced, is addressed to Alexander Tourguenief, the eldest of three brothers, men of great merit, and united by the most touching affection. Their father, a provincial governor, was connected with the famous Prince Repnin, the leader of the sect of the Martinists in Moscow, and had inspired his sons with some spiritualistic tendencies, which always continued to animate them.[1] Alexander Tourguenief, at the time when his relations with Mme. Swetchine commenced, was filling an important place in the ministry of public instruction and worship under Prince Galitzin. There are in existence at least three hundred billets of a similar nature to those that follow; and they would of themselves suffice to give one a fair idea of the writer's activity of mind and heart: —

Please, my dear Tourguenief, excuse me to our ladies. I cannot go to the meeting this morning; and it is the less inconvenient for me to remain away, as I have no petition to present. Do me the favor of obtaining the matron's memoranda, — that is to say, the names and lodgings of those to whom board is furnished. We have, in all, thirty roubles a month. This month the poor people have not made application, and I do not know how to dispose of it. If there happens to be no meeting, please let me know.

Pardon me for giving you so much trouble. It is written that I shall never cease to do so; and this necessity I shall

---

not call fatality, like the Turks, but predestination, like a true Jansenist.

The Countess . . . has received no further communication from a certain individual. Could you not, with your accustomed kindness, hasten the progress of her affair? She is in a state of actual agony. Patience does wear out, like every thing else ; and we, poor mortals, are not rich in any thing. Good-morning.

Wednesday.

The bearer of this is an honest man, named Zilbrecht. He is extremely poor, and as such has received some slight assistance from the philanthropic committee. He would like a situation ; but, as he does not know German, I fancy it will be quite difficult for him to obtain one : and it seemed to me that you were the only person who could indicate to him the means of success, — if success be possible.

You must remember the merchant Hiedapol. His wife remained here ; and she finds herself very much annoyed by the police, who will not renew her permission to reside in St. Petersburg, and insist on her departure : would you not be so kind as to explain to M. Gorgoli, that these people are not vagrants? Her husband is well known to the Empress Elizabeth, her children are under her protection, and the woman herself under the care of a physician in Her Majesty's pay. A thousand pardons for the trouble I am always giving you ; but the truth is, when there is a good turn to be done, you are the first person that occurs to one's mind.

Thursday evening.

It is very gratifying that you would fain believe me omnipresent, like the superior intelligences; and I myself regret that I have never yet succeeded in being in more than one place at a time. I never felt the inconvenience of this state of things so much as to-day, when you paid me a visit, positively knowing that I was somewhere else. Depend upon it, if divination answered me instead of knowledge, this should never have happened.

However, I shall not confine myself to bantering a man as amiable and obliging as yourself. I feel bound also to torment him. Consequently, I beg that you will come and see me to-morrow morning, whenever you can spare me an hour.

I very much want a Bible with parallel columns in ancient and modern Greek; and you will confer a great pleasure by procuring one at your earliest convenience. What you tell me of M. . . . confirms my instinctive suspicions. I must confess that I have no taste for hazardous proceedings; and I firmly believe, that, when a thing is useless, it is no longer matter of indifference, but positively harmful. I am much more mortified at the idea of foregoing five hundred roubles from the government of Toula; but, where we are not satisfied, we must submit. Good-morning, my dear confidant in all my official anxieties.

Monday.

You cannot imagine how earnestly they are asking at Moscow for Polish and Italian Bibles. Have you not some which contain versions in these two languages in parallel columns? I have no alternative in this matter but to apply to the distributor, whose complaisance is worthy of the most high-flown of Oriental encomiums.

Will you be so kind as to borrow for me two requests which I presented at the last meeting? They were from two peasants to whom we allowed five hundred roubles; but, as they have not yet come for the money, I want to know where they lodge. The place is marked on the requests, which I will immediately return. I hope to see you this evening.

Friday.

Will you be so kind, my dear Tourguenief, as to ask M. Sayger to send me Viller's book on the Influence of the Reformation? I would like it this minute: but, as soon as I have obtained the information I want, I will return it; and I beg that he will keep it as long as he desires.

Do not forget, either, to give me Philaretus'[1] book, and to send me the Princess Alexis'.[2] May I keep Goethe? and will

---

[1] Archbishop of Moscow. It is customary to designate simply by their baptismal name the dignitaries of the Russian Church.

[2] Princess Alexis Galitzin, née Countess Protasof. She had married Prince Alexis Galitzin, grandson of the field-marshal to whom Russia owes the victory of Pultowa. She became a widow in 1800, and was one of the first Russians who embraced Catholicism. Her sisters, Countess Rastopchine and Protasof, and the Princess Vasiltchikof, soon followed her example. She had, moreover, the happiness of winning to the true faith her eldest son, Prince Peter; and her daughter, who died in America, a nun of the Sacred Heart. The Princess Galitzin was all the nearer to Mme. Swetchine in that she was bound by so many ties to

you not add the "Kleine Prosaische Schriften" of Schiller, one
volume of which I already have? Pray refuse, if you need
them ever so little. Permit me also to borrow your Müller.
I want to take a few notes from it; but I will not keep it long.

Thursday.

You relieve me of embarrassment, my dear friend, even
when you cannot come to my assistance. Could you not obtain
a courier for Moscow? I have a multitude of packages to
send, and I cannot avail myself of to-day's messenger. I have
barely come back to life; and the sufferings of yesterday have
left me in an indescribable state. I would like to be soothed
to sleep by Arabian tales. It is the literature of a people still
in its infancy, and I assure you that I have returned to mine.
I have just learned that the invitation is for six o'clock. Nothing
could be more inopportune. So Ouvarof[1] wants every thing
of a piece, and no European element in the meeting. I shall
assuredly attack him on this point.

Friday.

You were here yesterday, my dear and good Tourguenief;
but I had not forgotten, before they told me, that it was an
enormous while since I had seen you. I shall be invisible another
week, but not to you, whom I naturally associate, not with a
system of privation, but with all that is needful to repose of
heart and mind.

Sunday morning.

There was a calm and serious tone about your yesterday's
letter, which touched me peculiarly. It was like an impulse to
prayer in one who habitually consults his reason. May God

Count de Maistre; and the two ladies corresponded constantly till the time
of the Princess's death, which took place at St. Petersburg, on the 28th of
October, 1842. But, though strict in the observances of the Catholic faith,
she maintained in society and the court the rank which her birth, her
intellect, and her virtues awarded her. Like M. de Maistre, she liked to
preserve her impressions in writing, and has left several manuscript volumes, whose publication may one day furnish fresh proof of the fact, that
religious sentiments, so far from extinguishing patriotism, purify and
strengthen it.

[1] Head-clerk of the Minister of Public Instruction, and subsequently
Prince Galitzin's successor.

preserve you, dear friend! There is the material for ten good men in your head and heart; and your first idea and dearest desire must needs be to do the work of those ten men in one.

Tuesday.

I was sure that you would be affected by Countess N.'s letter. I think it needs but a single revelation of character to assure us of an individual's capabilities. Tell M. Muralt, that nothing could suit me better than the hours he can give me. Charge him not to put it off later than Thursday. I should have wanted him to-day, were I not, for the greatest wonder in the world, going to the theatre. It seems like going back to my childhood, for I am to be carried; and that, I think, will amuse me.

Saturday.

I am tired of seeing you with so many people about. Please come to-morrow morning, at whatever hour suits you. My doors will be closed to everybody else. Till to-morrow, then, dear friend.

Saturday.

Here is your paper, my friend. Believe me, in religion as in politics, it is a bad plan to wish to remain neutral, and belong to no party. In a purely intellectual sphere, this may answer; but, when thought is to be wrought into action, we ought to know exactly where to classify it. Try to be at M. Karamzin's early. I dine with the Princess Alexis; and immediately afterwards, — that is, about half-past six, — I shall go to Mme. Mouravief's, and thence to M. Karamzin's.

Sunday.

Here, my dear friend, are all the books I have had from you; viz., four volumes of Herder, two of Klopstock, and three of Müller. You must allow me to keep Butterwerk, — the volume on Æsthetics. I have removed the marginal notes from the others; but, in this case, it would oblige me to recommence a preparatory labor. Graef has promised to get it for me in a few days.

Monday morning.

MY DEAR TOURGUENIEF, — Fischer speaks, in one of his letters, of a man named Hausen, a German and Moravian, who is settled in Astracan, whence he has made several journeys into Persia. Engaged at first, it may be, in mercantile pursuits, he conceived a passion for botany on his travels, and has collected specimens of all the most interesting plants and grains which he could find. At present, he is extremely anxious to resume his travels, with the same end in view. Several individuals—among others, Count Alexis Razoumofski—have provided him with the pecuniary means; and all he now needs is such facilities as might be derived from the recommendations he would like to take with him. My husband has written to the Governor of Astracan, whom we know; and I, too, have just despatched a letter to Mazorowitch. But Fischer charged me to ask Ouvarof for a letter for Abas Mirza; and you would do me a great favor by procuring it for him. I trust it will not inconvenience him; and countenance of this sort, in some shape or other, cannot fail to be useful to Hausen. If you think of any other way in which we might serve him, let me know. One is always glad to encourage disinterested scientific effort; and it is a still greater pleasure to contribute to the happiness of a wise man, who is so far from being exacting on his own account.

Tuesday, half-past three.

Do not come this evening, my dear friend; for I am going out. I have had a fancy not to see you this morning. I am ready for you at all moments; and, as to days, I need not say, only to-day is perhaps one of the least favorable. I imagine that these congratulations were only invented to console the people who were never congratulated on any thing else. Come to-morrow, dear friend. You know that I ask and obtain this perpetually.

Making no distinction of nationality, or of faith in needy cases, exhausting all the resources of her own generosity before calling on that of others, Mme. Swetchine was always discreet and prudent in her appeals. This character of universality and circumspection about her benevolence is especially conspicuous in the following billets:—

Tuesday.

The poor woman who will hand you this, my dear martyr, has met with losses whose amount is stated by M. Romanof, governor of Witepsk, in the accompanying paper. She came so late that she obtained nothing from the great collection. Prince Galitzin and Countess Kotchoubei are interested in her case, but can do nothing. Her husband is sick; she has two children; and her intention is to return to Witepsk, having no means of subsistence here. We voted her two hundred roubles, out of our poverty, at the last meeting; but this is insufficient for the transportation of herself and her children, and to meet the indispensable preparatory expense. If you could obtain two or three hundred roubles for her, it would be charity well applied, as I have taken care to ascertain from M. Wassiltchikof and the Countess Kotchoubei. I have made a rough estimate of the requisite sum, rather in the fear that I should get too much than too little. What I know of the generosity of the Countess Strogonof makes me fear an excess. I am sure that this sum will take her to her province; and that any thing more belongs, of right, to those who are poorer than she.

The woman is a Jewess. I conceive this to be no objection, and that true charity will make no distinction between suffering Samaria and Jerusalem.

Thursday.

Count de Maistre has written, requesting me to mention to you a poor Polish woman, named Zazeski, in whom we were disposed to feel interested. M. de Maistre did not know her particularly, and only recommends assisting her on condition that the preliminary information which you obtain corresponds with what he has heard of her.

Forgive me, my dear Tourguenief, for ever returning to the charge, and making such constant demands on your indefatigable goodness.

Sunday morning.

MY DEAR TOURGUENIEF,— The unfortunate mother who here solicits some aid from Her Majesty has been, for a long time, supported by the Patriotic Society, whose enforced inaction leaves her in absolute want. She has decided to return to her province, where she hopes to find an asylum; but she has no means wherewith to prosecute her journey, and hence she has had recourse to the unbounded charity of the Empress. As I am distrustful of a generosity which so often leads her to overstep the bounds of strict utility, please inform Mme. Longuinof that one hundred roubles will be quite enough. I know that it is extremely improper for me thus to limit the amount: so, pray, keep my secret, but insinuate adroitly something approximating to the sum. I am actually jealous for these consecrated riches; and, even in a case of necessity, I scruple to covet them.

———

Saturday morning.

My dear Tourguenief, — Will you do me a great favor by suggesting some method of procuring a situation for a little girl nine or ten years of age, of whom I have taken charge, and about whose condition I would like to feel at ease? Could not one, by paying her board, obtain her admission into the House of Industry? I know of no one but yourself who could afford me, in this emergency, the information and assistance needful to the success of the plan I have fixed on. Take pity on my embarrassment, and relieve me of it by some good advice.

———

Friday, June 30.

I return the note to M. Goucharewski, trusting it will act as a reminder of the interest you promised to take in procuring a place for my poor dear little girl. You have given me so many proofs of friendship, that, without hesitating for an instant for fear this should be the last, I can assure you it will make me more grateful than ever. Please, if you experience any difficulty, try to get her received at my expense. I am anxious that the child should do as well as possible. By " well," I mean only that she shall have a safe asylum, and an education suitable to her station, which shall one day insure her a subsistence. The more simple that education, and the more strictly confined to manual employments, the better I shall like it.

When you write, be so good as to tell me what the prospect is for her. It will set my mind at rest.

While these various cares occupied the mind of Mme. Swetchine, a new tie was binding her to St. Petersburg. This was the marriage of her sister to Prince Gregory Gargarin, a young, distinguished, brilliant man, who had already achieved success in many different lines, and was high in favor at the court.

A friendship which remained paramount with Mme.

Swetchine as long as she lived also originated at about this time. Mlle. Roxandra Stourdza, afterwards Countess Edling, was also residing with her parents at St. Petersburg. The Stourdza, a family of Greek origin, and owning considerable property in Moldavia, had emigrated, with their children, after the Treaty of Jassy, in 1791, sacrificing their hereditary interests and influence to invoke the protection of a Christian power.[1]

M. and Mme. Stourdza received a distinguished welcome from the Empress Catharine; and one of their daughters, Roxandra Stourdza, — born at Constantinople, on the 12th of October, 1786, — was appointed maid of honor to the Empress Elizabeth as soon as she had attained her sixteenth year. The affection and confidence which she soon won from this princess attracted to the young girl the notice of superior minds. Count de Maistre came to share their intimacy; and some words of his will help us to a better understanding of the friend of Mme. Swetchine and the companion of the empress, who received, by courtesy, the title of madame : —

MADAME, — I must be wholly destitute of persuasive talents, if the homage I render to your merit does not occupy a prominent place among the things which you do not feel at liberty to doubt. I have never wavered, in this article of my faith, since the happy moment of my entrance into Greece.[2]

How can I describe my joy and relief at the tidings brought me by your amiable friend about your honored father? My pleasure is proportionate to the pain which the contrary announcement caused me. I was upon thorns, — seeing the

---

[1] The family of Stourdza has furnished two hospodars to Moldavia. Jean Stourdza was invested with this office in 1822, and reigned till 1826. Prince Michel Stourdza, destined by Russia for the hospodarate, received the investiture of the Porte in 1834; and retired, in 1849, on the consummation of the deed of Balta Lémani. The fathers of Prince Michel Stourdza and the Countess Edling were brothers.

[2] M. de Maistre means his introduction to the Stourdza family.

sword suspended above my excellent Roxandra's head, without knowing where to go for further information. Mme. Swetchine was so kind as as to send me, without the least delay, the more favorable news, which doubtless she received from you. But you were wanting there. No one should be ill at your house when you are absent. I wanted, and I did not want, to write. I wanted, and I did not want, to go to Tzarskoe Selo.[1] I wrote to Mme. Swetchine, and waited, with extreme impatience, for her reply. It came, and was favorable. Instantly, at seven o'clock in the morning, I hastened to mingle my congratulations with those of our mutual friend, who had shared all my distress. What a miserable world! — trouble if we love, and trouble if we do not love: a few drops of honey, as Chateaubriand says, in a cup of wormwood, " The rod, my child! it is for thy good!"—"Much obliged, but I prefer sugar."

Rodolphe de Maistre having been admitted into the Russian military service, M. de Maistre thus expresses his anxieties to Mlle. Stourdza: —

"Since your departure, my soul has been busy with misfortunes. My son has left me. I see our excellent friend, Mme. Swetchine, as often as possible. She understands me, and comforts me very much; and I need it sadly.

"When shall we have you to ourselves again, my dear and esteemed friend? and when shall we have another chat around that table where the tea is only a form?

"Our good friend Sophia is the same as when you left her; that is, good and lovable to the last degree, but *without any fixed principles about her health.* I cannot tell you how this sort of disposition vexes me. At the first glance, she appears perfectly well, and one can never feel sure about her. It is her sole deception. Still, she is better than little Nadine, who appears to me to have made very bad progress. They call her better; but I have not much confidence in it. I am sensible how necessary her sweet companionship is to the excellent lady; and, if things take an unfavorable turn, as they may, it will be a terrible blow to her."

The letters of Count de Maistre have already revived the memory of the Countess Edling. Those of Mme.

---

[1] A palace about five leagues from St. Petersburg, the favorite summer residence of the imperial family.

Swetchine will suffice to clothe her name with an undying interest.

This precious correspondence will give us a picture, not merely of Mme. Swetchine's life at that period, but of her inner self, — of the unconstrained workings of her mind and heart: —

"If I did not fear a silent reproof (these are the only ones I fear), I should tell you that my heart is absorbed by regrets at our separation; and that, since Monday, every moment at my own disposal has been replete with the emptiness left by your absence. One may not consult one's personal interest, but it is very difficult to hush its voice entirely. Yet my eyes and head are so weary with the light and din that reign at Kameni Ostrof, that I delight to think of you among your beautiful, shady alleys, where I, with my uncivilized nature, should ask only a little more solitude. I should like this residence of Tzarskoe Selo extravagantly, if there were fewer people here, and on condition that you were one of them. The more I think of it, the more analogy I discover between my situation and purgatory. Our recollections will preserve all their pristine force: love, prayer, suffering, and hope will make up the lives of the inhabitants, — all except *ennui*, of which life has more; and this inclines the balance considerably in favor of purgatory.

"Speaking of prayer, I never knew so many circumstances to unite in disposing me to it as on the occasion of the consecration of Prince Galitzin's chapel, which I attended this morning. I thought much of you, my friend, and regretted that you were not there. I have never witnessed a more magical effect, — the graceful form of the chapel, which is decorated with simple elegance; the mellow, golden light with which it was irradiated; the melodious voices, issuing one knew not whence; the quiet pomp of the service, — Philaretus in the midst of it all; the assembly of three hundred persons; the silence which piety demands and maintains; in short, my friend, a species of actual enchantment, whose remembrance even now transports me. Ah, how such situations favor meditation! I actually thought myself alone, and only recovered from this illusion to enjoy the sight of so many persons, differing widely among themselves, but absorbed for one moment in a sentiment common to all. It is only religious thoughts which can produce this effect; and it is always wonderful. The very

words which stir to their depths the souls of the simple and
ignorant denizens of the desert seemed to-day to fix the attention of frivolous spirits, and excite emotion in the enervated,
and perhaps tainted, souls of creatures intoxicated by prosperity."

Among those who will one day kneel in the chapel of
Mme. Swetchine, none will have read without emotion the
lines in which she foreshadows and describes, so many
years beforehand, what she herself was yet to realize at
Paris. It is her inexhaustible charity which is illustrated
by the next letter : —

My DEAR ROXANDRA, — We have had, this morning, a
stormy meeting, which distressed me, and will long continue to
do so. The Countess Orlof had set her heart upon having
Mme. da C. received in her place when she goes to England.
She applied to me, and I told her that all I could do would be
to propose her name. After sounding our ladies, one by one,
I found that they were horrified at the idea of admitting among
them Mme. de C., with her very doubtful reputation. Yesterday, at the close of the meeting, Mme. Orlof pressed the
point, and, in spite my entreaties, would have it put to vote.
It was rejected by an almost unanimous negative, and the
most unpleasant reasons adduced ; and all my precautions have
been unavailing to shield Mme. de C. from the humiliation
which she owes entirely to Mme. Orlof's obstinacy. How true
it is, that a malicious enemy is better than a clumsy friend ! , I
am far from condemning the ladies who opposed the proposition ; I agree with them about the desirability of maintaining
order in our establishment ; but I must confess, dear Roxandra, that, if these scenes occurred often, they would go far to
disgust me with it. Besides, I cannot strike one in the face in
this way. I believe I am capable of sufficient zeal and strictness : but when it comes to publishing so unfavorable an opinion,
and making parade of one's severity ; to crushing any woman,
or causing her to blush, however just it may be, and however
much one's duty, — I feel that I am incapable of it. The thing
surpasses my firmness. You can judge how all this suits my
love of peace, which is such that I have always suspected that
the soul of the Abbé de St. Pierre had passed into mine by
means of metempsychosis.

At that period, Mme. Swetchine was enjoying a great deal in her family relations. The Princess Gargarin was residing at St. Petersburg. The two sisters lived apart, but indemnified themselves for their separation by renting a country-house together through the summer, when the two households were united, either on the isles of the Neva, or in the vicinity of Peterhof and Tzarskoe Selo. In the course of a few years, the Princess Gargarin had five sons. The two eldest were the objects of Mme. Swetchine's especial partiality, though all were tenderly loved. "They are all my nephews," she used to say; "but the two first ones are my children." She joined in their plays and their lessons, and watched with delight the development of their young intellects. Remarking the extreme deference which Princess Gargarin's second son, Eugene, paid to his elder brother, Gregory, she said of him, " He even tries not to grow, for fear of outstripping his brother." The children, for their part, confounded mother and aunt, and were impatient of any thing which kept the latter away from them. Mme. Swetchine was sometimes obliged to lock herself into her room, in order to pursue her beloved studies in peace. The little boys then armed themselves with their noisiest playthings, collected outside her door, and made all the disturbance in their power, to induce their aunt to desist. Many a time, Mme. Swetchine yielded to this uproarious summons; sometimes, however, she remained inflexible ; but, the moment she unlocked her door, the children forced an entrance, sure of being received, not with chiding, but with smiles and kisses.

This sweet family life lasted till 1811. At that time, General Swetchine petitioned to return to active service; and, while he went to meet the French, Mme. Swetchine retired to her estates in the provinces of Nijni and Saratof. At the same time, another woman, pursued by the hostility of Napoleon, fled from Vienna, crossed Poland, and reached St. Petersburg by way of Kiew and Moscow. Even Petersburg was not the limit of that long journey, which constitutes, together with "Corinne," the eloquent Odyssey entitled "Ten Years in Exile." Mme. de Staël believed herself secure only in Stockholm; and when Mme. Swetchine returned to the habitual centre of her existence, she found there only a brilliant memory.

The meeting which she regretted having missed, and which the two would equally have appreciated, was reserved for Paris.

CHAPTER IV.

Invasion of Russia by the Emperor Napoleon. — Mme. Swetchine is appointed president of the Soldiers' Aid Society. — Letter to the Abbé Nicolle. — Correspondence with Mlle. Stourdza during the years 1813 and 1814.

THE sentiment of duty was always so strong with Mme. Swetchine, that patriotism could hold no secondary place in her soul. The time at which she lived, and, still more, her deliberate convictions, inclined her to that order of ideas which awards to one's country the right of demanding every sacrifice, and which recognizes in the sovereign the natural centre of all patriotic regard, affection, and devotion.

As soon as Russia was menaced by France, the Emperor Alexander put the finishing touch to the enthusiasm of his subjects, by taking the head of his army in person, and associating, in a few words, simply and nobly spoken, the cause of his crown with the cause of the people and of justice. "I will be with you," he said, in his first proclamation to the Russian nation, — "I will be with you, and God will be against the aggressor."

The military courage of Alexander was proved equal to his political ability. In the midst of a warm engagement, the General, Prince Wittgenstein, sent one of his aids to the Emperor to beg him to be less reckless of his life; adding, that his presence deprived him of the coolness necessary to military operations. The bullet which cost Gen-

5

eral Moreau his life, before Dresden, covered Alexander with dust.

The humane feelings of the Emperor, which had always been lively and sincere, were conspicuously manifested during this war, so disastrous to both the contending parties. He visited the French and Russian wounded, without distinction, as they lay upon the frozen ground. More than once he shed tears, as he listened to cries of anguish and last adieus, uttered in every European tongue. All the soldiers who could be moved were collected in the hospitals; but there again they were decimated by epidemic diseases. The Duke of Oldenburg, brother-in-law to the Emperor, was seized with typhus, and died. It was no check upon Alexander, nor could any representation prevail over his desire to superintend and relieve the cares necessitated by so much suffering. In order to render his oversight more efficient, he was careful to preserve a strict incognito. One day, when he was telling the Countess de Choiseul of the care he had been taking of a poor Spanish prisoner, the lady asked him if it was true that he had been recognized on his visit to the hospital. " Yes," he answered simply, " in the officers' room; but generally they take me for one of General St. Priest's aides-de-camp."[1]

Such examples fire the heart of a nation; and all Russia desired to emulate the Emperor Alexander in relieving the countless victims of the war. A ladies' society, for investigation and distribution, was organized at St. Petersburg, under the patronage of the Empress Elizabeth. The most distinguished ladies hastened to join it, moved by the spontaneous impulse which animated rich and poor, lord

---

Memoires de M. de Choiseul, p. 161.

and peasant, merchant and soldier. Mme. Swetchine was chosen president. She was then thirty years of age.

We find evidence of her activity, and of the value already set upon a few of her words, in a letter preserved among the papers, and afterwards among the posthumous effects, of the Abbé Nicolle. The latter, justly affected by the sufferings of his adopted country, had desired to give her some proof of his gratitude; but he did not forget that he was a Frenchman. He thought to reconcile conflicting duties by sending anonymously to the Aid Society the sum of three thousand roubles. This delicate precaution could not deceive a delicacy equal to his own; and Mme. Swetchine wrote him as follows : —

MONSIEUR L'ABBÉ, — I will only say, that I recognize you. Perhaps this simple expression may fail to convey to you an idea of my personal gratitude; but I should have been mortified to be obliged to *learn* what I so easily divined. Even if Prince Galitzin had not soon betrayed you by exhibiting the pleasure one always has in revealing the author of a good action, the incognito in which you shrouded yourself would not have served you. Do not, however, attribute this to my penetration, but to that public opinion which ever does you homage : for several of our ladies had the same thought; and, the moment it was expressed, others shared it. So you can see whether or no it was in our power to respect your wishes, and keep the matter secret.

The south of Russia had recently been ravaged by the plague. The Abbé Nicolle seconded the Duke de Richelieu in his noble charitable labors, as well as in his attempts to civilize the people. They have both been seen, with their mattocks, going from the houses of the infected to the cemetery, to dig, with their own hands, the graves of the dead. " Odessa owes her life twice over to the Duke de Richelieu," — such was the cry of Russia, sweet for a Frenchman to repeat. Mme. Swetchine closes her letter as follows : —

"I know that no place of residence can be as pleasant to you as Odessa. There you find at once repose and activity, constant and agreeable society, and, what must still more attach you to the place, the certainty of being useful. But may you not be so everywhere? And if a clear sky and a fine climate are a source of daily enjoyment, the South pays dearly for it in the plague which has desolated her so long. The personal interest which makes me so earnest for your return exaggerates to my mind the dangers to which you may still be exposed; and, when anxiety about pestilence is added to the regrets of friendship, I know of no arguments strong enough to combat them. Try to come back to us soon. Have you not here, as well as there, books and friends?"[1]

M. de Maistre, whom we always love to see beside Mme. Swetchine, wrote, at the same time, to the Abbé Nicolle: —

Aug. 13, 1813.

A pestilence is one of the most searching of sermons; and one need not be constituted like you to derive great spiritual profit from such a scene. It distresses me to think of you as undergoing so cruel an experience; and I am no less anxious about M. de Richelieu, who has found, in this scourge, an opportunity of showing himself, not only better than others, but better, if possible, than himself. What a trial! What exertions! Thank God, it is over!

The wave of invasion had spent itself in Russia; but events outside had only advanced from one crisis to another.

In 1813, the Emperor moved his head-quarters to Germany. It had been the wish of the Empress to accompany him, but she had not carried her point; and Alexander's indifference was thought to have had more to do with his refusal than the embarrassments of war. Her Majesty was obliged to be content to follow her husband's march at a distance; and she repaired successively to Riga,

---

[1] See the Life of the Abbé Nicolle, by the Abbé Frappat.

to Weimar (whose grand-duchess was Alexander's sister),
to Berlin, and to the other German capitals, in the line of
military events. Mme. Swetchine's friend, Mlle. Stourdza,
accompanied the Empress on this long and painful journey.
The letters of Mlle. Stourdza to Mme. Swetchine are no
longer in existence. Those of the latter have been piously preserved, and they suffice to admit us to the souls
of these two friends. They are marked by infallible
rectitude, and constant elevation of judgment. We see in
them the development and the growth of steadfastness,
breadth of view and disinterestedness, and are struck with
respectful astonishment, as we follow these two women,
step by step, in their intimacy. Young, brilliant, connected
with all that has ever been most sounding and seductive in
human affairs; they drew therefrom only grave lessons in
politics and morality, and aspired only to impassioned
friendship, philanthropy, or solitude. The letters bear no
date; but the facts to which they allude refer them in-
contestably to the close of 1812, and to the year following : —

Tuesday evening.

Your note, my friend, was not the cause of my incurable
regrets ; but it intensified them. I was not expecting it: the
address was in an unfamiliar hand ; and when I opened it, and
recognized your writing, it seemed as if I had never lost you,
but was even then experiencing the agony of parting. To feel
grief intensely, one must needs have been a long time happy,
or supposed one's self so ; for, in a colorless existence, one but
passes into a deeper shadow, through almost imperceptible di-
minutions of light. Doubtless, my love will be a consolation to
you : I am sure of it; but that word " consolation " is so sad,
when it has any meaning at all, that I would rather you found
my friendship a superfluity amid other more worthy and precious boons. I am often surprised to find myself envying those
whose impressions are light and variable. The sponge passes
over the slate, and leaves no trace ; and perhaps it is the fittest
type of the nature of man, whose pleasures are for a moment,
while his pains are for a lifetime. If he have but moral dignity !

But you are not the one to rest satisfied without it. So try to submit to your destiny. It is an eternal one. I think of nothing but your sufferings. The state of your health troubles me exceedingly. How have you borne the severe cold which has prevailed since you left? I am awaiting your letter from Riga with indescribable impatience. I am confined to my room; and the twenty-five or thirty degrees of cold of the last few days have increased my habitual chronic ills at least twofold. What effect must they produce upon you, with your impaired health? I am convinced that the inhabitants of the North will have nothing but an inferno of ice. Fire, in any shape, would be welcome to them. Tell me particularly of your health, and take the utmost care of it. Dilate upon the measures you have taken. Whatever interest you may feel in your own preservation, others feel yet more; and what would be a piece of egotism in many people will be specially benevolent in you.

I am writing in great haste. If you will believe it, I have scarely had a moment to myself since you left. I feel keenly that movement is not diversion; and that one unchanging idea may dominate over all the cares which share one's life between them, but cannot fill it. Adieu, my friend. How many times already has that word filled my heart with bitterness! The head of Medusa is no exaggerated image. I trust your health will improve. Seek help of God; use your strength without abusing it; and, when the conflict becomes too unequal, abandon it, and ask divine grace.

My husband, who has conceived a strong liking for you, charges me, as does also Nadine, to present his respects. Adieu, once more, dear friend. I cannot bear to close this letter. As if a paltry piece of paper could give back to me the joy of your presence!

While I was at our estate, which was a perfect limbo, Count de Maistre thought he did a prodigious thing to send me a short letter, or rather a long note, every month or six weeks. You had been gone but three weeks wanting two days, when he mentioned having written to you; and, shortly after, he sends you an immense packet: and who knows if the quality be not more outrageous than the quantity? The song says, -

> "Sans un petit brin d'amour,[1]
> On s'ennuie même à la cour."

I do wish you would add this to your other sources of enjoyment, and then you would experience to the full the persecu-

---

[1] Without a little spice of love, it is tedious even at court.

tions of prosperity. Only do not rob the poor of their pittance, and let all have their share. Mine, last evening, was a very pleasant one. M. de Maistre came. I was slightly indisposed, and he took pity on me. Hence more sleep, more dogmas, and a good deal of kindly indulgence. We laughed; we chatted; took turns in telling stories; and retired, contented with ourselves and the world. . . .

The armistice[1] at first shut the mouths of all the boy-prophets. They hung their heads, and folded their wings, to think they had not foreseen the great event. Since then, however, they have regained their inspired and threatening tone; and I perceive that nothing is harder than to disconcert a fabricator of hypotheses. There is an English piece called "All in the Wrong;" and a clever man remarked to me, that Europe in general seemed to be playing this comedy, in which all the *dramatis personæ*, from first to last, are involved in a series of blunders. My soul is too weak long to endure the activity of hope in any matter. Conversely, when everybody is desponding, the very uncertainty and instability of events afford me some consolation.

Thursday.

What are we to think of the extension of the armistice? They say the news is contained in a letter from Lord Cathcart. On the other hand, it is claimed that the Emperor's commands to Prince Gortshakof are of quite another tenor. Meanwhile, a reliable man, lately from Moscow, tells me that the first tidings of the armistice which has just expired were received with unmixed consternation, and that those who were beginning to rebuild suspended operations.

Monday, 26th.

I confess that I am beginning to be seriously sick of my privations, and that an interesting grief is a thing I can no longer imagine. As we advance in life, the circle of our pains enlarges, while that of our pleasures contracts; and, among the latter, I know of none more alluring than a sweet and confidential converse which begins with an interchange of ideas, and ends with one of sentiments, — a seemingly accidental communion, which, when earnest, is among the best gifts of Providence. All this I have found in our intercourse, and particularly in that part of it to which you allude. It is a long time, dear,

---

[1] This fixes the date of this letter at the commencement of 1813.

since I have experienced such genuine comfort. Believe me,
we never know any persons perfectly, save those whom we divine at first sight.   A thorough mutual understanding; the
power of penetrating into all the recesses of another's being,
and attaining that perfect acquaintance which lays his whole soul
open to our eyes, — these are dependent upon a sort of analogy
of character, a likeness in dissimilarity.   It always seems to me
as if souls sought one another in the chaos of the world, like
those kindred elements which have a tendency to re-unite.
They come in contact; they feel that they agree; and confidence
is established between them, often without their being able to
assign any valid cause.   Reason and reflection come afterward;
place upon the treaty the seal of their approbation; and think
it is all their work, like those subordinate ministers who take
credit for their master's transactions, for no better reason than
that they have been permitted to sign their names thereto.   No:
I fear no mistakes with you; and only the fulness of my recognition can equal the perfect confidence with which you inspire
me. . . .

    We have had two days of the liveliest anxiety, due simply and
solely to the vagueness and mystery in which they shroud the
news, which is not so alarming now that all is known.   But
here, as elsewhere, I suppose, there is a vast number of people
who oscillate between the predictions of Jeremiah and the in-
credulity of Thomas.   Certainly, for one's own peace and that
of others, one ought to take different examples from Scripture.
It is droll enough, that people will not learn even to doubt with
diffidence; but it is not the first time that scepticism has found
itself dogmatic.   Intolerance in politics is carried farther than
ever.   Woe to him who speaks, and woe to him who is silent!
Woe to him who suspends his condemnation, and woe to him
who does not overdo his praise!   There are two or three stories current here about eagles floating and soaring above the
Marshal's [1] remains.   I know of no more successful fable since
the days of Herodotus, whom you are reading.   It is very well
to say that man has need of faith.   He has another need also;
namely, to aim unceasingly at a higher degree of folly than
has been assigned him.

    Count de Maistre came to see me yesterday; but I was not
in, and therefore could not acquit myself of your commission.
He misses you; and I need not tell you, dear, whether or no

---

[1] Marshal Koutouzof died at Bunzlau on the 10th of May, 1813.   His
body was solemnly transported to Russia; and the people pretended that
an eagle constantly hovered above his coffin during the funeral march.

this is a new point of contact between him and me. I wish my friendship for him made him fond of my society; but he must needs have yours in connection with it. With both of us, he appeared content. He seemed to say, like Peter upon Tabor, "It is good to be here." How heartily would I, too, say it, if I were with you! Rudolf[1] goes to-day, or rather to-morrow. When I know that he is fairly gone, I shall get the Princess Alexis to visit his father with me, and use every effort to distract his mind from his sorrow, in the only way in which I conceive such distraction to be possible; that is, by sharing it.

Thursday evening.

If you were not away, my friend, I should enjoy much, and my pleasures would have a keener zest. I need not tell you that I pass my days in the study of ethical medicine, and passive obedience will always be the basis of my system. Slander it as you will, I have never been at peace elsewhere; and when one has found a rest for the head, even upon marble, one should not change one's position. I have never met with any palliative which was not superseded by the grand remedy, save occupation: and I sometimes long to give myself up to it; for the greater part of the time my ill-health subjects me to the fate of Tantalus, who, when we meet in the valley of Jehoshaphat, will probably have nothing to tell me.

I told Count de Maistre your story of the German baron, — a story whose patriarchal turn, embellished by all the poetry at my command, I thought, should have conquered him. He charged me to tell you that it was "shocking." So much for the success of my poetry upon your prose! Being unable to let the matter rest, he started from the points that the divorce having been defended by I know not what council, in I know not what year, &c.; and thereupon followed a beautiful discourse, rather theological than sentimental. Do what we will, my friend, —

Rome se met toujours entre lui et son cœur.[2]

Have I not produced a fine verse?

As for me, who am not bristling with arguments, and, in the matter of dogmas, have a singular aptitude for that of sacrifice, I must confess that there was something preternatural in that

---

[1] Count de Maistre's son.
[2] Rome is always coming between him and his heart.

act of self-devotion which powerfully attracted me.   Adieu, my
friend.   I cannot imagine the continuation of obstacles which
could long withhold me from writing to you.   I await impatiently your letter from Berlin.   Tell me fully of what you are
doing, and particularly of your mood of mind.   There are a
thousand situations from which one can only extricate one's self
by the extreme of heavenly resignation, or the extreme of
worldly levity.   You know nothing of the latter.   Try to have
recourse to the former, and so complete the recovery of your
strength.   I embrace you with all my heart.

September, 1813.

I have been longing to write to you, and all yesterday and
to-day have actually been lying in wait for a moment in which
to do so.   You, too, my dear friend, have had a broken
and fatiguing day, although of a very different kind.   I have
thought at intervals of all your grandeur; picturing to myself my dear Roxandra with a tranquil exterior, but sorely
ennuyeé at heart.   Has it not been so?   Yet I do not so much
compassionate those people in the amphitheatre, who, like you,
can indemnify themselves by observing others; but the poor
observed, — when they play their part, — is there any patience
equal to theirs?   I would quite as soon be the counterpart of
St. Simeon Stylites on the top of his column.   To-day, however, I fancy that I could bear any thing, even that, with
the utmost philosophy; the excellent news which we continue to receive puts me in such "high spirits."   I am more
hopeful than ever.   We can never make blunders enough to
paralyze so many resources, and betray so brilliant a beginning.   Since Count de Langeron has beaten the enemy, it appears extremely probable to me that he will continue to do so.
If we are not deceived, and our force is what they say, only
misunderstandings and low jealousies can prevent it; and it is
to be hoped, that, for once at least, quarrelling will be in abeyance till the common enemy is worsted.   I cannot tell you how
deeply I have been affected by the misfortune which has fallen on
the good cause, in the person of Moreau.[1]   What a subject for

---

1 General Moreau, transferred to the United States in consequence of
the lawsuit which Bonaparte had commenced against him, landed at Goth-
embourg in the month of July, 1813.   He entered into relations with the
allied sovereigns through the medium of his old companion in arms, Bernadotte, who was then Prince Royal of Sweden.   The armistice had just

a pompous exordium on the part of the monster! and to what account will he turn it in impressing the French mind! But when I think that the same blow might have fallen on the Emperor, and what an immense peril we have escaped, I must confess that I dare not complain. It is not simply an affectionate anxiety that I feel when he exposes himself thus: it is a noble and righteous wrath, the strongest I am capable of feeling. It is a wholly false notion of real courage which lures him on; and I, who spend my days in pardoning erroneous ideas, do not feel the slightest toleration for this.

Count de Maistre, who has just left me, brought me the news of the death of the younger Prince de Broglie.[1] My heart bleeds for his poor mother, who, in several years, has scarcely recovered from the loss of her eldest son. What times we live in! "Woe to the fathers!" says the gospel. In this deplorable age, there is scarcely an individual who does not tremble or suffer.

The poor Princess Alexis has been in a state of terrible anxiety. She knew that the regiment of Sémenowsky, where her two sons[2] are, had been engaged; and, having received no news of her children, she has feared some misfortune. At present, she is somewhat re-assured, and, I think, with reason. If there had been bad news for her, she would already have received it. I do not know why they are so careless about sending the lists of the killed and wounded. Suspense is crushing, and the incoherence which pervades the reports is itself a species of torture.

I am in so little haste, my friend, to speak of Nadine, that

---

expired. The allied armies marched from Bohemia into Saxony to attack Dresden, which was, at that crisis, the centre of the Emperor Napoleon's operations. At the attack on Dresden, on the 26th of August, 1812, a bullet fractured Moreau's right leg, passed across his horse, and carried away a portion of the left. Amputation of both limbs was performed upon the spot. He died during the night of the first or second of September. His body was embalmed at Prague, and then carried to St. Petersburg, where it received the same honors as had been awarded to Marshal Koutouzof.

[1] Francis Ladislas de Broglie Revel, grandson of Marshal Broglie. Born in 1788, he was but a year old when he left Paris with his parents. At the age of ten, he entered the First Corps of Cadets at St. Petersburg; was appointed ensign in a regiment of the Imperial Guard; and slain in the skirmish at Culm, in Bohemia, 29th of August, 1813.

[2] Princes Paul and Peter Galitzin.

you will rightly have concluded that she is better. The remedies work well; and I am beginning to believe that youth will triumph over a malady which rends my heart by the suffering it entails, apart from its dangerous nature. As soon as the frost is out of the ground, I shall take her into the country: where, I do not yet know. Countess Tolstoy has been kind enough to write to her husband to procure me a suite of rooms at Oranienbaum, the air of which place the doctors recommend for Nadine; but I do not know whether she will be successful. Good-night, dear Roxandra. I am going to bed; and I shall not close my letter till to-morrow, which will give you the trouble of deciphering a few more minute pages.

Tuesday, 9th.

Less of choice than of necessity, I find myself at length relieved of my august presidency; and, like all who have ever abdicated sovereign power, I had my regrets. I long ago formed the determination to leave in the spring; and Nadine's illness gave me the courage to execute it. If you think it necessary, please inform Her Majesty. I hardly know whether to believe those who tell me that I should have asked for her commands before she left; but I must say, that, when there is a question of making advances, I feel them to be inconsistent with my character, and all the sophistry in the world comes at once to the aid of my shyness.

I am truly glad that your relations with the Empress are satisfactory; but you know very well that I am not influenced by motives of vanity, even where those I love are concerned. It has seemed to me that you behaved like a person whose feelings have been hurt; and wounded sensibility is so often mistaken in this world for offended vanity, that I could not bear to have the slightest suspicion of pettiness attach to you. I am inclined to think that there is nothing more flattering than a naked truth, boldly uttered; but, all the same, those who can bear it are the rare exceptions in human nature.

The last news from the army, announcing the victory won by our dear Emperor himself, has re-animated our spirits, strangely depressed by perpetual alternations of hope and fear. God grant that all these efforts and this devotion may be crowned by a period of dear-bought repose! The word "glory" no longer affects me. The string it once caused to vibrate in my soul would seem to be broken; and I would gladly beg, for the world as for myself, a little tranquillity, if ever so tame. The death of M. de Saint Priest[1] moved me deeply; and that of Count Strogonof was keenly felt. His mother encounters this affliction with a courage and resignation which some people are unjust enough to attribute to insensibility. They seem to forget, that every thing, even the pride with which she is so bitterly reproached, conspires to increase the poignancy of her regret. Countess Strogonof bears the blow meekly, suffering with sweetness and submission. This is enough to excite doubts as to the character of her very just and natural affection in the minds of those who are ever on the watch for something to relieve them of the responsibility of compassion and respect. Ah, my friend, how dull and illogical are narrow minds! They judge only by appearances; or, it may be, more guilty still, they refuse to believe the evidence of their senses, that they may wrong others at their ease.

We are soon to lose M. Tchitchagof,[2] and I am very sorry for it. He has great faults, he has not the greatest virtues: but he has a fine mind and a strong character; and these suffice to make him a lovable being. We are great friends; and, though one can never answer for these gentlemen, I, at least, am sure that I shall always be a friend to him. He is as inconsolable as ever; and I need sorrow, as well as something better, to enable me to love him. The Emperor has just granted him permission to go to England, and I am glad that he was not thwarted in this project; for I am certain that a residence

---

[1] Count de Saint Priest, brother of General Viscount de Saint Priest, Duke of Almazan, was killed March 17, 1814, before Reims, in a fight with Marshal Marmont's army corps.

[2] Admiral Paul Tchitchagof was a son of Admiral Basil Tchitchagof, who left a name illustrious and revered in the Russian fleet, which he repeatedly led to victory. His son Paul — himself a distinguished man — was educated in England, which country was ever afterwards the object of his avowed preference. He married Miss Elizabeth Proby, the daughter of an English admiral. The loss of his wife, to whom he was passionately attached, plunged him in inconsolable melancholy. He lived in retirement thenceforward, and soon fixed his residence in England. He died at Paris, in September, 1849, aged eighty-two. He had been, for some years, agent of the Russian marine, and bequeathed to this agency those of his papers and notes of travel which seemed likely to be of use to Russia. Among these papers were found a number of letters from Count de Maistre, which have recently been published at Paris, thanks to Baron Korf, director of the imperial library.

there will eventually make the place distasteful to him. Lord
Walpole remarked, in speaking of him, " He is restless ; " and
this disquietude will yet restore him to the native land, by
whose prejudices he is alienated.

Apropos of Lord Walpole, I think that you have judged
him very severely. If you had looked closer, you would have
seen that his is not a spirit of contradiction ; and his conversation, on many subjects, is interesting and suggestive. I see
him often : he inundates me with English books ; and I should
be at a loss to determine to what extent these books influence
my opinion of him. It is always understood, at St. Petersburg,
that one's days are to be spent without pleasure or profit. It
is positive plunder ; and I regret what I save more than what I
lose. I have such need of leisure ! The confusion of the life
I have been leading renders me almost a stranger to that inner
self which never expands to fulness of life save when I can give
myself up unrestrainedly to the impulses of affection, to nature,
and to that world of mind which sometimes makes us forget the
other. I have so much of the past in my heart, that to live
with old regrets and the new emotions which they awaken is as
necessary to me as the hope of happiness to the young souls
that believe in it. God has been very good to me in relieving
my anxiety about Nadine ; but, if I were denied the outpourings of perfect confidence, my whole life would be disenchanted.
I feel sometimes so keen a need of confession, that I would go
to the world's end to open my heart ; and often I have started
involuntarily from my chair, as if it depended upon me to
hasten my deliverance from the weight that oppressed me.

The Countess —— is always the same. Ages loaded with
experience might pass over her head without her eternal youth
getting older by a day.

Now for your admirer, Sayger,[1] who pretends that with
you went all the happiness he ever enjoyed in Russia. He
sends you his kindest regards. The departure of the grand-
dukes has not deprived him of his fees ; but I fancy that he is
somewhat harassed in money matters, beside his domestic
troubles. He was very sad the last time I saw him. I believe him to be somewhat wrong-headed, and strongly suspect
that he makes no struggle against afflictive circumstances.
Did I tell you that the two lessons which Sayger gave me did
not answer? I have engaged another German master, who
comes every day, and under whose tuition I make rapid progress. If you hear any thing from Count de Lagarde, please

---

[1] Professor of German in the imperial family.

let me know: I have had no intelligence since he crossed to Frankfort, and I miss it. 'Tis a good sign, that nothing is said of him. Military men are in the same category as women, — they are most fortunate when they are not talked about. I send you a letter from Count de Maistre. He had one from his son yesterday, which was perfectly satisfactory.

If you are having it cold at the South, we are almost warm here in the North. The river has broken up, to my great delight; and the three windows of my study present to view three beautiful Vernets, whose genuineness no one will deny.

I have read Mme. de Staël's "Germany," and find, as in all her other books, some admirable pages and some hasty judgments. My professors of German literature, Ouvarof and Tourguenief, do not find her account, in all respects, accurate. Please give me your opinion on this matter. If you could send me a book on magnetism and its effects, not too voluminous, but which would give me a fair idea of the subject, you would do me a great favor; for I like nothing better than to be interested in all that interests you, from alpha to omega. Adieu, my dear friend.

Last Friday, the Princess Alexis and I passed the evening with Count de Maistre, who, under the pressure of the duties imposed by hospitality, did not allow himself a moment's sleep. He came off conqueror in the terrible struggle; but who knows what it cost him?

Universal benevolence has been the romance of the second period of my life. When one renounces the hope of living uninterruptedly in a single soul, it takes the whole race to fill the place of that one. Nothing is more common than to make up in number what we lack in quality.

The better I come to know you, the greater need I have of your constant presence. If I live ten years longer, and continue to advance in the same direction, I shall finally arrive at the point of lunacy, — I shall believe that I am your shadow.

Apropos of books, I send you some volumes to-day, at the request of Count de Maistre. He has just returned a pamphlet which I lent him, entitled "A View of French Literature in the Eighteenth Century;" and returned it enriched by very interesting marginal notes of his own. The book is excellent; and his observations, though a little severe, are remarkable for their tact and acuteness. Count de Maistre is like a huntsman's dog: he scents, at a prodigious distance, all which has a direct or indirect bearing on the ideas of his age. He tolerates no deviation from fundamental principles. If this obliquity manifests itself in ever so slight a degree, neither eloquence nor elevation of thought or sentiment will atone for it.

Your character reminds me of those happy turns of expression for which great writers are remarkable. The admiration which these combinations excite springs from the fact, that
genius has the art of uniting words which were never meant to
go together. Ah, well! your character is a collection of op-
posites which would naturally be thought incompatible, but
which constitutes your greatest charm. You say, perhaps,
that this charm is of my lending. Something must, of course,
be attributed to motives of retaliation; but please remember
that we only lend to the rich.

Do you share with me the thought most calculated to alle-
viate the dread of death? Do you believe in the eternal re-
union of souls which have comprehended one another here
below? It seems to me to be the heart's own doctrine. Religion leaves us entire latitude in this respect; and the universal
assent, or, rather, presentiment (the strongest of proofs in a
matter of feeling), seems to me a warrant of its truth. I know
that a pious soul may anticipate the delight of re-union with the
Supreme Being; but would heaven be quite heaven to us, if we
could not unite to the sublime thought of our future destination
some sensible ideas? Where would be that personality without which they say that immortality would be but a vain gift,
if memory had vanished, and the *ego* ceased to exist? and if
that *ego* finds itself again, what region, what degree of felicity,
could obliterate the memory of that which was once identified
with it? No one will ever make me believe that the soul of my
father, when I meet it, will be no more to me than that of the
Chinaman in whose company I may make the last journey. I
know well that we must take care not to judge heavenly by
earthly things; but are not these a shadow or an echo of those?
and what is a shadow or an echo but a picture or a voice, feeble, indeed, and indistinct, but ever faithful to the original?
Ah! if this soothing theory were supported by the most positive
proofs, the aspect of Death walking with lifted hand ready
to smite those we love, or snatch us away from those who love
us, would still be "awful," as the English say so expressively.

Dear Roxandra, one ought to bless Providence, when, like
you, one has much to lose; still more, when one has, like you,
a thousand chances of repairing loss. I know, by instinct, the
happiness which you will enjoy; and I desire it for you with all
the united strength of your heart and mine. I see the outlines
of your destiny. You will be a wife and mother; and in the
centre of these blessed affections you will pass peaceful days,
whose very reflection will brighten those of your friends.

What poignant regrets must fill the soul of the poor Empress, who has had the cup of felicity put to her lips only to

be made more sensible of the bitterness of having it with-drawn![1] I can well understand the impulsive feeling, that you would give your life to restore to her the possession of what she regrets. My God! if one did but dare! if one might some-times be as good as one's heart! If a little power over nature had only been accorded to those whose sensibility removes them, lifts them, so to speak, above themselves! But how long would be the list of our desires! Things seem arranged upon a plan which the germ of evil in the human heart explains only too clearly, but which one would fain see suspended at the word of such as would interrupt the course of general laws for the sake of others only. Then we should see angels upon earth protecting other angels, and the world would be the better for it. What do you say to this arrangement?

I find, in all the distractions which would divert us from our sadness, the contrast which pained you on returning from your walk. All that is discordant, or directly opposed to our feel-ing, irritates and wounds us. If grief is to be mitigated, it must either wear itself out or be shared. It is the idle, the importunate, and the tiresome, — and their name is legion, — who have invented that multitude of ceremonies, formulas, and trite observances, with which it is customary to surround the afflicted, who thus have added to their original trial that of an enforced publicity of grief. My recipe would be this: Per-fect solitude, which would allow of utter abandonment to one's feelings; or, better still, the mingling one's grief with that of another in such a way that the souls as well as the sorrows would coalesce. I should say that these were distractions which might attain the desired end, because they would not attempt it prematurely. . . .

Those romances which present a faithful and artless picture of the human heart and its mysteries seem to me to be history *par excellence*. Names void of interest, barren facts, dates which we know to be useless, — these are what should be called romance, if we mean by the word a wearisome motley, which adds nothing to our experience, and has no tendency to ame-liorate our condition. That plan of collecting and preserving your reminiscences is charming. Do not abandon it, dear Roxandra, — you who forget nothing, and are never forgotten.

I am truly glad that you have discovered the sterling qualities of Mlle. Walouef.[2] She needs to control her first impulses somewhat: she will be reasonable in the end; but it is often a

---

[1] The Empress had lost two infant children, and was childless.
[2] Superintendent of the Maids of Honor.

long time first; and this is a more serious disadvantage to herself than to any one else. She is satisfied with you, and will one day appreciate you fully. The atmosphere of Tzarskoe Selo is that which suits her nature best. There she is diverted and amused; and, although you may not know it, 'tis none the less true, that/our sufferings have much to do with our faults.) . . .

You are right in thinking that we must be generous in order to be just. If a painter would produce a perfect representation of nature, he is obliged to embellish her. Since he cannot impart to canvas the velvet softness of the skin, the freshness of coloring, and the grace of nature, he must supply their lack by another species of perfection; and it is only by giving too much in some directions, that he succeeds in giving enough. Morally speaking, we are painters of those on whom we pass judgment; and, having no exact measure of the good qualities which we perceive, let us at least palliate the defects. Here, perhaps, lies the sole secret of producing mental likenesses which shall be perfect as a whole, and, better still, agreeable. . . .

I am harder to cure than the King of England.[1] How great, then, must be your skill, if you are successful! Ah! you are right, — I am very weak in action; and, what is more, it is an organized, systematic weakness, which manifests itself in a multitude of ways. If I lose this fault, shall I have one virtue left? Judge for yourself, my dearest friend. If I had ever dared ask for aught, should I not, with my native impetuosity, ever ready to carry me beyond bounds, have become exacting in all my relations? If I had not made haste to shroud my life in a sombre veil, could I have borne the thought of death? If I dared indulge hope in any matter, would it not weary my soul too much? I am like the globe, according to Buffon's theory of its formation: detached, like that, from a burning sun, I have been cooling for many years. I am not quite arctic in temperature; but, without the comfort you have afforded me, I should have been so ere this. At all events, I should have given one leap over the temperate zone; for there I have never been able to abide. To remain on the hither side of it is much easier for me. For instance: if I had had an immoderate dread of the abuse of speech, I could have become a Trappist with perfect ease; and absolute silence would have cost me less than retrenching twenty words each day. Every thing in me which savors of exaggeration in the practice of things praise-

---

[1] George III., who was partially insane.

worthy in themselves is but disguised weakness. 'Tis this alone which I fear; 'tis this alone which gives me the resigned and indifferent spirit with which you are pleased to credit me. You tell me of the future and of new cares, as I have often told myself; but it is time for the rule of Reason (who is no goddess) to begin. (We are no longer required actually to shun ourselves; but we must dare look ourselves fully in the face, and cease to call on phantoms to vanquish realities./ I assure you that this is my last word, and that I shall now proceed to establish a mixed government over myself. I shall assign to my several powers the part suited to each one. I shall permit no encroachments; and out of this arrangement, perhaps, will spring the equilibrium which has so long been a desideratum here. If you were but at the helm, my friend, the bark would soon arrive at a good port. What a medley! What an exalted idea I must have of your indulgence to try it like this! While I write, the horrors of moving are going on around me. Nadine is very busy and important: she has at least six copy-books to put in order; and, as you may imagine, she has had to consult me on the subject a hundred times. . . .

It is splendid weather. The air is pure; the sun warm, but not oppressive. There are trees; there is verdure; there are walks, and people who enjoy them: better still, there are those who do not enjoy them alone. How happy are such! If we have superfluities, we can dispense with necessaries. I am interrupted. Adieu, dear friend. Perhaps you are writing to me at this very moment: the thought makes it harder than usual to leave you. . . .

When you say, "Have you experienced this?" or, "Do you understand that?" you may be sure that I can truthfully answer "Yes." I have felt and reflected much, and in the matter of human affection and passion have traversed an immense circle, and penetrated to the very antipodes. I have taken a doctor's degree in this law, and am not at all mystified by things which are inexplicable to those who have lived only in externals. Experience has not even taught them to spell, and how should they understand reading? It is in the precinct of my own heart that I have learned to comprehend the hearts of others; and a knowledge of my single self has given me a key to those innumerable riddles which we call men. The idea that every individual is a microcosm has always approved itself to me. I have sometimes dreaded to have sleep come, and interrupt the delicious reverie in which I lay quiescent between memory and hope; but oftener I have shut my eyes, as children do, that I might not see the phantoms of the night, and sought to persuade myself that I slept, so as not to be too sensible that my heart was awake and suffering. In truth, my friend, if I did not believe that the habitual unrest which I experience, and which interferes so sadly with my serenity of mind, were due to my health, it would seriously disturb my gratitude to my Maker. I have sorrows, — who has them not? but, if life had always smiled on me, if every thing had been propitious, could I have deserved, have kept, have guarded, my happiness? should I not have been utterly devoured by that restlessness which is at the bottom of all minds of a certain order? I have deserved the greater part of the griefs I have known; yet God softens them, as if they had been only tests, not punishments. I meet with kindness; I inspire it: my need of esteem is satisfied. I have known the most illustrious of my kind. My craving for love is also filled. My heart has been so fortunate in the matter of friendship! Why, then, should I not finish with courage a career whose close is already in view? I assure you, my friend, that, when my prostration is not physical, it resembles a calm and sweet tranquillity. . . .

To produce any thing valuable, I need to be absorbed; and, when I work only by fits and starts, I experience fatigue without pleasure. It is one of the greatest inconveniences of the life which I lead, to such a character as mine, that I must parcel out my day, and leave empty spaces in it. Melancholy effects so easy an entrance into these breaches; and then it cannot be dislodged. When shall I be able to spend a long morning with you, reading from some good and pleasant book by my own fireside? . . .

The example of Mme. de S. ought to disgust me with self-love. Has she not always lived for herself? and yet how has her happiness ever been at the mercy of troubles, trifling in their causes, but poignant in their effects! What has she gained by making herself the centre of her life? It reminds me of that English verse : —

> " To each his sufferings. All are men
> Condemned alike to groan:
> The tender, for another's pain;
> The unfeeling, for his own."

Judging by the sad impression which misfortune makes, it would seem to be new to us every time we encounter it. Have you reflected upon this strange but incontestable fact, that the thought of death is terrible in an arid existence, when no love or compassion can come to sweeten its bitterness, while it is almost pleasant at the two moral extremes of life, — su-

preme sorrow and supreme joy? In the first instance, it is a
change, and seems like a deliverance. In the other, there is
a feeling that there is nothing beyond but God; that a genuine affection is a preparation for eternity; and that eternity
comes, not to interrupt, but to perpetuate, all which makes
life dear. To whom do I say this? 'Tis time that wears on
tender, loving hearts. Eternity is their asylum. . . .

My sister and I go Saturday to Peterhof to see the house
which I am to occupy. Count de Maistre tells me that he is
sorry to have me go: and I can believe it; for I, too, shall be
extremely sorry to see him less often. I spent yesterday evening with him: we sat till two o'clock. He was sad; and, to
divert him, I conversed on his favorite subjects, which I do not
understand in the least. We went from Greek to Hebrew by
a way that I knew not. Finally, the conversation flagging, I
quarrelled with him; and then he revived. This is my method
of entertaining my friends. Count de Maistre will write you;
and I have undertaken to forward his letter. That cold face
of his conceals a profoundly sensitive soul. I do not wish to
boast; but he has sometimes said things to me that were very
sweet to hear. I leave you to guess which of these sayings I
have prized the highest, and shall be able to repeat most accu-
rately after the lapse of two or three months. Now rack your
brains. Have you done it? No: you are wrong. Then
speak to your heart, and speak of mine. It is enough: you
have guessed.

Friday, two o'clock, P.M.

My letter will go this evening; and I wish to add one word.
The court lackey who brought me yours so promptly told me
that I might send mine in the same way; and this gives me all
the facilities I could desire. You will not show this letter?
It is not out of vanity that I ask it, but that I may feel at ease,
and always dare to be myself. If it is impossible that I can be
wrong in relying so utterly on your comprehension, it is
equally so that the confidence which I repose in you should
extend to those about you. As to your own letters, nothing
could be more superfluous than to request me to keep them
private. My native egotism, so prompt to see profanation in
the touch of indifferent persons, is sufficient to put me on my
guard. Mme. S. is kind enough to say, that, for some reason
or other, I am like the bee. If I were one, I should assuredly
prevent the flies from approaching the flowers whence I made

my honey, whatever good or bad reasons they might allege for
so doing. . . .

My health is not very bad; and, in view of the equal division it makes of my time, I am tempted to apply to it the
parable of the seven fat kine and the seven lean kine. I have
my good days, when activity reigns, and then others in which I
neither sow nor reap; and the latter, my friend, in a thoughtful existence, are very dull. Nevertheless, I do not complain
of this, nor of any thing else. It seems to me that I grasp
God's intentions concerning me. I feel that I am under his
influence, and treading the path which his pity has marked out
for me. Is not such a mood of mind in itself one of the greatest of blessings? You are right to desire nothing but what
God wills. / I am keenly sensible of our utter ignorance about
what is best for us. (I have seen so many more bitter tears shed
over fulfilled than over disappointed hopes, that, if I were invested with supreme power over my own destiny, I should beg
to be relieved of it without delay. It is good to depend upon
the Being who made all things; and, if aught could render
the human creature more miserable than he now is, it would be
one more degree of freedom.) These are old thoughts of
mine, dear friend. Their germ was within me in days when
the air was still fragrant; when surrounding objects were resplendent with beauty and freshness; and when, though my
heart had her sorrows, the consciousness of existence was still a
constant exhilaration. . . .

In the country where you are sojourning, when they see a
superior person who dares to be herself, and remain natural
and quiet where others are affected, instead of conceding the
superiority which such a line of conduct suggests, they attribute
it to the perfection of art. This is perfectly explicable. There
are ears on which the word *merit* grates, but which the word
address does not alarm. One point upon which I feel perfectly
easy is the Empress's judgment of you. She is too clever not
to appreciate a character like yours, and has every thing to gain
by intercourse with superior minds. There is nothing so advantageous as the observation of others for those characters which
deserve the praise so hackneyed, and yet so high when just, of
improving upon acquaintance. All which bears the impress
of unity is true; but, in whatever is factitious, there is always
a tip of the ear sticking out. I can very well understand why
persons of exalted rank are prone to hesitate long before giving the slightest confidence. They feel that a genuine friendship would be very sweet; but, all the same, they know that
they compromise more than others, if they make any but an
excellent choice. . . .

M. de Maistre has given me an abstract of the advice with which he has favored you (it is droll, — is it not? — that we should take it upon ourselves to advise you, who might well lead us both) ; and I have smiled more than once at his grand theories, which could not possibly be reduced to practice. There is surely some method (which is never applied) of sparing the pride of man ; but, as regards the vanity of woman, none such has ever been discovered. I believe the simplest way is to make up one's mind to sacrifice it; to advance slowly, and repeat one's self often, and thus to gain strength. Do right, whatever betides. Moreover, we must not attach to trifles an importance which they do not possess. Good as well as evil is transitory; vanishes, and leaves no trace. People caress you, and then sulk at you, or overwhelm you with demonstrations of interest, after loading you with proofs of dislike. We are all of us, in this world, more or less like St. January, whom the inhabitants of Naples worship one day, and pelt with baked apples the next. The saint, who is very good-natured, performs the same number of miracles each year. Let us imitate him; and let the miracle wrought on ourselves be the attainment of patience and balance of character, so difficult of preservation in the midst of so many vicissitudes.

Count de Maistre has gone on a pilgrimage to visit the hermit Tchitchagof, who is very comfortable at his Oranienbaum. The grief of this man interests me. It is of more service to him than he suspects. He is hot-headed, and needs some fixed point on which to concentrate his ideas. If, in his position, he had been given over to ambition, and left at the mercy of all its attendant annoyances, he would have suffered thereby: he would, I think, have had no power of resistance. But now he offsets against these influences a sorrow which enlarges and ennobles the man ; and, at least, all the original force and dignity of his character is preserved. . . .

I believe that our rulers are to be pitied for the strait to which they are reduced; but, I must say, I should not understand them, if they could help despising inwardly the example just set by M. de ———. Thus to change, at a critical moment, from one party to the other ; and to carry one's betrayal so far as to deliver over to the enemy all the important bills and papers which one has in possession, — fie, what meanness ! This man would have saved Russia only to blow his brains out afterwards, if I should suspect his intentions! Our good Emperor is too noble to give his confidence to such ; and, if I did not think so, I could not be easy. If any one should hear me say this, I know very well that my opinion would be anathematized; it would be an unpardonable sin: but, unless all one's ideas of justice and honesty are to be reversed, I do not see how any other is to be entertained.[1] . . .

You are closing your blinds to keep out the sun; and we, my friend, would fain multiply and make warmer the few scattered rays he sheds on us. Our spring exists nowhere but in the calendar; and, if the river had not broken up, it would require the faith which we exercise in all mysteries to prevent us from despairing of it. In the North, one imagines a new beatitude, — "Blessed are the warm!" I cannot possibly tell you how sorely I need a different climate, and another kind of life than that which I now lead. I should need, for my regeneration, a benignant atmosphere; and, for the complete re-animation of my broken spirits, the combined blessings of a fine climate, poetic scenery, much leisure, and more friendship. But this is just what I only find in samples which make me long for the whole piece. I am attached by a thousand ties to my native land: but these would not break, even if they were loosened for a few years; and the re-establishment of my moral force would make me fitter to enjoy them. We find as many rare and lovable persons at St. Petersburg as elsewhere, — perhaps more; and I shall not light my lantern, like Diogenes, to seek them out, I have known so many in my day. But that precaution would be very useful, if it could assist me in shunning the crowd of commonplace individuals whom we meet on our journey, whose mediocrity, versatility, and, too often, their malice, are not atoned for by an instant's pleasure in their society. What you tell me of your circle would make me long for it, even if you were not there; and, were I to follow you, dear friend, I should claim a little interest in your name from those whose friendship you have already won. It is so pleasant to be in your debt! . . .

I do not prefer others to myself, but it is others only that I really love; and it is in them that all my selfishness centres, and all my comfort, unless I am living bound up in self. I have never felt that any person owed me any thing (you understand

---

[1] This impulse of manly honor should have its place in a memoir of Mme. Swetchine; but the reader ought to be made aware that Gen.——— and his friends have recently published a justification, which may be found at length in the "Vie Militaire du Général Comte Friant; par le Comte Friant, son fils." This justification rests principally upon the watchful jealousy of Berthier, who saw, in the Baron de ———, the sole rival whom he had to fear, and upon the nationality of the Baron ———, who was a Swiss, and not a Frenchman, by birth.

the latitude with which I use the expression) ; yet I have always
thought I should be quite miserable, unless I owed all to others.
This may render the character strange and eccentric; but it is
easy and safe, and will not repel even the ungrateful. . . .

The rumors to which Count de Maistre alluded have come
to my hearing; but I know, better than any one else, how active
is malevolence, and how cheap falsehood. I have been afraid
they would reach you, and such things always give pain. . . .

Your letters will be sent to-morrow morning. I enclose one
from Count de Maistre, who replies to your intention of writing him. . . .

I am expecting my husband daily. I long for his return,
and the end of his nomad life. It is a good while now that
we have been like M. Sun and Mme. Moon, who are never
seen together. Speaking of my husband reminds me that it
was St. Alexander's Day when the news of the victories reached
Moscow. The cathedral had been consecrated that very day:
there was an illumination in the evening, transparencies and a
prodigious crowd in the streets. Conceive the contrast between
this *fête* and those ruins ! But it is perfectly natural. Are not
all our merrymakings over tombs? and what is the earth,
half a fathom below its surface, but a mass of formless remains?
Forget! so says Providence, in its kindness, touched by the
misery of man. . . .

Count de Lagarde writes me from Vienna. He says that
the enthusiasm of the Austrians for the Russians is at its height.
Every thing, even to the dinner-plates, is *à la Cossack*. They
report a brilliant victory, won by the Prince Royal.[1] It will
remind you of that verse of La Harpe, —

"Tombé de chute en chute au trône académique."[2]

My constant fear is, that, from one defeat to another, the monster will go on to greater glory than ever. . . .

I have just discovered a new pleasure, which I am exhausting. It is that of dying of fear. I read Macbeth every evening
alone in a dimly lighted room. I fancy I hear the owl's hoot
of terror, the incantations of the conspirators, the hasty step
of the assassins, the broken moans of the dying. I see the
daggers drawn in the darkness, the shadows coming and going:
and, when terror has fairly got possession of me, and I begin
to shudder, and cast doubtful and horrified glances about, I say

---

[1] The Prince Royal of Sweden, Bernadotte.

[2] Plunging, from one depth to another, down to an academic throne.

to myself, the representation is perfect; and I go to bed with my imagination full of absurd fancies. . . .

When I was in the country, the day the gnats came, I was mortally impatient with them; but, after a while, I let them sing and sting, and even get into my eyes and ears, if I was not paying attention. They were as intolerable as ever, but I had become accustomed to them; and I have had very much the same experience with incorrigibly sulky people. If I were to recount to you the remedies I have employed to soothe the irritable susceptibility of Mlle. Walouef, the list would exhaust even your patience. Nothing would do; and finally I decided to do nothing. It troubled me, because it is always painful to witness suffering, and because, moreover, one must always have some reason to fear that one has not acted quite for the best; but after seeing all the ground lost which I thought I had gained, and spending my breath for naught, and often prejudicing my own interests instead of advancing them, I learned to fold my arms, and make some approach to quietism. It is the system I should always adopt for this sort of emergency, if my naughty nerves did not occasionally interfere with my philosophic practice. Trust me, all you can do in these cases is to be passive and calm. Let the fickle people always know where to find us: it seems to me that this is all the concession we can make to them. When you told me that all was going well between you, I believed it for a moment; and then, like old men loaded with years and experience, I smiled at your illusion, without caring to destroy it. These annoyances make no serious difference to you, who are goodness and delicacy itself; nor to me, who recognize in her the good qualities which atone for disagreeable faults: but I cannot think without regret what an immense price she sets on the favor of the Empress, and how unlikely she is to attain and preserve it. The least she can expect is the ridicule and mortification which must await the failure of her ends. . . .

C. de Maistre passed a part of the morning with me, and left a thousand tender remembrances for you. "Tender" is the word, and, in fact, the most moderate one I could employ; for, if his feeling for you were analyzed, God knows what heterogeneous elements it would be found to contain! Good-by, my friend. Forgive me for having written like a cat, and chattered like a magpie.

CHAPTER V.

Connection between Mlle. Stourdza and Mme. de Krüdener. — Correspondence between Mme. Swetchine and Mlle. Stourdza continued.

THE character of the Emperor Alexander — flexible, mobile, and prone to emotion — passed through the same phases as his empire, underwent re-actions, and preserved some trace of every crisis. His heart was divided between the seductions of youth and the teaching of events. Seldom now did sovereign power appear to him clothed with the inviolable charm of its prerogatives, but under the severe, and at times forbidding, aspect of its responsibilities. The love of his subjects remained steadfast; but, again and again, their stupidity, their dull faces, their melancholy glances, called on him to give an account of the use he had made, or was intending to make, of so much confidence and devotion. Often his aids-de-camp had seen him turn aside, and traverse alone and with hasty strides the alleys of Tzarskoe Selo, or fling himself into his carriage, and burst into tears. But, at last, to the lurid glare of the burning of Moscow succeeded the brilliant gleam of the day of Leipsic. Napoleon, vanquished by all Europe, seemed to owe his defeat immediately to the Russian arms. Alexander was once more exposed to the allurements of fortune, of glory, and of pleasure. The gravity of recent catastrophes cast a shade over his *entrée* into Paris; but he was unanimously hailed as a generous arbiter and a wise ruler.

But as soon as Napoleon had been naïvely confined in the island of Elba, and monarchy restored in France in the midst of spontaneous and sincere enthusiasm, Alexander started northward Vienna detained him. He lingered there for a long time, quite as much to enjoy the congratulations and the rejoicings of Europe, which believed itself delivered, as to preside over the doings of a congress whose duties had ceased to be of an urgent or alarming nature.

A few obscure and melancholy minds were still under the influence of fear. Among these, there was a woman unknown in the political world, and only half revealed to the world of letters by a romance strewn with ingenious thoughts.

Julia Wittinghof came of a family which had counted two masters of the Teutonic Order in the fourteenth and fifteenth centuries, and was the grand-daughter of Marshal Munich. She was born at Riga, in 1764; and married, at the age of twenty, Baron Krüdener, then Russian Ambassador to Venice, but soon separated from her husband, and made her way alone to France, Switzerland, and Germany, where she abandoned herself to the guidance of an excited imagination. Chance led her to the Grand Duchy of Baden at the time when the Empress Elizabeth, still separated from Alexander, was awaiting under the roof of her brother, the Grand-duke, the return of the conqueror of Napoleon.

Mme. de Krüdener, then in her fiftieth year, was, for the time being, devoting herself entirely to religious preaching. Some Protestant ministers from Geneva and Baden were her companions, alternately inspiring, and inspired by her. She was a kind of Mme. Guyon, for whom Fénélon and submission to Catholic authority were replaced by a few adventurous apostles without traditions or precise aim, who were first instigated, and afterwards swayed, by the *philosophe inconnu*, St. Martin. Mme. de Krüdener began her relations with royalty by a passing intimacy with Queen Louise of Prussia. She then traversed Germany, at one time resuming, to some extent, the·habits of the world; at another, sojourning with the Moravian brotherhood; and then again lending an ear to the *illuminé*, Jung Stilling,[1] and preaching with him to the poor dwellers in the lonely valleys of the Danube and the Rhine. With no more originality of doctrine than any of the sectaries of Germany, England, or the United States, she yet created an impression by means of her sex, her birth, her brilliant success upon another stage, and her language, which, though it never bore the stamp of simplicity, yet breathed, at times, the romantic charm of *Valerie*. At the little court of Baden, Mme. de Krüdener found herself the descendant of one of the most illustrious servants of the empire, and the widow of a Russian ambassador; and, by virtue of these titles, she easily attained to familiarity with the Empress. From time to time, her glance rested on the young favorite who accompanied her; and, either from sincere sympathy or calculation, Mme. Krüdener made Mlle. Stourdza the confidant of the thoughts which were agitating her soul, and which all gravitated towards the Emperor Alexander.

After the pacification of France, the allied sovereigns quitted Paris for Vienna, whither their principal ministers

---

[1] Jung Stilling had been a noted oculist, but had become one of those German theosophists who testified so much interest in the fate of the masses. He was established at Baden as a member of the Aulic Council by the Grand-duke Frederic; and Mme. de Krüdener made his house her head-quarters on her arrival at Carlsruhe.

followed them, and soon formed themselves into a congress. The Empress Elizabeth finally left Carlsruhe to rejoin her husband. Mme. de Krüdener remained at Baden, but kept up her intimacy with Mlle. Stourdza. In her letters, the Emperor Alexander is called the " White Angel," and the Emperor Napoleon the " Black Angel ; " and she constantly reproaches the statesmen of the time with ·the frivolity of their pleasures and the rashness of their policy. This austere tone, contrasting strangely with that of the world in which Mlle. Stourdza then lived, easily created a revulsion of feeling, and so wrought upon the pure and high-minded, that they, somewhat uncritically, confounded declamation with eloquence.

Mlle. Stourdza did not conceal this correspondence from the Empress, who, ever desirous of recalling her husband to more serious thoughts, took care, in her turn, to mention it to him. Thus encouraged, Mme. de Krüdener re-doubled her calls to the Christian life, and even ventured upon prophecy. On the 27th of October, 1814, she wrote from Strasburg : —

" No : the poisoned cup quaffed by the multitude will not tempt you. I speak strongly, but I live at the foot of the cross. The events of life are hastening. The visions of time, the voice of the apostles, the miracles which God lavishes on the unworthy creature who addresses you, — all these excite my conscience, and I must speak strongly. The time for hesitation is past. Let the giddy masses amuse themselves. They have but this melancholy pleasure.

" The angel who marked with saving blood the doors of the elect is passing ; but the world sees him not. He is numbering the people." The judgment approaches : it is ready, and there is a volcano beneath our feet ! We shall see guilty France, which, by the decrees of the Eternal, was to be saved by the cross which had subdued her, — we shall see her chastised. . . .

" These lilies which God had preserved ; this emblem of a pure and fragile flower which broke an iron sceptre, because he willed it so ; these lilies, which should have been symboli-

cal of purity, piety, and repentance, — have come and gone.
The lesson has been given; and men, more obdurate than ever,
dream but of tumult. Alas for these men of the torrent!
They are in dry deserts: they are flung out, by their passions,
upon a stormy ocean, where they see the shipwreck of others
without even wishing to escape their own. Can men dance,
and array themselves in rich draperies,[1] when dark enmities
rend the human race? What! will you never learn to tremble
at these audacious festivities, which spring from the mourning
of nations, and plunge them in it again?"

To these words, which referred to Europe in general,
Mme. de Krüdener adds some more precise remarks concerning her mission to the Emperor Alexander:—

"To love, with me, is to conform to sacred things. . . . You
would fain tell me of the depth, the power, and the beauty of
the Emperor's character. I believe that I already know him
well. I knew, long since, that the Lord would grant me the
joy of seeing him. I have great things to say to him, for I
have experienced much on his behalf. The Lord alone can
prepare his heart to receive my words.[2]

"There is an old sinner at Vienna, to whom I am strongly
attached, — the Prince de Ligne. There are such everywhere.
He used to call me the Gray Sister of the heart; and we once
loved one another. His natural disposition is excellent. I am
so dead to the world, that he would fear me now as one fears
the departed. But I should care neither for his fears nor his
smiles, if I might but see him come to the life which saves from
eternal death. He used to have moments when his conscience
was awake. He wanted me to become a Catholic, and I
wanted him to become a Christian."

At the very moment when this letter was read at Vienna
by the Emperor Alexander, its effect was heightened by

---

[1] One of the most fashionable amusements at Vienna during the congress was *Tableaux-vivans.*

[2] All these details are taken from the "Life of Mme. de Krüdener,"
by M. Ch. Eynard, who has drawn the materials for his very interesting
work from authentic sources. M. Capefigue is wrong in assigning an
earlier date to the connection between Mme. de Krüdener and the Emperor Alexander.

the sudden death of the Prince de Ligne, under circumstances calculated to impress the imagination of the Czar.

As the time of the startling escape from Elba approached, Mme. de Krüdener grew more precise and urgent in her warnings. On the 14th of February, 1814, she once more wrote to Mlle. Stourdza, still dwelling on the Emperor Alexander : —

> " Yes, my friend, I am persuaded that I have things of immense importance to say to him; and, though the Prince of Darkness do his best to prevent it, and to separate him from those who might speak of sacred things, the Eternal will be too strong for him."

" At the very moment," says her biographer, " when Mme. de Krüdener was writing thus to Mlle. Stourdza, she was commanded by a revelation to repair to a mill near Schluchtern, in the Electorate of Hesse, and there await the fore-ordained meeting." And there she was met, though not surprised, by the news of the landing at Cannes, and the entry of Napoleon into Paris, on the 20th of March, 1815.

The Emperor Alexander, on his part, left Vienna, and hastened to his head-quarters, a prey to the sharpest anxiety, overwhelmed with remorse for his want of foresight. He had refused to appear at the splendid reception prepared by the Bavarians, and was with difficulty persuaded to accept the hospitality of his uncle, the King of Wurtemberg. At nightfall, he retired to his apartment.

> " I drew breath at last," he wrote with his own hand to Mlle. Stourdza, who had stayed behind with the Empress, " and my first impulse was to take a book which I always carry with me ; but my intellect was obscured by sombre clouds, and failed to take in the sense of what I read. My ideas were confused, and my heart oppressed. I dropped the book, and thought what a consolation it would be to me at that moment

to converse with some pious friend. This thought reminded me of you. I remembered, also, what you had told me of Mme. de Krüdener, and the desire I had already expressed to you of making her acquaintance. 'Where is she now, and how am I ever to meet her?' I had barely expressed this thought, when there came a knocking at my door. It was Prince Wolkouski, who, with an air of great irritation, declared that he was exceedingly sorry to disturb me at that unseasonable hour, but that it was his only way of getting rid of a woman who was determined to see me. At the same time he named Mme. de Krüdener. You may imagine my astonishment. It seemed as if I were dreaming. 'Mme. de Krüdener!' I cried, 'Mme. de Krüdener!' This sudden response to my thought could not be accidental. I admitted her instantly; and, as if she had read my soul, she spoke to me strengthening and consoling words, which calmed the trouble which had oppressed me so long."

This timely apparition was followed by an interview which lasted no less than three hours. At intervals, Alexander wept profusely, and covered his face with his hands. Mme. de Krüdener would then pause, and beg pardon for the strength of her language.

"Go on, go on," said the Emperor: "your words are music to my soul." And when, on taking leave, she made a last apology, the Emperor said, "Give yourself no uneasiness. All you have said recommends itself to my heart. You have given me a new view of myself: I thank you for it; but I need such interviews often. I beg you not to go away."

From that day forward, the Emperor looked on Mme. de Krüdener as a beneficent genius, from whom he could not be parted, and whose inspirations deserved respectful attention. She followed him to Paris, and the influence which she exerted there is historical. The origin of the connection only belongs to our subject; and this glimpse was necessary to a full appreciation of the correspondence which ensued between Mme. Swetchine, in Russia, and her

friend, whose lot was cast amid the most dramatic complications of the epoch.

In what concerns Mme. de Krüdener, we shall recognize
the plan of advice which Mme. Swetchine always adopted.
More alarmed than dazzled by the allurements of the Py-
thoness, disturbed by the enthusiasm of her friend, but
ever modest in the expression of her own opinion, we
shall see her avoiding proper names, sifting and combating with discretion the ideas which she resists, but
boldly bringing forward those which commend themselves
to her judgment.

On looking back, we find correspondence of Mme.
Swetchine's extending from the first Restoration to the
second, and embracing these events between the spring of
1814 to the close of 1815, which we have summarily reviewed.

I share to the full your admiration of our dear Emperor.
How blessed a thing it is to be able to praise sincerely! No
one knows what it is worth, who has not been overtaken by
the vicissitudes of life; and it may be, that happiness is even
more needed than suffering to temper the soul, and rouse its
energies. This memorable epoch will, I doubt not, exercise
a marked influence over the Emperor. He is already raised
above other men by the glory he has won. The influence of
religion will lift him above himself. His will was always good,
and now he will dare all he has dreamed. Let us hope that it
is the dawn of a better day for Russia. Ah, if his heart, now
that it has received a serious impression, could also be warmed
toward her who has suffered so long, and with so noble and
resigned a patience! Has not the day of usurpations gone by?
Do we not see vice everywhere yielding? I cannot tell you
how deeply I am pained by that suspension of correspondence
of which you tell me. What! can he not allow her to taste, in
its fulness and purity, the joy even of these happy events? ...

My husband sighed over the word in your letter about the
Countess ——. His regrets, which are slightly materialistic,
are principally for the loss of her beauty, whose remembered
image he still dotes upon. He values it so highly, that I believe he would avoid seeing her for fear of losing the impres-

sion. It is very seldom that I see in the guiltiest woman any thing but an unfortunate victim; but I must say, that indecency. in addition to weakness, dries up my charity at its source. What is to be hoped from one who dares defy all that is respectable? . . .

We have a more backward spring than any which I remember. Enormous masses of ice float down the Neva; and one would say, that, for eight days past, the whole North had been breaking up. My friend, when body and mind are ill, a temperate climate is very desirable. To feel disheartened in the midst of an ice-bound landscape is to feel death within and without one. . . .

The assurance that you were happy would console me for much care and anxiety. It would be every thing to me. But —poor creatures that we are—we can do nothing for ourselves, and, what is worse, nothing for those others who are more to us than ourselves. We are flung into life like malefactors, bound hand and foot; but the greater our impotence, the more our movements are trammelled, and the more the mainspring of the great watch acts for us. It is when we are motionless as blocks of marble in the hands of the sculptor, that the action of the Supreme Workman begins. I have often been reproached with what people call my familiarity with God; and it is quite true, that, starting from the principle that no one who loves is offended by confidence, I take him aside, as it were, and tell him of my sorrows, my joys, and my wishes, as well as my regrets. Prayer is for me a tête-à-tête *par excellence;* and I pity those with whom it is nothing but a monologue. I have sought this tête-à-tête with the best of fathers. Your image, dear Roxandra, made a third in our interview, and acted as a stimulus to my garrulity. . . .

How much trust and consolation for you and for myself have I not gathered there! And why may I not transmit my experiences to you? They make me smile a smile of peace, and give me new life. . . .

While I write, they are giving a serenade under our windows, for whose benefit I know not. The varying harmonies of voices, fifes, and wind instruments, succeed one another alternately. The river is perfectly still, the air balmy; and, from time to time, I rest my pen, sink back in my *fauteuil,* and indulge in a momentary dream. In an interval of silence, the clock of the fortress strikes one, and seems to tell me that it is time to go to bed. I have chosen to misunderstand it, you see; for I am writing still. My letter, however, refuses to take a fresh start. If I sit up, you are no longer there even for a pretext; and I speak only for myself. More than an hour ago, Count de Maistre ordered me to bed in the most peremptory manner. He treats me like Basil. He tells me that I have a fever; but I have nothing of the kind. I have only a bad cold, accompanied by cough and hoarseness. . . .

I already know Mme. de Krüdener, Jung, &c., as well as if I had seen them. But the most interesting acquaintance I have made through you is that of M. Pollier:[1] first, for the reason which you know, because he strikes a sensitive chord in me; and then for that trait of devotion to his young pupil, which has raised him very high in my estimation. I am sufficiently inclined to be metaphysical, and even mystical; but a single impulsive deed like this appears to me far to outweigh all the sublime conceptions and exalted delights of the third heaven. . . .

Among the thousand items which escaped my memory the other day, I forgot to speak of the book which you lent me. It gave me a great deal of pleasure, and has left an ineffaceable impression. It is truly the *rationale* of Christianity, and seemed made on purpose for me; for it answered objections which I have met in no other work, but which have often had the effect of unsettling my mind. If it developed no other idea save that the Scriptures are not revelation, but contain the history of revelation, this idea, ingenious, just, and fruitful, would have been enough, in my opinion, to make the fortune of the book. When it was presented to me, you would have laughed to see me spring from my chair, drop my book, and clap my hands, — three signs which denote the highest degree of admiration of which I am capable. Prayer never fails me; but I must own that I have sometimes been inclined to accuse myself of impiety, so wearisome do I find the best devotional books. I yawn at the first page; and it is long since I have been able to get as far as the second. A theologian who talks of religion affects me less than a man of the world who is penetrated by its spirit: the one has the air of fulfilling a duty; the other, of consulting an inclination. It is difficult to strike the balance between those who are convinced and those who are persuaded. I know very well that the greatest divines have been both; but even so their ascetic and peremptory tone is against them, — a tone which the gospel,

---

[1] M. Pollier was tutor to the young Prince Wasa; and, when the crown was finally removed from the ancient house of Sweden, and given to General Bernadotte, M. Pollier redoubled his devotion to the despoiled prince.

as Jennings[1] well says, never adopts. I have already made one person read the book, who has been greatly pleased with it; and I should like to repeat the experience.

February 22d.

Ah, my friend! do not you begin to mourn over the pitiful interests of this life. Can you not rise above the vicissitudes to which you are condemned? It is God's voice, do not doubt it, which replies to yours. It is not for the dew-drenched earth to complain. Only the parched and burning desert would have a kind of right to believe itself forsaken by the powerful hand whose mere withdrawal is a punishment. . . .

What you tell me of the Emperor pleases me very much. At last he is having justice done him everywhere. God grant that he may lead to a successful termination the noble and generous enterprise whereof events bore the germ which he has so successfully guarded and developed! There is no use denying it, — the mass of men are just only when they are happy, and the vulgar will sympathize only with success. Have you taken my advice, my friend, about your behavior to the Empress? have you alluded to what she has to bear; and have you done it frankly, earnestly, and affectionately, as you really feel?

When I am with you, I have a sense of calmness and depth. It is just the atmosphere which suits me; and, though I am not mad like Saul, there is something in your voice, I know not what, which recalls the effect of David's harp. Ah, how soothing is the thought that we are exciting interest! You say, in your letter, that I never speak of my own experiences. My friend, always till now I have made it a matter of dignity, moderation, and reason, to avoid dwelling on my troubles; but do you think I care for all that, where you are concerned? In my intercourse with you, I speak or am silent, receive or give, on the impulse of the moment; and, if I say nothing of myself, it is not from indifference or reserve, but because I like to hear you a hundred times better than to speak. . . .

I woke early from a sleep worse than death. At the age of nineteen, I threw myself into the arms of God, with a passionate fervor unexampled in my experience. For several years, my religion was of that stamp; and, if you will believe

<hr/>

[1] Jennings, born in England in 1704, is the author of a treatise on the "Evidences of the Christian Religion," published in 1774, and translated by Feller.

it, my friend, five minutes of religious exaltation sufficed to obtain every sacrifice, and give direction to the remainder of my life. It was grace; and, I say it with the deepest conviction, I deserved none. Later, Providence took away my milk and leading-strings. How weak I felt when it became necessary for me to walk alone, and climb instead of leaping! . . .

I know the needs of a character like yours; but your imagination, which I love as a part of yourself, might have proved a snare, if you had been led astray by ordinary seductions. And so I own, that, since your departure, I have often been fearful — sometimes to the point of despondency — that a specious brilliancy, and the very success you were achieving, would induce you to create for yourself a future where realities and my affection would hardly find access to you. I said to myself, " If the hopes and pleasures of the world, its vain ambitions and frivolous pursuits, ever permanently occupy her mind, I shall love her still; but our intimacy will not be the same. The perfect analogy which unites us will have been destroyed, and the hopes formed for a lifetime will have been but the dream of a day." This is what I have said to myself a thousand times, with an inexpressible pang at my heart, which is now converted into a most lively joy. The tests which they used to apply to novices were child's play to those which you have passed through. Try to use your triumph discreetly. The moral of this fable is, that happiness is only possible among our equals, in a situation where one is exposed neither to envy nor to indifference; and that all we can derive from the best of human intercourse is a firm persuasion that God's service is the only source of repose and well-being for his intelligent creatures. I hope, that, amid all you have seen, you have gleaned some ideas that may be realized in our dear native land, which, like childhood, contains as yet only germs and elements. . . .

My health is more miserable than ever, and is only kept up by ruinous remedies. My superstitious confidence in Leigthon has yielded a little to reason; and I have decided to consult Grigthon, who promises me some palliatives, but persists in saying, that, if I will not have recourse to violent measures, it is absolutely necessary for me to take four seasons of different waters. The advice is very good, — so good that I had administered it to myself in advance. The only trouble is, it cannot be followed. I should have to make up my mind to leave my husband, which I cannot do. He urges it upon me; but, the kinder he is, the less I am disposed to profit by his kindness. If illness or misfortune should overtake him in my absence, how could I forgive myself? . . .

The report has been circulated here, that the Empress was

going to Paris. Nothing but the announcement of your immediate return could give me greater pleasure, if I could but feel
sure of it.[1]

August 10th.

I have just come back into my little solitude, after a season
of forced dissipation. In the good society in which I have
been moving, retirement is as artificial as enjoyment; and I
have not been able to find a moment in which to add to my
letter a word for your good brother. Spite of my neglect, however, he would be doing me great injustice if he doubted the
strength of my attachment. The place I have just quitted
bears off the palm for busy idleness and monotonous excitement. I should prefer Thebaïs to passing my summers so.
There are several of the individuals from whom I have just
parted, who, separately and singly, would have been pleasant
company; but, taken collectively, they induce a sense of lassi-
tude and emptiness. I never exactly understood Rousseau's
wanting to be separated from his beloved, that he might have
the pleasure of writing to her; but I comprehend perfectly, that
one must retire from the world occasionally, if one would not
become disgusted with it. And so the grand wall of China
between one's summer and winter life appears to me as
necessary as well conceived. One compensation for the trouble
of my goings and comings is the pleasure I experience in
being re-united to my sister and her two cherubs, of whom
their mother's educational tact has really made two little won-
ders. I have no hesitation in saying to you, that I cannot conceive a finer character than my sister's. Every day strengthens
the good, and weakens the evil. . . .

It seems to me that your good angel is very busy about you,
and is covering your thorns with some few flowers. How I
should like to be charged with the visible execution of this
charming mission! If your candor and good faith did not
re-assure me, I should perhaps fear, that, unconsciously to yourself, all that you have heard — the opinions by which you have
been surrounded, and whose organs were calculated to captivate
your imagination, as well as your heart — might have produced some lasting effect upon you. But if a novel impression
could have given a false direction to your thoughts, your deviation would have been less serious than another's, since you
have in your excellent brother, whom I like so much, a true
counsellor, and a guide equally capable of reproving and sus-

---

[1] The report had no foundation. The Empress never went to Paris.

taining you.   As for myself, I have but one thing to say in this
connection: Distrust that cant of "simplicity" and childlike
docility, which the system-makers preach so authoritatively,
while they fail of it themselves at the very outset.   True simplicity consists in following, step by step, the gospel teaching, without involving one's self in those introverted speculations which are reserved for the very few, in weighing our
actions by the shekel of the sanctuary, and in submitting
humbly to life, rather than in soaring vaingloriously above
it.   It has been my lot to see many an Icarus in this enterprise. . . .
    How grateful we ought to be, and especially to our be-
loved Emperor!   I am glad that I always dimly foresaw in him
what has been so gloriously manifested to-day.   Certainly, he
is one of humanity's heroes, and will be so always and everywhere.   I seem to see all my dreams of moral dignity realized
in his conduct, and discover, at last, in this union of religious
fervor with liberal ideas, the long-sought resemblance to my
ideal type of character, — a type which might, until now, have
been deemed the fantastic creation of an exalted fancy.   Our
adorable Alexander satisfies my demands, and gives permanence to my ideas.   It is possible, then, for a king upon the
throne, surrounded by a tumult of unchained interests and passions, to be a man, a Christian, a philosopher; to pursue the
wisest and most generous of plans, and to throw into their
execution all that is noble in human nature, from the loftiest
equity to the most affecting modesty.   And this wonderful
young sage is our master!   My friend, if the Russians always
feel his worth as deeply as now, they will be only too happy.
The fall of Napoleon is such as we should have expected from
divine justice.   If he had died on the field of honor, it would
have been a noble close to an unworthy career; and his character would have remained one of those problems in nowise
doubtful to such as understand moral or even political laws,
but leaving some points capable of being seized on by those
wrong-headed individuals who are born hero-worshippers.
God has not allowed it.   Napoleon is judged in the sight of
all men, and for ever.   As to the happy change which has been
wrought in the temper of the French nation, it has not in the
least surprised me.   Their misfortunes prepared the way for
it.   Moreover, for them to change is to remain the same.
Their return to right principles reminds one of the bourgeois
gentleman and his hymn; and when La Fontaine wound up one
of his phrases with "*Vive le roi! vive la Ligue!*" he gave
expression less to his own thoughtlessness than to the mobility
of his countrymen.   Doubtless, my friend, there are individu-

als who ought to be exempted from this judgment, which, like so many others, would be unjust, if it were universal. . . .

You and I have different conceptions of religion, and the aids and means of advancement which it offers us. A certain novelty and formality about the step you have taken would constantly disquiet me, were not my heart full of the blessed effects which it has produced upon you. You are, doubtless, one of the people whose imagination sometimes carries them away; but then your singular purity of heart classes you with those for whom all things work for good, and who soar on the wings of inspiration to a height which others attain only by painful efforts, and a slow and sad success. I trust we shall often return to this most interesting of subjects ; and I am quite sure, that, though our opinions may not always harmonize, no temporary divergence can really separate us, our point of departure and our end being the same. It is so good and so profitable for two to travel arm in arm, supporting one another, towards that region which we may not call the unknown. . . .

Yet once more, my friend: can it be possible that the animation of our discussions should degenerate into acrimony, or weaken an attachment so thoroughly reciprocal? You and I must be other than we are, before I could even fear such an event. Nothing could be more eloquent or fascinating than what you say of the rapid progress of the impressions which now sway you. One could easily be carried away by the immense range which the system you adopt offers to emancipated thought, free to roam at will through the vastness of the visible and invisible creation ; but, in this soaring of the mind, which marks perhaps its point of highest culture, do we see, as you do, any trace of the character impressed upon religion in the primitive days of Christianity? I see but one approved route, and every species of deviation severely censured. I see the imagination and its brightest dreams dreaded as the source and the effects of illusion ; a boundless submission to what is established by common consent; a respect for tradition, almost equal to what is accorded to the Holy Scriptures ; and a perfect oneness of opinion with all true Christians, to whom we are bound by the tie of a fraternity which is charitable without being weak. No, my friend: my faith is not so ill-assured that I can fear to examine the bases upon which it rests. I say, with you, the Christian religion is not merely the religion of love, but that of science too. The more I learn, the more I reflect ; the more spiritual and thoughtful the life I lead, the more firmly do I believe. But I am not sure that every species of science is directly and immediately serviceable to Christianity ; whether or no it may not nourish our pride, which feeds on any thing ;

and whether, when one has found faith, — true faith, — it be
not wiser quietly to cultivate the virtues of the heart, than to
leave the intellect to wander in the labyrinth of those ideas,
— ingenious, it may be, — but to which human faith alone has
given a divine significance.   Yet I too, dear friend, have
plunged into studies looking to the same end.   I keep as much
as possible to the main route there, where one needs at least that
Ariadne's thread which you will find in yourself.   I advance
slowly and painfully; my only consolation being my sense of
a steadfast wish to grow in the knowledge and love of the law
of that God of mercy in whom we have such need to hope.
How sweet it will be, my friend, to unite our hopes, and cherish
them together!   Ah, how much worthier we shall be, both of
heaven and earth, when our souls are penetrated by the blessed
peace that follows mutual outpourings! . . .

Forgive me, dear Roxandra, for having neglected so many
days to send you this additional note from Count de Maistre.
He would never pardon the delay; but, since you will pardon
any thing, please keep my secret.   I press you to my heart. . . .

I cannot tell you how much what you say of Mme. de
Krüdener and her daughter has interested me.   Since I cannot
lay claim to the not very rare honor of having made up my
mind in advance, and since, by a whim which would be severely
condemned at St. Petersburg, I hold (if it be not boastful
to say so) to having somewhat exact notions of a question
before passing judgment upon it, my opinion of the Theosophists of Germany is in a state which would drive the
orthodox wild with indignation and fear.   One can make great
progress in so vast a field: and it has always seemed to me
very natural, that, in the laying of foundations, some should be
busy in removing bricks which they think useless, while others
are adding new; provided, always, that the lavishness of these
last does not defy heaven by a second Tower of Babel.   I believe I am very tolerant; but I have always found, upon reflection, that it was better to follow religion in its simplicity than
to make of it a science, whose most able professors are not
always most attached, as Christians, to the precepts which
identify practice with theory.   When we abandon ourselves to
the transports and the abstractions of divine love, it is very
rare that pride fails of her share, and dies of inanition.   The
war-cry of this sacred army is always "Simplicity," "Abnegation of self and self-love;" but this fine medal unluckily has
a reverse, which displays all the correlative vices.   Over and
above these considerations, suggested by a certain society,
there is another which would have decided me against it; and
that is, its pronounced aversion for every thing which savors of

association. I have never understood how one could be bound by his opinions; and, if ever I am a member of a sect, it will be of an independent one. My confidence and esteem are awarded to character only; and the romances of Mrs. Radcliffe would terrify me less than the thought that I was in the clutches of a religious party constituting a separate body within the body of the Christian Church. Try, my dear friend, to save yourself from this. It is not as easy as you suppose. These people, however estimable in other respects, have always this mental reservation; and propagandism is lukewarm compared to the ardor which they throw into it. Hear them, if they interest you, but do not adopt their opinions. Take from them what will warm the heart without influencing the judgment. Your brother has read me Mme. de Krüdener's letter, a copy of which you sent him. I thought it admirable, and so did he; although he was not perhaps quite as willing as myself to admit its perfect good faith. But none the less do I beg of you to hold fast by that *collier's faith* to which I come back after all the oscillations which reproduce, to some extent, in my poor head, the fermentation of opinions that took place in the sixteenth century. Do you know your brother has contributed materially toward making me a better Greek-church woman than I ever was before?[1] . . .

Though nothing positive is known of the plans on which you are dependent, I presume, according to all appearances, that the Emperor will soon take a fresh start, and that you will remain in foreign lands till he returns to our own; that is, for the indefinite period during which the Emperor is occupied with the affairs of Europe, of which he is really the attorney-general. Setting aside all personal considerations, — a habit of mine which has become almost mechanical, — I am glad of it. A further residence in Germany will protract for you that life of enchantment which never lasts too long. Moreover, this lengthened stay appears to me to be favorable to the restoration of our angel's happiness. Far from hostile and jealous looks, and the machinations of intrigue and cunning, there will be, I fancy, fewer obstacles to a change in her lot. For myself, I feel that I am incapable of illusions: the premonitory symptoms are unmistakable. My head has nurtured so many chimeras, that I have come to distrust the most suitable

---

[1] M. Stourdza was at that time preparing a book, entitled "Considérations sur la Doctrine et l'Esprit de l'Eglise Orthodoxe." Stutgard, 1816. This book was refuted by Father Rosaven, in a volume entitled "L'Eglise Catholique Justifiée." Lyons, 1824.

combinations which I have arranged for others; the very
desire of seeing them realized being enough to give them the
old flavor of the soil. . . .

I have had two letters from you, whose reception I have
never acknowledged. The last was from Baden, and contained,
like its predecessor, a most lifelike, and, so to speak, palpable
picture of the animate and inanimate nature about you. Ah,
my friend! every day strengthens the preference which I award
to landscape over historical painting. I envy you your privilege of wandering through one of the loveliest countries on
earth, in the midst of magnificent ruins, clothed with all the
wealth of vegetation, and of marrying your reveries to the vague
sweet tones of Æolian harps. But it does not make me in the
slightest degree covetous to see you surrounded by every development of the human heart, and reaping the dubious delights
of observation. . . .

You have good reason, my friend, to call your destiny a
strange one. It will not, however, on this occasion, appear
inexplicable to those who love you. There is nothing so
attractive to noble souls as a noble soul. . . .

It is natural that prudence should seem a quality of an
inferior order, to characters like yours; but, trust me, it is the
only one which you constantly need to exercise. The eyes of
all those who follow the career in which you have engaged will
be ever upon you. Irritated by your advantages, they will find
matter for discussion in your most insignificant steps; and, if
you do not meet them with great reserve and caution, you will
involve yourself in troubles which may be despised theoretically,
but which, in reality, one feels. Really, my dear friend, were
it not for your extreme goodness, I could not preach to you.
If I could only do it like Julia![1] . . .

What a blessed thing it would be, if those who are raised
by their rank above others, and by popular enthusiasm above
even their rank, did but know the value of their opinion, which
might so easily be made to subserve the purposes of reward
and punishment. There is something positively magical about
the intellectual sway exercised by that invisible sceptre which
deals blows so authoritative, and so salutary when they strike
home. The misconception which should lead any one to attempt
to make you an instrument of his elevation is exceedingly
droll; but, dear Roxandra, it is your own fault. Why do you
conceal so much finesse under the simplest and most artless
demeanor? . . .

---

[1] Julia was Mme. de Krüdener's Christian name.

In your first letter you said that M. de La Harpe had come, but that you had not seen him. In the second, you said nothing about it. Please, a little more information on this subject. I want very much to understand it. All I have heard pleases me, even the blue ribbon, which it was natural for the Emperor to offer him, but which he need not have accepted, to prove that he deserved it. This act, on which I dare not pass judgment, since I am ignorant of his motives, which might silence all objections, has nevertheless confused my ideas about him. Will M. de La Harpe return to Russia? I envy you your ability to associate faces with all these famous names. I should like at least to know those of all the persons in whom you feel an interest, were it but to gratify the passing caprice of an idle moment. This M. de Berckheim,[1] of whom you tell me, is entitled to more consideration, to judge by the two or three strokes of the pencil which give me his portrait. I have read "L'Homme de Désir,"[2] which he lent you. It is a very fine poem, the scene of which is laid in the clouds. When we read, we seem to see earth from the eagle's stand-point, aloft in the air. But does the work open the soul to real heavenly impressions, or quicken its love? I think not. Appealing to the imagination, rather than to the sensibility, it elevates the mind, but scarcely touches the heart. Such, at least, is the effect it produces upon me; and it is the same with all religious writing which has not the antique simplicity of the gospel and its divine wisdom of expression. Over-boldness is a human foible, and does not come by inspiration of the Holy Spirit. I read much, my friend; and, the more I read, the oftener I go back to those first principles which are so simple that childhood itself can lisp them. I confine myself to these, and desire only to purify the vase which receives them. The outskirts of our estate are peopled by *rascolnicks*;[3] and yesterday, when I

---

1 Son-in-law and disciple of Mme. de Krüdener.

2 "L'Homme de Désir" is a work by St. Martin, published in 1790, and thus described by M. Sainte Beuve: "He commands the attention, both of the serious and the profane, by the vivid beauties which gleam out from the depths of his obscurity, and by certain effusions and emotional hymns, in which he announces a harbinger." — *Causeries de Lundi*, vol. x.

8 "Niet, mamouchka iaidou staröi dorogöi tchem bog blagoslovil." The word *rascolnick* means, in Russian, *schismatic*. They include, under this title, all sects dissenting from the Russian Church. The adherents of the most formidable of these adopt the name of *staroveres*, or old believ-

asked a poor woman from one of the villages which most abounds in them if she were one, she replied, " No, my little mother : I walk in the old way, and take what the good God gives me." . . .

For one born under the light of Christianity, is not this the highest exercise of reason? and would it not be wise for the brightest and best of us to imitate my poor woman and her answer, and the deep feeling which was depicted on her countenance, and seemed to have dictated her reply? I think as she does to-day : to-morrow, who knows but I shall be troubled by the old fruitless speculations? . . .

My good friend, curiosity is as powerful as it is ancient; and you have excited mine to such a degree that I understand Eve better than ever before. I know not whether I shall have the courage to put to sea with you; but this much is certain, — if I cannot keep you in port, I will follow you with my vows. Are they not such as insure good fortune? I have sometimes feared that your imagination would be too much excited by the atmosphere in which you live; and that, if the truths held by the superior men whom you admire were not purged of error, you would take the error along with the truth. But I feel re-assured, when I reflect that your naturally reverent mind never seeks to transcend the limit of man's powers. The old faith is proved to be a positive faith by the very fact that it has traversed the ages unchanged. Let us cling closely to this main truth, however widely our gaze may range. All that is true is ever ready to combine with the one truth divinely revealed and universally diffused; and the presence of an alloy is betrayed by its very refusal to unite. . . .

---

ers. No difference of dogma separates them from the Established Church. They attach extreme importance to external forms, insignificant in themselves. They also refuse to use the liturgy corrected by the Patriarch Nicon in the seventeenth century. What gives their dissent a serious character is their persistent refusal to recognize in the Church of Russia the true church of Christ, since it ceased to be independent of the temporal power. The government does not recognize them; but they constitute an immense organization of five millions of men. They lay great stress on freedom of conscience. During the Crimean War, their sympathy for the allies was very pronounced. The news from Sevastopol was known among them before the official journals published it. We see by the woman's reply to Mme. Swetchine, that those who do not share the opinions of the *staroveres* treat them as innovators, and consider themselves the genuine old believers.

I keep forgetting to tell you that I have seen much of Prince Ypsilanti and his family. The father appears to me, as to every one, a man of great talent and vast information, to whom the contrast between his Oriental costume and his thoroughly European manners imparts a piquant charm. But I must acknowledge, that, as a disciple of Lavater and pure instinct, I should not feel disposed to trust him implicitly. Something scrutinizing in his glance; something hard and penetrating; an uncertain and dubious expression about the countenance, which is undoubtedly the accent of the face, — these would have kept me on the defensive, even if I had had good reasons for trusting him. I made several experiments upon him, which I will describe when we meet, for the purpose of proving to what extent simple frankness and good-nature could surprise and disconcert finesse, subtlety, and all those qualities in which the intellect confides. As to his eldest son, Alexander, I believe that he pleased me thoroughly. He could not be more modest or more loyal. I am greatly mistaken if that young man is not as honorable as he is brave. Perfectly simple, without a touch of egotism, his calm and slightly melancholy air wins him more suffrages than he could obtain by more brilliant advantages.[1] . . . My friend, even if the Empress did not attract by her own peculiar charm; if the grace of her mind and manners did not amply atone for these irregularities of temper which disturb you, — a mere sense of justice

---

[1] The family of Ypsilanti had given, in 1774, a hospodar to Wallachia, Prince Alexander Ypsilanti, taken prisoner by the Austrians in 1788. In 1799, his son Constantine was appointed Prince of Moldavia; and, in 1807, Moldavia and Wallachia were once more united under the same government. Prince Alexander was then living in retirement at Constantinople. The English ambassador, foreseeing the wrath of the Sultan at the news of the re-union of the principalities, had a frigate placed at the disposal of Prince Ypsilanti. He refused this means of escape, and contented himself with the reply, "At eighty-five, we await death, not shun it." He was executed at Constantinople on the 8th of March, 1807. The person here mentioned was his grandson. This young Prince justified Mme. Swetchine's judgment at the time of the Greek insurrection. Greece bestowed on him the official title of Lieutenant-general of the Greek nation; and, in the public prayers, he was called "our prince." After the Battle of Dragachan, which was fought contrary to his orders, and in his absence, he attempted to cross Austria incognito, but was arrested, and held in custody. He died at Vienna on the 23d of July, aged thirty-six.

should prevent one from dwelling on them. Think of the deep wounds constantly inflicted upon her heart! She is doomed to suffer, and to have her sufferings indefinitely multiplied by every capacity, every weakness, and every want of our poor human nature. Under a trial so dull, so disenchanting, so calculated to imbitter, the soul of an angel would succumb. How easy it is to be amiable in the midst of happiness and success! But when we have a right to every species of homage and devotion, and feel within us, but can never develop, the power to inspire the same; when every thing fails us at once, — what can we show the world but a conflict which is not, and cannot be, always successful? Think of this sad lot, my dear friend, and regulate your devotion accordingly. . . .

I approve strongly of your calmness and moderation; but do not let them be mistaken for indifference. The shade of difference is so difficult to define, so easy to apprehend. Loving is the first condition of being loved. Rest assured that all imaginable merit and all possible service will fail of winning confidence, unless their object is informed by an unerring presentiment that the source of our devotedness is a deep and living affection. Do not fear to yield to such a sentiment, and you will soon cease to be misunderstood. I should not perhaps have advised setting your affections so high; but, since you have been led to it by circumstances (so variously interpreted by the all-wise mass of men), utilize, in the noblest sense of the word, the means afforded you. . . .

The Empress has always appeared to me the most interesting of human beings, and the one possessing in the highest degree the charm which is the reflection of a beautiful soul; but I have thought more of her than ever of late, since her hopes and ours have become dim and uncertain. I love the Emperor sincerely; I appreciate him; I honor his fine qualities: but I have, I must confess, a grudge against him for resisting, as he does, the sweetest and most holy seductions of virtue. How can any thing else win his regard, especially when that other thing is so different, so inferior? There is no woman on earth capable of solving this hard problem. Delicate discernment almost always accompanies our weakness; and it is a rare thing for a superior woman to love much without a groundwork of esteem, — the thing of all others most agreeable to the vanity, and most conducive to the lasting attachment, of the best men. I am glad of the confidence which the Empress seems to repose in you. Attach yourself unreservedly to her destiny, and, believe me, in time you will secure much more than her esteem. . . .

Your scene from the Capuchin convent makes a fine pic-

ture, which would not disgrace the richest gallery. It breathes
the religious philosophy of the artist, who trusts that people of
different opinions may all be equally right.   Christianity in
broad touches captivates me.   Yet, in giving my faith so wide
a latitude, I am embarrassed by the thought of that "straight
gate" which they say we must needs enter; and my heart
grows heavy and my thought confused, when, disregarding the
harmony of the *ensemble*, I endeavor to find truth in the mass
of details.   And who shall say that it is enough to feel one's
self penetrated with the spirit of religion? and, if we neglect
to seek and embrace the absolute verity of positive dogmas,
can we hope to find ourselves clothed with the wedding garment? . . .

Your heart outstrips your reason, and leaden-shod prudence wills that they go together. To think of my preaching
so frigid an alliance! As to that project of a convent equally
accessible to the professors of the three religions, its success
would demand a far more conciliatory spirit than obtains
among the rival mistresses of a Mahometan seraglio. Ever
so slight an observation of men shows them to be more obstinate and intolerant in their opinions than exclusive in their
feelings. Add to this the immense difficulties which would
arise from the inevitable fermentation of religious ideas, from
the fanatical zeal with which each would defend his own and
reprove and anathematize those of the others, and you will
see, my friend, that, for the accomplishment of the work you
meditate, there would be required a different age, a different
place, and different men. We must not forget, that, in religious discussion, as well as religious philosophy, we are still a
virgin nation; and we can but fear that the natural growth of
this element will lead us through the storms of the sixteenth
century, or carry us, at one leap, into the dazzling darkness
of Germany.   I do not need to remind you that I have neither
prepossessions nor prejudices: the unsettled state of my own
opinions does not entitle me to such, and, besides, they are
inconsistent with my character; but none the less do I abhor
sects.   The unjustifiably harsh and intolerant spirit which
possesses them condemns them in my eyes, and makes them
intolerably repugnant to me. I do not know whether the
dreams of Mme. de Krüdener and Jung resemble those of
our own sectaries; I only know their general character; but,
if the spirit of yours is narrow and inquisitorial, other fruits of
the same tree are doubtless similar. . . .

As for me, my chronic ailments continue to be mitigated
by the pure air which I breathe, and the independence of this
country life. If the situation were only a pleasant one, I

should be perfectly contented. If no aspects of nature are entirely dumb, it is certain that all do not appeal to our souls with equal force; and hence my fancy for two or three rooms connected with some royal palace. My first requisition is pleasant surroundings which do not belong to me; for proprietorship entails so many troubles, that it would oblige me to renounce that quietistic repose which I never want interrupted by sublunary affairs. I hesitate about confessing it, lest it should injure me with you, my friend, whose imagination the fields, the woods, and the meadows have captivated, and, so to speak, *idyllized*. But we ought to prefer truth to success: and, I must own, blushing for my artificiality of taste the while, that I have no fancy for the country. I like neither to plant nor to sow nor to cultivate nor to adorn; and I could enjoy myself only in a spot which had been planted, sown, and adorned without any interference of mine. I like very well to gather fruit; but, if I were to spend a hundred years in one spot, I should leave no trace of the sojourn of an intelligent being. I want vegetation to do without me, and every thing to come as if by magic, and independently of any law of mine. Rousseau, with his silly reveries in the groves of Montmorency, which he was fortunate enough not to own, is a kind of mole, whom, but for his genius, I should take great pains to avoid. . .

"The universe," says some one, "is but the symbol of a great thought." It seems to me impossible to doubt that there exists a unity between the moral and physical world; that the latter is but the manifestation of the former,—the sheath which preserves its forms, and follows its contours. But I hold it to be a somewhat dangerous belief, that the indefinite perfectibility of man, either individually or collectively, could ever result from progress in this direction,—that the key of the great book could be attained thereby,—especially that a single religious truth could thus be added to what is revealed. Man may perfect himself, so far as his nature allows it, better by action than by speculation; for the grandest flights of the latter will teach him nothing beyond the simple and sublime precepts contained in the Lord's Prayer. The key of the great book is still a kind of philosopher's stone; and as to religion, for the very reason that it is divine, it must needs have been perfect from the beginning. We corrupt rather than perfect religion, if we either add or take away from the Nicene Creed; and it should not, I think, be hard for us, in our day, to seek our rule of faith in an age of miracle, saintship, and sacrifice. Such, dear friend, are my views on this important subject; but I would not set myself up above those who think otherwise, nor deny myself the pleasure of studying the most diverse systems. Tell me always about those which impress you; but take care, I beg of you, not to be carried away by them. Think how pure and beautiful our faith is, and consider, that, since so many careers are open to one of your fine imagination, you ought all the more willingly to close this by your own submission. Do not exercise, in matters of doctrine, an indifference which would be truly culpable. Think what religion would have become, if the first believers had not been faithful to their precious trust. . . .

My husband has just returned from Moscow, where he has been very ill; and, although I did not know of his danger till it was passed, I have been exceedingly anxious. . . .

When shall I thank God for your return? The reports we get are utterly contradictory; and I anxiously wait the decision which will probably follow the Emperor's journey to Munich. If any further complication takes place in political affairs, who can foresee the end of so many inextricable difficulties? My timid nature shrinks at the approach of a conflict which promises to be long protracted, although a favorable issue seems certain. The state of suspense in which we live is very painful. All we can do is to lay before God our uncertainty, and our confused sense of fear, — fear of a personal character; for revolutions are impending on all sides, and we cannot hope that any part will remain sound in the midst of the general corruption, nor immovable upon its foundations when there are secret mines or visible ravages everywhere. The spirit of God broods over fiery volcanoes as well as over green and tranquil meadows; and this must be our consolation for living at the present time. For my own part, I am far from regretting the age in which I live, — so fertile in the events which awaken great thoughts. If we were to be annihilated after a single day of life, I should wish that day to be perfectly fair; but storms, hurricanes, all the grand spectacles of nature, — which are, it may be, but an image of human ravages and commotions, — are better suited to a being who bears within himself the pledge of his immortality. . . .

Philosophy has been speculative in other times; in our own, it is practical. Its truths have become intuitive; we breathe them in the air; if we do but resolve not to repel, we become penetrated by them. And the shocks and overturns we witness suffice, even without personal contact, to induce that passive submission which otherwise is either the result of misfortune, or the chef-d'œuvre of wisdom. How finely you are situated, my friend, for the study of all these vicissitudes, which are especially striking in high places! What a view you must have from your stand-point! How insignificant the objects which the vulgar invest with grandeur must appear in your eyes! You can judge of human affairs just as they are. From the top of the Saltzburg Mountains you admire the natural heaven; and in the presence of earth's potentates, and in the midst of their conflicting interests, one may study with profit the action of God, who smites with vanity and nothingness what he seemed to have lifted highest. My friend, you must have completed your course of experience; and, if you have gained no happiness thereby, you have garnered a multitude of useful ideas and observations, whose influence will extend over all your life. Its effect, so far as regards an acute discrimination of good and evil, is assured to you: only try to add to this the regulation of your external conduct, and its restraint within the bounds of moderation and prudence. Preserve your independence, as the source of all that is noble, strong, and elevated; but do not let it appear on the surface. Those who are incapable of it themselves would take it for *hauteur*; and it is our duty to prevent unjust misconceptions. Oh! when shall we be together? When will it be given me to share your impressions immediately, and modify them by the very fact, that I do not possess, in the same degree as yourself, what pleases and suits me so perfectly in you? We both love truth; and we both love it undisguised and unveiled. What hope for advancement does not this disposition authorize? Never before, my friend, have I desired so earnestly to render myself worthy of all God has done for me in giving me a tender heart, and the power of loving virtue passionately, and of sacrificing myself to my friends. I am neither troubled nor perplexed, but I am often sad that I make so little progress in a route whose beauty and magnificence I see so plainly. How I have followed you in your journey over the mountains of Saltzburg! Your description is enchanting, and consoles me for the fact that I am probably doomed to see nature only in pictures: yours are full of warmth and life; and richer coloring never animated a pencil. How pleasant it would be, if we could make landscapes together! You would take care of the *ensemble*, — of the trees, the water, the effects of light; and I should beg to be allowed to place, in one of the dimmest corners, some mouldering monument, some burial-stone, or a figure whose grave and melancholy attitude should announce meditation or sorrow. If that fine landscape of Poussin's had been our joint production, my part would have been only the inscription, "And I, too, was ——."[1] I should have liked that sufficiently well. When

---

[1] An allusion to a celebrated picture of Poussin's, representing a tomb, the sight of which hushes all the sounds and extinguishes all the light

I want actual delectation, I dream of travelling with you,—that we are traversing glorious countries, where beautiful landscapes suggest noble thoughts, thinking of heaven while we admire earth. Will it ever come to pass?...

I cannot tell you, my friend, with what an intensity of desire I yearn for an existence apart from the crowd! I have seen a good deal of society this winter, and given myself up to it more entirely than I had done for several years; and the result of the experiment is, that at heart I am more alienated from it than ever. It is impossible for me to have, in any human relation, only the trifling stake of cool and rational mortals. Even general benevolence — a sentiment so minutely divided that it is well-nigh reduced to nothing — assumes an actual consistency in my case. Every thing that I see always inspires me with more or less interest; and the result is a vague emotion, fatigue without compensation. I know not the art of speculating on the amusement afforded us by others; and what are deemed flattering successes are so for me only when I can suppose them to have planted some germ of kindness in the hearts of my fellow-men. My own embraces so easily the whole creation, and every individual in it; my natural impulse is so surely to sympathize with another's feeling, — that I am constantly shocked by the dryness, insensibility, and coldness which I inevitably encounter on my way. What shall be said, then, of that malevolence which has too little idea of self-concealment; of that irritable envy which cannot be appeased; of that aversion, under the mask of indifference, to every thing which suggests the most miserable advantages of a miserable life? And, in the suffrages which we rely on most, what a sense of disappointment and emptiness succeeds to the agreeable feeling which they excite!...

That journey into the Vosges,[1] which you were planning

---

of life, in the midst of the joy-breathing landscape. Youth and love hardly heed the lesson: they but glance that way, and pass on. The shepherd on the left — less young and less happy, for he is alone — feels it more deeply. But the figure in the foreground, of one who has lived his life, lost his crown of verdure, and is already bowed with age; the shepherd who stoops to read the inscription, " Et in Arcadia ego ——," tastes its sadness, and muses on its application. He personifies the sentiment of Mme. Swetchine. For others, the charming landscape, its shadows and its distances; for him, the monument.

[1] They were talking of visiting the Ban-de-la-Roche, or Oberlin, a Protestant pastor, greatly revered, who drew around him spirits like Mme. de Krüdener. It was a place for retirement, preaching, and good works,

with Mme. de Krüdener, will afford you a variety, and a great
pleasure. But who knows, my friend, whether to breathe for a
fortnight, instead of a week, a perfectly calm atmosphere would
not cure you of this fancy altogether? I have always heard
the most experienced seamen say that a calm was pleasant
immediately after a storm; but that, if it lasted ever so short
a time, it became insupportable. When I see you believing
just what you wish to believe, you seem to me a true descendant of those Greeks whom the hierophant of Thebes treated
like children. How shall one know one's own will, when, caught
with difficulty upon the wing, it escapes us, soars off, and re-
produces itself unceasingly under new forms? As often as its
vague unrest is soothed, it arises anew from its ashes, ever
craving satisfaction, but never satisfied long. I am not surprised that you should desire a change, and I believe you to be
perfectly sincere in your longing for repose; but you probably
deceive yourself in supposing that it would suit you, for you
embellish it with all the colors with which we always adorn
what we lack. Prolonged repose suits very few people, and no
one less than you, whose active mind needs something to feed
upon. You do not yet know what it is to be constantly thrown
back upon yourself, — the fatigue and depression which result
therefrom, as well as the need of being called out of self by
external objects. On this subject I could make out a little
memorial, which should be a simple recital of facts, and which,
like a good many other things, would be useful as material for
an immense work on the extravagances of human misery. . . . .
The unreliability of the post, mistakes and misdirections, —
all the obstacles which ill luck can accumulate, combined, my
friend, to prevent my receiving before yesterday your two letters, — that of the 12th of July, forwarded in the Galitzin
packet; and that of the 18th, written after the Emperor left.
As to the letter which you sent by the august individual who
previously had been only the messenger of Heaven, I never got
it, — unless, indeed, you were mistaken about the date, and it was
the same that was put in Helen Galitzin's packet. It is very
certain the Emperor did not forget it; for he was kind enough
to say to my husband, that he had a letter for me, and that he
would forward it to him. My husband said no more to me
about it; and I do not know whether the letter received is the
letter in question. How what you told me of the interview [1]

---

which M. Ch. Eynard describes as "one of those oases which the Lord
prepares for his weak children in the desert of the world."

[1] First interview of the Emperor and Empress after the Restoration.

affected me! What sweet and tender tears I shed! For more than a month, my eye has been fixed upon this point; and my hopes and wishes have anticipated the moment which was to realize them. There was, too, a mixture of fear; for, do what I will, black predominates on my palette. But with what rapture do I wipe off that ugly black to-day, and abandon myself to the enjoyment of the perfect confidence which that part of your letter inspires! In that longed-for re-union, I seem to see the sole triumph which virtue had to win, — evil vanquished in its last intrenchment, and under its last aspect; and the dawn of a new day of favor and blessing for Russia. Heaven will complete its work, and renew in our midst the solemn act of pardon which divine compassion, variously expressed, seems proclaiming to the universe. For what means the late succession of happy events, if not that suffering Europe has made full atonement for guilty Europe, and the time of reconciliation has come? Ah! let us be worthy of it; and let our own regeneration be the first pledge of that alliance to which God, more unmistakably than ever, has invited man. Dear friend, my heart is full of joyful emotion. If, in spite of ourselves, we are appalled, oppressed, afflicted, by the prosperity of the wicked, the triumph of virtue strengthens our faith, augments our elasticity of spirit, and gives us a share in the deep content of the victors. In such moments, one feels happy and strong, simply because there are those who have persevered till they have won power and happiness. . . .

You were right in concluding that I was not one of those who looked for a marvellous run of unexampled good fortune to establish the Emperor's credit. I have made some experiments in this connection. No surprise has been occasioned by events, nor have his noblest actions excited any. My admiration is not as exalted as yours; for my soul, like the antediluvian earth, has all her pristine force: but it is genuine, and such as a recluse may experience, bearing principally upon the things least appreciated by the multitude. The interest which the Emperor testifies in you is enough to awaken your gratitude; although one does not need to have danced with him before one can say, from the bottom of one's heart, that he is the best prince in the world. If his kindness to you, my friend, leaves you the possibility of rendering him a service, profit by the opportunity; but do it with great tact. We are responsible for the employment of such credit as we have with others; and I charge you not to use yours to flatter that vanity which we must combat in ourselves, and never encourage in others.

CHAPTER VI.

Album of Louis de Saint Priest, and unpublished thoughts of Count de Maistre. — Death of the Princess de Tarente.

THE volumes of extracts, always carefully continued by Mme. Swetchine, take a new form in the year 1814. On the first page of a small album, we read, " Last gift of Louis de Saint Priest on his leaving Russia, Oct. 29, 1814." The binding of this album bears a vermilion scroll, on which are engraved these words: " I, too, knew him." The volume opens with some verses of M. de Saint Priest, addressed to Mme. Swetchine. They close as follows: —

> " Heureux qui toi ressemble, aimable violette;
> Heureux qui comme toi cherche à vivre oublié:
> Aux yeux indifférents cache bien ta retraite;
> Mais qu'elle soit au moins ouverte à l'amitié." [1]

These verses, which bear witness to the unfailing modesty of Mme. Swetchine, attest also by their signature the value attached to relations with her. The volume under consideration is wholly consecrated to religious thoughts, mingled with fragments from the conversation of Count de Maistre. Some of these coruscations have been preserved in his writings; but here we find the original flash, the accent of spontaneous inspiration. The greater part have never been published.

---

[1] " Sweet violet! blessed are those who, like thee, seek to live forgotten. Still do thou hide thy retreat from careless eyes, but let it be ever accessible to friendship."

"The Turks shut up their women," said Lord Byron, "and are all the better for it."—"Yes," replied Count de Maistre: "they need either the four walls or the four evangelists."

Genius does not seem to derive any great support from syllogisms. Its carriage is free: its manner has a touch of inspiration. We see it come, but we never see it walk.

The greatest sin against grace is to accord too much to it.

To restrain the desire of a Russian is enough to make it explode.

I would gladly preach to kings and people simultaneously, and my sermon would be as follows: I would turn to their majesties, and say, with a profound bow, "Sires, abuses lead to revolutions;" then, addressing myself to the people, "Messieurs, abuses are preferable to revolutions."

In the language of the Orient, a woman is a speaking flower. M. de Maistre defined a child as an angel dependent on man.

"Thou shalt not kill,"—where is the man who even knows what it is to kill? In how many ways, to what different degrees, life may be withdrawn, obstructed, destroyed! The Devil, who was a "homicide" in the beginning, has been so always, and throughout his kingdom; and it is by no means with the sword that he has cut off the majority of men.

A legend which M. de Maistre greatly admired represents, on the one hand, the arrival before the throne of God of the penitent souls whom his pity admits into the eternal city; and, on the other, Satan reproaching God with his injustice: "These souls have offended thee a thousand times, and I only once."— "Hast thou ever asked for pardon?" replies the Eternal.

It was in the same spirit that M. de Maistre altered the following verses of Boileau, which doubtless he found too Jansenistic:—

> "L'Évangile à l'esprit n'offre de tous côtés,
> Que pénitence à faire et tourments mérités!"[1]

These lines are written in Mme. Swetchine's hand, without index to their source, and followed by these words: "M. de Maistre alters them thus:"—

---

[1] "The gospel everywhere offers to the soul the choice of repentance or merited torments." M. de Maistre would substitute "free grace" for "repentance."

"L'Évangile à l'esprit n'offre de tous côtés,
Miséricorde offerte et tourments mérités."

"No man has ceased to believe in God until he has desired to annihilate him."

"Submission, which exposes one to believing too much, exposes to nothing. Pride, which exposes one to believing too little, exposes to every thing.

The play of children is business, and the business of men is play, — *n'est ce pas*, madam?

The last thoughts are in Count de Maistre's own hand, preceded and followed by selections from Massillon and Pascal, and German poetry, also in his writing.

Verses inscribed by Count de Maistre on the Monument of Descartes.

"Esclave dans les murs du cloître et de l'école,
La raison n'osait rien. Je vins briser ses fers.
Je flétris de vieux mots la science frivole,
Et c'est moi que donnai Newton à l'univers."[1]

We have already had a glimpse, through Mme. Swetchine's correspondence with her friend, of her rapid prog-

---

[1] "Immured as a slave in the cloister and school, Reason was powerless. I came to break her chains. I branded as obsolete their superficial science, and it was I who gave Newton to the world."
Although M. De Maistre cannot be considered a detractor of Descartes, I hesitated to attribute these verses to him merely on the faith of the ambiguous compilation which precedes them. In addressing M. Cousin, I believed that I was submitting my doubt to the man most capable of resolving it. I had the honor to receive from him the following reply: "The verse which you send me is both beautiful and true. It certainly was Descartes who gave Newton to the universe: for the supreme difficulty was to comprehend that the problem of the construction of the worlds was a problem in mechanics; and Descartes was the first who so conceived it. The problem, once fairly stated, has been resolved by Huyghens and Newton successively. It is then to Descartes, as to the first discoverer, that we must refer the system of the universe, and a portion of Newton's glory. M. de Maistre, therefore, was perfectly right; and his verse was true *in toto*. I cannot say whether this verse of M. de Maistre's is generally known; but it was new to me. Besides, upon what monument of Descartes could it have been placed? Descartes never had

ress in pious emotions and instinctive aspirations after truth. In this healthful movement, much was due to her association with the French *emigrés* and their example. We are now to note another link in that invisible chain which associates with France the last struggles and the definitive victory of that great soul.

The Chevalier d'Augard had recently died, as he had lived, in a frame of the most exalted piety. The Princess de Tarente, in her turn, was near her end. She had never dreamed of quitting the land of the stranger, while the house of Bourbon still languished in exile. With her, as with the rest of the world, the Emperor Paul had caused disgrace to follow swiftly upon favor; but the society of St. Petersburg had never ceased to lavish upon her every testimonial of affection and respect. Count Golowine had offered her rooms in his house; and that house was almost a home to her. Count Golowine's daughters divided their devotion between their mother and their illustrious guest. The Princess de Tarente held her sway rather by the authority of virtue than by superiority of mind. Her political ideas were remarkable neither for depth of wisdom nor acuteness of penetration; but they were mixed

---

a monument: when his remains were brought back from Sweden to Paris, they were temporarily deposited in St. Geneviève; and his disciples of every rank assembled to hear his funeral oration, which was to be pronounced by M. l'Abbé Lallemont, the university orator of the fourteenth century. A mandate of the king arrested the ceremony, and closed the learned orator's mouth. The body of Descartes was at St. Germain des Prés. At the Restoration, it was transferred to the cemetery of Père la Chaise. His head has been handed about in the amphitheatres of the Museum of Natural History. There has not been, for forty years, a complete French edition of his works. My own is unworthy of him. I was too young for such an enterprise. I therefore honor Count de Maistre, if, as I suppose, he wrote this verse to be engraved on the monument which he desired to have erected to Descartes."

up with such stately traditions and such pathetic misfortunes, that one easily forgave her fixed contemplation of the past, and never approached her without being lifted above one's self by veneration and tenderness.

As soon as the news of the Restoration resounded in St. Petersburg, society, *en masse*, and by a spontaneous impulse, hastened to Count Golowine's to congratulate the Princess de Tarente, and rejoice in her joy. This Restoration was the signal for her return to France. She began immediately to prepare for her departure, but with a certain moderation, — the last tribute of gratitude towards her friends. The Emperor Alexander, on his part, desired to assure her a passage on board a man-of-war which should be worthy of her and of himself. She seemed to be touching the limit of all her soul's sorrows and sacrifices; but it was an everlasting reward which she was about to receive.

The eldest daughter of Count Golowine has kept a faithful and very affecting journal of the last moments of this noble life:[1] —

"'Every emotion of happiness which new events occasioned her seemed,' says Mlle. Golowine, 'to mingle physical suffering with her joy. An indescribably sweet melancholy pervaded her features. We had never seen her happy, and we thought this was her way of being so.'"

On Ascension Day, May, 1814, when at mass, she felt seriously indisposed. A severe chill seized her; and this

---

[1] Prascovie Golowine married Count Fridero, a Pole, aide-de-camp of Prince Poniatowski, and after the reconstruction of Poland, in 1816, marshal of the court of Warsaw. Mme. la Comtesse Fridero has long resided in France. To her I owe the communication of this precious journal, and much other information. The friends of Mme. Swetchine should be unspeakably grateful to her.

accident — the day and the place — appeared to her like a warning.

" 'Before leaving us for ever,' resumes Mlle. Golowine, 'she must needs give us an example of the sole virtue which she had not yet been called upon to practise. During all the course of her malady, her goodness never failed. She had not the self-conscious delicacy of the world, which, under the specious pretext of sparing others fatiguing cares, would conceal the sufferings of that body on which we set so high a value. She submitted to the most painful prescriptions with that simplicity which was a part of her nature, and which everywhere made her at home with all that is good. She always had that kindly forethought which understands the means of giving pleasure. Several times she praised me in my father's presence, endeavoring to compensate me by his gratification for the sacrifice which she regretted to impose. Every time my father entered her chamber and approached her bed, she received him with as much politeness as if she had been in full health, and never once failed to concern herself about the place where he would be most comfortable.' "

One morning, guided by a thoughtful affection, the Count and Countess Golowine sent to the Princess's room a lily in full flower. The invalid contemplated it fondly, clasped her hands, and cried, "Dear lilies, may Heaven always protect you!"

Father Rosaven bestowed upon her, with deep tenderness, all the consolations of his ministry. In the intervals of his visits, Mme. de Tarente had Mlle. Golowine read to her holy books and prayers. She was particularly moved as she listened to the prayer for patience. The first day they read it to her entire; but, perceiving that it specified many kinds of patience, she said on the morrow, "My child, only read the part about sickness: I have no injuries to forgive." — "And yet," replied Mlle. Golowine, "you have many wrongs to forget." — "No," answered the worthy friend of Louis XVI. and Marie Antoinette, "no one has wronged me; or, if I had forgotten it, this is not the moment to renew the remembrance."

When they heard her speak thus, and hold unceasing communion with her God, they lost all hope of keeping her long on earth. "But," adds Mlle. Golowine, in her pious narrative, "I never ceased to listen to her; and I would rather have followed than detained her!"

When Father Rosaven, after having administered extreme unction, exhorted her once more to an utter renunciation of earthly ties, she replied with energy, "My God! thou knowest that I long ago sacrificed to thee what I held dearest,—the happiness of seeing my king in his native land." These words were almost the last which her dying lips were able to articulate distinctly; and, after a brief agony of a few hours, she expired on the 22d of June, 1814.

It was Count Golowine's wish, that her remains, at least, should not be detained in exile. The Russian physicians proceeded to embalm her; and that heart, so profoundly French, came to France, to rest in the chapel of Videville, under the guardianship of the last of the Châtillon,—her sister, the Duchess of Uzès.

The Princess de Tarente followed a rule of spiritual life which had been given her by the Bishop of Boulogne. This code, which embraced and provided for the slightest actions of every day, was communicated to Mme. Swetchine, and copied in full in her own hand into the volume of M. de Saint Priest, together with several eloquent and fervent prayers. The whole is prefaced by these lines: "Copied from a little note-book in the handwriting of the Princess de Tarente, and found among her papers. Copied on the 15th of August, 1815, at Bariatinski House."

Sundry notes from Count de Maistre, carefully preserved

by Mme. Swetchine, are evidently to be referred to the same epoch, although many of them have no dates : —

The anxiety I have endured on your account, madame, can hardly be expressed. They said to me, at your door, *Otchen ne khorocho.*[1] It did not need so much as that to put me in the same case. I trembled in all my limbs, lest your indisposition should become an illness. The fears of all your friends are quieted; but I should thank you for your courtesy, if you would be so kind as to relieve me, in particular, of these alarms in future. It was with the most lively and tender disquiet, madame, that I haunted your door for information about your health. I regard in the light of lost moments those in which we stood somewhat in awe of one another, and seek to indemnify myself for them by the fulness of love and confidence that I owe you. On your side, madame, you will do as you please : but I also count a little on your indulgent kindness; for I would neglect nothing which might help to maintain, in its integrity, an attachment which I prize so highly, and by which I am so infinitely honored.

Since I became androgynous, I have necessarily been a trifle dissipated. This evening, I am going to a ball. It is the thing I dread most on earth, after a cold bath; but, when one is of both sexes, one must dance. Previously, I shall dine with the Princess Belosselski and twenty-five or thirty particular friends. But, still earlier, I shall have the honor of paying my respects to you between twelve and one o'clock, and of telling you, by word of mouth, a part at least of what, in my own opinion, I am expressing here so feebly. My whole seraglio embraces you tenderly : you are often spoken of here, and in the highest terms, I assure you.

———

Tuesday, 3d.

The Tuesdays pass, madame, and the Fridays follow them, and you are not at home. What are you doing inside your cage? When I reflect, that yesterday we could not linger, after dinner, upon the terrace of M. le Baron Blom, I fear that you are pierced and transpierced by the sea wind.[2] I do not see that you have in your vicinity a single person capable of being either your *mi*, *sol*, or *do*. Now, when one string sounds alone, it may be as pure and sonorous as you please;

---

[1] Not at all well.
[2] An allusion to Peterhof, which is situated on the seashore.

but it will never be music. You see, madame, that, even in a
note, I cannot help falling into metaphysics. But there is no
metaphysics about the friendship which constantly takes me to
your cage, and makes me dread all the winds (draughts and
other) of the land and sea. His Excellency, M. le General
Rodolphe, is going to-day to take leave of the Strellanians.[1]
I charge him with this billet; and I charge him still more
strongly to see you face to face, if possible, and bring me
news of you, which will not prevent, in case your beneficent
hand should make me a present of a few lines, my receiving
them with gratitude. Still, I do not ask for them; for I do not
want to weary you.

I am leading here the life with which you are familiar. It
has some agreeable interiors; but the rest,—*ne vaut pas le
diable*, and I don't see the slightest gleam on the horizon.
The chain of destiny leads him who obeys, and drags him who
resists it. Let us advance with a good grace, only praying
that we may be allowed to halt whenever we encounter some
good fortune on our way; as, for instance, a cage inhabited by
a bird like Sophie, whom I love and venerate with all my
heart.

Apropos, madame, if it was proposed to pay you a visit
with the ambassador, for instance, what time would suit you
best?[2] Here, madame, is a small treatise, which is presented
to you as a friend of the house. I wish that, under this mitigated form, it might obtain a new reading from you.

Have you, dear madame, the treaty of the 30th of May?
There is your friend declared an alien to France, to Savoy,
and to Piedmont.[3] We shall see whether Providence has in
store any unexpected compensation. I am prepared for any
thing; and I am particularly prepared not to be astonished at

---

[1] Strelna is an imperial pleasure-house, around which are grouped
some elegant residences, occupied by personages of the court and their
families.

[2] The ambassador of Naples is meant, the Duke of Serra-Capriola,
with whom Count de Maistre was very intimate, and in perfect intellectual sympathy. This colleague of M. de Maistre was the only one to
whom he confessed (as we see in this note in which they are also confided
to Mme. Swetchine) his incessant trials with the court of Sardinia. •

[3] By the treaty of 1814, Chambéry remained with France, and M. de
Maistre continued ambassador of the King of Sardinia. Savoy was
restored to the sceptre of the King of Sardinia, only by the treaty of
1815.

any thing. Meanwhile, I have asked, with fresh importunities, to be allowed to remain where I am; but the thing appears to me so just, so reasonable, and so natural, that, to tell the truth, I quite despair of it.

What think you of the death of that poor Princess de Tarente? Yesterday, at five o'clock in the afternoon, after an extraordinary illness, she left us for heaven, where she will meet again Moreau and Rapatelle: for the laws of Menu, the son of Brahma, in whom I believe with all my heart, assure us that all soldiers dying on the field of battle are certain of salvation. We may say with truth, that Providence is convoking a new assembly, and dismissing, one after another, the members of the old. Ah, how little he needs us! The Princess fulfilled her duty perfectly; yet she believed, like so many invalids, that she had not yet reached the end of life. You may rely on this. Those of the St. Petersburg ladies who are most learned in medicine (and there are a good many of them), say that it was a very bad thing to consult only three English physicians, — Rogerson, Chrigton, and Leygton, — since physicians of the same nation never contradict each other, and it is quite like having only one; whereas a German would have pulled her through (perhaps!). Upon this point, however, madame, as on so many others, I am quite of your mind.

This death will have a great influence on the household that witnessed it. They carried the Princess from the room which you know, into the library. She had the best attendance, as you may imagine; but care and medicine were alike useless. She died at the age of fifty precisely, and, what is very singular, at the very moment when nature was calling her for the last time by her *nom de femme.*

The last offshoot of the house of Châtillon dies at St. Petersburg, while the King of France, stiffened by the gout, is supported upon the arm of his cousin. Such is the law. Rome perishes; all things change; every thing is precipitated towards the mighty ocean.

> " Et rien afin que tout dure,
> Ne dure éternellement." [1]

It was Malherbe who said that; and it is not so bad.

Adieu, a thousand times, dear madame! If you believe that we are becoming used to your absence, you deceive yourself gravely. I am mortally tried, and mortally isolated. It

---

[1] " And that the universe may endure, no one thing endures for ever."

seems to me that my berth is getting uneasy, and that I am not wanted here. Ah! if I must needs go somewhere, I am ready to go with Mme. de Tarente. I have nothing more to say. Accept, madame, my sincere and affectionate homage. Many compliments to good Nadinka. What do you think of the state of her health?

Count de Maistre was not deceived in his presentiment of the influence which the sight of a beautiful life and death would exert over a family worthy of so lofty a lesson. The Princess de Tarente discharged her debt of hospitality, by leaving behind her the worship of the true faith united to the worship of her memory.[1]

More than fifty years afterward, Mme. Swetchine, in her turn, received the affectionate hospitalities of the feudal castle of Fleury, which had passed from the hands of the Prince de Tarente into those of his nephew, the Prince de Talmont, and the Countess Larochejacquelein. It was there that Mme. Swetchine addressed to the author of the journal of Mme. de Tarente's last moments the following lines:—

TO THE COUNTESS FRIDERO.
FLEURY.

MY DEAR PACHE,[2]—You must be very lonely without your son. I do not doubt that you rule your lonely state with courage; but he who speaks of ruling implies coercion, and suggests something which, for that very reason, has not the charm of the running stream. In a little apartment occupied by the Princess Talmont, and which they had occasion to open the other day, I was moved to see, among the pictures which adorned the walls, the interior of the library Rue de la Perspective, with the inscription, "Mme. la Princesse de Tarente, in the cabinet of Mme. la Princesse Golowine." These relics of the past are always affecting. Adieu, my dear Pache! My best love.

---

[1] The second son of Countess Fridero embraced, in France, the ecclesiastical profession.
[2] Pache is a familiar derivative of Prascovie.

CHAPTER VII.

Conversion of Mme. Swetchine.

WE have now arrived at the epoch when Mme. Swetchine formed the determination of resolving her doubts by a course of searching study, which issued in her acceptance of the Catholic faith.

The life of St. Petersburg, crowded as it was for Mme. Swetchine by numerous family cares and benevolent engagements, which she neither could nor would evade, was incompatible with the laborious research in which she longed to engage. The General's health had been temporarily impaired: he was entering upon his sixtieth year; and, though phlegmatic by nature, he felt keenly every absence of Mme. Swetchine. The Princess Gargarin was devoted to the education of her five children, and could not leave St. Petersburg. Mme. Swetchine therefore sought to accomplish her object without putting between herself and her loved ones a distance which would involve complete separation. One of the noted men of Russia, Prince Bariatinsky, possessed a country-seat which went by the name of Bariatinsky House, in the neighborhood of St. Petersburg, and agreeably situated on the shore of the Gulf of Finland. Mme. Swetchine obtained from Prince Bariatinsky the rent of this peaceful and picturesque dwelling, and retired thither in the early days of June, 1815, accompanied only by her adopted daughter, Nadine, and a carefully selected library, which she proposed to exhaust.

A small number of friends received her confidence. Count de Maistre was in the first rank of the initiated; but he refused her his approbation. He disliked the plan, and doubted its effect. The volume of correspondence published by his son contains a long letter in which M. de Maistre sums up his objections with eloquent frankness:—

"Never, madame," he wrote on the 31st of July, 1815, "never will you reach the goal by the way which you have taken: you will be overwhelmed by fatigue; you will groan in spirit, but without unction and without consolation; you will be a prey to an indescribable dry anguish, which will rend your heart-strings, one after another, but never relieve either your conscience or your pride.

"At present, you are reading Fleury, who was condemned by the sovereign pontiff, that you may know exactly what doctrine to hold concerning his sovereignty. That is very well, madame; but, when you have finished, I advise you to read the refutation of Fleury, by Dr. Marchetti. Then you will read Frebonius against the Roman see, and subsequently, in the capacity of a judge who hears both parties, the Anti-Frebonius of the Abbé Zacharia, — there are only eight volumes octavo: that is nothing! Then, if you take my advice, madame, you will learn Greek, that you may know precisely what is meant by that famous *hegemony* which St. Irenæus attributed to the Romish Church in the third century, in accordance with ancient tradition: you will want to know, in short, whether the word signifies the *pre-eminence* of the Romish Church or the *supremacy* of the Romish Church, or the *principality* of the Romish Church or the *jurisdiction* of the Romish Church, &c. The celebrated Cardinal Orsi undertook to refute Fleury, and found so many errors in him, that he determined to write a new history of the Church; being of the opinion that a good history is the best refutation of a bad one. He began upon his new history, and died at the twentieth quarto volume, which does not complete the sixth century. You must read this too, madame, I assure you, or you will never find peace."

Count de Maistre supposed himself to be uttering a defiance. He was but tracing a programme which was followed in detail. During the brief days and interminable nights of the Russian autumn and winter, Mme. Swetchine was unceasingly occupied in examining the most contradictory documents, which she had laboriously amassed in advance. She ascended to the sources of history; she compared dates; she studied languages; over and above all, she gave her soul to prayer. The Princess Alexis Galitzin, already a Catholic, had composed an invocation to God, in which she interceded for the conversion of her friend; and this prayer she had repeated daily, ever since the 10th of January, 1810.

Of the innumerable elements which entered into her conversion, one only has been preserved to us intact, — the one which, of all others, exercised the most enlightening and subduing influence upon her mind, — Fleury. Bossuet was also one of her favorite authors; and, in the album of M. de Saint Priest, we find a long extract from a discourse on the unity of the Church, bearing this date: " Sept. 2, 1815. Bariatinsky House."

The searching analysis of Fleury, in which she engaged, may be found entire in a folio volume of four hundred and fifty pages, filled with the closest and finest of her writing. This volume, like all the rest, consists of separate note-books, subsequently bound together, and bears the title, " The Ecclesiastical History of Fleury; comprising in twenty-four volumes the thirty-six of the Paris edition. Caen."

Her exquisite good sense had early taught her, that the question at issue between the Latin and Greek churches was not, strictly speaking, a question of doctrine, but, primarily and pre-eminently, an historical question. She therefore analyzed most carefully the acts of the principal œcumenical councils assembled in the East; noting particularly whatever in those acts attested most clearly the

supremacy of the pope.   Her attention was also directed
to the history of Photius, — his intrusion into the see
of Constantinople, his deposition, his restoration; and to
the overwhelming proof, incidentally furnished by these
events, that the authority of the sovereign pontiffs was
recognized and accepted at Constantinople.   Through this
historic labyrinth, a guide was indispensable; and Mme.
Swetchine desired one who should be impartial, and, as
far as might be, respected by both parties.   She was confident of finding this union of qualities in Fleury.   Plato,
the celebrated Archbishop of Moscow, lauded him to the
skies; the Protestants spoke of him with respect; and he
was not absolutely rejected by the Catholics.

The parts of her works are so closely interdependent,
that it is impossible to detach any thing from it; but perhaps the volume in its entirety may one day be published
with profit, and dedicated to the whole Russian nation.
Only the mottoes and some marginal notes will be introduced here, since they give some clew to her intellectual
preferences, and the passages on which her thought loved
to dwell.

The motto on the first note-book is : —

" Doubt is always ignorance."

The motto on the second is in the English language : —

> " To take up half, and half on trust to try,
>   Name it not faith, but bungling bigotry."

Several passages are accompanied by marginal notes or
braces in pencil.   Some of these notes dispute the text;
others complete it.   In the second book, Mme. Swetchine
marks with a pencil-line the following definition of faith :

" Faith is a compendious knowledge of the most necessary
truths.   Science is a conclusive demonstration of what we

have learned by faith. Philosophy is a preparation for the faith on which science is founded. Saint Clement says that it is weakness to fear pagan philosophy. The faith which can be shattered by such arguments is very fragile. Truth is impregnable : error destroys itself."

Motto of the third book : —

"The first truth which it is necessary to believe is, that we must believe nothing lightly."— *Tertullian.*

In the third book, there is a peculiar mark appended to the following lines. It is easy to understand that they had a poignant application for Mme. Swetchine.

Tertullian says of Christian marriage : —

"The blessing of the Church is its seal. The angels carry it to the heavenly Father for ratification. Two believing souls bear the same yoke: they are one flesh and one mind. They pray, they bow, they fast in company. They instruct and exhort one another: they are together in the church, at the Lord's table, in persecution, in consolation. They conceal nought from one another: they do not weary one another. They may visit the sick freely; give alms without constraint; take their share of sacrifices without anxiety. They sing psalms and hymns together, and incite one another to the praise of God."

Pencil-mark : —

"The fear of renouncing pleasure deters more persons from Christianity than the fear of death."

Pencil-mark : —

"The Lord says in the Gospel, 'I am the truth,' and not, 'I am the custom.'"

Marginal note : —

"How many times have we seen the destruction of religion ready to be consummated! — and, after each severer test, she rises again, grander, stronger, more majestic than before. I am not sure that there are not as many proofs of her divinity in her combats as in her victories.

"A young Roman virgin, Theodora, had resisted outrage, and was condemned to death. A Christian, named Didymus, enters her prison, disguised as a soldier, and releases her. The pretor causes Didymus to be seized, and led to execution. Theodora learns it, and immediately presents herself to the executioner to dispute his right to the martyr. ' It is I,' said Didymus, ' who was condemned.' ' But I,' said Theodora, ' will not be guilty of your death. I consented that you should save my honor, but not my life. I fled from disgrace, not death. If you had deprived me of martyrdom, you would have wronged me.' The prayers of both were granted: they died together."

To this passage is appended the following marginal note:—

" How far below the beauty of this is the most touching incident of pagan antiquity! The generous devotion of Orestes and Pylades was dictated by friendship: the sorrow of surviving one another urged them to it. Here we have nothing of the human *me*, nor of its duality, which is more human still, but a broad and warm charity, the fruit of regeneration and grace. How admirable are the dialogues of the martyrs among themselves or with their judges! We admire Corneille less in Polyeuctes, when we come to draw from the sources whence he drew, and to which he owes his most magnificent scenes. Many minds despise the simplicity of these stories; and yet, beside their essential sublimity, they contain new laws, new ideas, and new manners; and, as ever in the early days of nations and of institutions, here we find traces of that eloquence which the lapse of ages always weakens. Here are lightning-like flashes of thought and feeling, nobility, unstudied power. All which can lift us above ourselves, all which exalts and fortifies the soul, may be found in the sublime utterances of that army of martyrs of every age and condition. Often eternity interrupts them, and in eternity they finish the canticle of thanks and praise which they began in tears and torture."

Motto of the sixth book:—

" O God of grace! let me not perish in the vortex of my own thoughts!"— *Werner, February 24th.*

Pencil-mark at the close of a passage on the Trinity:—

" Human knowledge goes no further. The cherubim cover the rest with their wings."

Marginal note:—

"The fragment of St. Hilary on the grounds of his conversion appears to me very fine. His thoughts are linked together, and his convictions follow unresistingly along the swift declivity which conducts from genuine philosophy to true religion. Christianity, even before it is accepted, is, as it were, outlined in truly noble souls. It is deposited there in germ; and the little seed grows up in the shadow of humility to be an impenetrable asylum from every storm."

Motto of the eighth book:—

"There were no vain disputes for the display of intellect, but a steady investigation of truth."—*Fleury, speaking of St. Augustine and his disciples.*

Pencil-mark:—

"Prudent suggestions for those who would hold intercourse about divine things, by St. Gregory de Nazianze: 'Not that we should not always think of God: we should think of him oftener than we breathe; but we must only speak of him at suitable times.'"

Motto of the ninth book:—

"Sincere effort is rewarded."—*Werner, February 24th.*

Pencil-mark:—

"I have desired to illustrate the truth, that to unite political to sacerdotal power is to blend incompatibilities. Antiquity had priests who were judges. The Egyptians and Hebrews were long governed by their priests; but, in my opinion, since this divine work has been humanly managed, God has separated the two orders of life. He has declared the one political, and the other sacred. The one he has dedicated to material things; the other, to himself. Politicians are to devote themselves to action; priests, to prayer. Why would you join what God has put asunder, and impose on us an unsuitable charge? Do you need protection? Address yourself to him who administers the laws. Do you need God? Go to the bishop."

Motto of the twelfth book:—

"God draws near to those who are uninfluenced by passion, and in the frame of mind which suits him; but, when one acts in wrath, how can the Holy Spirit come to him? that Spirit which passion would expel even from a soul where he had previously dwelt."— *Synesius to Theophilus of Alexandria.*

Motto of the thirteenth book:—

"The Church must light its candle at the old lamp."— *Waverley.*

Mark:—

"St. Gregory to Domitian, who had been to Constantinople to preach: 'Though I am grieved that the Emperor of Persia is not converted, it does not diminish my joy in the fact that you have preached to him the faith of Christ; for you will have your reward. The Ethiopian may come out of the bath as black as he went in; but none the less is the bath-keeper paid.'"

Motto of the fourteenth book:—

"True faith is never shaken."

We find by the dates, that the ardor and intensity of her work redoubled as it advanced. The books in the second half of the volume follow one another weekly. From the 1st to the 25th of November, Mme. Swetchine composed and wrote three hundred pages of enormous size. In two days, from the 25th to the 27th of November, she wrote twenty-six.

Motto of the fifteenth book, 8th of November, 1815.

"Prejudice sees not clearly; but aversion sees not at all." — *Letter from St. Isidore de Peluse to St. Cyril.*

Pencil-mark:—

"As to images, we must not portray what has never been; but since, in the incarnation of God, all was real, he was born, he wrought miracles, he suffered, and rose again, I would to God that heaven, earth, and sea, all animals and all plants, might reiterate these marvels in speech, in writing, and in painting!"— *St. Germain.*

Motto in the sixteenth book, 16th of November:—

THE PATRIARCH NICEPHORUS TO LEON THE ISAURIAN.

My lord, do not disturb the order of the Church. The apostle says that God has ordained priests, prophets, apostles, teachers; but he does not speak of emperors.

A marginal note of "Admirable discourse" is appended to the following passage: —

"When Zacharia was ordained Bishop by Photius, he desired to reply. The Secretary of Constantine then mounted the tribune, and read a long discourse in the Emperor's name, exhorting schismatics to re-union. 'Sound,' said he, 'the depths of your conscience, and you will find that you did wrong to withdraw. We are at the last hour, my brethren: the Judge is at the door; let him not surprise us outside his church. Let us not be ashamed of revealing our malady in order to seek relief. If you fear this mortification so much, I will show an example of self-abasement. I will be the first to prostrate myself upon the pavement, despite my purple and my diadems: mount upon my shoulders; walk over my head and over my eyes. I am ready to suffer all, if I may see the church re-united, and save my own soul."

Motto of the eighteenth book, Nov. 25.

"Truth is only developed in the hour of need: time, and not man, discovers it." — *Bonald*.

Motto of the nineteenth book, Nov. 27.

"The heavenly hosts have only one will: men have many." —*Words of St. Arsenus, the recluse*.

The last pencil-mark is appended to the refutation of the fable of Pope Joan.

At the end of the first book, we read, "Finished the 9th of June, 1813." On the last page of the completed volume, "Dec. 4, 1815." This prodigious compilation was thus undertaken and accomplished in the space of six months.

Before Mme. Swetchine had achieved this labor, light dawned upon her mind. We may safely say that truth never won a more complete victory over a heart at once more sweet and more refractory. From a Christless education, from the scepticism which shrouded her youth, she did not arrive by a single leap at Catholicism. Subdued, in the first place, by the proofs which establish the divinity of Jesus Christ and the inspiration of the gospel, she began by the submissive and loving practice of the Greek religion. She paused then to consider the constitution of the church universal, the organization of the hierarchy, and the pre-eminence of St. Peter's successor. Finally, she comprehended, that, in the presence of two separate and mutually exclusive churches, she could not remain neutral; that one only could merit the sacred title of the bride of Jesus Christ; and that, this church once identified, it was necessary to belong to it. Naturally distrustful of sects and innovators, — as we have seen in her correspondence with Mlle. Stourdza, — instinctively inclining towards tradition, she could not long endure a state of vague and unsatisfactory opinions on religious subjects. She therefore took her way across contradiction and doubt, but without precipitation, by measured steps, and never planting her foot upon the earth till she had become convinced of its solidity. Once introduced to the heart of the Catholic Church, the magnificent organization of its priesthood constantly attracted her intellect, and transported her with admiration; and she more than once expressed her astonishment, that M. Frayssinous, in his lectures, should almost entirely have disregarded it.

The papers of Mme. Swetchine have been vainly searched for a record or precise souvenir of her conversion to Catholicism. Her unwillingness to speak of herself, and especially to adduce herself as an example, doubtless deterred her from making such. She had also an additional motive, originating in the same virtue. With a sincerity and depth of faith which, while she lived, was never for an instant belied, Mme. Swetchine always attributed the good in herself to the pure grace of God alone.

We should thus have lost all trace of the most solemn and precious day of her life, if her constant habit of interspersing the notes she took with some of her own private thoughts had not accidentally surprised and fixed a confession. In the tenth volume of her collected extracts, without preparation or indication of any sort, we read as follows : —

BARIATINSKY HOUSE, Aug. 31, 1815.

Happy day! when the darkness of my mind yielded to the *fiat lux!* spoken by a celestial voice in the depths of my conscience. Cloudless brightness does not yet pervade my soul; but the harbinger of day has appeared, and has shown me the path I am to follow. My God! thou art as merciful as I am obstinate. My God! thy will be done. Teach me not merely to submit to it, but to love it, to delight in it, to take it for the sole guide of my actions and my thoughts. I owe to thee, to-day, the first moments of happiness I have tasted for many years. Thou wilt perpetuate this happiness, O compassionate Father! if only to encourage me in my sacrifice, and give me strength to accomplish it. Inspire me : it is thy truth I seek. Thy truth, I trust, I have found : thy truth I adore. If I should go astray (oh, let me die sooner!), may a miracle of thy goodness restore me to the frame of mind from which, as I have reason to believe, a miracle has delivered me. O God! have compassion on my sorrows past, on the sufferings whose memory is almost wiped out to-day, on the hopes which sustain my heart at this moment. I feel happy : yes, I am so. Can it be transitory? Shall I be condemned to lose the faith which thrills me? to sink once more into dimness and uncertainty? Doubtless, I deserve it; but, O my God! dost thou regulate thy favors by our deserts? dost thou not rather make them infinite, like thyself? I throw myself into thy arms! I beseech thee! I offer thee my tears and my joy! Deign to enlighten me fully, and inspire me with the desire of living to thee alone, and with the strength I need to remain steadfast to this resolution. I ask it in the name of thy son, our Lord Jesus Christ. By his cross and passion, I hope to obtain it.

Tuesday, quarter before twelve.

A note of similar character, left loose in a shapeless note-book which was not even thought worth binding, gives us some further information. The note is as follows : —

My last Greek communion, on the 20th of June, 1815, in the chapel of Peterhof, was partaken with the sole purpose of disposing of my remaining hesitation. God, in his goodness, did not despise my choice of means; and, on the 27th of October (8th of November), in the same year, I accomplished my abjuration. In memory of the aid vouchsafed me, in part, by the holy apostles Peter and Paul, I composed the following prayer two days before their feast at Vichy, which I attended in 1837 : —
"O holy apostles, Peter and Paul," &c.

Finally, in the twenty-fifth volume of her extracts, between this thought of Mme. de Rancé, "So act, that your fidelity may be your thank-offering, and your works the expression of your faith," and the funeral oration of Daniel O'Connell, by Father Ventura, we read, interlined in minute characters, "Day blessed a thousand-fold! a beloved anniversary! Tours, 1847, the 8th of November."

Neither in her conversation nor her correspondence does she afford us more circumstantial details. Two letters to the Duchess de Liancourt contain the two following allusions merely. The Duchess had written to Mme. Swetchine that her letters reminded her of Bossuet. Mme. Swetchine replies : —

"I can only explain what you say of me by my passionate and exclusive admiration of Bossuet, amounting even to injustice to Fénélon. All my life, I have said, that, if I had but one crown, I would give it to Bossuet; and, of this hidden fire, some sparks have reached you, as there is always a sort of relation between one's own adoration and the object of one's worship."

MY VERY DEAR FRIEND, — I cannot specify the precise date at which one becomes sensible of a disagreeable tendency

in Fleury. At the time when I read him, I was outside the
centre of unity. The more delicate shades, which ultimately
are seen to constitute an essential part of truth, escaped me;
my end being quite special, and only taking me as far as the
Council of Florence. At the very time that I was reaping so
much benefit from the book, I heard a great deal said against
it; but my confidence remained unshaken, as has my gratitude
since. This by no means proves, even to me, that Fleury is
irreproachable; only the life which I owe him establishes an
unquestionable relation of parent and child between us. It is
with books as with men, the good they do cannot be adduced
as proof that they are faultless.

The prayer to the apostles has not yet been found; but
two meditations, which evidently commemorate the same
event, have been preserved just as they were first thrown
off, as is evident from the hasty character of the handwriting, and the presence of two or three superfluous words.

In the first of these meditations, we find, mingled with
personal acknowledgments, expressions and views of hers
concerning situations which had come under her observation. The second meditation concerns herself alone, and
contains her soul's whole history.

"There is a species of sanctity which, by virtue of its regular, balanced, harmonious character, I shall call classical. This
sanctity, perfectly self-poised and in keeping, its present a
logical sequence of its past, and harmonious in all its elements,
has a sphere, a spirit, a walk, and laws of its own. God holds
perfect sway over this sort of sanctity: he rules it justly and
kindly, and has pleasure in it, as in the most perfect image of
the regular and immutable laws of creation. Another kind
of holiness there is, freer, more individual, more bold, swifter
in its flight, more ardent, more devoted, more self-aban-
doned, it may be, in its love. It is the holiness to which those
are called whom I should name the children of Providence;
those whom God has sought out; whom he has found in the
midst of all sorts of snares and perils; whom he has folded in
his bosom, as if to shield them from his own right hand's gesture
of dismissal. A piety so different in its origin (when considered in reference to human events fructified by divine grace),
so dissimilar, also, in its vocation, cannot imply a perfect

identity of duty. Let the performance of prescribed duties continue to be the soul of Christian life to the first; but woe to the others, if, after having ignored or neglected, in all their most serious relations, reason, prudence, and a wise and careful moderation, they should pretend to inaugurate them when they enter upon the spiritual life! Woe to them, if, after having a thousand times risked or compromised, in the ardor of their merely human passions, health, fortune, and personal consideration, they should begin to be careful of these things when they walk in God's way!"

MEDITATION ON THE GOOD SHEPHERD.

"I am the good shepherd, and I know my sheep, and am known of mine."

"*I am the good Shepherd.*"

"Thou givest thyself a name, O God! to our softened and believing hearts. Was it not, then, affecting enough for them to recognize thee; to designate thee as their compassionate Saviour, their only Saviour? But thou wouldest that thy word should confirm thy presence, because thy presence on earth was not to be eternal, like thy word. I am the Good Shepherd. Yes: shepherd, and at the same time God, father, master, mother, friend, and brother, of these poor sheep, who will hear no voice but thine, and obey no other crook."

"*I know my sheep.*"

"O Lord, who knowest me, what dost thou see in me? What seest thou there that does not merit thy reproof, even in the good with which thou hast endowed me, — good which I have let perish, and become corrupt, although, like a faithless steward, I have taken no account thereof. And yet I love thee, Lord: yes, I love thee. It would be a false humility which should deny it. But is it not still thyself who hast been the first to move my soul by a divine look? who hast plunged me in the pool to purify and heal me? Hast thou not called me twice, by a bitter disgust with the world, and by the authoritative and mighty attraction of thy grace? What part have I, then, in my life, such as it is, if thou takest away my faithlessness?"

"*And am known of mine.*"

"Yes, Lord, thy sheep know thee, and ask to know thee still better, that they may love thee more. My God! not always have I known thee, not always have I loved thee. It is long, happily very long, since thou didst come, and touch my heart, and will that I should love thee. In the beginning, it was a feeble ray; now it is a great sun. It was first a grain of mustard-seed, which, grown into a mighty tree, protects me with its shade, and gives me food and shelter. For a time, O my Lord, — a time which I cannot now conceive, — thou wert everywhere as now, and I saw thee nowhere. Yet at last I had glimpses of thee amid the crowd of objects which hid thee from my view, and soon thy adorable head lifted itself above others, and asserted its supremacy. I saw it — that divine head — dispensing pity, enduring insult, exposed to many a blow. Thy divine beauty, the malice of thine enemies, who were also those of virtue, overpowered me. I began by often turning my eyes to thine; then oftener: at last, I removed them no more; but that dear sight became inseparably mingled with all others, and made me better and wiser. I had advanced so far, and thought to advance no farther, when it came to pass, I know not how, that one day, one hour, — one swift and blissful hour, I ceased to see aught besides thee! O my God! then it was, in thy presence, that all which thou wast not appeared imbittered and smitten with nothingness. I saw my dear Jesus aright, and the poor sheep knew its true shepherd!"

CHAPTER VIII.

Mme. Swetchine has occasion publicly to profess the Catholic faith. — Her departure for France.

THE Emperor Alexander, when he returned to his dominions, brought back some new and salutary impressions. His soul had been deeply stirred in that brief interval of years by great disasters and great victories, great sorrows and great joys, an unparalleled personal triumph and bitter personal trials. God moves in his own ways. Fascinated at first, but soon fatigued by the incoherent and barren predictions of Mme. de Krüdener, the Emperor, nevertheless, came back more regular and serious in his private life, — more religious in theory, but more troubled and uncertain than ever in practice. The great virtues of the Catholic nations, of which he had just had a near view; the heroic endurance of the Spaniards; the angelic purity of the sovereign pontiff, Pius VII.; the noble and sympathizing qualities of France, — all these had given him occasion to reflect upon himself, his ancestry, and his country. Still he hesitated about touching the knife to the sores which were everywhere revealed. Like most sovereigns, and especially absolute sovereigns, he had to contend against the prejudices and interested passions of those about him. The politicians of Russia fought for what they called national tradition. The light-minded were either concerned or bored to behold their master, and consequently their model, inclining towards what they denominated mysticism. The nearest friends of Alexander, who, like him, were ready either for lively or serious impressions, formed themselves into bible-societies, or dreamed of the regeneration of their native land by the transforming action of masonic lodges. Thus statesmen, men of pleasure, and theorists, all clogged and opposed the Emperor in his strivings after truth.

The Catholics now became, more than ever, objects of suspicion at the court of Russia; and Mme. Swetchine believed it her duty, in the first instance, to sacrifice to those who were dear to her the public profession of her faith. Her abjuration was made in secret. Her first confession was heard by Father Rosaven, in a saloon with open doors, and in momentary dread of a surprise.

She supposed herself condemned, for an indefinite period, to this painful mystery, when a generous and spontaneous impulse unexpectedly freed her from her self-imposed rule of prudence.

It is well known, that, during the storm which burst upon the Jesuits, in the course of the eighteenth century, Frederic of Prussia wrote to Voltaire, that he was preserving the seed of the order, that he might some time furnish it to those who should desire to cultivate so rare a plant; and that the Empress Catharine held the same language, and adopted the same line of conduct. On the death of Frederic II., his successor dispersed the Jesuits; but Catharine collected them again, and soon four colleges —at Polotsk, at Vitepsk, at Orcha, and at Dunabourg— were flourishing under their direction. Paul testified still greater confidence in them by admitting the celebrated Father Grüber into his most private councils. He summoned the Jesuits to St. Petersburg, placed in their hands the University of Vilna, and confided to their care the colonies of the Volga. Alexander continued to show the same

favor to Grüber, who perished the victim of a fire on the
night of the 26th of March, 1806, praying for the prosperity
of his order, and blessing his friend, Count de Maistre,
who had hastened to the very scene of the catastrophe.
Father Thadeus Bzrozowski, who was elected general of
the order in his stead, continued his work.   Alexander
opened to them Siberia; and they hastened to its murder-
ous deserts for the consolation of the exiles.   The Duke
de Richelieu and the Abbé Nicolle claimed their assistance
at Odessa; and there they discovered a field for mis-
sionary labor, and had marvellous success in inducing
the tribes of the Chersonese and the Crimea to accept the
blessings of Christian civilization.   At the time of the invasion of Russia, the Jesuits excited the veneration of
the French and Russian armies alike, by the aid which
their zeal lavished impartially on the wounded of all
nations.   Napoleon visited them at Polotsk; and the soldiers of Marshal Victor and Marshal Gouvion de St. Cyr,
had particular reason to congratulate themselves on their
devotedness.

While the Jesuits were restricted to reconstructing their
society with the remains of the shipwreck, the Russian
clergy and corps of instruction took little umbrage at
them; but when the favor of two emperors, and their own
rapid success, had placed them upon a broader stage,
jealousy began to hatch its ordinary plots.

Count de Maistre, who, in the leisure left him by the
duties of the Sardinian Legation, considered himself, and
justly, the ambassador of great truths to a great nation
and a sovereign worthy to hear them, — Count de Maistre
took up the pen, and refuted, in five famous letters, addressed to the Minister of Public Instruction, Count
Rasoumowsky himself, the accusations and insinuations

which incessantly found their way to the ears of Alexander. These five letters created an immense sensation: they resulted in the erection of a new university in the interest of the Jesuits; but this triumph was their last. Hostility took a fresh start during the long sojourn of the Emperor in Germany and France. The earth was mined under the feet of the order. Every conversion was spied out, and signalized as an act of infidelity to the country and treason to the sovereign, the absolute master of consciences as of hearts. On the 3d of January, 1816, a first ukase was extorted with Alexander's signature, which banished the Jesuits from St. Petersburg and Moscow. "They have," said the ukase, naïvely, "turned aside from our worship young people who have been confided to their care, and certain *women of weak and inconsequent minds.*" Some months later, the proscription was extended to the whole empire. Schools were closed, missions interdicted, and Russia presented to Europe the singular spectacle of a monarch who had cast his sword into the balance of the most gigantic of conflicts, and caused his voice to prevail in an assembly of crowned heads, but who did not hesitate to avow his dread of a few religionists, possessing naught in his empire but the right to live, and to speak of God. Russia, under two sovereigns such as Catharine and Paul, under the malevolent empire of the prejudices of the eighteenth century, had constituted herself the shield of the proscribed company; but at the epoch of universal restoration, when Russia had dictated to Europe her most generous thoughts, she resumed for herself the narrowest traditions and the most arbitrary blindness.

This situation wrung cries of anguish from Count de Maistre.

0 LIFE OF MADAME SWETCHINE.

"Who will dare," he wrote,[1] "speak the truth to him who is
all powerful, and who has never heard it?

"Russia boasts of her toleration, and allows it to be lauded;
but there is a twofold mistake. Russia tolerates all errors, —
because errors are always friends to one another, and ready for
a mutual embrace. It is not so with the truth, or with the
Catholic Church, if you will, — which is nothing less than
tolerated.

"Certain very knowing individuals pretend that the Emperor
of Russia — disgusted by the religious scandals at Vienna —
has contracted an incurable prejudice against the Catholic
religion. In one sense, the Prince was right, if the report
is true; for, unhappily, these scandals are only too well founded.
But he needed a courageous minister at his side capable of
saying, 'You think, sire, that you see Catholicism. You see
only the absence of it. You see the work of Joseph II. With
the fatal impatience and impetuosity of an inexperienced young
man, he undermined the power of the sovereign pontiff in his
dominions. You see the result. There is hardly more religion
at Vienna than at Geneva, or than there will be in your own
realm when certain forces which you choose to ignore shall
have received their full development.'

"There is no truth more indisputable than this: *In the
present state of the human mind in Europe, Christianity can
only be defended by the Catholic principle, which refers all to
authority.*

"But how can this principle be developed, if the courts persist in their blindness? In one sense we may say that all
princes are dethroned, since there is not one who reigns as did
his father and grandfather before him; and since the sacred
character of kingship is daily becoming weakened in proportion to the growth of the irreligious principle, no one can yet
foresee the extent of the misfortune with which Europe is
threatened.

"There is an inflexibility in the teachings of the Catholic
Church which is displeasing to temporal authority. The latter
does not feel herself mistress, or sufficiently mistress, in the
presence of another power which she cannot control at will. . . .
She does not heed the fact, that this independence and ascendency are the natural and necessary characteristic of truth, —
that where *they* are not, *it* is not. What prince ever dreamed
of combating mathematics?"

---

[1] Letter to the Marquis ——, on the state of Christianity in Europe.

In yielding to the sentiments and influences which Count de Maistre thus describes with his usual imperious eloquence, the Emperor Alexander was not exempt from perplexity and disquietude. His personal acts seemed often to enter a protest against his official measures. When the ukase of banishment was announced to the Jesuitical order, each of the Fathers received from the Emperor's private purse pecuniary assistance and furs to protect them from the inclemency of the journey. Mme. Swetchine could no longer be resigned to subordinating her faith to prudence and mystery. The proscription of the Jesuits outraged her love of justice, besides wounding her personal respect and confidence; and her unfailing sense of honor must needs declare itself openly. As soon as the proscriptive measure was announced, Mme. Swetchine avowed herself a Catholic, hastened to the cell of Father Rosaven, placed at his disposal and that of his companions in misfortune all the means of alleviation at her command, and allowed no obstacle and no personal consideration to interfere with her pleading the' cause of the calumniated and proscribed, as her heart dictated. Until lately, the Emperor had testified for Mme. Swetchine nothing beyond the affectionate regard and consideration which all the imperial family bore her. But, after his return, — whether it was that he had become cognizant of her correspondence with Mlle. Stourdza, or that he naturally felt more drawn to her by the new turn his thoughts had taken, — their relations became closer and more intimate.

Those who had groaned over the influence of Mme. de Krüdener were yet more alarmed to think of the sway which a reason, lofty and pure as that of Mme. Swetchine, might come to exercise over a susceptible mind like Alex-

ander's.   But this time the woman who represented
religion and virtue to her sovereign, was actually worthy
of the honor; and the men whose prejudices or interests
were wounded by her ascendency, convinced that they
would look in vain for a stain on her irreproachable life,
found means to wound her by directing their intrigues
against General Swetchine.   The wrath excited by his honorable course at the time of Paul's death was not extinct;
and it seized this opportunity to gratify without betraying
itself.   A fault committed by a subaltern under his orders
was made the pretext for organizing perfidious machinations against himself.   The General scorned to justify
himself in the beginning; and when it appeared that his
enemies, old and new, had obtained a hearing, his pride
was wounded, and he took the course of leaving Russia.
His departure involved that of Mme. Swetchine,—a result
both anticipated and desired.   The Czar, baffled and
irresolute, testified his regret to Mme. Swetchine by begging her to write him on her journey.   This correspondence
was kept up until Alexander's death.   Mme. Swetchine
carefully preserved the Emperor's letters, and he accorded
the same honor to hers.   On the death of Alexander,
—whether by his express desire, or through the delicate
kindness of the Emperor Nicholas,—Mme. Swetchine's
letters were returned to her at Paris.   This complete
interchange of thoughts—whose interest may easily be
estimated—was still in her possession in the year 1845,
—when she permitted an eminent statesman of that day
to examine the letters.   No trace of them has been discovered among his papers.   We are at a loss whether to
believe that these documents were burned, like so many
others, amid the alarms of 1848, or merely returned to
Russia,—in which case they will, doubtless, one day see
the light.

As for Mme. Swetchine herself, the thought of travelling in Europe, and particularly in France and England, stimulated her passion for study, and allured her imagination. Since peace had opened the world to every species of investigation, she had frequently expressed her desire to share in the new freedom. Her intentions went no further. She said so repeatedly to the numerous friends whom she left behind her. In a note to her friend Tourguenief, we find an explicit statement to this effect.

My dear Tourguenief, — Here I am again at my eternal petitions! But I leave so many unfortunates here, that what is useless to one may be serviceable to another. Be so kind as to look after them a little; and sustain your courage, if it is ready to droop, by the reflection, that, in spite of myself, I must soon leave you at peace. Ah! my friend, if I had nothing else to bind me to my native land save these children and poor people whom I leave behind me, the tie would still be stronger than all foreign allurements. What I constantly experience in this connection is the best proof of the yearning which will restore me to my country sooner, it may be, than I myself suppose.

Mlle. Stourdza had not returned to Russia with the Empress. In 1816, she had married Count Edling, who held a conspicuous post at the court of the Grand-duke of Saxe Weimar, and the Grand-duchess Mary, Alexander's sister.

Another friendship no less strong and faithful had acquired an equal right in the heart of Mme. Swetchine. Mlle. Marie Gourief, daughter of Count Gourief, who was for a long time Minister of Finance, had married Count Nesselrode, Secretary of Foreign Affairs. Totally unlike the Countess Edling by nature, but with a mind equally acute and a heart equally warm, albeit under a colder exterior, Mme. de Nesselrode had consecrated to Mme. Swetchine one of those friendships which, throughout the longest life, afford only consolation and support. We shall see her, during forty years of separation, as active a friend, and, so to speak, as constant a companion, as if their mutual affection had matured in the narrow and intimate circle in which it originated.

Mme. Swetchine took with her a magnificent crayon portrait of Count de Maistre, who presented it, accompanied by the following stanza, which he inserted in the frame : —

"Docile à l'appel, plein de grace
De l'amitié qui vous attend,
Volez, image, et prenez place
Où l'original se plait tant."

---

1 Docile to appeal, and thankful for the love that awaits you, fly, my likeness, and take your place where the original loves so well to be.

CHAPTER IX.

Arrival of Mme. Swetchine at Paris. — Correspondence with the Duchess
de Duras.

MADAME SWETCHINE did not protract her journey from Russia to France. She came to Paris to
pass the winter of 1816 and 1817, at the age of thirty-four,
in the full vigor of her own intellect, and at the political
era which best answered to her own ideas.

She had known just so much of the crimes of the Revolution as the indignant memory of Europe had retained.
She had judged of the injustice and blindness of the passions of the mob by the noble victims to whom she had so
cordially offered her share of hospitality. She had also
observed closely, and with no less keen an eye, the abuses,
the violence, the infatuation, of unlimited and uncontrolled
power. And although called to no public action, and
though her sweetness and timidity revolted from the idea
of direct collision, it had been impossible for her to witness
the conflict of contradictory principles, so fatal alike to the
hopes and delusions of humanity, without arriving, in her
own heart, at fixed principles and conclusions. She assumed, in the first place, an attitude of perfect impartiality
toward all those who might conscientiously and sincerely
represent a generous idea; then she fixed irrevocably her
own preferences, friendships, and views on the side which
promised the longest duration to limited power and enlightened freedom.

The Restoration realized this type. Mme. Swetchine

gave it the approbation of her heart and mind. She was at once at home in the epoch and the society which she had come so far to visit. Friends whom she had already proved in her native land were the first to welcome her, — the Marquis d'Autichamp, whom she found Governor of the Louvre; the Count de La Garde, who received one of the first family embassies; and the Duke de Richelieu, who at once placed her on intimate terms with his two sisters, the Marquise de Montcalm and the Countess de Jumilhac.

The Duke de Blacas had lived much at St. Petersburg in the years which preceded the Restoration; and he had a great admiration for Mme. Swetchine. Up to his latest years, when saddened by a noble and voluntary exile, his cold and stern face expressed emotion whenever her name was mentioned. But at the beginning of the reign of Louis XVIII., the Duke de Blacas represented the court darling, differing widely from her in opinion, and with no especial desire for reconciliation. It was by means of their learning, of which so many souvenirs remain at Naples and Rome, that the Duke de Blacas and Mme. Swetchine maintained their relations. M. de Maistre had sent to Mme. Swetchine a letter for the Viscount de Bonald, in which he said, "You never saw more moral worth, more talent, and more erudition united to so much goodness." And Viscount de Bonald replied, "She is a friend worthy of you, and has one of the finest minds I ever met, which may be either the effect or the cause of the most excellent qualities with which a mortal was ever endowed."

The charitable institutions of France excited in her an interest which established frequent and most amicable relations between her and M. de Gerando. The diplomatic corps had two assiduous representatives at her house in the persons of Baron Humboldt and Count Pozzo di Borgo.

The salon where Mme. Swetchine found herself most speedily at home was that of the Duchess de Duras. There she saw for the first time Mme. de Staël, and addressed a remark to her which has been often, though inaccurately, quoted. The Duchess de Duras, wishing to make up for the disappointment of St. Petersburg, invited them both to a small and very select dinner party. Always very reserved, Mme. Swetchine allowed almost the whole repast to pass in silence, and scarcely lifted her eyes to the illustrious guest opposite. After dinner, Mme. de Staël approached Mme. Swetchine. "They told me, madam, that you desired to make my acquaintance: was I misinformed?"—"Assuredly not, madam; but it is always the king who speaks first."

Mme. Swetchine met in that salon all the reigning intellects of the day. All shades and all ranks mingled there as they did in the political councils of the Restoration,—M. de Chateaubriand and M. Abel Rémusat, M. Cuvier and Viscount Matthieu de Montmorency, M. Molé, M. Villemain, and M. de Barante. Some of these men, particularly M. Cuvier and M. Abel Rémusat, became her friends, as they were those of the Duchess de Duras. Others who were more deeply involved in politics did not nevertheless forget their meeting with her, and cherished its memory fondly. Madame de Duras conceived for her one of the latest and deepest affections of her soul. Often straitened for means, in spite of her grand position; independent and devoted, zealous and thoughtful; in the world, but not of it; an earnest Christian, but with a heart that piety had not yet been able to satisfy and render calm,—the Duchess de Duras recognized, at the first glance, in Mme. Swetchine the only qualities which could prove alluring to her now,—sensibility without complacency, sympathy

and strength.   Some of the outpourings of the Duchess de
Duras will give us the best idea of what Mme. Swetchine
was on her arrival in France, of the confidence, the affection, the enthusiasm, she inspired at first sight.   This correspondence will be a mirror which shall reflect the light (so
to speak) upon the portion of the picture which we desire
to examine.

After a six months' stay in France, General Swetchine
decided that his presence was necessary at St. Petersburg
to baffle the persevering manœuvres of his enemies; and
Mme. Swetchine did not hesitate to follow him thither.

It was during this absence, which lasted about a year,
that the Duchess de Duras wrote the following letters.
We must, however, except the first, of which a fragment
only has been preserved, and to whose date we have no
clue, but which evidently refers to Mme. Swetchine's first
sojourn in Paris, and to the commencement of her intimate
relations with Mme de Duras : —

ANDILLY.

Was I unwise to bring hither two volumes of those memoirs
of Dangeau?   I hope not.   They amuse me.   They read themselves, like all that is written, — all books that contain proper
names, and every thing relating to Louis XIV.   There is magic
in that great name !   He has left one enduring trace of himself.
You will be struck by it, when you see Versailles.   There
nothing comes between him and us.   "He did us great honor,"
said a peasant of Rouergue ; and, with the French, that is every
thing.   What matters the individual suffering?   He had placed
France above all other nations.   This will perpetuate another
name beside his, — the name of one who deserves immortality
less, for he had neither his goodness nor his greatness.

So I chat with you, and it gives me pleasure.   I am so
sure that my letter will be received, as it was written, kindly
and simply.   I would have said to no one else what I have just
said to you.   How some people would enjoy commenting upon
it !   But, with you, I dread neither cavilling nor ill-will.   I
believe in you : friendship is faith.   But how did you inspire
me with this confidence?   Do not deprive me of it ; do not dis-

appoint me: it would grieve me too deeply. I shall return on Friday, and hope to see you in the evening. Come early.

My little house progresses.[1] I hope, in fifteen days, to be able to show it to you; that is, its walls. Every thing is to be done. You will need all your imagination to comprehend it. As for me, I am like an author thoroughly imbued with his subject. I see the *ensemble* and the details: nothing escapes me. If I can but live, and cure my diseased mind, I may yet be happy,—who knows? You have done me good, and that is what I did not believe possible. Clara[2] embraces you. Adieu till Friday!

PARIS, Aug. 24.

Here I am in Paris, dear friend; and you would believe in my devoted friendship, if you knew what I suffer in your absence. This cabinet is a desert: it reminds me of all I lack. I entered it with pleasure; but now it is a source of sorrow, because you will come hither no more. All my friends are absent, or worse than absent; and I have not the slightest chance of seeing any one the sight of whom can touch my heart, or lift the weight that constantly oppresses it.

Is it not better to be alone at Andilly? There, at least, all is new. We must endeavor, of course, to preserve equanimity of mind; but it is impossible. I felt the need of writing you the moment I entered here. Josephine told me that you came here. Why need I have lost a single hour of the few you could still afford me? But it was better so. Adieus are not needed, when one's future is as sad as mine. I have no news. The change in the ministry has not yet taken place, but it is only delayed. . . .

This is one of those conventionalities which amaze you, and which are so common in France. It would certainly be better to refuse to see people toward whom one feels in this way. Doubtless, such is the first impulse: but one dreads scenes, eclat, ridicule; and the result is a false and frigid intercourse, and factitious professions of interest, which, in the end, impart a fatal taint to the character, and destroy, along with sincerity of manners, that good faith of the heart without which there is no true worth. And then, dear friend, what is the use? Why should we give ourselves so much anxiety? Time moves on, and regulates all things. When we consider what hours,

---

[1] Mme. de Duras was preparing a delightful retreat at Andilly.
[2] Clara de Duras, afterwards Duchess de Rauzan.

months, years, and lives really are, it seems inconceivable that
we should torment ourselves.   It is pitiful.

The burning of that frigate was the work of the malecontents ;
and I have just seen the Duke de Raguse, who was sent to
Lyons, Grenoble, &c., to pacify and conciliate them.   Do you
know him ?   These are people who conciliate by cannon-balls !

There is a good deal of talk about the classification of the
peers.   They are to be divided by benches.   This is very well.
I wish every thing in the state was as clearly defined : it would
remedy one of the greatest evils in France, — the uncertainty
about what one really is, which paves the way for so many
pretensions.   A definite ambition is not dangerous : a vague
ambition makes us discontented with what we have, without
giving us an aim.   Oliver de Vérac received a letter from a
provincial lady asking a place for her son.   " He is qualified,"
she stated, " to be a sub-prefect, prefect, councillor of State,
or even minister."   Ah well ! heads are full of this in France. . . .

Ah, my friend, what chatter !   I am ashamed of it.   It seems
as if you were here upon the green sofa, and had devoted your
whole evening to me, so that we felt at liberty to be lavish, and
waste our time in idle talk.   Mme. Montcalm always does me
good ; and it was you who disarmed my prejudice, fortunately
for me.   Nobody fears her more than I ; and I never know
how to conciliate those who are alienated from me.   I should
always need a guardian angel like you.   I took Clara to the
ball yesterday evening, and am dead with fatigue.   I asked myself, whether, among all the young people, there was one who
would suit me for a son-in-law.   No : there is but one after my
own heart, and he has not the requisite advantages.   I discussed the whole matter fully with M. de Duras this morning,
and we quite agreed on the main points.   In short, he leaves
me entirely free : and then I have a year, at least, before me ;
and that year is too precious for me to lose.   I embrace you.
I am impatient to receive tidings of yourself and the journey
to Moscow, and to get the first word of promise with regard to
your return.

Albertine[1] has come.   She is going to La Grange, which is
lent her by M. de La Fayette, who is absent.   I love her
tenderly.

ANDILLY, Sept. 8.

MY DEAR FRIEND, — I have had no news of you since your
letter from Strasbourg, and that did not quite please me.   I

---

[1] Albertine de Staël, afterwards Duchess de Broglie.

should like to unveil my heart to you, and you would be satisfied. I love you more than I should have believed possible,
after what I have experienced. I believe in you, — I, who had
become so suspicious. I feel secure in your friendship: I
would go to the ends of the earth, whatever might be my cir-
.cumstances, to seek it; and I should be sure of always finding
it the same. Why, then, should you not be content with me?
I give you all which it is possible to give in a life as confused
as mine. If you had come sooner, you would have found me
whole; but it is only my ruins to which you have become
attached. Your imagination has created an *ensemble*, but it is
no longer a reality. The griefs of which we ought to die, but
do not, disarrange our characters as well as our interests and
our whole existence. Harmony and equilibrium are broken up.
Henceforward, one is nothing. Since, however, nature ever
has a tendency to regain her level, we are tossed about on an
ocean of disgust and ennui; and life becomes but a melancholy
effort. Such is the poor creature whom you have deigned to
love, and who loves you with all the remaining strength of her
heart. I am constantly here. I have never been able to decide
to go to Tremblay;[1] and, when the time comes, I shall do just
the same about Lormoy[2] and Mouchy.[3] And yet I do not love
solitude. I am too much with myself, and that is not good for
me; but to be with others is more intolerable still.

I have had M. de Humboldt and M. de la Tour du Pin here
for a few minutes, and also M. de Chateaubriand, who came to
pass three days in Paris. I made a flying visit there. His
money matters are arranged, which gives me positive pleasure.
He is now independent, for, thank Heaven! politics have nothing to do with the arrangement. I found him in his best
mood, amiable, and having quite renounced that terrible idea
of self-expatriation. It is the continuation of his autobiogra-
phy which has benefited him so much. He has told the story
of seven or eight years of his youth, — from the age of twelve
till his entrance into the service; of the first efforts of his
genius; of his reveries in the Bois de Combourg; and, finally,
the prose history of which René is the versification. It is charming reading; but I trust he will not allow himself to read it to
anybody but me. I should be sorry, for a good many reasons.
His present intention is, that the memoirs shall not appear till
fifty years after his death. The number of years is of little

---

[1] Estate of the Marquis de Vérac.
[2] Estate of the Duke de Maillé.
[3] Estate of the Duke de Mouchy.

consequence, provided he is not living. He will return in two or three weeks to look out a lodging, and prepare himself for the Chambers. He has a good deal to say. The Concordat agitates all minds. Benjamin Constant has written a pamphlet on the elections, which is simply a song with the refrain, Nominate me, nominate me! The ministers are quizzed in it from beginning to end. If there was a courier, I would send you the work.

The Abbé Nicolle has been somewhat indisposed. I have not discovered that Mme. de Montcalm is angry with you for not having written her. I am longing for a letter from Moscow, saying that you can and will return. It must be, dear friend. You know that I have the misfortune to believe only in actions, which is very vulgar.

Apropos of subtilties, I have finished Waldemar,[1] and am indignant at it. I cannot endure such a mixture of truth and falsehood. There is an accuracy of reasoning, and, at the same time, a falseness of sentiment, which revolts me. I can excuse an error of the intellect, when the heart is right; but these ultra refinements of sentiment are intolerable, — this love which is not friendship, and friendship which is not love! Good Lord! to love is to love; and when two people love one another sufficiently to have every thing in common, — thoughts, interests, affections, tastes, — they can do no better than to marry, and become mutually attached, each to the being who has doubled the other's existence. All the eloquence of Jacobi will not alter the case; but he has some admirable passages, and his system is ingenious and fascinating.

Adieu! How can I send so far what I should say in my own chimney-corner? Let us not think of it. The autumn is fine. Why should you not see our poor France in this beautiful weather? It is another and a better thing than any spring. I embrace you, my dear friend. Ask my forgiveness for your letter from Strasbourg.

Clara loves and mourns for you. She has much to say to Nadine.

Sept. 20, 1817.

I showed you, my dear friend, some of the letters of my poor friend ——. You admired, with me, the superiority of her mind, her high tone of feeling, and the delicacy, the wounded pride, which have so long been imbittering her life, — for there is, in my opinion, no situation more cruel than one

---

[1] A romance by Jacobi, translated by Vanderbourg.

in which our own conduct misrepresents us. We are judged
with so much severity, and yet the humiliation is so painful!
And when one has won the admiration awarded to beauty,
grace, wit, and elegance of manners combined, and when one
has enjoyed that admiration, and then feels that it is disputed,
how terrible must be one's reflections! add to this a sensibility wounded or misunderstood, and the unrest of a heart at
war with itself, but too proud to ask aught of others!

In short, my dear friend, the situation has produced its
natural effect, — her brain is affected, her imagination is disordered, she has lost her reason. I cannot tell you how
much pain this gives me. My poor friend is very glad to see
me. Her insanity is not violent, but it is harrowing. She is
smitten with fear: she thinks she is to be assassinated; that
every thing she takes is poisoned; that we are all to perish
sooner or later by a conspiracy, but that she is especially
doomed; that all her servants are half-pay soldiers in disguise,[1]
— in fine, a thousand vagaries. She has been confessed. She
constantly believes that she is to die the ensuing night, but says
that she is happy. She charged me to justify her after her
death, to say that she did not deserve to be abandoned as
she had been: in short, many things in which one discovers —
spite of her madness — the trace of thoughts which I know
too well have been habitual with her. This is heartrending.
In this situation, — with all disguises stripped away, — we see
how sweet a soul hers was, and how great her capacity for suffering. Forgive me! you never saw her, but you know her;
and I am so absorbed by my poor friend, that I must needs tell
you of this first of all. I cannot believe that so recent an
attack is incurable, — horrible thought! Alas! what has she
done, as she said yesterday in her ravings, that she should be
treated so? People will say, "How was she treated? She was
at liberty to do as she pleased," &c. You hear it where you are.
But the wrongs which the heart resents most keenly are impalpable and invisible: they are like cactus-thorns, which make
bad wounds, though one cannot see them. Can it be possible
that there is no tribunal before which offences that have gone
unpunished in this world shall be judged? You will sympathize in all this. I know only M. de Chateaubriand and you
who could understand me on this subject. He will be much
distressed. I wrote him only three days ago. I hope her
dreadful condition will be ameliorated, but thus far she has
only grown worse. I can think of nothing else. . . .

---

[1] Military recently discharged by a measure which had excited **great**
discontent.

Did I tell you of the marriage of Louis de Saint Priest? He married the daughter of Caraman, — one of the most remarkable young women of the present generation, who will make him a lovely wife. She is Victor's[1] sister, and twenty years of age. Her fortune is the only point which is not satisfactory. She has no patrimony whatever, and her treatment is so uncertain. Mme. de Montcalm has received your letter from Saltzbourg. I see her tolerably often; but it is hard for us to feel at ease with one another. We need you: you were the link between us; and it is not here only that your absence makes itself felt. . . .

Mme. de Boigne has returned from England. That country is more disturbed than ever by the Jacobins. London is their centre. They have made several attempts to liberate Napoleon at St. Helena: new plots for an escape are daily discovered. How abominable for strangers to engage in such manœuvres! If it were Frenchmen, it would be rash, — criminal, if you will; but it would not be villanous. But to throw from a distance the match which kindles the fire, and to watch from a place of safety the misfortunes one has caused, there is no chastisement too severe for such enemies.. . .

Since M. Molé has been in the ministry, people pretend to dread the Jacobins. Both sides are apparently making advances to the royalists; but I do not believe it will lead to any thing. There are too many obstacles, and especially too much suspicion.

I have seen Auguste de Staël. He is still unlike himself, and has not recovered from his affliction. He described to me the awful silence which had reigned in the family since his mother's death. She stimulated them all. The animation of her presence communicated itself to every thing else. Now they had the old routine, but the life was gone out of it. . . .

I received your Munich and Saltzbourg letters at the same time. They gave me great pleasure; and I am glad to rest in the hope that your affairs will permit your return. I have spoken to M. de Humboldt of all the countries you have traversed. I should like to transport myself thither, and be with you.

October 3.

They tell me that there is a courier, but he starts to-day; and I have only time to write a few lines. Still, dear friend,

---

[1] Victor de Caraman, son of the Marquis de Caraman, created duke on his return from a mission to Vienna in 1828.

I do not want him to go empty-handed; and, ill as I feel, I have seated myself at my desk. I am none too well. I have the blues badly; that is nothing, and I do not want to talk of it. It will have passed when you receive my letter. But is it not deplorable to be in that state where your well-being depends upon a breath, a mere nothing? Find me a remedy for this evil. I know very well what you will say. It is quite true; but to embrace that assistance requires all the strength it can impart, and that is what I have not. So I only take palliatives, and remain essentially as ill as ever. I received your good letter from Vienna, and sent to Georges,[1] that I might question him. He swore that you were well, and not over-fatigued. But how your letter aggravated me! Might you really have stayed? The thought is too trying to dwell upon. I regret you, and shall as long as I live. No other society pleases or suits me like yours; and your affection was not the sole cause of my happiness, or, rather, it was not your praise, but the feeling which dictated it, that made me happy. There was no truth in it all; but you thought it, and that was enough; and so it is with any sentiment. We love feebly where we judge impartially; and there is no deception in letting a soul believe itself worthy of what is given it. And then is it not really a means of improvement? I believe that you have actually rendered me estimable; but you need not have left me. . . .

Come back, my friend! It is what I must constantly reiterate.

I have just had recommended to me a Russian lady, the Countess Lieven.[2] I have not seen her; but I have a grudge against her, because she is a Russian, and is not you; and, notwithstanding the wonderful stories they tell about her, I will lay a wager I shall not like her. They say, moreover, that she is what they call in London "a leader of fashion," which is something I cannot endure; for to hold that place necessitates a degree of effort and occupation with petty things which I believe incompatible with simplicity and elevation of mind. . . .

I have left no room for politics. M. de Chateaubriand has not yet arrived; but the turn things are taking makes one fear, more than ever, that reconciliation is impossible. I embrace you, dear friend, with all my heart! Come back, come back! I need you every instant.

---

[1] Count Georges de Caraman, attached to the embassy of Vienna.

[2] Afterwards Princess Lieven, *née* Benckendorf. It should be remarked, that this celebrated woman, who made a profound impression on European society, was not known to the Duchess de Duras when this judgment was pronounced.

October 22.

My dear Friend, — Although I wrote you eight days ago, I cannot let the Abbé Nicolle go without a letter. I have none from you. I feel your absence whenever I am with any of the persons who composed our little soirées. M. de Chateaubriand has returned. M. de Humboldt leaves Friday, to pass five days with his brother in England. . . .

Here all is unchanged. The opponents protest they want to be friends; but, the truth is, they do not. I expect this session will be consumed, like the last, in tacking between the two parties. My poor friend has a year or two before him in which to arrange his affairs, and *nous verrons* is the refrain of the song. They are blazing away at the Duke de Raguse, for his conduct at Lyons; but I imagine that these great events, which affect us so sensibly, look very small at your distance. The great figure of the Revolution is broken into a heap of minute débris: but, whether considered in detail or as a whole, it is still the Revolution; and these elements are perhaps none the less dangerous when they are disunited, and when one is attacked and wounded by them on every hand without the possibility of seeing or seizing them. . . .

Tell me that you are coming back, and that you do not forget me. M. de La Garde gave me a fright about you the other day. He told me that you would cease to write to me some fine day, and yet that you would be always the same. Do not believe it. I do not understand all this, but they may think what they please. All the sophistry in the world will not alter my opinion. You know that I am vulgar enough to believe that actions speak a thousand times louder than words. . . .

Do you know what M. Greffulhe did at his house the other day? You must know that he is subject to fits of suffocation in the night, and that one of the things that help him most is to go into fresh sheets and another bed. He has keys to all the chambers in his castle,[1] and he promenades these all night long. The other day, he arrived late in Paris, and went to bed without a word to any one. It was warm; and, in the middle of the night, the suffocation seized him. Where should he go to bed? He remembered a chamber occupied by Mme. d'Audemare. Mme. d'Audemare was away, and the chamber empty. M. Greffulhe arose, and, armed with a lantern and a *passe partout*, he traversed a long corridor, opened the door, entered a chamber, and prepared for repose. He approached

---

[1] Bois Boudrant, near Melun.

the bed, and what do you think he saw? Mme. de Crillon sound asleep, who had arrived the night before unknown to him. Our new Scipio retired to his own apartment, and at breakfast gave an account of this fine adventure, — which surprised Mme. de Crillon a good deal, since she had never waked. It will take its place among the castle legends. How foolish to write you all this nonsense. Adieu, dear friend! I am in a hurry. Write me, and give the lie to M. de La Garde; and especially come back, come back, come back! If I should say it till to-morrow, I should not feel that I had said it half as much as I desire it.

PARIS, Oct. 31.

Nothing in my life has changed! All is as it was when I knew you; but I have made up my mind that you alone could do me good, and now I am minus the happiness and reposo which your friendship afforded me. Tell me in detail what has necessitated this sad sacrifice. It is something sudden and unlooked for, because you were coming, in spite of your sister's change of plans. Write me word about it. I need to come to an understanding with you. It is I whom you have sacrificed; but, if it was your duty, do not think that I blame you. No! I certainly should not wish to owe your presence to any thing which might disturb your mind. Your letter to the Countess Stanislas[1] troubled me in more ways than one. I am jealous of her: you love her very dearly. You will tell me that she came too late; but I imagine she is better worth your love than I. She has such an air of repose. She pleases me, but I am not at my ease with her. That will come, perhaps, when we talk of you. I do not yet understand why, when she has lost so many children, she should have deserted this one. You know my doctrine of actions. They are every thing. The finest words are of no account. I have seen the Emperor[2] pass. Only the King and princes have more to boast of. The Princess Bagration persisted in the cruelty of not giving us even a night. As for me, I should have been satisfied with a day. The Emperor used to be graceful. He is always handsome, and I perceive that he has grown stout.

I am in the depths of despair since I have learned that you are not to return. It is an accident, but it is true. I need you, my friend, every moment; and this sentiment is strength-

<hr>

[1] Countess Potocka *née* Branicka.
[2] The Emperor Alexander on his return from England.

ened, rather than weakened, by my increasing certainty that
there are so few like you. My poor heart, which I thought
quite dried up, renews its strength to love and to regret you.
Who knows but we shall meet some day in another country
than this? The Jacobins, in consequence of the measures
they have adopted, are acquiring new power every day. It
might still be possible to reduce them to the insignificance
whence they should never have emerged, but people are too
blind. And then I believe in divine decrees. Perhaps we shall
yet admire together the natural beauties of Switzerland or
Italy, in that country-home which shall be the asylum of my
family and my friends from France. The money destined for
its purchase is all ready; and, when I find myself over-agitated
by the confusion and misery of the world, I meditate upon that
future, and instantly get calm. Adieu! write to me. I shall
give this letter to the Countess Stanislas, who is to pass the
evening with me at the Tuileries.[1]

November 19.

I have been troubled at receiving no news from you; but
here it is at last, only too summary in relation to your own
affairs. You speak to me of myself: that is not necessary,
neither is it reasonable. When friends are as far apart as we
are, they cannot answer, but they can address one another.
Tell me, then, of all your occupations; but do not waste these
precious sheets in replying to details which are foreign to us
both. What is not so, and what comes very near to my heart,
is your return. Do not attempt to dissemble the part which
I may have in it, nor underrate my share of gratitude. I accept
it all, and am equal to all, — for I love you. At the commencement of our acquaintance, I desired no sacrifices from
you, because I was not sure of my own affection; but at present
I would demand such sacrifices, since I am quite ready to make
them. I shall see you, then, dear friend, in a year, — minus
six days. Remember this, and see that you do not give me
a terrible disappointment. I will go where you will to meet
you, and we will spend a little time together. I should like to
spend my life so. I have not written you for a fortnight
because I have been anxious, and hoping to be delivered from
my anxiety, and able to tell you something positive.

----

[1] The Duke de Duras, as first gentleman of the bedchamber, was
lodged at the Tuileries.

Here Mme. de Duras enters into minute details about her plans for the marriage of her daughter Clara. She then resumes : —

" Perhaps my first letter will contain some definite information. I see that the letter which I sent to Just de Noailles[1] for you never reached you. The post is better every way. I should not care to have Pozzo read these details.

" Our little soirées have commenced. Everybody misses you, I most of all, and more just now than ever. M. de Humboldt has been in England for a fortnight. He will have witnessed the terrible affliction into which the country has been plunged by the death of that poor young princess.[2] It is a fine thing when the institutions of a country are such that a loss like this is a misfortune : still it is not an event which can materially influence the political existence of the nation ; and this of itself is a sufficient eulogium on the constitutional form of government. I believe that M. de Chateaubriand's work is not to appear. He is unwilling to do any thing at this time which might irritate, or be prejudicial to a reconstruction. I have made the acquaintance of M. de Villèle. He has an excellent head, but his manner is a little too confidential to suit me. I do not like 'asides' unless they are absolutely necessary. Possibly, it is a kind of affectation in him. I will reserve my judgment : I have only seen him twice, and never tête-à-tête. The Duke de Richelieu and M. Laisne are very much disaffected. I am persuaded they will be turned out, as the Duke de Feltre was. Royer Collard said yesterday, that the Concordat was a political crime, and that to sustain it was a political folly. This is the way these gentlemen treat one another ; and you know what happens to a house divided against itself. I speak of these men just as if you knew them ; but you know France so well, it is difficult to believe that any interest or any individual therein can be strange to you. I have diffused universal joy by the announcement of your return. A year minus one day, remember, dear friend ! My future is in that promise.

" I have received a delightful letter from a traveller.[3] He gives a minute description of Athens and Constantinople. A sin-

---

[1] Just de Noailles, Prince de Poix, at that time ambassador at St. Petersburg.

[2] Princess Charlotte, first wife of Prince Leopold of Saxe Coburg, afterwards king of Belgium.

[3] M. de Forbin.

gle small excavation between Phalerum and the Piræus brought
to light two monuments, two vases, and several statues and
bas-reliefs. In about a fortnight, he accomplished a great deal.
I do not think his absence will be very long. He has visited
Constantinople, in spite of the pestilence, enveloped in a great
cloak of waxed taffeta. He has seen the Bezesteins,[1] the streets,
the edifices, and the Sultan, — who is thirty-two years of age,
and very handsome. He says that the Turks elbowed him, the
Greeks laughed at him, and the Jews prostrated themselves before him, and the doves lit on his shoulders. The Abbé de
Janson has a superb moustache. He tries all the Arab horses,
and says mass every day. The cousins have a quarrel because
the Abbé de Janson[2] wishes to take the command of M. de
Forbin, and because they are infatuated like the late Bishop of
Marseilles.[3] *Apropos* of Mme. de Sévigné, I am to have her
crucifix, and a little trifle in sandal-wood, which belonged to her
writing-desk. One of them is destined for you.

   "Yesterday I supped with the Duchess de Luynes. M. de
X. was happy. There was a scandal on foot! Mme. de J.
and M. de la C. in the same room, seated side by side at play.
M. de la C. said to Mme. de J., ' I am very glad to see you ; ' and
the poor man was overcome. You can imagine the delight of
those who subsist on the follies of their neighbors. It is melancholy nourishment ; and the mind gets no good by it. Heavens !
what a pitiful thing is conversation at these great parties ! It
was the opening of the year ; and nonsense, scandal, and frivolity bloomed in all their freshness. It is very well to take a
respite in summer from what is called the great world. To
have a taste for and enjoy it would be the greatest misfortune
which could happen to heart or mind. Adieu, dear friend !
write me often, — so often, that, when September comes, we shall
have nothing to say to one another. We shall have the happiness of La Bruyère, ' To be with those we love is enough.' Ah,
how true this is ! and it is a happiness which will outlast this
life. In this thought I love to rest.

   "M. Benoist[4] desires to be remembered to you. His son is
charming. M. de Richelieu does nothing for him."

---

[1] Bazaars at Constantinople.

[2] The Abbé de Farbin Janson, afterwards Bishop of Nancy.

[3] A bishop of Marseilles belonging to the family of Forbin; see the
letters of Mme. de Sévigné.

[4] Count Benoist, director-general under the Restoration, father of
Viscount Benoist d'Azy.

In the ensuing letter Mme. de Duras returns to the details of her daughter's proposed marriage, and then adds : —

Jan. 29, 1818.

MY DEAR FRIEND, — You must excuse me for allowing myself to dwell upon what, I must confess, occupies me exclusively just now. I have no courage to speak of politics. If you read the papers, you know as much as I do. I have had news from M. de Forbin, dated at Jerusalem, Nov. 20. He was to be in Egypt at this time. I think we shall see him the ensuing summer. And you, — when will you come? The Russians here will not believe in your return. This irritates me extremely. Moreover, I do not like them, and scarcely see them at all, except the Galitzin for Catinka's sake. . . .

M. de Chateaubriand has broken one of the muscles of his leg, and is confined to a sofa for forty days. I go to see him; but you have no idea of the void it makes in my life not to have him in my cabinet for an hour or two in the morning thinking aloud to me. I am mortally sad. There is nothing more strictly internal than happiness; yet what are external objects without it? It is the light which illumes them: all is dull and lifeless when it is withdrawn. You write me very seldom, and speak neither of yourself nor of your associates. Our correspondence is not what I could wish. Have you seen the nonsense which is said of me in the English journals, — how a statement has appeared in them of the opinions of MM. de Fitz James and de Polignac, which I have reviewed and corrected? There is only one difficulty: these gentlemen do not come to my house. The King knows it perfectly well, and has said so: so that I should not care if I had not such a horror of having my name in print anywhere and for any cause. This piece of malice must have crossed the sea twice; for I will never believe that the Londoners take any interest in such gossip.

Feb. 2, 1818.

This letter is truly conversational. I wish I might receive one from you which should be equally confidential about your own interests. Speak particularly of your return, and of all which favors or hinders it. Mme. de Montcalm has been sick. She is better; but she is eaten up by politics. They are her vulture.

---

[1] Catinka Galitzin, Countess Edmund de Caumont.

M. de Humboldt is well.   M. M. Benoist, d'Harcourt — all
our friends are here.   I no longer see M. de Villèle, who is as
witty in conversation as in the tribune.   You know very well
that I prefer the other side.   In the matter of *ultras*, I like only
three or four distinguished men, — the generals : the rank and
file weary me to death, and I do not see much of them.   If M.
de Chateaubriand were to continue ill long, I should join the
ministerial party for very ennui, and the unreasonableness of
those who surround his couch.   Adieu !   I embrace you.

May 3.

Still no news from you.   Just arrived this morning, and
brought me nothing ; but at least I shall talk with him about
you, and that will be a pleasure to both of us.   Your silence
grieves and disturbs me.   You do not write, because you have
not the courage to tell me that you are not coming back ; and
as for me, my dear friend, I have not the courage to hear it.
Yes, I need you, — need you greatly !   There are so many
things to say which one cannot write, and especially at such a
distance, and with the experience I have had in lost letters.
To whom did they go?   I want to tell to none but you the
pains and pleasures of my heart.

M. d'—— dreads M. de Duras.   People who have committed political sins have singularly timorous consciences.
They imagine that men owe them a grudge for things long
since forgotten, and steps which Time has effaced a hundred
times over.   This is the true state of the case ; but the uneasiness which they experience themselves is much more difficult
to cure than that of which they suspect us.

May 5.

MY DEAR FRIEND, — I have received your good letter of the
30th of March.   Is it possible that the silliest rumor in the
world has reached you? — a rumor which lasted but two days,
and never had any foundation ; and which arose from the fact,
that M. de Duras, who had gone to see Mme. de Lubersac and
spend a fortnight at Ussé [1] during planting time, when he found
the season advancing, left, not expecting the recruiting law.
But our position is not in the least altered.   The King is always
the same to M. de Duras, and, without being any more in favor
with him, he is certainly no less so than when you were here.

---

[1] Chateau near de Langeais, in Touraine.

However, dear friend, you will make me regret disgrace, if it could have brought you to my side. You are ill. Our climate is necessary to you. Come back, I implore you! I am disconsolate that you have no fixed plans. Tell me, then, the nature of your difficulties. Your affairs are now in such a state, that General Swetchine might wind them up, and then rejoin you. Send me one decisive word. You repulse me in my uncertainty.

ANDILLY, July 8.

MY DEAR FRIEND, — I have received an adorable letter from you. It ought to be enough for one's happiness to know that there is, at the world's end, a being who loves one sincerely; and I always find that I am unjust to Providence when I ask any thing more. Yet I do ask him more earnestly than ever for your return. You are the only person who understands my position; and you give me good advice. . . . I wrote you about my cottage, where I have been established for a fortnight. I received this morning your beautiful strips of needlework. They shall be for the front of my sofa. I should like to adorn myself with your gifts. Nothing could be prettier than my little retreat. Why are you not here?

Your chamber is ready, and so is Nadine's. Come, come, dear friend! Life is so short; why should we waste it thus? I am anxious about your health. I believe our climate to be much better for you than the Russian. All feeble constitutions are recruited by the lovely weather we have had for three months past. I am very well. My stomach is astonishingly renovated. I sleep all night long, and they tell me I am growing stout; but I am incredibly weak after my illness. I, who was so strong, cannot endure the least fatigue without a relapse. I am like a building which presents a fair appearance, but has no stability. A breath upsets me. I have, besides, those singular throbbings of the arteries about the heart. I am convinced that the organ is enlarged; and what surprises me is, that I am still alive. I would give all the world if my poor Clara were only happy. I pity myself to think that I can be concerned about any thing else. What a letter! all full of *me*. How does it happen that I have such entire confidence in you? I did not suppose it possible any longer. It is the strongest proof of friendship I could give you.

Yet once again I beg for some precise information about your return. I need it more than I can tell you; and every day that passes is so much taken from the friendship which will be the blessing of our lives. Think of it, and do not let trifling obstacles detain you; and I call those trifling which are not insurmountable.

I go to Paris on the evening of the 23d.   Lord Wellington
has come; but I have no hope.   It makes no difference: one
must act precisely the same; but all I do will be nullified by
what my poor friend writes.   He is at his wit's end; and you
can judge what his pen will produce, when he has thrown off
all restraint, and writes from a place where the most exaggerated style of opinion prevails.   It is no use to hope.   There
are characters, and especially orders, of talent, which are always
persecuted, or fancy that they are so.   It would be forcing nature to rescue M. de Chateaubriand from this infliction.
When all is said, he will remain a French peer; but, if he
could lose this rank, you may be sure he would.   I have begun
a piece of work which interests because it does not fatigue me.
I am translating Glenarvon; and I beg you to be so kind as
to read it.   It is the freest translation possible.   I add and
take away continually; but I find so much talent and originality, and so many things that I should have said myself, that it
is thoroughly amusing.   I only manage to keep the thread of
the story; but that is a support, and I make progress.   Read
it.   You will readily separate the gold from the alloy; and
you will see whether I was mistaken about its original talent.
Nobody liked it; but did anybody like Adolphe?[1]

MY DEAR FRIEND, — You are almost here!   This is all I can
see in your letter.   What joy, what bliss, to see you again! to
be sure that you are coming!   I love you with all the ardor of
my youth!   I should never have believed it possible.   Yesterday the Countess Stanislas, of whom I am very fond, came to
see me at the Tuileries.   The first word she said was, that you
had left St. Petersburg, but that you were going to Rome.
She had learned it from the Countess de Nesselrode, who informed her, at the same time, that you were going by the way
of Vienna, and that she had sent my portrait thither; for I
have had my picture taken for you, dear friend, and Mme. de
Nesselrode had undertaken to forward the box to you.   Rome
annoyed me: still I dared not murmur, since it was your sister
you were going to see.   But what joy your yesterday's letter
gave me!   You are coming straight here, without that Italian
journey, which would inevitably have deferred your arrival till

---

[1] By Benjamin Constant.

spring. But no more changes. Do not take this comfort away from me : it would be too hard! I am so accustomed to trouble, that the sensation of joy confuses me. The 19th of October is so late a date for St. Petersburg, that I cannot believe Mme. de Nesselrode has the last intelligence. But you are suffering, and you do not say how. The journey, it may be, will fatigue you. The cold will be extreme, and the winter promises to be severe; and perhaps I am rejoicing when I ought to mourn. Yet, once here, the climate suits you better than that of Russia. I will take care of you : I will lead you to the waters : I will take possession of you; and it is my wish that not a pang, mental or physical, should visit you while with me.

This letter goes to Weimar; but perhaps you will miss of it there. I shall send it off at once. I embrace you a million times.

Mme. Swetchine achieved, not without difficulty, the end proposed by her journey, and became more and more convinced that the benevolent disposition of the Emperor Alexander did not enable him to enforce justice and impartiality about him. The prejudice against Catholicism was on the increase; and the soul of the Emperor grew melancholy without his becoming either more enlightened or firmer of purpose. The Count de Maistre had seen his moral authority contested at the very moment when his official position, along with the situation of the king, his master, resumed its normal aspect, and he had expressed a wish to leave St. Petersburg.

The Countess Edling continued to reside at the court of Weimar. The Countess de Nesselrode, who was involved, along with her husband, in the agitations of the highest political circles, could only consecrate to her faithful friendship those rare moments which she spared from her imperative duties. Finally, to complete Mme. Swetchine's privations, she did not, on her return to Russia, find her sister there. Prince Gargarin had happened to excite the jealousy of Alexander, and had been attached to the embassy at Rome. Mme. Swetchine was thus recalled to France by a double attraction; and, though she had not conceived the idea of a permanent establishment at Paris, she cherished a plan for a protracted residence in a country which had captivated her taste and won her affection at first sight. She arranged her affairs with a view to a long absence; and General Swetchine withdrew from a court which he had never frequented in the character of a courtier, and where he had more than once been subjected to unmerited displeasure.

Both quitted Russia towards the end of the autumn of 1818, — the General to return no more; Mme. Swetchine to make one last journey thither in the reign of the Emperor Nicholas, and attain thereby, after the Revolution of July, the privilege of an exceptional sojourn.

The Emperor and Empress permitted Mme. Swetchine's voluntary exile, as they had permitted the departure of the Countess Edling; holding both in affectionate esteem, but according their preference to intellects and hearts far less worthy. The more absolute a monarch is, the more he needs to be on his guard against the temptation of awarding to custom the place due to merit and services. Inferior natures flatter, and to some extent corrupt, their masters, even when they are not, consciously and voluntarily, sycophantic and unprincipled. Without effort and without premeditation, they stimulate and cherish a prince's constant enjoyment of his superiority; and, without being exempt from vanity or infatuation, they are incapable of raising these two elements of resistance to the height of sustained dignity or sturdy complaint. Only too happy to obey with a show of advising, they are restrained from contradiction even more by sterility of thought than by lack of courage.

CHAPTER X.

Unpublished letters of Count de Maistre. — Mme. Swetchine's earliest connections in Paris. — Notes of the Abbé Desjardins. — Departure of Mme. Swetchine for Italy. — Correspondence with the Marquise de Montcalm.

COUNT DE MAISTRE embarked on board a Russian vessel on the 27th of May, 1817; landed at Calais on the 20th of June; and, on the 24th, arrived in Paris. It had been his wish to see France before revisiting his native land; but he was soon at Turin, yielding himself unrestrainedly to the sweets of domestic life, which were almost unknown to him. He put the finishing touches to several of his works, brought out his book on "The Pope," and prepared the "Soirées de St. Petersburg." Three of his letters have been preserved. The first, dated in Russia, speaks of the regret caused by Mme. Swetchine's departure, and invokes her memory in the name of her sorrowing friends. The two others are subsequent to M. de Maistre's return to Piedmont. The three are given consecutively, notwithstanding the difference in their dates: —

St. Petersburg, Aug. 17 (29), 1816.

I am charged, madame, by your good friend the Countess Razoumofsky, with a sad message for you, — to acquaint you, namely, with the death of her good mother, the poor Baroness de Maltzen, whom yesterday we accompanied to her last resting-place. She died on Monday, the 14th, about five o'clock in the morning, in the arms of her daughter and the faithful Carizé. Mme. Viollier, who is occupying at present a little country-seat on the road from Catherinhof, close to Peterhof, has very opportunely assumed charge of the poor Countess, and taken her home with her. I am going to see her. The Princess Sherebatof is making great exertions in her behalf; and, in short, we are doing what we can. But how we miss you! and how your absence has been regretted on this sad occasion by the unhappy widow! for such she is.

Mme. de Maltzen took remedies which burned her; and, when she swallowed them, she said, "You are killing me!" After her death, the physician decided that she had an abscess in the chest which he had not suspected. Thereupon, the poor Countess tore her hair, and would have it that she was to blame for not having prevented the use of those remedies. You can imagine what a dispute she had with Stoffsin. O medicine! we are constantly seeing new triumphs of thine! The Grand-marshal leaves to-day or to-morrow, in a deplorable state. It is nothing more or less than a consumption of the bowels. He goes accompanied by his daughter, who is *enceinte*, his son, and a physician; but, consumed by a frightful dysentery, he will die in some neighboring inn. You are simple enough, it may be, madame, to ask the foolish question why he goes. Ah, you know nothing about it! The Emperor has given him a hundred thousand roubles for his journey; so he must go, that is plain.

To return to your afflicted friend. She had a great desire to return immediately to town, and take a lodging near the church; but it could not be. Her house, as you know, madame, is disputed property: it is not known to whom it belongs. The Emperor came to no decision before his departure. The syndics say they are syndics no longer, since the promulgation of the imperial ukase, and refuse to accept their arrears of pay. There seems to be no reason why this state of things should not continue. I hope, by God's grace, that the house will be destroyed before the question of its ownership is settled.

Yesterday, the poor lady's last word before we parted was, "You will write to her, — will you not?" You may be sure, madame, that my promise was readily given. As soon as your friend has recovered some degree of strength and calmness, you will receive a long letter from herself.

I have no information to give you about myself, madame, except that, according to all appearances, I shall yet pass the winter with you. The destiny which awaits me under other skies will be better discussed in conversation than by letter. In one way or another, I hope to find myself once more upon your track; and, while looking forward to our re-union, I shall not cease to mourn for you. You certainly ought, madame, to ask for Prince Kalsofsky's [1] place at Turin. You are not as

---

[1] Minister from Russia to the court of Sardinia.

heavy as he, but you have more weight; and, though your mind may be "weak and illogical,"[1] ours will easily accommodate themselves thereto. Take my word for it, my good Sophie, and come forward.

You cannot guess, madame, how deeply I am obliged to that good princess who has never failed to give me tidings of you. Every Wednesday and Saturday I institute an inquiry. I know not, when I arrive, but you are already burned:[2] but when she has said "She speaks of you, M. le Comte," then all is said. Happily, it is a good deal.

I kiss the hands of Sophie with respect, and beg her to hold me in remembrance, — mine of her is eternal.

So I finish, as our fathers used, with a prayer that God will have you in his safe and holy keeping. Nothing can be fitter. May he shield you, and enlighten you, and bless you!

Your very humble servant and eternal friend,

PHILOMATES DE CIVARRON.

Did I ever tell you, madame, that this is my Latin name?[3]

———

TURIN, Oct. 26, 1819.

MY DEAR AND HONORED FRIEND, — I received your Vienna letter on the 13th of September. Pray, do not wonder at my silence. I have been constantly on the move since my departure from Paris, and have resumed no regular correspondence. In the first place, I went home, where I spent six days in a kind of perpetual enchantment, surrounded by brothers, sisters, nephews, nieces, and cousins, — male and female, — caressed, fêted, glorified, spoiled, after an incredible fashion. I then repaired to Turin, where I was patched up most artistically. Then to Genoa, to my sister, Mme. de St. Real, who set about demoralizing me anew. But here I am at last, surrounded by the best of remedies, and I do not believe that my attacks at Chambéry and Genoa will have any serious consequences.

I know no more of my future than on the day when I first

———

[1] An allusion to the terms of the ukase which proscribed the Jesuits.

[2] The Princess Gargarin was accustomed carefully to burn her correspondence with her sister.

[3] Philomates, derived from the Greek, signifies a friend of science; and Civarron is the Latin name for Chambéry. The Cardinal Chigi, who became pope under the name of Alexander VII., had already, in the seventeenth century, adopted the pseudonym of φιλομάτης.

set foot in this august capital. My position is indefinable. I
wish you were here to see; but, while I await the *finale*, of
which I shall inform you, I am not in the least impatient. I
have seen others in these twenty years. You shall be apprised
of all that occurs to me; and I hope you will treat me in the
same way. There must be no divorce, or even separation,
between us.

Ah, how those absurd ideas of geography and chronology
will keep occurring to my mind, when I think of you! My
poor vine! when beaten by the storm, to what elm will you
cling? when your heart swells with bitterness and contradiction, what will you do? will you crush it between two stones?
Do not, in God's name! But, when you are so inclined, write
to me. I shall never get accustomed to your absence, to
the impossibility of calling upon you to give an account of
your thoughts, your joys, and your sorrows. When you are
fairly settled, send me a sketch of your cabinet, that I may
see your table, your arm-chair, and the place for your books.
I am doing my best to add to your stock; but I am constantly
thwarted in one way and another. If I succeed, it will be a
great affair. The Duchess de Duras was calmly oblivious of
the work upon her desk. She had never bestowed a thought
upon it, still less upon its author. When M. de Chateaubriand at last informed me of the fact, with all sorts of polite
apologies, I burst out laughing in perfect good faith. It was
very well for the Duchess de Duras to forget me; but, for myself, I never think of her without recalling the utter failure I
made in her hôtel. I felt *gauche*, embarrassed, absurd. I did
not know to whom to speak, and I did not understand the
others. It was one of the strangest experiences of my life.
It seems to me that I told you about it at Paris.

I cannot yet satisfy all the anxieties of your friendship on
my account. What you say has certainly been said here, and
many other things besides; but nothing is decided, nor even
probable. What amuses me is your idea about Rome.[1] I
shall amuse you, too, some day, by telling you what other
person, or personage, has conceived the same idea. In effect,
as far as I personally am concerned, nothing would suit me
better; but the slightest observation of my surroundings will
reveal to you obstacles which are almost insurmountable.
This permanent separation from my son is a species of damna-
tion: I cannot think of it without rage.

---

[1] Mme. Swetchine was surprised that M. de Maistre was not appointed ambassador to the sovereign pontiff.

You say what is very pleasant and very true, whether agreeable to reason or not. Poor woman! It is too true: she is always accused of thwarting us at every point.

Adieu, my good, my excellent, my esteemed friend. Do not forget that I cannot do without your regard and your affection. My thoughts will always follow you. My heart will ever feel the value of yours.

Rest your aching head upon some soft cushion. Sleep sweetly. Genius and virtue will shield you from every evil dream. I kiss your hands reverentially, as well as those of your amiable companion, — with her permission.

I beg that you will not fail to forward the enclosed hymn. It can go by the post, if there is no other way. What you tell me about the probable arrangement of your affairs, enchants me. May it quickly emerge from the sphere of possibilities into that of realities! My respects, if you please, to your husband.

TURIN, July 22, 1818.

MY GOOD SOPHIE, — Though suffering the acutest grief, I have strength enough remaining to inquire the reason of your silence. On the 24th of last December, I wrote to you in Moscow, whence you yourself had written me, but received no reply. On the 2d of last May, I wrote you again at Vienna, in the care of M. Artaud: still no answer.

I have lost my brother, the Bishop of Aosta. He has just died in my arms. We were planning a fraternal re-union for the 19th. Almost all my family were collecting from different parts of the empire, to enjoy at my house one of those unspeakable meetings of which we have been so long deprived. On the morning of the 18th, he who was chief among us died after an illness of only four or five hours, which we had taken for a trifling indisposition. We are desolate, thunder-struck, — more dead than he! A famous orator, apostle, theologian, and man of the world, as much admired at Geneva as among ourselves; an excellent brother; my childhood's friend, — this is what I have lost. Ah, madame, it is a terrible blow! It is with difficulty that I pen these lines, which I cannot extend; but I was unwilling to lose the opportunity. Pity me; and, if you have not forgotten me, tell me so.

If you were here, would you not be in the very room where I write? I kiss your hand, while I bathe it with my tears.

M. de Maistre did not long survive the Bishop of Aosta. He died on the 26th of February, 1821, at the age of

sixty-seven, in the fulness of his powers, but oppressed
by sad forebodings of the future of Italy and France. His
portrait, which Mme. Swetchine kept constantly before her,
was hung in her favorite saloon, between that of the Countess de Nesselrode and that of the Duchess de Duras.
The three pictures were wrought by different artists, and
in different countries; but, by a singular coincidence, they
were of precisely the same dimensions, as if their prox-
imity had been fore-ordained. The memory of M. de
Maistre continued, so to speak, to brood above the life of
Mme. Swetchine. We shall have occasion to remark here-
after the deep feeling which his name never failed to
awaken, and to see how indissolubly the great soul remained attached to the great memory.

Among many attractions which contributed their share
towards fixing the residence of Mme. Swetchine in France,
we may safely affirm, that the first and strongest was the
freedom, the dignity, and the charity of the Catholic
Church. For the first time in her life, she calmly contemplated religion in all the majesty of its social achieve-
ments and institutions, came in contact with minds as
vigorous as her own, and felt herself understood. In seeking a director for her soul, however, Mme. Swetchine had
regard neither to brilliancy of position nor the prestige of
eloquence. A venerable ecclesiastic — the Abbé Desjardins — was living under the shadow of the towers of Nôtre
Dame, in a modest retreat, laboriously occupied and
piously absorbed by the incessant duties of his apostolate.
Mme. Swetchine obtained an introduction to him, and perhaps it would be proper to confine ourselves to this simple
statement; but after we have displayed, in the correspondence of Mme. de Duras, the homage paid her by rank
and wealth, is it not fair to show, in the tender regard of

the humble priest, a reflection of the first years of Mme. Swetchine's Catholic life? Is it not also just to honor in M. Desjardins the exquisite type of the old French clergy, and recall to the mind of a generation somewhat prone to forgetfulness its potent qualities of meekness, urbanity, and self-devotion?

The first letter of the Abbé Desjardins is dated previous to Mme. Swetchine's journey to Russia. An acquaintance with her of less than a year had been enough to inspire him to write as follows : —

MY VERY DEAR AND GOOD DAUGHTER, — It is by force of habit that I give you the second epithet, and because, up to this time, you have deserved it in a remarkable degree. But, if it were possible for you to forfeit it, you would do so to-day. Certainly, it was no good angel who inspired you to make me a superb present. Would such an one have suggested to you to engrave upon silver gilt what your heart had to say to mine? If you only knew how this outlay wounds me! A trifle, such as you are accustomed to offer, would have been much more flattering. Still, the dread of wounding your feelings induces me to keep your gift. After all, it is a memorial of your affection, and I will read the inscription over every day, if only to correct it.

I want to put my own principles in practice. I shall offer you no splendid gift, yet one which will not be without its value to you, — a reliquary, made from the wood of the true cross, which I have carried in a little portfolio, and used for six years, and which I had with me in my imprisonment.[1] I add a book from my poor library, and present these offerings along with my tender farewells. There is also a book of meditations for good Nadine : it is all simple, like my own soul.

You are going away: shall I ever see you again in this world of sorrow and care? We know not, neither you nor I. Let us both strive after a meeting in a better land. Let us emulate one another in the love of Him who has bought so dearly the right to our affection.

I cannot let you go without informing you of some events which are likely to alter my position. You only, of all the

---

[1] Under the empire, during the persecutions of Pius VII.

world, know that the bishopric of Blois was offered to me, and that I felt obliged to refuse it; although I have procured for my best friend the adjoining one of Orleans. Afterward, I was offered either the cure of St. Thomas Aquinas or a place in the bishopric, with a salary of ten thousand francs and an honorable title. I have not made my choice. It seems that one place or the other will be given me; a matter which I leave to my superiors, though I have begged them to leave me in peace. I would not allow my daughter, who is at the same time my worthy and honored friend, to remain ignorant of this; and I beseech her never to think of me without a prayer for my eternal safety. Adieu! You may rely on my promise: I will never approach the sacred altar without presenting your name along with my sacrifice. Be so kind as to give Mlle. Nadine my magnificent present, and assure her that I do not wish to see her parted from you. Allow me also to retain my place with you.   DESJARDINS.

This 18th of August, 1814.

P.S. — The blessings of the poor of my parish are added to my own gratitude for your kind care of them. Do not forget the Rue des Brodeurs at St. Petersburg, where you never went but to do good.

Neither the friends nor the superiors of the Abbé Desjardins could overcome his modesty; and he persisted in refusing the episcopal dignities, as he here states in such simple terms. They were unwilling, however, that his light should remain entirely hidden; and, on Mme. Swetchine's return to France, she found him grand-vicar of the Archbishop of Paris, along with M. de Quélen, who always professed and retained the tenderest veneration for him. M. de Quélen himself had recently been appointed co-adjutor of the Cardinal de Perigord, who died, at a very advanced age, in the month of March, 1821.

The majority of the ensuing notes from the Abbé Desjardins are undated, and no attempt has been made to arrange them methodically. Their value lies in their tone of feeling and charm of expression.

I consecrate to God the first moment of the new year; and to you, the second, my amiable and indulgent daughter. Upon my *prie-Dieu*, — having finished my orisons, but while still upon my knees, — I offer you my vows; or rather I address my supplications to our common Master, that he will open wide his hands, and bestow on you the treasures of his pity.

I learn from little L. some circumstances which will give pain to your household, and oblige the Prince and Princess to adopt other plans for the education of their dear children. I advise with L., and reserve the right of a father and an old man to lecture him. The little man has upset my first surprise. "He has sucked no bears' marrow," as they say.   Ph. D.

You are here, then, my best and worthiest friend! How I shall delight to see you, and repair, by a little chat, the void of your long absence! I shall come to see you; but, at all events, you may be sure of finding me at the Archbishop's palace to-morrow, and Wednesday until noon. Thursday I am at the Missions from early morning till half-past one. I am tormented, and must quit you abruptly for some tiresome people, who know not that they are so. My best respects.

What an event was that yesterday at St. Geneviève![1] A princess, who had never appeared in higher health, falls ill, and is taken out a corpse. I am so shaken by the blow, that I have only strength to cry for mercy. Let him who standeth realize that he may fall, and fall stone-dead, with no further preparation than that afforded by blooming health.

I will be ready for you to-morrow, if it be still allowable to put any thing off till to-morrow.   Ph. D.

I have, indeed, received the letter of my dear and worthy daughter and friend. but I have not seen young Gravel; and I must see him before I can talk the matter over with you, O best, kindest, and most generous of creatures!

I shall pay my respects as soon as there are more than twenty-four hours in the day; for I get behindhand a little at each turn of the wheel. Still I want very much to see you. Receive the assurance of my respectful affection.   Ph. D.

------

[1] The death of the Duchess of Bourbon.

MY EXCELLENT DAUGHTER AND FRIEND, — You will do me a great favor by sending me some news of yourself: I was sure you were suffering. God only spares those of whom he can make nothing, as the architect does not cut the stones which he cannot use for building. I am using the language of dedication. Let us celebrate the service to-morrow. Let us reconsecrate the temple, — the true temple worthy of God's presence, the pure mind and the heart which glows for him alone. Adieu! Accept my respects for yourself and the Princess.

MY VERY DEAR FRIEND, — I am distressed by your useless journeys. Will you come Monday at one o'clock? I will be at home to you alone. Come at noon even. We shall have a little leisure to speak of what is near our hearts, which comprehend, and will always comprehend, one another so perfectly. I would that you might have nothing but consolations: but God does not will this, and so it cannot be best for you; for he is good, and understands our affairs thoroughly. We will never cease to confide them to him, and to love him; and that will be some compensation for the loneliness to which the pettiness of this life condemns us. The King came here yesterday in procession. He had the extreme goodness to stop, and ask after my health with the grace you know to be his. The Dauphin did the same, and even the Dauphiness. 'Tis a pitch of favor which takes away my breath, when I consider my own insignificance in comparison with such a distinction. But, thank God! I do not think I am puffed up by it. Monday, at about noon! I pray without ceasing for my excellent daughter and friend.

MY VERY DEAR DAUGHTER AND WORTHY FRIEND, — I am tormented with remorse for having left almost without warning, and without bidding you adieu. Yes, I have quitted Paris, Conflans, the Seine, and the world, to come and draw breath at Courteille.[1] One feels as if one had said good-by to the universe in this beautiful retreat. The earth and its creatures are wholly changed. Nothing here resembles what is left be-

---

[1] Courteille was the home of the Countess de Courteille, who lived there with her daughter, the Marquise de Rouchehouart, and her grand-daughter, the Duchess de Richelieu.

hind, unless it be the heart and the faculty of loving; for there are hearts in this place which are very kind, and own a benevolence marvellously like friendship.

And then you draw breath in the sweetest shades, and ramble about, without either climbing or descending, by a variety of paths which communicate with one another, and only take you back to the house when you have lost your way. You will say that it is a small merit in a garden to have no rising ground, not even an apparent precipice; but, dear, you are not sixty-six years old, and the proprietors with whom I am staying are eighty and more: besides, I shall have enough of hills and valleys when I return; so let me take comfort in the smoothness and the level walking.

I am reading a sort of pamphlet which amuses me, but which I should like to read by your side. It is Rulhiéres on the Revolution in Russia which raised Catharine to the throne. I must acknowledge that I am horrified by all I read; and what I want to know is, whether it be true. As for the results, they are indisputable; but the details seem to me to have been made up by some profligate, for the sake of bringing contempt and hatred upon the authorities.

My dear Daughter and incomparable Friend, — I have received, read, and pressed to my lips, your little letter from Vichy, dated the nineteenth of the present month. I hasten to reply, helpless as I am. Fortunately, I am less so in my hands than in my legs, which are larger, just now, than a young lady's waist. Whence comes this? you will say. Ah, whence comes it? Whence comes the wind? It is the wind that has caused all the mischief, and compelled me to accomplish in a few days a very different journey from that to Mount Doré. In short, it was a case of perspiration checked suddenly by an icy chill. Then came paroxysms of fever, bloodletting, emetics, purging, convalescence, and swelling of the limbs, which it is to be hoped will close the comedy. The Archbishop has taken me to Conflans, where I am resting, and whence I reply to all your affronts.

It is not decided that the journey to Mount Doré shall take place. The Faculty is deliberating. Let us await its oracle. I await it resignedly, and find myself as well here as at the waters. Do not think, my dear daughter, for all my pretended insensibility, that I can pass by Vichy without halting for a few hours to assure myself that the waters are doing you good. I wish my doctors would send me to Vichy: the pleasure of being with you would cure me. I hope our time may not have been lost, and that we shall encourage one another to turn the miseries of life to good account for eternity. Ah, my dear daughter, how the view of that boundless future enlarges the soul, and makes it long impatiently for the breaking of its chain! How long and hard our exile seems to me! When will our time come to fly away to our native land?

Ph. D.

Yes, yes, my dear daughter and incomparable friend, go to God, who is our protector and our all, and render thanks for the varied benefits which he has been bestowing ever since we came into the world.

I was going to offer thanks to him for you and for me, when people came, and I had to quit his presence. But he is everywhere. In these days of ice and hoar-frost, he receives us by the fireside, even by our own, repairing thither in his goodness.

Receive my wishes for the opening year. I ought to think that this will be my last. "He that hath ears to hear, let him hear." Pray, my dear friend, that my end may be peace, and continue to lay up treasure for a few years more. One can never have enough. Forgive my idle hand and worn-out brain. My heart remains, and is still true: you hold in it the next place to our Master. Adieu!

My very dear Daughter and excellent Friend,—Our Lord, I think, will find wholly superfluous the account which you expect to have to render him. I shall give it him at once, and transmit any message he may have for you.

I learn that you are suffering, and that you have bad nights. If I were less feeble, I would tell you all that is in my heart towards you; but I am sinking away. Pray for your dying friend.

To this fatherly guidance, so precious to Mme. Swetchine, deeper friendships were added, day by day. The connections formed with the Duchess de Duras and in her salon were enlarged and fortified by intimacies born of the community of all lofty inspirations. By the side of M. Cuvier and his family, M. de Gérando and M. Abel Rémusat, ranged themselves the Viscount de Bonald, the Count de Divonne, the Baron Eckstein, the Marquis of Quinsonnas. The Marquise de Pastoret, the Duchess de la Rochefoucauld, the Duchess de Damas, the Duchess de Maillé, the Marquise de Lillers, the Countess de Saint Aulaire, and the Countess Octave de Ségur were already being drawn towards the two sisters of the Duke de Richelieu by the tie of a common affection, and the sway of a common charm. This grand naturalization of intellect and heart had already transformed the salon of the Russian stranger into one of the most select and delightful firesides of the best French society, when an incident in her private life caused Mme. Swetchine suddenly to resolve upon a journey which she herself considered in the light of a second expatriation.

Nadine Staeline had never left her adopted mother, and had grown into an accomplished and attractive young lady. The Countess Octave de Ségur had three sons. The youngest of the three, Raymond de Ségur d'Auguesseau, astonished at once his mother and her friends by making known his fixed determination to marry Mlle. Staeline, foreigner though she was, and in feeble health. Mme. Swetchine, who was the last person in the world to make use of an affection to promote an interest, no sooner learned the sentiments of young De Ségur, than she began to reproach herself severely for not having foreseen and discouraged them. She did not confine herself to the resistances and remonstrances of a frigid reason, but determined to sacrifice herself, — to quit France, and not to return thither till she had tried the effect of absence and forgetfulness. In selecting the place of her voluntary exile, Mme. Swetchine turned her eyes towards Italy, lured thither by her religious fervor, her passionate fondness for study, and the presence of her sister. Her absence, and the situation which necessitated it, lasted two years.

Some fragments of the correspondence of Mme. Swetchine during this journey have been preserved. They may speak for themselves : —

TO THE MARQUISE DE MONTCALM.

TURIN, Sept. 24, 1823.

How happy I was to find a letter from you here! and how much I thank you for letting me hear the sound of a friendly voice in the midst of this crowded solitude! Absence has a marvellous effect in assigning things to their true places. If I had undertaken the present journey for any purposes of pleasure, or curiosity even, I give you my word that I should have turned back a hundred times. This necessity for looking out for one's time and one's money every moment is intolerable; and the prose of travelling encroaches so far upon its poetry, that our best moments seem to be too dearly bought. You cannot imagine the petty vexations to which one has to submit in the cities. Everywhere a jealous and annoying surveillance reminds one of the most troublous times. Every official exceeds his duty in order, apparently, to be sure that he fulfils it. What a pitiful arrangement! and how many suspicious circumstances may be discovered when one is on the watch for them!

Savoy, in spite of its severity of aspect, struck me as charming. Its lofty mountains prepare one insensibly for the majestic grandeur of the Alps. As you come down on the Piedmont side, the transition is abrupt. Three hours after leaving the Convent of Mont Cenis, I found myself in the pleasant little town of Suza, in the midst of a square, still enlivened by a fair which had taken place the night before; and, two paces from my window, a rope was stretched, on which a mountebank was exercising his talent. Every thing along the route I have followed reminds one of France. Savoy is wholly French, and Piedmont half so. The Savoyard often speaks French better than the French peasant himself; and the Piedmontese mingles it with his bad Italian. But how incomplete the illusion is! and how often am I reminded that I am outside that dear France which no foreigner ever loved as I do! I shall write you from Florence, perhaps sooner; and, meanwhile, I beg you often to recall the fact, that the slightest proofs of your remembrance are infinitely dear to me. To-day, the Austrian troops finally evacuate the Sardinian territory.

FLORENCE, Oct. 31, 1823.

With the exception of three or four days passed pleasantly at Geneva, my journey, since leaving Turin, has been painful, and the latter part of the way even dangerous. I would describe it, had I not determined to spare you, the mountains, the torrents, and the sea, — all the grand effects, in short, which are particularly agreeable to those impassioned natures whom you desire never to hear mentioned again. The farther I penetrate into this country, the more I regret not having seen it ten years earlier. I might not have observed it to better purpose, but I should certainly have enjoyed it more. Italy has all the brightness, all the *naïveté*, and all the inspiration, of youth; and I feel that it is impossible to arrive at a just appreciation of her by judging her coolly. It is not enough to be transiently enchanted by the contemplation of her treasures. We must forget every thing under her skies, and be so fascinated by the twofold enchantment of nature and of art, that we shall be absorbed in our pleasant emotions, and scarcely heed those which are painful. I am very far from this state, and am constantly lapsing from the enthusiasm which certain objects excite in me to the severity called forth by certain facts. It is from a heart thoroughly French that I thank God for this happy issue[1] of the great undertaking. The King of France is now restored for the third time to his throne; and I hope this time all is well. This success ought so to strengthen the government, that it may be confident of reducing friends and enemies alike if it will, and of making them walk in those ways of wisdom and moderation which thus far have appeared to suit neither party. This is no reason for despairing of their cause; for I see so many people who mismanage their own affairs, that I consider it an immense gain not to be one's own worst enemy. Who can say as much of us? Alas! not I nor you.

ROME, Dec. 2, 1823.

My sorrow for having neglected writing to you so long ought to move your heart, if you had not made it the most selfish thing possible by persuading me that I have no chance of a word from you which I have not provoked. The truth is, that, as to affection and the marks thereof, you are still under the old *régime;* and all my gratitude for the note I have just re-

---

[1] The deliverance of the King of Spain.

ceived cannot obliterate my regret for the silence which preceded, and that which will probably follow it. This frame of
mind will not let me enjoy the present; and I should forgive
you more readily, it may be, if this habit of yours were not the
effect of a *system* which you ought to have sacrificed to common
sense, as I have done. My journey hither occupied about
eight days; and, immediately after my arrival, I became so ill,
that, for ten or twelve days, I was incapable of the slightest
exertion, and could only enjoy the delight of finding myself
once more quite *en famille*, warming myself in the rays of the
bright sun of Rome, and reposing, in short, upon the breast of
that *dolce far niente* which has its value even under the most
unfavorable auspices. I find they have a charming establishment.[1] They have fitted up simply, but in very good taste, one
of these Roman palaces,[2] which cost no more than very common
lodgings at Paris, and are thus enabled to unite in their dwelling the peculiar advantages of both countries, — comfort and
beauty. The hall where we dine is covered with frescoes by
Albano; and, at the foot of the courtyard, we have a fountain
which elsewhere would adorn a public square. The magnificence of the buildings, and the materials employed in them, is
incredible. These marble columns explain the taste for porti-
cos. Surely, I have not been insensible to what I have hitherto
seen in Italy; but it is nothing, compared with the lively, profound, and ineffaceable impression made by Rome. She is the
queen of cities; a world apart from that which we have
known, where all is unlike what we encounter elsewhere, whose
beauties and contrasts are of so lofty an order, that one is
wholly unprepared for them; and their effect can neither be
imagined nor described. Every lack we find at Rome adds to
the impression she produces. One would not see her Cam-
pagna cultivated, her well-nigh deserted suburbs repeopled,
or the inhabited portion of the city enlarged. Rome, bearing
the impress of antiquity, must needs be a little sad to corre-
spond with so much subverted power and grandeur in the dust.
Your ideas are enlarged here, your emotions more deeply religious; your heart is at peace; you hardly dare to suffer in the
sight of spots which recall so much suffering, nor fail in fortitude where so much has been shown.

I have found the Duke de Laval,[3] to my great joy; and he
makes himself very agreeable to us. We see him often; his

---

1 Prince and Princess Gargarin.
2 Palazzo Verospi, Corso.
8 Ambassador of France to the Holy See.

society is genial; and he is a good conversationist, if only
because he enjoys conversation so much. The Duke de Rohan[1]
has also been to see me. He is less savage at Rome, and has
promised not to be at all so to us. Nothing, assuredly, could
place him higher in the public esteem than the mode of life
which he has embraced. It suits his mind; and, fortunately
for him, his manners are adapted to it. We talked much of
you, — he with infinite interest, and I, as you may guess, with
even more.

ROME, Dec. 17, 1823.

How shall I describe the lively impressions which succeeded
one another during my first excursion in Rome, — the charming variety of views, the interest increasing at every step? I
seemed to myself to be in a new world, and with reason; for
Rome comprehends within its vast boundary all which elsewhere you must go far to seek, — city and country, the noise of
the multitude and the most silent solitude. Yet there are no
abrupt transitions here. Nowhere do you find a wearisome
mélange of objects not in harmony with one another: one
would say that every thing has been arranged with a view to
imparting the most perfect unity to the picture, and rendering
the study of it easiest. St. Peter's, the Vatican, and all its ap-
pendages, form a complete whole. Returning from the Palatine
Hill, the abode of the Cæsars, you pass the circuses, the race-
courses, the hot baths which belonged to their palaces; and
all the Republic is still living in the Forum, and the Coliseum,
which adjoins it. Not only are the objects grand and beautiful
in themselves, but they are beautifully and poetically arranged;
all the historic epochs are in view at once, each separate and
distinct. Each appears to have impressed its own character
on its surviving monument, to have its own proper horizon,
and, so to speak, its peculiar atmosphere. One feels here a
need of living in the past, which conflicts strangely with the
natural impatience of man to rush into the future. He is
struggling with two eternities; and the present, which still
he cannot escape, appears to him more than ever fugitive
and miserable. I beg your pardon for this little attempt at a
sermon or an epic. One must either say nothing about Rome,
or give vent to the emotions which she unceasingly excites.

---

[1] Afterwards Cardinal and Archbishop of Besançon.

Rome, Jan. 9, 1824.

I like Rome better and better, and the kind of life I lead here, which is, in some sort, that of a scholar, who has come to live in the places, and with the people, he has encountered in his books. Those tastes of mine which had slumbered without being extinguished, have taken on a new life. I have found great resources here of every description; and, in my calmness of mind and general well-being, I am reaping the natural fruit of a true harmony between my thoughts and feelings, and external objects. This last test is decisive for me. I see clearly to-day what my self-distrust has but allowed me to suspect hitherto; viz., that a very retired and serious life is the only one which suits me perfectly. This discovery will follow me to Paris, the seat of the society which allures me most, and the thought of which mars all my pleasure. In fact, one can scarcely propose to one's self a more magnificent holocaust than that of all the seductions, sacred and profane, of the Eternal City. If it were only for the charm of her climate, the sacrifice would be worth something. Thus far we have had no frost, and but few days when we have not revelled in cloudless sunshine. Winter here no more precludes fine weather than troubles in youth interfere with happiness. I constantly take delicious walks in the beautiful villas at the gates of Rome, which are no more like the country-houses of France or Germany than Rome itself is like other capitals. All the gardens here are arranged with an eye to the season when we dispense with the beauties of nature in other places. Evergreens are planted everywhere; oaks, cypresses, and Italian pines (the most picturesque of all trees) abound, all the walks are tapestried with orange and lemon trees, which are covered with fruit without losing any of their rich foliage; while we tread a turf worthy of spring. Fountains always playing, the profusion of statues, the beautiful architectural lines, and the horizon of mountains which you might believe transparent, — these are beauties which one must come to Rome to see, and of which it is impossible to give any idea. If one could render one's self independent of those impressions which cannot be transplanted, and which attach one to the spot which gave them birth, it is surely here that one would pitch his tent; and I am not surprised that Rome should have been, in all ages, the fatherland of those who had lost their own; the true Elysian Fields for the shades of departed power and social distinction.

I have spoken in this letter only of my joys. I could have told you also of a grief which augments with the arrival of every courier. . . .

ROME, Feb. 12, 1824.

My internal life is perhaps more at Paris than at Rome. When I come back, there will have been no interruption to it. God grant that there may be no external change! I have never felt so keenly the need of cherishing the affections, and resuming the habits, which are to be those of my life. Unhappily, this need of permanence is only a personal matter, and there is the germ of all uncertainty in the circumstances by which I am surrounded. The most imperative considerations press upon me. You will easily understand them; and the only thing, I fear, you will not understand is what this is costing me.

We have noticed the feeling of identification with France, which pervades all the letters of Mme. Swetchine. We find further proof of it in a letter addressed to the Duchess de Damas : —

ROME, Feb. 9, 1824.

I owe to M. Dorian, madame, one of the greatest joys which could have been vouchsafed me, — that of talking of you with one who could understand me, and of receiving a mark of that kindness so precious in my eyes, that it makes me as proud as grateful. Among the tokens from France which spoil all other gifts for me, yours, madame, is associated with regrets to which the past itself is no stranger. Every moment by which I have failed fully to profit comes up before my memory; and, if I were not already too severely punished, I should demand of myself account of my time. Your indulgence for me, which profanes — allow me to say so — expressions which, in their full force, are applicable to none but yourself, can only be explained by the deep reverence of which I should have liked to give you better proof. I do not think, madame, that I ever left your presence without saying to myself, that nothing could be more useful or delightful to me than habitual contact with so accomplished a person. I have shared your joy, and that of your daughter, at the return of your grandson,[1] and his brilliant conduct. It was the indemnification he owed you for all your cares and solicitude, and surely it was a happy exchange. I have been no less interested than yourselves in the succession

---

[1] The Marquis de Vogué, who had distinguished himself in the Spanish campaign.

of events which have recommenced so gloriously the history of ancient France; and it is with a heart wholly hers that I celebrate all her successes. Alas, madame! I live so constantly and so actively in your midst, that it almost unfits me for the enjoyments offered me here.

We will return to the correspondence with Mme. de Montcalm, which will give us the sequel of Mme. Swetchine's residence in Italy: —

ROME, Feb. 13, 1824.

. . . If I were ten years younger, I should make light of so brief an interval; but, when the future is wasting, it concentrates itself into each moment, which is bright or colorless, according as it is connected with our dominant life-interests or no.

When we have renounced self in good earnest, and have firmly resolved not to resume it again, I know not what sweet and soothing unction mingles with all our sorrows, and imparts to us that elasticity which enables us to rebound under blows which would else have been crushing. I find it so inconvenient to have become so utterly French at heart, that I am doing my best to become thoroughly Italianized in mind. I approach Rome from every side; I review all her resources; I go deeply into her literature; I am initiated into her mysteries, and the marvels of her monuments and arts; I study her history under this glorious sky, which seems to give new life to all it shines upon. At every step, it is necessary to pause, to study and meditate. I have already told you, that all my fêtes are held in the open air, like those of the ancient Romans, and that my seclusion from society is complete. In the evening, I no more stir from my arm-chair than you from your couch; and I hear unmoved the recital of all the gayeties which are in progress, and which will, when the carnival comes, degenerate into absolute folly. A charming entertainment has just been given by the Ambassadress of Austria;[1] two French comedies were enacted, among others; and, of the eight or ten men who played in them, only two were of the same nation, and not a single one was French, — a fact which should tend, you see, to strengthen your faith in the universality of your language. Once a week, there is an English tragedy played by the best London company. It

---

[1] Countess Appony, née Nogarola, afterwards ambassadress to Paris, where she has left an enduring memory.

succeeds pretty well, save for an attempt at English music, — fit to outrage Italian ears. Every evening, there is an opera, a ball, or a crowded re-union, which always begins with the cardinals, who must be invited to every entertainment which is given. They hew out the block, and then go away if the character of the fête does not suit them. The Duke de Rohan, whom I should like even now to see cardinal, is forced, by the habits of this country, to modify his own a little, and exercises his virtue in complying with custom, and conforming to the world, — just as he did before in withdrawing from it. He enjoys here a well-earned consideration; and, if he obtains the preferment spoken of, he will meet with even more favor at Rome than at Paris. The Duke de Laval is very conspicuous. Mme. Récamier is not at all so, and appears sincerely to prefer a life of retirement. I do not think she has aimed at effect; and it is fortunate, for her beauty and celebrity are on the decline. Ruins make no great sensation in a country of ruins. It would seem, that, to feel her attraction, it is necessary to know her better; and, after so brilliant a career, nothing surely could be more flattering than to count almost as many friends as one formerly had adorers. Without wishing to detract from her merit, I cannot help saying, that, perhaps if she had once been in love herself, their number would have been considerably diminished. A passion exclusive in its nature wounds the vanity of aspirants even more than their sensibility.

ROME, May 16, 1824.

Paris will be of no use to a young man who has finished his studies, but has not yet arrived at the age when one begins to think of resuming them. Still it is in this interval that tastes and habits are formed; and it is important to occupy it in such a manner that it may not prove wholly useless. Unless one could travel like M. de Humboldt, I have always thought travelling the most frivolous part of the lives of serious people; but it is also the most serious part of the lives of worldly people. Do what they will, they always learn something by it, — if only, in the case of the Frenchman, the substance of the verse : —

"Plus je vis l'étranger, plus j'aimai ma patrie." [1]

My stay at Rome has augmented my fondness for my nephews, who are truly charming. The two eldest are par-

---

[1] The more I saw of foreigners, the better I loved my country.

ticularly dear to me ; and, in character and good conduct, they are almost men, — I should say, estimable men, if the word were not incongruous with their cherub faces.

We are planning to leave in a few days for the north of Italy, to avoid the extreme heat. We shall begin with Bologna and Venice, and finish with Milan and the lakes. From every part of Italy, Rome, I am sure, will always attract my longing. There one lives less with his brethren than with his ancestors, and this mingles a filial element with every impression.

You ask whether I was pleased with Holy Week. I admired its pomp, which was, however, rendered very incomplete by the absence of the Pope.[1] But the imagination so easily divines and surpasses all possible magnificence, that surprise added nothing to my admiration, unless in the case of the music, whose solemn and religious character and astonishing execution are above praise. This music makes one dream, with Pythagoras, of the music of the spheres, and all the marvels attributed to it in the early ages of the world. It is truly the sublime, and the sublime in angels' language. Pardon expressions which appear hyperbolical, in consideration of the rapture which you, I will answer for it, would have shared with me. I have not spoken so on other occasions, which is at least a proof of my sincerity. I must acknowledge, that, if I were consulted, I should require more calmness and order in the solemnities of religion than can co-exist with a noisy crowd rushing abruptly from one chapel to another, and subordinating all propriety to the demands of its eager curiosity. I could wish, also, that the services called together only humble minds, if not hearts, that are truly one ; but I must confess, that this crowd of haughty and sneering strangers made me regret, more than once, that any charm should allure them to us, especially at a time when one would so like to forget contradiction, error, and pride.

Rome is being forsaken day by day, that is, by strangers; for the Romans themselves prefer neither watering-places, travelling, nor the country.

---

[1] Leo XII. had just succeeded to Pius VII.

CHAPTER XI.

Excursion to Carlsbad. — Return to Rome. — Continuation of the Correspondence with the Marquise de Montcalm. — Letters to Mlle. de
Virieu, the Countess de Sainte-Aulaire, the Duke de Laval, Montmorenci, and Mme. Récamier. — Extracts from her journal.

THE hot season was approaching. Mme. Swetchine was
suffering exceedingly from liver complaint, of which
she had never been entirely cured ; and the physicians
advised her to try the waters of Carlsbad, in Bohemia,
taking the north of Italy on her way. Mme. Swetchine
obeyed their orders, uncertain whether, after her season
at the Springs, she should return to Paris or to Rome.
Her decision was in abeyance to the motives which had
determined her departure. Two letters only furnish us
with some details of her stay at Carlsbad : —

TO THE MARQUISE DE MONTCALM.

CARLSBAD, Aug. 3, 1824.

The order which forbids my writing during my convalescence is accompanied by such fearful threats, that, with the
exception of business letters, and those which I cannot safely
defer, my correspondence is entirely suspended, and I bargain
with myself for the briefest billet. But to learn that you are
suffering, and that you have remarked my silence, makes it
impossible for me to wait ; and I write to-day, as I should have
hastened to your house, to open my heart to you, and to tell
you how much it costs me not to convert into action those
sincere and tender sentiments of mind by which you profit so
little.

I found a numerous company assembled here, offering precious advantages to those who are disposed to avail themselves
of them ; but new faces alarm me in proportion to my love for
the old ; and my shyness, although in a measure overcome, is

not yet sufficiently so for my life to be other than habitually secluded.

You know already, that, after having despaired of meeting Mme. Nesselrode again, I have been so happy as to have her here, and to insure our mutual friendship against the sad effects of protracted separation. She has often inquired for you, and begged me to remember her to you. Adieu! This letter is only a certificate that I am alive; but after leaving Carlsbad, or rather Saltzburg, where I shall stop for a few days, I shall most certainly resume the dear and delightful habit of writing to you regularly, and, I may add, of being independent of your silence. My own impetus is so strong, that I can dispense with any on your part. Whenever you are good and just enough to write to me, address your letters to Rome. I shall not return thither much before October; but my sister will be nearer me than you, and will know better how to direct.

TO MLLE. DE VIRIEU.[1]

CARLSBAD, Aug. 31, 1824.

M. de Ferronnays is here, whom I have never met before, but whom I like exceedingly. Chance was favorable to both of us. I mentioned you, I know not on what occasion; and he exclaimed that he knew you, and spoke to me of you with a degree of interest, penetration, and tact, with which the heart had quite as much to do as the intellect.

On her return to Rome, Mme. Swetchine describes minutely to Mme. de Montcalm the circumstances which must prolong her residence in Italy, and then adds:—

ROME, Nov. 9, 1824.

It is long since I wrote you, but this time I am not anxious about your conclusions. First, because you do not suppose me to be very happy; and secondly, because of the joy it gives me to be able to fix my return for the early spring, with a reasonable prospect of accomplishing it. I have been able to set aside other projects, and to make every thing bend to my constantly increasing desire of returning to France. You will agree, that to labor for this end is better worth my while than writing.

---

[1] Daughter of Count de Virieu, a distinguished deputy from the nobility of Dauphiny to the States-General, in 1789.

I have seen, with sorrow, that you are suffering more than
ever, while no deep and heartfelt consolation has yet come to
your relief.   You are still seeking in this miserable life what it
cannot give you.   Before it can yield you the nourishment you
need, your heart must become less exacting, or your intellect
less keen.   All our faculties, when too highly developed, become of necessity self-involved, if they are not absorbed in the
Infinite.   They must either rescue us from ourselves, or lay
waste all that is within us.

I hope to pass a part of the winter with Mme. de Nesselrode, which will be delightful.   She is coming here about the
middle of next month; and I count upon making the trip to
Naples in her company.

TO THE COUNTESS DE SAINTE-AULAIRE.

ROME, Dec. 7, 1824.

I have received your letter; and it is very sweet thus to be
assured, from time to time, of your remembrance.   In turn, I
can assure you of mine : but you alone deserve credit in this
matter; for, outside of Paris, the absent are lost in shadow,
while, for those same absentees, Paris is the only point of light
in the whole picture.

How I regret that you were not at the head of that caravan
of your compatriots which has recently arrived!   M. and
Mme. de Montmorenci, Mme. d'Hautefort, &c., — I have not
yet seen them; but we are to meet at the Duke de Laval's to-
morrow.   Mont Cenis can be crossed in all weathers.   Do
arm yourself with a little courage, and come and surprise us.
With the exception of the month or six weeks which I hope to
give to Naples, I shall be at Rome all winter, and start for
Paris early in April.

We live a life of perfect independence, far surpassing, in my
opinion, the boasted liberty of Paris, for the very reason that
society offers fewer seductions;   and therefore one escapes
more easily one's taste for that, and for general attention.
Moreover, if we formed any attachments here, they must be
for strangers, since the people of the country extend us no
welcome, and we only meet them at the great parties which
constitute the whole of society here.   Our own circle is numerous, and varies very little.   Among its members, I must
not forget to mention M. Blank, a Neapolitan, whom you saw
at Paris, and who can fully appreciate the charm of your
mind.   He is a very witty man.   I do not always agree with
him; but, beyond the circle of ideas which constitute collec-

tively the life of the intellect, every thing can be borne but mediocrity and bad faith. True eminence always compels us, in one way or another, to examine and approve it. I doubt whether you would find great resources here, even in individuals. That every-day life, of which you are so impatient, soon resumes its rights. It is so easy to get accustomed to solemn and grand effects, and one is so sure of ending by dining and sleeping at Rome, that there are multitudes who do nothing else. I did not know Lord Byron, but I have mourned him. So, probably, have most people. Your remark struck me as very just. Only a severe virtue is worthy to be associated with heroic successes, as sweet voices are needed to sing the woes of Zion. Did not the adoption of his daughter by the Greeks remind you a little of the daughter of the nation? Only the natural order is reversed, and the parody comes first. The abandonment of the Greeks must ever be an indelible stain. Never did the prudence of the age so deserve to be branded. The governments of Europe recoiled from an enterprise, — hazardous it may be, but imperatively demanded, — as we recoil from needful sacrifices. Well, what is the result? God snatches from us what we will not give. I should not be surprised if war were the result of this shameful inaction: in fact, I should be glad of it; for we must desire the good of the whole world. On the other hand, I want the Greeks to go on, from one success to another, independent of the world.

I have been very glad of the species of truce spontaneously agreed on by all parties in France. The acts of the new reign [1] have been calculated at once to surprise and to gratify; but it is not by acts alone, however honorable to the authorities, that we can explain so lively and general an enthusiasm. The charm of novelty has its share in the same. Were you not pleased with the article of M. de Salvandy on St. Denis? I thought it admirable. It was all *fused* in his own mind before he wrote it.

My sister charges me with a thousand remembrances for you. She is more of a home body than ever. Her children are lovely, and I am foolishly fond of them. If I am ever pope, I fear I shall hardly escape the charge of nepotism.

Adieu! Write and tell me when you will come; and, if you are not coming, write to console me for the sad delay. ·

At about the same date, Mme. Swetchine addressed to Mlle. de Virieu the affecting confession which follows: —

---

[1] That of Charles X.

" Since writing you, I have received the sacrament of con-
firmation, which is not valid as administered in the Greek
Church. I have taken the name of Joan, for the sake of St.
John the Evangelist, for whom I have always cherished a
peculiar and devoted affection. I hesitated some time between this name and that of Mary; but I comprehended the
friend better than I can ever hope to comprehend the mother,
and the former prevailed."

In the midst of so many varying emotions, Mme. Swetchine could not forget her friend the Countess Edling. A
great change had taken place in the life of the latter.
Germany had been variously agitated during the years
which had witnessed the bursting of the storm of revolution
in Italy and Spain. Count Alexander Stourdza had been
insulted and threatened with death in the performance of
his duty as the representative of Russia; and, from that
time, the Countess Edling conceived a strong desire to
withdraw from Weimar, and return to her own country.
She had no desire, however, to encounter other storms and
fresh political complications. Her fancy for a life of
meditation, of which we have already had transient glimpses
in the correspondence of Mme. Swetchine, developed and
ripened. Count Edling was not averse to it; and in 1823
both adopted the resolution of residing on their estates in
White Russia, while they chose for their winter habitation
the flourishing city of Odessa. The Emperor and
Empress, who had often heard Roxandra Stourdza in her
youth express her ideas on charity and Christian civilization, desired that she might at least take with her to her
retreat the consolation and the power of carrying out
her designs. Ten thousand deciatines of land beyond the
Dniester were gratuitously ceded her by the Crown in
the valleys but lately overrun, though not improved, by
the nomad race of the Boudjac Tartars. The Count and

Countess Edling cleared up this wild land, planted fir trees and vines, and built villages in a desert which, until then, had lacked husbandmen, cottages, and water alike. They then erected for themselves a vast habitation called Mansir; and in the midst of labors over which they maintained a constant supervision, and surrounded by happy beings who flocked in increasing numbers to this remote spot, they fixed their own residence. Thither was addressed the only one of Mme. Swetchine's letters from Rome which has been preserved : —

ROME, Dec. 1, 1824.

MY DEAR ROXANDRA, — I live, and I love you. This is what I fancy you will be glad to know, and what I feel a constant need of telling you. If our love had not united us once for all, we could not thus set custom aside, and doubt would attack us with all its disheartening power; but I cannot help judging your heart by my own, and in the depths of my being I test all your emotions. How would it be with us now, dear friend, if we had been drawn together simply by mutual attraction and conformity of tastes? In a matter of mere pleasure, one is interested, — one wants each moment to bring its share of profit and delight; but our souls have touched, and the actual happiness of our connection would have been less enduring, if the tie itself had been indissoluble. I always wear your little ring upon my finger. This symbol, fragile like all symbols, will never leave me. Doubtless it will survive me; but I do not envy it, for I am sure that the sentiment which makes me value it so highly will survive the trinket in its turn.

Despite the small chances in my favor, I still cherish the hope of seeing you again, and of sitting up with you. 'Tis so pleasant a chimera, that it mingles with all my comforts, and oftener still comes to fill the void where there are none. This new establishment which you are planning — this thoroughly religious civilization which you propose to summon into the deserts, where, but for you, man would not be, or would only vegetate miserably — allures your imagination, which is haunted by dreams of virtue. I love to see you good and lofty like yourself, suiting your actions to your character; and yet, my dear friend, I am impatient under the weight of the necessity which detains you far from me. If you had not exchanged your beautiful, green, picturesque mountains for desert plains,

I should have seen you again this year; I might perhaps see
you next, and, in default of actual possibilities, the hope at least
would have been left me. I admire in you the courage which
undertakes. I have hardly that which perseveres. The day
seems to me so far spent, and the sun so surely to be tingeing
all my remaining objects with his last rays, that I feel as if I
should scarcely have time to reach home.

You will be surprised that the date of my letter is still
Rome. My plan last year was certainly to return to Paris.
There has been nothing voluntary in my determination, or I
could not have enjoyed this seeming independence without
positive self-condemnation. It would be too long a story to
detail the conflicting motives which appealed to my conscience.
This summer I took a long journey for the benefit of my health.
I left Rome, which I love as much as one can love any place
which has no part in one's future, to seek a little strength in
the depths of Bohemia. It is folly to wish to get cured; above
all things, to shrink from suffering: for every one must attend
to his own business, and suffering is ours. Besides, I have
never thought that lots were so unequally distributed in life as
they sometimes appear, especially if we set aside those ills
which are of our own creating. The most fortunate are those
who employ heavenly forces to preserve their balance amid
earthly ones; and it is with the deepest gratitude, my friend,
that I observe in myself, as the result of so many vicissitudes,
the strongest and most sincere desire to take thought for one
thing only, — ameliorating the condition of others.

This Greek struggle, so noble, so heroic, which excites
such just and sacred hopes in you, has my warmest wishes also.
We are so distracted in this world, and so absorbed by selfish
interests, that general interests, which move the mind more
deeply, no longer find their proper aliment. How else can we
explain the fact, that all who judge for themselves have not
been won to awarding a constant attention to efforts, the
purest and most praiseworthy in principle which have ever been
made for a holy cause. The liberals of Europe generally repel
and vex me; but the liberals of Greece, religious and political,
appear to me worthy of all admiration. Sad and dangerous
dissensions, perchance individual ambitions, sometimes mar
attempts as noble as this; but where, in an imperfect world,
shall we look for cloudless and unshadowed brightness? I
have never thought that any cause could long sustain itself here
below, if one had the misfortune always to see men where one
ought to look only for principles. The devotion of Lord Byron
and his premature death have doubtless touched you. It was
natural for a great poet to die where poesy herself is all alive;

but, as some one[1] said to me, "it would seem as if Providence found his character unworthy to furnish so noble an example."

Adieu! Tell me that your love for me is unalterable.

Mme. Swetchine had pleased herself with the thought of seeing Mme. de Nesselrode again that winter. The latter was true to her engagement with her friend; and the two passed some weeks at Naples, of which a few souvenirs have been preserved.

TO THE MARQUISE DE MONTCALM.

NAPLES, Jan. 8, 1825.

I came here a week ago, having been almost dragged away by Mme. de Nesselrode, but for whom I should have held Naples and all its beauties very cheap. My mind is so far from free, that it requires a great effort of the will for me to derive any advantage from *things*, always so far from supplying the place of persons to me. You would have pitied me, if you had seen my struggles, my anxiety, my distress. Placed in the centre of a thousand diverse interests, it is by my experience that I must weigh all the conflicting elements; and I can but sympathize, with all the sensibility I possess, in sorrows so prolonged and so deep, and joys which can be only fleeting. How many things there are in this world which can only be judged by their results; and how many righteous and pure intentions are foiled by a superior power! All we can do is to act in accordance with our light, and with that unselfishness which is the logic of the heart.

Mme. Récamier had arrived at Rome, accompanied by her friend M. Ballanche, and M. Charles Lenormant, who was to marry her niece. The French embassy fêted her, and the Duke de Laval hastened to bring her and Mme. Swetchine together. The latter soon modified her previous judgment, and yielded to the fascination of Mme. Récamier's rare and sterling qualities. In the early days of December, 1824, we read in a note of Mme. Swetchine's to the Duke de Laval: —

---

[1] Mme. de Sainte-Aulaire. See the preceding letter.

" I will not wait till you come, to thank you for the visit which I have received, and which I had intended to prevent. I found your friend just what you have always described her. Your portraits are more than like. They have all the expression and all the grace of the original. Friendship is happy when it can enable others to divine its own knowledge.

" Mme. de Nesselrode is slightly indisposed. I am going to pass the evening with her; and I wish you would be so kind as to send me your little sketch of the Duchess of Devonshire,[1] whom she desires to know. You shall make a third with us. It is the very best way of enjoying a tête-à-tête."

From Naples, Mme. Swetchine addressed to Mme. Récamier the following letter : —

TO MME. RÉCAMIER.

NAPLES, Saturday.

We have been favored with the finest possible weather on our journey; no disturbances and no delays. In short, I have enjoyed every thing except being away. As we got farther from Rome, the sky grew brighter and the air softer; and I regretted more and more that I had prevented you from coming. Yet I would do the same again. I think that a voluntary sacrifice always compensates us for troubles of which we have a greater dread.

I have found myself enslaved before I had dreamed of being on my guard. I have yielded to the indefinable thrilling charm whereby you enthral those even for whom you do not care. I miss you as I should if we had spent much time together, and had many common memories. How can one be so impoverished by the loss of what yesterday one did not possess? It would be inexplicable were there not in some moments a little of eternity. One would say, that, when two souls meet, they are

---

[1] Georgiana Spencer, wife of Lord Cavendish, Duke of Devonshire, was born in 1746. She was the author of several poems. Delille made a metrical translation of her Passage of Mont Gothard, and addressed to her a letter of dedication, in which we read, —

> " Je crois voir, à côté de l'aigle de Pindare,
> La colombe d'Anacreon."
>
> *Œuvres Completes de Delille*, vol. x.

I seem to see Pindar's eagle beside Anacreon's dove.

stripped of all the conditions of this miserable existence, and, in their new freedom and happiness, already obey the laws of a better world. We arrived here at nightfall. A little later, the moon rose above this beautiful bay. To-day I have seen the sunrise; and I leave the enchanting picture only to write to you. Whatever fully satisfies our love of the beautiful awakens with unparalleled force our craving for happiness, which is as enduring as our faith in the same. One may well ask, by what mystery of ingratitude it is that admiration does not suffice us. And only suffering makes answer, that, to enjoy any thing, we must have all. Perhaps you have not felt this as I feel it. Sometimes the most congenial hearts respond differently to the same influences. You have been very kind to me, — very kind in manner and in speech; but I was peculiarly touched by those glimpses of a confidence which as yet you were not quite ready to award me. When you know me better, it will be only an act of justice. To-day it is a favor; and I am like a good many other people, — I would rather receive than deserve. Already I would give all I have, and all I have not, to know that you were happy. May you be so soon, independently of me! But I do most resolutely claim a share in your sorrows. This letter, as you see, is merely meant as a continuation of our last conversation, which left on my mind an impression at once so sweet and so sad. We have too many indifferent speeches, even for indifferent people.

Adieu! Remember me to the Duke de Laval, whom I associate so gratefully with my affection for you.

Italy produced on Mme. Swetchine its infallible effect on high-toned minds. Her habits of industry were not broken up, but stimulated, by the variety of the scenes she witnessed; and besides the hastily written pages of her correspondence, where her anxieties for others occupied as large a space as her own impressions, there is a volume specially consecrated to the galleries and to topographical and archæological studies. Many pages in this large volume are devoted to an exact analysis of the course of study which she industriously pursued at Rome with the celebrated Professor Visconti. But, from time to time, the pupil speaks by the side of the master; and it is from this portion that we borrow a few extracts.

" I pass over in silence," she says in one of the earlier pages,
" the wealth whose acquisition implies only time and money;
and come to the pictures, the memory of which never forsakes
those who have studied them *con amore.* Every picture is a
new idea. The impression which it makes remains with us as
a precious souvenir, mingling with our deepest emotions, and
recalling them all."

TURIN. — " In the palace of the King of Sardinia, which is
more loaded with gilding than any other I have seen, I was,
as usual, not much impressed by any thing but the pictures.
The following struck me most : —
" Two Vandykes, — the one representing the children of
Charles I., the other Cromwell and his wife, — beautiful pictures; but they make one regret that the same pencil should
have drawn Charles I. and Cromwell.
" Two pictures by Guercino, which are above praise. The
prodigal son on his knees before his father, imploring his mercy.
Guercino has so placed the prodigal, that his face is not seen;
perhaps with the same thought as the artist who veiled the head
of Agamemnon.
" The other is the most admirable thing I ever saw for beauty
of attitude, grouping, and marvellous simplicity of drapery.
It represents Saint Frances standing and holding an open book,
and an angel by her side in nearer perspective."

GENOA. — " Architecture should owe nothing to color, any
more than sculpture. Beauty of coloring, truth and nobility of
expression, for painting; proportion, grace, harmony, for the
others. These are the perfections at which the arts must respec-
tively aim. Whatever destroys unity of impression may improve
the details, but adds nothing to the general effect. Each art has
its limits; and there are few usurpations in the world punished
more severely than transgressions of these.
" Instead of taking the street of the Faubourg Saint Pierre
d'Arena, we followed the shore; and I can never find words
for the emotion which seized me, when I beheld, on my left, the
sea in all the wondrous beauty of its vast expanse. The sun
was already low; and his rays struck obliquely upon the transparent waters, which sparkled with a thousand fires. The
water between the two piers was green as chrysolite, but
towards the horizon it was tinged with the purest blue. A light
breeze agitated the surface of the waves, ever varying in their
motion, and yet always the same. After passing the gate of the
Lantern, you take in at one view Genoa the Proud; and if you
keep to the centre, which serves as a base to the amphitheatre

14

formed by her edifices, astonishment mingles with admiration at every step. Here all dreams and all magic are surpassed. Here the word which has pronounced the majesty of nature subordinate to man receives its full accomplishment, while yet he is unceasingly recalled by the sight of the infinite to a sense of his dependence. How great must he be in his own eyes, when he casts them over the vast basin in which, so to speak, he holds the sea captive; upon the ships which are the monuments of his progressive science and his indomitable courage; and on the palaces which lay so long hidden in the bosom of the earth! And, on the other hand, before the infinitude of the sea and of the sky, and before the depths of his own heart, how feeble and powerless must he feel himself to be!

"I have to-day passed through the celebrated streets, Nuova Nuovissima and Balbi, which are doubtless destined to mark the extreme limit that luxury can attain. I was sorry that so much magnificence should not have been reserved for public buildings. To be sure, almost all the wealth in the world was concentrated among the individuals who built these beautiful palaces; and these same individuals sustained sieges, levied armies, &c. Nevertheless, such pomp, and such an employment of treasure, are almost inconceivable; albeit, we cannot be sure that we should have made a better use of it. And we, with our poor and narrow ideas, we who are no longer individuals but masses, cannot grasp a notion which transcends our contracted customs. The Roman sewers strike us as forcibly, and in much the same way, as the palaces of the Genoese nobles. Sacrificing every thing to the selfish interest of the moment ourselves, we ask how it was possible to consume fifty years in building a palace, or to continue from one generation to another the erection of a public edifice. Alas! if our plans are more reasonable and prudent, it is not because we are more self-forgetful, but because we are afraid that we shall not soon enough reap their fruits.

"Genoa makes one idle. It is so delightful to sit at the window, that it is not worth while to go far in search of objects of interest. It is enough for the traveller to revel in the vast sea-view, in the magnificent port which is, as it were, its vestibule, in the forest of masts swaying with the waves beneath his eye; and he cannot tear himself away. The life and movement which disport and display themselves under a thousand diverse forms, the light boats gliding between the motionless ships, the confused voices mingling with the dull sound of the waves, the cries of the sailors softened in the distance, their picturesque costumes, their expressive faces, the blue sea, the clear sky, the vivid light, the breeze so fresh and yet so soft, the arch

which encloses the picture without its suffering the loss of a
single detail, — and all this at a glance! Here, surely, to
breathe is to enjoy; to look is to be happy. Doubtless there
are many seaports which afford a varied and extensive view;
but, setting aside the magnificence which one must seek in vain
elsewhere, the different levels on which the city of Genoa is
built seem like terraces prepared for the express purpose of
enabling her inhabitants to enjoy the perpetual ναυμαχία displayed before them.

"When a sovereign builds a city out of his own good pleasure
and to serve as a suburb to his palace, it is speedily abandoned,
like Potsdam or Versailles. When, on the contrary, commerce,
facility of communication, beauty of aspect, and fertility of soil,
determine the site, every thing conspires to inaugurate a free
and spontaneous movement, which is perpetuated and protected
in the common interest. Revolutions, failing fortunes, change
of masters, all the vicissitudes, in short, which states undergo,
leave things very much as they were before. Genoa is no
longer Genoa the Proud; but not only are her population, her
commerce, and her industry, still prosperous, but her beautiful
palaces and marvellous suburbs still echo to the old names,
whose representatives, in spite of the excessive reduction of their
patrimony, have submitted to every sacrifice rather than not
preserve the monuments of the wealth and luxury of their
ancestors."

From admiration of the palaces and the panorama at
Genoa, Mme. Swetchine passes to her visit to the hospital,
which she examined with especial regard to the care bestowed on the poor, and is gratified at the decency and
gravity which always attend the pauper's burial.

"The tenderest cares of charity," she says, "appear to me
incomplete, if they do not follow man to his last asylum. The
contempt shown the remains of the poor man in the French
hospitals has oftened saddened me. Since they grant him a
little earth, why should they refuse him prayers and a parting
benediction? Let us not forget that He whom we adore has
placed the burial of the dead among works of piety; and to
bury means here, not to hide from the sight, but to confide
to the earth with religious reverence, the seed reserved for
a glorious resurrection; while we hasten, by our prayers, that
deliverance which one day — and it may be soon — will be
invoked for ourselves.

" English *comfort* is the exact antipodes of luxury, as the Italians conceive it. Their palaces are absorbed in vestibules, staircases, and galleries. Their churches are vaster than their promenades and public squares. But the heir of an illustrious name, in the palace of his ancestors, is not much better lodged than the advocate whom he pays, or the artisan whom he employs. The universal privation of all the comforts, elegances, and refinements of life, puts widely differing ranks on the same level ; and, under this aspect, there is perhaps less difference between the rich and poor in Italy than elsewhere. All may enjoy in common the beautiful horizon, the clear, soft sky, where clouds are only an accident, and these rich façades and churches, — faithful types of the heaven which all may inherit."

FLORENCE. — " Near the Duomo is the little chapel of the Brethren of Mercy. This society was formed in 1244, at a time when Florence was often exposed to the twofold scourge of pestilence and civil war. A church-bell summons the brethren who dwell in the city. The moment the sound is heard, they leave every occupation, and repair to this point of rendezvous. Here they are instructed in their duty ; and in case any one is wounded in the streets, or a workman has a fall, or any person needs to be carried to the hospital, the litters are always ready. Each brother puts on the black robe of the penitent, covers his face, and goes to the performance of his task. Almost every day I have occasion to witness this pious spectacle, when I go and sit on a bench which runs along a wall parallel to the cathedral. The Brethren of Mercy are, for the most part, young men from good families in Florence. I learned yesterday, that Dante used to come and sit on the bench I am so fond of, to enjoy the cooling breeze."

RAPHAEL. — " The gallery of the Grand Duke of Tuscany contains a good many Raphaels ; and here one may study the great master in his widest range of manner and of subject. An immense value attaches to master-pieces considered separately, but variety adds to the charm of a collection ; and, though genius may be more surprising in the heights it attains than in the extent it embraces, it is difficult not to be confounded, when we see the same man trying his hand at all subjects and all styles, and creating models in all.

" Can there be a more beautiful portrait than that of the Fornarina? But it is only a portrait ; and Raphael in the perfection of his imitative, but not of his creative, power. He copied with rigorous accuracy the object before his eyes, without even idealizing it ; so entirely did the nature of the sentiment which animated him hold him enchained within the sphere of a purely human loveliness. The Fornarina, beautiful as she is, does not cross the threshold of sense. She is a woman.

"It has been remarked, that there is something of the Fornarina in the head of the Madonna della Seggiola; but, though they show equal ability, what an infinite distance there is between the two pictures! They are a world apart. Thus, painting, like philosophy, proceeds from the known to the unknown. From the culminating point of terrestrial beauty, it rises through infinite spaces to divine beauty. The two kinds of beauty here represent the two orders of love. There is a grace in this Madonna della Seggiola,—a delicacy of feature, a divinity of expression, and a harmony of coloring, which will for ever defy the most skilful copyists. There is nothing else approaching the sweetness of the head of the Virgin, the majesty of the infant Jesus, and the unction and ardent devotion of St. John. Every thing about these two children is prophetic. The one revolves in his thought the destinies of the world: the other is already consecrating his to its service.

"A little further on, this same St. John has become only the child of the desert and preacher of repentance. We see him standing in the midst of wild, natural scenery. His young and graceful limbs are hardened to fatigue; his coloring is full of vigor. The inclement weather he has braved has banished the delicate tints of youth from his cheek; his mouth is opened to preach salvation to the world, and the emotion depicted on his brow is sadness, — that he should too often speak in vain. He might be of any or all ages, by his aspect; his expression is at once naïve and serious; he is both child and man,—a man in devotedness, a child in years. We feel that all human wisdom is confounded by the thoughts that are written on his brow. In one hand he holds a roll, which perhaps contains the good tidings; in the other, he lifts a cross, which is as yet but a broken reed, — a luminous reed, relieved against a dark background.

"Portraits of Leo X., Julius II., Cardinal Bibienna, and Cardinal Inghérami, all from the pencil of Raphael, may be found in the Pitti Palace. Imitation can go no farther. The figures stand out, and seem to be alive.

"But there is something very unlike nature in a small picture near by, — the amazing Vision of Ezekiel, — one of the finest poems that the genius of painting ever conceived. Truly, it is a vision. Torrents of light dazzle the spectator. He feels as if he were seized by the arms of fire that upbear the prophet. It is not merely the coloring which astonishes you. There is, in the drawing of this little picture, an energy, a boldness, and a richness which are incomparable. It is indeed Jehovah, the true God of the Old Testament, who is revealed to Raphael, — more poet than painter here. It is a strophe repeated from the divine songs. Elsewhere Raphael has done well, but he never soared higher."

ANDREA DEL SARTO. — "The *chef d'œuvre* of Andrea del Sarto is the picture called the 'Dispute of the Four Doctors.' The beauty of the several figures, the purity of design, and the effect of brilliant coloring, carry our admiration to the pitch of enchantment. Andrea del Sarto is superior to himself. His manner rises till it is lost in the heights where individuality ceases. It is not a universal rule, that we must cease to be ourselves, if we would become greater than ourselves. Are not the depths of art sounded on the same conditions as the depths of morality? Are not the same devotion, the same renunciation of vanity and frivolous tastes, and the same self-concentration, demanded of the artist? Must he not also come out of himself, and live in his worship and in his love? Who has not felt, in approaching the sanctuary of the arts, a kind of reverence and religious calm, the purity of whose principle is none the less manifest because the objects offered to the contemplation tend to lower or profane it? It is like strength which has been consecrated to virtue, but of which passion has obtained the mastery. Is not beauty in one sense eternal, like truth? and, if so, how close is the alliance between religion and art! And those proud Reformers, whose incomplete law proclaimed their divorce, — how poor was their inspiration!

"Observe, when you study the essence of art, whether the faculties through which it acts upon you be not the very ones which religion seizes and sways most powerfully; and, on the other hand, see if it be not on the religious masterpieces that art has founded almost all its theories. What does not painting owe to religion and to Christianity? What would they be without her? She might have numbered Davids, Teniers, Wouvermans, possibly a Titian; but would she have had a Raphael, a Michael Angelo, a Domenichino, a Guido, or a Guercino? Deprive artists of religious subjects, and what is left them? Cold history, colder allegory, battles, nature without life, figures without expression, or the melancholy resource of those violent passions so incompatible with human beauty and dignity!"

ROME. — "Whether the doubts cherished by many minds, about the strictness of Italian monasteries, be well founded or not, the religious houses for women have completely escaped these unfavorable prejudices. Not even calumny has been able to excite against them the suspicion of grave offence. I have always been struck by the urbanity, affability, and un- obtrusive kindness of the Italian monks; and I found these qualities, in a yet higher degree, in the female convents. The benevolence of the nuns is so affectionate, that it wins the heart; and so sincere, that it would be impossible to detect the slightest trace of constraint or effort about it. The most prac- tised and watchful eye cannot discover a single movement which is not dictated by that charity whose secret it is to be universal, without seeming to be mechanical.

"Their horizon is limited, as regards human science; but, on the other hand, their few ideas tread over and over again the way marked out for love by divine revelation; and, with piety for their teacher, they have nothing to regret. They ascend and descend and re-ascend, without ceasing, the steps of that miraculous ladder which enchanted the prophet's vision. They sit at the Samaritan's well, climb the heights of Calvary, repose upon Tabor, bathe like Mary Magdalene the Saviour's feet with tears and perfumes, or adore his cross. They have no cares for the earthly morrow, no fears for the terrible mor- row of eternity. The same hours bring the same labors, and are associated with the same thoughts. They know that they have chosen the good part, and that they possess the pearl of great price. No doubt or anxiety disturbs them. The type of their faith is as simple as the type of the virtues they practise, — 'humble plants,' as saith St. Francis de Sales, 'who have grown up in the shadow of the cross.'

"And the future! that cannot mar their joy and their settled peace; for they have no past, and, consequently, no memories nor objects of comparison. The light of the world has become a feeble twilight before it reaches them; and any divergence from their ideas is regarded as a misfortune and a danger. How hard it is for them to admit gradations in religion! In- complete truth is as much falsehood for them as the grossest error; and they can hardly appreciate any thing beyond the alternative of being in the world or out of it. Of course, this rigidity and these set colors are unfavorable to the breadth and flexibility of the intellect; but, on the other hand, is not virtue thus preserved in all its integrity, and is there not always a little danger in understanding perfectly what we are to combat? The Italian woman, raised and ripened in the shade of the cloister, may have a small share in the noble freedom of hu- manity; but of that share she is secure, and her place is midway between militant virtue and the inviolable bliss of the angels.

"One of the proofs of the truth of Catholicism is its response to the heart's exclusiveness. Other communions think to simplify religion, and render it more accessible and more attractive, by extending to all alike the promises of its divine Author; but this is a strange misconception of our real needs. The more positive, exclusive, austere, and exacting a rule is, the more attraction it has for us, — by virtue of that vague instinct which makes us feel that our mobility needs to be arrested, our weakness strengthened, our thoughts recalled and set in order. No one will be passionately attached to any religion, who believes that others are just as good; and a jealous God knew this well. When a thing has ceased to be, I will not say the best, but the only perfect, good, what call is there for choice or preference? Why should we concentrate, rather than divide, our homage and our love? The *esprit du corps* has always seized upon this concentrative force to accomplish great things. It has always tightened its bonds within, when it would increase the power of its action without. Language itself bears witness to the fact. Thus, inside the universal and all-embracing religion, there is, in the phrase of the different monastic orders, the religion of St. Dominic or St. Francis or St. Theresa, — in short, the religion which, in the mouth of the *religieux*, often means only the rule of his order, which constitutes, in his individual eyes, the abridged type of truth and perfection here below."

"THE REGINA CŒLI, A CARMELITE CONVENT IN THE LUN-GARA. — This is the first convent I have seen in Rome; and I was very glad to begin with the Carmelites, as a piece of just and spontaneous homage to their founder, St. Theresa. One is so struck at Rome by the vanity of all human greatness, that one is better prepared than elsewhere for the sacrifices of Christian self-devotion. One becomes familiar with what are called extraordinary courses, which are yet, to the eyes of faith, such simple and necessary courses. The saints, who elsewhere are little more than types, — fantastic beings whose idealized virtues are merged in inimitable and unapproachable perfection, — become at Rome, what they really are and always have been, the true ancestors of the faithful, — their predecessors, beings like themselves, their guardians and models only. When you issue from the catacombs, you have a new appreciation of that tyrannous necessity which induced rare souls to conceal their devotion in life, as the martyrs did theirs in death; and you go from one sacrifice to another, and acknowledge that he who burns his holocaust slowly is not the less meritorious.

Before I visited this Convent of the Lungara, my mind had

dwelt only on the sacred authoritativeness of its rule, and the strictness which extends to the most minute details, and seems calculated everywhere to substitute grace for nature. I believed that I should find its inhabitants happy; for where is the heart that God has touched, which does not own a pious felicity, even in the midst of suffering? But I imagined them saddened, as one is, by the solemn thoughts and deep emotions which subdue the poor human heart. What, then, was my surprise, when I found myself surrounded by bright faces, indelibly stamped with that assurance which constitutes the joy of virtue! The first compliments were hardly passed and returned before ease and cordiality had replaced the slight embarrassment which always attends the meeting of strangers; and soon a frank, childlike, playful pleasure was expressed by the holy sisters, and communicated itself to us, who, alas! bore in their midst souls less pure, and hearts less content, than their own. We remained together about three hours; and I brought away from Regina Cœli the conviction, that, next after the merit of desiring the only thing that cannot be bought too dearly, the best thing is to know exactly what we do desire.

" The aspect of these religious retreats leads one to draw a singular comparison between their material arrangements and the ideas of the ancients. Strange as it may seem to be reminded of the old Romans by these poor nuns, it is certain that their habitations are arranged upon the plan of antique institutions. Thus, with the ancients, the individual was completely absorbed and sacrificed to society. All which was calculated for private use was small, contracted, poor, and shabby; while luxury and magnificence were displayed in all public monuments. So the house of the wealthiest citizen was entirely out of proportion with the surrounding edifices; and, even in this contracted dwelling, he occupied only a dark, close, crowded nook, that more space might be afforded for the *atrium* and *triclinium*. The social instinct with them was paramount to the desire for personal well-being. All was done for all, and nothing for one only. The temple of the gods, the basilica, the portico, the triumphal arch, flattered the love of national glory; and they cared for nothing else. There was something grand in all this, which Christianity came to reclaim and consecrate, along with whatever else of truth and virtue she found upon the earth, and to reproduce it upon a loftier and more perfect scale. Thus, in the life of the cloister, which is the flower of perfect Christianity, all the straits of evangelical poverty are for the nun, and all the luxury for the community: for the *religieuse*, the coarse garment, the meagre fare, the hard bed, a cell hardly larger than the spot her tomb will occupy; for the community, vast and airy spaces, refectories, cloisters, gardens, infirmaries, and, above all, the splendors of the Lord's temple. . . .

"But what surpasses all the marvels bequeathed us by the past, and all which the imagination can restore, is the incomparable view from the terrace of the Villa Spada. The richness of its details makes the view an extensive one, as the memorable events it recalls put ages in the place of days. On the left, you distinguish the portico of the Convent of St. John and St. Paul; the garden of the monks who bear the name and the signs of the Passion; the Villa Mattei, St. Sylvester, and the Baths of Caracalla, which bound the view on this side; St. Balbina, with its high tower; the Claudian Aqueduct; St. Sabas, with its numerous arcades. In front, you have the arch of the imperial theatre, the Circus Maximus, and, beyond, the Aventine and its edifices. At the right, the Arch of Janus, the Temple of Vesta, the Tiber, and the Janiculum; the little pine-grove between the Villas Lanti and Corsini; the majestic façade of the Aqua Paolina; and, finally, the dome of St. Peter's, which towers above all these glorious realizations of human thought, like a great king ruling over a great people."

"SEA VIEW, BY VERNET. DAYBREAK. — Waves of vapor inundate, and at the same time illumine, this picture. The sky, the air, the water, — all have that magical transparency which those who have not been in Italy cannot allow even to nature."

"THE DEATH OF GERMANICUS, BY POUSSIN. — The coloring of this picture is not flattering: the flesh-tints, for the most part, are carried up to black; but the composition is so fine, the arrangement so simple, and at the same time so imposing, that these merits suffice to award to this painting a prominent place among pictures of the second class. It is one of those whose principal beauties are least spoiled by engraving."

"A VIEW OF CASTLE GANDOLFO, BY CLAUDE LORRAINE. — This little picture is enchanting. The lake, the sky reflected in it, the trees which shadow it, the sweet mist in the air, the vibration of the light, — in short, it is Claude and nature."

"THE CENCI. — A lovely head, by Guido. This unhappy girl has only the excess of her wretchedness to offset against her crime. There is nothing consuming, nothing active even, in the grief which her features express. Her profound sadness seems to say, that she cares as little for the eve as for the morrow, and that destiny's only favor to her had been the scaffold which is now preparing. The Cenci is an enchantress of beauty, youth, and melancholy. Those sweet eyes have wept so much! That brow must have flushed so deeply!"

"A MAGDALENE, BY AUGUSTIN CARACCI, which they say is a very beautiful thing; but which I do not like much better than the Magdalene of Tintoret at the Capitol, which I detest."

"A HOLY VIRGIN, WITH THE CHILD JESUS, BY TITIAN. — I do not know how Titian dared to paint the mother of Christ. All his genius rebelled against it. I wish to read the life of Titian. It will probably confirm me in my idea, that no person is so utterly a stranger to the inspiration and light of Christianity as he who, born in its bosom, has rejected its spirit and its love."

"A DESCENT FROM THE CROSS, BY RAPHAEL. — This picture is in the second manner of this immortal man; and I, for my part, see in it the apogee of his glory. The picture was painted at Perugia, and it was this *chef-d'œuvre* which raised the fame of Raphael to such a pitch, that he was summoned to Rome. This beautiful composition is a perfect poem. Nicodemus supports the lifeless head and arms of the Saviour, and a young man lifts his feet. St. John, with his head bowed in all the abandonment of grief, fixes his eyes on his adorable Master. A woman holds one of his hands in hers, expressing at once the most poignant sorrow and the most sacred love. His mother, pierced by the divine sword, has fainted in the arms of some young women. Words cannot express the beauty, the purity, the richness, and the artlessness of this marvellous picture. Its variety equally transcends praise. There are no two heads alike; none, where the expression of the common sentiment is not varied. Here we have united all mental anguish and all physical beauty, and a splendor of imagination so discreetly employed, as to combine the glorious prodigality of youth with the thoughtful sobriety of ripe age. No: Raphael could not do better nor rise higher. Those of his masterpieces which are most resplendent with majesty and genius have nothing to compare, in my eyes, with the perfume of spirituality which exhaled, perhaps for the last time, from the descent from the Cross."

"TWO LANDSCAPES, BY CLAUDE LORRAINE, IN HIS FIRST MANNER. — No part of these two pictures corresponds with the unrivalled glory of Claude Lorraine; and yet they are youthful attempts which he would not disown in all the might and magic of his genius. These waters, this sky, these trees, are not the inimitable Claude; but Galatea was not herself the moment before she received the divine breath."

"THE ECCE HOMO OF GUERCINO.—In this picture, the God-man has, as it were, anticipated his own glory. He reigns already by the sublimity of his expressive and majestic beauty. The excess of sacred sorrow has penetrated all his flesh; it is like an internal fire, which colors, while it consumes, his transparent cheeks. His eyes are raised to heaven; and in that look what power of prayer, of will, of yearning, and of pity! All human plagues and sins are present in an incomprehensible unity to the Saviour's thought. They rend his heart; but we feel that he has not a moan for himself. Ah! He whom earth saw but for a moment, that she might adore and mourn him for ever, is here before us, in this lofty and evident union of two natures, whereof the invisible is the one that appeals most powerfully to the intellect and the heart."

"A FINE PORTRAIT OF PHILIP II., BY TITIAN.—The *pose* is stiff, more supercilious than proud; and there is something narrow and sour in the face, which, nevertheless, tries to smile."

"THE FORNARINA, COPIED FROM RAPHAEL BY JULES RO-MAIN.—What an immense distance between this copy and the original! It is like that commonplace translation of the Iliad, of which somebody has said that it rained down."

"HOLY FAMILY, BY CARLO MARATTI.—The artist has taken too much pleasure in feeding the divine child on the ambrosia which Olympus lavished upon its infant gods. These blooming and voluptuous shapes are not in harmony with the Christ for whom wormwood was mingled with his mother's milk, and the bread of affliction with a diet always meagre and severe. The Holy Virgin has also, in her beauty, something which is rather attractive than chaste and regular. We feel that the carelessness of drawing, in the works of this master, sometimes borders on a deterioration of ideas. When the latter have lost their original purity and severity, something effeminate, which may be taken for an excess of tenderness, begins to detract from the dignity of the subject, and even from that of the art. To please becomes then the highest aim of the artist; and, little by little, he descends to the level of the public, which has descended before him."

"VENICE.—The glory has departed from this land, where its traces still linger. There is nothing to unite the present with the past; and the Cathedral in the midst of Venice produces somewhat the effect of the Egyptian obelisks at Rome. It is a monument which retraces the annals of another race, and tells a story which the present generation either know no longer, or know too well."

"RIMINI. — Who would forget, among the souvenirs of Rimini, the most poetic of them all? Of all the treasures which Rimini has amassed for us, the most precious legacy is Dante."

"BRESCIA. THE ADULTERESS, A BEAUTIFUL PICTURE BY TITIAN. — The figure of Christ is full of majesty. It expresses, in the highest degree, divine and uncreated wisdom, so superior to human wisdom, and yet so perfectly in harmony therewith. The woman is surpassingly beautiful, and in her coloring Titian seems to have excelled himself. Her countenance is modest, but expresses neither confusion nor penitence; it is the judges who have dragged her into the Saviour's presence, not the cry of her own conscience. By the expression of his face, one feels that the noble words of pardon have not yet been pronounced, and that the miracle of conversion awaits the miracle of mercy.

" All the great names of architecture meet us at Brescia. In the midst of her numerous palaces, we distinguish a building by Palladio, whose façade is noble and simple; and also a charming house, by the same Palladio, — a house with three windows as delicious as Rousseau's romance in three notes."

" PAVIA. — If the eyes of the Carthusian were not turned inward, what a difference there would be between the lot of the Carthusian of Pavia and that of the Carthusian of Naples. How unlike are these horizons! Nature has refused every thing to the Carthusian Convent at Pavia, and has spread out beneath the one at Naples her utmost grandeur and loveliness. He who has watched the moon (and the moon of Naples!) from that lofty and well-chosen site, reflected in the bay or striking the rock of Capri, which seems to interpose itself between us and the vast sea, like those slight obstacles which arrest us on our way to the infinite; he who has caught the sun's rays falling on that arid Vesuvius, whose aspect at least does not belie, though it conceals, the menace of destruction and death, — he, I say, has but one step more to take to rise above all created things, and pass from their glory to that of the Infinite."

The reasons which had induced Mme. Swetchine's withdrawal from France no longer existed. General Swetchine quitted Italy, while Mme. Swetchine was visiting Naples with the Countess de Nesselrode. They met again at Paris in the spring of 1825.

CHAPTER XII.

Permanent establishment of Mme. Swetchine in Paris. — Death of the Emperor Alexander, and accession of the Emperor Nicholas. — Salon of Mme. Swetchine. — Mme. de Nesselrode's residence near her. — Death of the Duchess de Duras.

ON her return to Paris, Mme. Swetchine established herself permanently.   Until then, she had lodged in the Rue de Varennes, in the neighborhood of the Duchess de Duras.   She now took, on a long lease, a house in the Rue Saint Dominique, a suite of rooms where she could enjoy, in the heart of one of the most brilliant quarters of Paris, the sunshiny quiet of the country.   Situated at the foot of a court, the Hotel No. 71 was occupied only by herself and the proprietors, who testified a regard for her which has been transmitted through thirty years, and to two generations.   The garden of the hotel was not large ; but it adjoined other gardens, and the views from the first story, which was occupied by Mme. Swetchine, embraced a long stretch of lawn, flowers, and beautiful trees.

She sent to Russia for some of the pictures, bronzes, and porcelains which her father's care had amassed, and which had interested her childish gaze.   With these she adorned, though not profusely, a drawing-room and a second apartment, which she had transformed from a bedroom into a library.   Her bed, which was only a little iron couch, was removed to a back cabinet, and brought every day into the library, or into the drawing-room, for her brief intervals of sleep.   The rooms occupied by General Swetchine were up-stairs, and every thing was so arranged as to insure the complete freedom of his habits.

The return of Mme. Swetchine was saddened by the death of the Emperor Alexander, to whose memory she had always remained faithfully attached. The long distance which separated her from her native land had never impaired either her affection or her penetration. The Emperor Alexander expired on the 19th of November (1st of December), 1825, at Taganrog, an obscure little town on the confines of Russia. His last days were involved in mysterious conspiracies, his life threatened with imminent outrage, and they succeeded in screening from his dying eyes the dangers which threatened his successor, — dangers which blazed out on the advent of Nicholas, and which were only to be mastered by heroic firmness.

On the 23d of April, 1826, Mme. Swetchine wrote to the Countess Edling : —

"To tell you what I have suffered on account of our poor country since the late cruel events, would be impossible. I have lived more in Russia during the last four months than in the thirty-three years I passed there. Her misfortunes and her dangers have been my one absorbing thought. What a terrible way in which to have one's patriotism fully awakened! That black plot, those crimes projected in darkness, and, as it were, in cold blood, fill me with unutterable horror. What novices in this frightful career! They began where the greatest villains have ended. Our young sovereign and his noble conduct are my only consolation. The touching traits which are ascribed to him acquire a new value when we remember his courage, which was calm to the verge of impassibility. But how much he will have to do, and how needful it is that he should go to work at the foundation! To direct the present generation, it is necessary to curb it; a poor and inadequate method. It is by education that he must make himself master of the rising generation; and he must look for solid results only as the fruits of a wise and slow culture.

The most unhappy circumstance is, that the national elements
are lacking. Most of those men who are more enlightened
than the rest, have drunk from poisoned sources. The longer
I live, the more firmly I believe that strength lies in doctrines,
and not in men."

Mme. Swetchine proceeded to address, in the name of
France, this touching appeal to her friend, who was then
in the full tide of creation at Mansir : —

"Nothing can be more practical certainly than your vines
and your sheep, nothing more rational or more convenient than
the money they will bring you; but please do not become too
much absorbed, either in the idyl or in the purse. Think that
your friend is pining for you, and that our days are short as well
as evil. Make haste, my dear, good friend! Does not every
thing hasten within and around you? I promise you all that
you can desire. We will pass our lives together. We will
enjoy the same things. My friends are yours already, and they
think you are delaying too long."

The salon to which the Countess Edling was summoned
with such tender eloquence was in reality numbered
among the most attractive centres of Parisian society, at
a time when Paris could still boast of many delightful and
distinguished circles. This salon was neither a narrow
guest-chamber, nor a literary coterie, nor a school. Mme.
Swetchine would have been indignant, if the word "disciple"
had been uttered in her hearing. She was as averse to
ruling as to serving. It was the incomparable superiority
and the unvarying sweetness of her presence alone which
created the impalpable tie that bound so many hearts to
her; and in the end established a kind of community
among them, whereof she was the soul, and not the teacher.
With no other motive than her love of all moral elevation,
and as free from envy as from ambition, she excelled in
accommodating herself to the most diverse characters and

the most dissimilar minds; in making prominent the good in some, and excusing the weakness of others. Souls, which else would never have met, assembled instinctively under the shadow of that inexhaustible charity, where each in turn found sympathy, aid, and strength. What eminently distinguished Mme. Swetchine was, that her qualities, her virtues, and her powers were so distributed, that the result was a perfect equilibrium. She was sensible and enthusiastic in about the same degree, because it was her rare privilege to have been endowed with as much reason as imagination; because she thought as deeply as she felt; because, though often a man in intellect, she always remained a woman in heart; and, finally, because her self-abnegation was neither feigned nor studied. She lived first in the life of others, then in public events, and thought of herself only after she had taken thought for every one else. She disliked egotism, without ever needing to repress it in herself, so fully had she experienced the richness and sweetness of the contrary sentiment. Her soul referred all to God, without ignoring a single human interest. Her mind was constantly growing in knowledge; but she loved science for science' sake, without making the slightest pretension on her own account, and without seeking aught beyond the delights of discovery and of thought in which she revelled. She was free from prejudice, alike in her religious and political opinions. She was no less so in matters of art and literature. We have just seen how fully she appreciated Italy. Her taste was classical, but classical in the widest sense; not confined to the cold literary propriety which began with Boileau and Pope, and ended with the official literature of the empire, and had nothing in common with the mighty qualities of Homer and Virgil, Sophocles and

15

Corneille. She was as keenly alive to the bold and mas-culine beauties of Shakespeare and of Dante as to the exquisite finish of the seventeenth-century writers. She admired Goethe and Schiller, no less as revealers of the deep sorrows of their country and their time, than for their poetic genius. Then, like all persons of sound and clear judgment, she thought much of composition and form. The vague terrified her; it disturbed her like indecision of character and mind. She dreaded to discover in it the absence of that moral rectitude, which, above all things else, was dear to her. Feeling, moreover, the necessity of reserve and caution in one's judgments, she willingly allowed the tide of fashion and infatuation to sweep past her; and was chary alike of her praise and her blame in regard to contemporary reputations. She was never ultra, either in her admiration or her criticism. She considered that the embellishments of life and the pastimes of the mind possess a legitimate charm, and furnish a species of relaxation, which, when partaken in moderation, unbends and tempers the powers. She did not look upon poetry and art as fit masters of the heart, the thought, or the speech, but as the servants of God, when worthy so to be, and instruments of his secondary designs upon the earth.

She took a keen interest, and expressed herself strongly, in matters of philosophy, history, and politics, although she generally shunned those subjects under their abstract and scholastic forms. There has not been an important work published for fifty years in any of the principal European languages, of which she has not made a careful estimate in writing; yet it very seldom happened, that she made use in conversation of pedantic technicalities, or terms borrowed from a foreign idiom. As a Christian, she was perfectly entitled to a philosophy which was summed up in Christianity, and always conducted to it. For saints, and candidates for saintship, it was an ascetic philosophy; for the mass of society, a living and practical philosophy, the conducting wire between history and morality and active life; for the heads of nations, it was a rule of duty, and a standing treaty for mutual education between different social ranks. She never pretended that theology restricted the Christian to the natural science of the days of Thomas Aquinas, or any such era. She thought, on the contrary, as Leibnitz had proclaimed, and as the Church had never denied, that it was important to introduce largely into the sphere of Christianity all such acquisitions of the ages as were compatible with its teachings. She appreciated every effort of human genius, without believing that it could dispense with Christian doctrine. She did not believe in the possibility of studying man in himself, — inferring the Creator from the creature, — and arriving at what has been called natural religion, and, more recently, naturalism, independently of a living and personal God. She did not admit, that, without God, all the celestial mechanics of a Laplace or a Lalande could issue in a perfect understanding of the principles on which the system of the universe rests. But no discovery, improvement, or progressive movement ever found her indifferent at its outset; still less, hostile.

In politics, she was firmly and profoundly monarchical, but strongly on her guard against any tendency towards absolute power. She beheld in monarchy a system supported upon principles the most favorable to a people's development, as well as most conformable to the order established by God in the constitution of the family and the hierarchy of the Church. She saw in it a state in

which equity prevails over force, and in which neither
equity nor moderation are transient accidents, but strict
obligations and indefeasible duties. She did not believe in
the divine right of kings, in the absolute sense of the word.
She saw and heard the warnings of history from the time
of the beginnings of empire; but she adhered with un-
swerving confidence to the chief grounds of authority.
She recognized its two essential conditions of power and
fruitfulness, — first, a national and popular root, a complete identification between people and sovereign, the
people's autonomy being shadowed forth and represented
in the person of the sovereign, without the sovereign's
having the right to absorb or confiscate it to his own
advantage; and, secondly, the consecration of the ages, the
prolonged intertwining of a people's destiny with the
destiny of a royal family, in whom the people respected
and glorified itself, giving to its obedience the dignity of a
high motive, and saluting in its prince an undisputed chief,
but not a master. Outside these limits, which were never
overstepped, Mme. Swetchine held in aversion every
thing arbitrary, violent, or hypocritical: she considered it
an offence against human conscience, moral life, and the
lasting prosperity of nations.

Resting upon these great principles, she contemplated
events and men with serenity. She did not lightly espouse
the cause of the victor; but she refused to throw herself into
a fever of excitement at the bidding of any one of the vanquished. She did not enjoy herself, nor did she approve
in others, one-sided laudings or denunciations. It was impossible for her to adopt an argument or a cause, because
it personified a conventional or private interest. She saw
and loved the fugitives of all our successive *régimes*,
aristocratic, bourgeoise, and even republican. But, however

distinguished they might be for intellect, talent, or goodness, she held them all slightly in suspicion, until she had
fairly estimated the social state which had been born or
developed in their absence. Before all and above all, her
desire was to examine, to weigh, to test: she employed all
her energies, and she excelled in separating motives from
deeds. She dreaded lest her opinion, which always required the seal of conscience, should be engulfed in the
whirlpool of hasty judgments. She strove to penetrate
into the true spirit of her time, its actual movements and
tendencies; and, even when she held a decided opinion, she
sought intercourse with those who defended the opposite
view. "Of what use would it be to live," she used to say,
"if one heard only one's own voice?"

More than once her friends murmured against this
toleration, and would fain have compelled her to opinions
or indignations more conformable to their own: she would
then desist, smilingly or sadly according to the importance
of the conflict, or the affection she bore the combatants;
but she never allowed herself to be influenced. Sometimes, to be sure, she had to endure sharp reproaches or
protracted sulking from those who were unable to enter
into the clearness of her views or the charity of her
sentiments, or to comprehend how far in some cases equity
transcends vulgar justice. Justice follows the letter,
applies the law, and is in danger of becoming pharisaical.
Equity, more free, more magnanimous, and more essentially Christian, constituted, in Mme. Swetchine's eyes, the
best policy of great minds.

These petty resentments faded away before her calmness, and especially before her affection, which always
remained unalterable; and, in the end, it came to pass, that
her friends let her impose on them a relative and tempo-

rary impartiality.   Her salon came by degrees to be neutral
ground in the midst of Paris, — not neutral in sentiments and
ideas, but neutral in respect of passion, exclusive absorption,
and violence.   One reproach only had power at times to
touch and wound her: it was when people said, "You
cannot feel this or that as we do: you are a foreigner."
She would then repeat the ungrateful word in strict confidence, without complaining or telling the speaker's name,
but with tears in her eyes.

It was not enthusiasm which people sought at Mme.
Swetchine's, although she was so rich in it.   Enthusiasm
is God's gift.   If we have not its germ within, it cannot be
communicated.   But she excelled in inciting to reflection,
rectitude, sagacity, and patience; and what she said bore
the impress of an incomparable unction of the heart.   She
rarely gave what is called advice, an absolute solution of a
given problem: her humility made her shrink from direct
responsibilities; in no case did she take the initiative,
and rather shunned than provoked confidence.   "God
only gives us grace to answer," she used sometimes to
say.   But, if you opened your heart to her, she extended
you her hand, and never drew it back again.   She did not
lecture you.   She did not set herself up as a model or
guide.   She did not say, "Walk thus," but sweetly, "Let us
walk together;" and so, without making the slightest pretensions, she often guided those she seemed to follow.

Under the influence of that gentle will, whose rectitude
and charity made it all powerful, one could not deviate
long: it became necessary either to withdraw from her
entirely, or to yield to the ascendency which she exercised,
— an ascendency unrealized in most cases without violence,
without flagrant contradiction, without collision or vehemence of language.   If each one of us could descend into

himself, and take note of the alien influences which have been at work in the formation of his thoughts, and the origin of his resolutions; if, without wounding our own vanity, we could arrive at a clear understanding of the extent of the modification which has taken place in our souls, — how many of our contemporaries would find in themselves, their characters, and the principal acts of their lives, traces of their intercourse with Mme. Swetchine!

And when we come to scrutinize the method of action, by the aid of which she exercised, and extended into the most diverse spheres, that influence which was ever on the increase during thirty years of an epoch prone to shake off every influence, we are amazed to discover that it consisted, first of all, in rejecting any methods, simple or complex. Even in her conversation, Mme. Swetchine never aimed at effect. Her timidity was never overcome. Her first remarks were generally uncertain, and even obscure. She needed to be carried out of herself by the emotion of the interview and the interest of the subject. No novelty of diction, no attempt at paradox, no being carried away by eloquence, but truth in all things, truth in style as well as in thought, without excess of ornament, though never bare. Her very absence of all pretension constituted her first claim to originality. Aside from the moments when nature overflows, and the most humble need to give vent to their emotions, — moments of *abandon* which she could always control and limit, — she was never brilliant, she did not astonish. You loved her and admired her instinctively, long before it was possible to give any account of what it was in her that charmed and subjugated.

Mme. Swetchine's household was very carefully ordered, though without affected refinements of any sort.

She never invited her friends to a set *soirée* or dinner; but she delighted to assemble about a small, round table, a few persons, who were glad to meet one another in her presence. Her repast was then served with elegance, and she presided over it with the thoughtful attention which she bestowed even on little things. Her drawing-room, open morning and evening, was almost always adorned with some flowering plant, or some object of art, loaned her by a friend, and which an artist considered it a great favor to see displayed in her room. The splendors of the Hermitage had given her a taste for brilliant light. In the evening, except in the very last years of her life, her saloon sparkled with lamps and candles, which gave, on your first entrance, a somewhat worldly air to the scene. This exterior was, in fact, destined for the eyes of the world. She wanted her guests to find there the peculiar refinements to which they were accustomed, and by which their lighter tastes were gratified; but you soon saw that the interior belonged to God, and that she who possessed these advantages was not possessed by them. It was just the same with the first impression created by her conversation.

There was nothing austere or grave to begin with. Social intercourse was there, as elsewhere, trite or superficial or languid, at the outset; but presently a current of superior intellect began to renovate and vivify the atmosphere. A good word fitly spoken, a gleam of intelligence, an impulse of affection, changed and enlivened the scene. People arrived at last at a degree of earnestness which no one had foreseen or prepared for; and thus it was, that numbers of worldly people, persons of light and wavering convictions, who would have been on their guard against premeditation, and stiffened themselves against

attack, yielded to the undeniable charm of sincerity and
novelty. More than one visitor, who had obtained an introduction to Mme. Swetchine from motives of curiosity or
vanity, found in her presence what he had not come to
seek, and went out other than he came in.

At all periods, Paris, the capital of European society,
has counted political, literary, and æsthetic salons. The
salon of Mme. Swetchine neither disclaimed nor affected
any of these titles; but it was above all, without ostentation or premeditation, a Christian fireside. The catholic
spirit did not aim at ascendency there, but it naturally
irradiated the place. Mme. Swetchine had never arrogated to herself a mission. She knew too well that missions are not improvised, and come only from above; but
she made it a point of duty to be unfailingly affable. She
regarded it as the tribute due for her birth, her fortune,
and her intellect. The least worldly advantages were, in
her eyes, instruments of Providence, whereof all, without
exception, must render an exact account. She had had no
previous ambition to establish a celebrated salon; but when
that salon had grown up of itself, through the attractive,
latent, involuntary virtue which dwelt in her as in the
magnet, her very modesty would not allow her to evade
her responsibility. Without appreciating all the good she
did, she had too much sagacity and too much experience
in human nature not to have glimpses of the pre-eminence
which so many hearts and so many diverse minds accorded
her; nor did she fail to comprehend that she ought — as
far as this might depend on her action and her example —
to bring nearer to God all who came near to her. Soon,
hers became a ministry of conscience; and, from that time,
neither her sufferings, which were excruciating, nor her
tastes, which often made her sigh for study and retirement,

were any check upon her self-devotion; and she finally came to look upon herself in the light of a sentinel who has received his countersign, and must keep it until death.

This sentiment alone can explain her inexhaustible patience. No one ever surprised in her an emotion of irritation or of *ennui*. At one time, she was confronted with presumptuous self-conceit, which laid down the law to her on matters in which she might have instructed the world; at another, she had to deal with representatives of science or polemics, who pertinaciously seized upon her *soirée*, and appropriated it for the development of their favorite subjects. Yet again, when the conversation was especially to her taste, the door would open to admit some idle lady, or some one of her modest friends who were strangers to the world, and all subjects of general interest. But never did these fatigues, these usurpations, or these untimely interruptions, elicit the slightest symptom of vexation. The humble was never sacrificed to the proud, the tedious to the agreeable, the poor to the rich. A woman with a great name tormented her salon and her friends for fifteen years; she burst forth like a tempest on any and every occasion, multiplied her questions without waiting for replies, and the announcement of her name was the signal for a general dispersion; but she never met with a hesitating or a cool reception. Mme. Swetchine calmly discouraged all the attempts against Mme. de X., by saying sweetly, "What would you have? Everybody avoids her; she is unhappy, and she has no one but me." Mme. de X. died in old age; and, in her last days, it was Mme. Swetchine who sought her out, and lingered longest by her death-bed.

Sometimes, also, implacable antagonists met in her salon, and this reduced her to mute but utter despair.

There was, for instance, a standing quarrel between Chevalier Z. and M. Y. When the Chevalier Z. had had the good fortune to arrive first, plant himself before the fire, and give himself up to the triumph of a dissertation on some oriental manuscript, without an opposing voice; if M. Y. made his appearance, he at once relapsed into silence, glided behind the arm-chairs, and gained the door unobserved. Mme. Swetchine only followed him with her eyes, softened his flight by a graceful *"au revoir,"* and sometimes even had the courage to reproach the conqueror.

Women who are not ordinarily accessible to the influence of another woman, were confidential and docile to Mme. Swetchine. Young and old acknowledged her sway. That which gives rise to hostility among women, did not exist in Mme. Swetchine. She never awoke a sentiment of rivalry, because no one ever detected in her a temptation to win admiration at the expense of others, or to eclipse any person whatever. Her disinterestedness won pardon for her superiority.

This woman, who, when she could snatch an hour of solitude, gave herself up to the severest studies, and, as she sometimes confessed, plunged into metaphysics as into a bath, was all grace and gayety the moment a young lady entered her salon. Beauty, elegance, freshness of age and emotions, gave Mme. Swetchine unaffected pleasure. All who were just entering life appeared to her peculiarly interesting, and needful of support. Her taste in matters of the toilet, as in every thing else, was fine and unerring. She, whose simple dress never varied, and consisted only of a costume of brown stuff, made up in one unchanging fashion, did not condemn dress in others, when that dress was in harmony with their station. Young ladies loved to display themselves to her in the evening, in all the brilliancy of their ball-room attire. It gave Mme. Swetchine sincere pleasure to admire them, to praise them, though not in the hackneyed language of compliment, and gently to indicate what she thought excessive. And so it often came to pass, that, after that swift evening apparition, the young girl came back in the morning, at the hour of *tête-à-têtes*, influenced by graver thoughts, and soliciting a very different kind of advice. It was then that sick or erring hearts came and revealed themselves to Mme. Swetchine in all sincerity, and then that she shed upon them, sweetly and gradually, light, truth, and life. Sometimes she struck at the very root of the evil; sometimes she arrested its development, and then again she applied herself to healing old wounds, or indicated the most efficacious mode of curing them, or neutralizing their effect. God only knows what passed in those interviews, how much was quietly done for his service and his glory in those secret conferences, which often ended in tears, when they had begun with the frivolous chat of the drawing-room. Hence it was, that so many young souls loved in her a spiritual mother, and vowed to her a sort of worship, whose ardor, checked and repressed by the very mystery of its origin, was only freely revealed after she had been taken away.

Mme. Swetchine, in her turn, drew from this intimate intercourse, added to her own exquisite penetration, a knowledge of the human heart which amounted almost to divination. A word, a gesture, a glance, a remark, or a pause, unnoticed by the world, became a whole revelation to her; and when you subsequently came to her, thinking to tell her every thing, you at once perceived that she knew all in advance, both virtues and defects. She knew already what had never been told her, and sometimes even what one was striving to hide. She knew the science of the soul, as physicians know that of the body. Common men see in a plant only its form and its color: the botanist perceives, at first sight, the family to which it belongs, and the laws which it obeys. He needs but a glance at the flower you hold in your hand to be able to say, "You come from the mountain or the plain, from the south or the region of snows." Such was the glance of Mme. Swetchine. A feature, a lineament, sufficed to enable her to recognize and reconstruct a whole moral nature.

Mme. Swetchine's days were divided into three distinct parts. She reserved the morning exclusively to herself; but her morning began before day. At eight o'clock, she had heard mass, and visited the poor. She then came home, and her doors were closed till three o'clock. From three to six, her drawing-room was open; it was closed from six to nine. At nine, her *soirée* commenced, and rarely closed before midnight. The *habitués* of the afternoon and evening were generally different. Certain persons who passed every evening with Mme. Swetchine, had never encountered or made the acquaintance of others who had chosen the morning. The Marquise de Pastoret, for instance, who came to Mme. Swetchine's every day, came there only between four and six o'clock, when she returned from visiting the hospitals, and after the accomplishment of her countless works of charity. In the evening, with a grace and dignity equal to those of Mme. Swetchine, Mme. de Pastoret did the honors of her husband's house, either at the chancellor's residence, or, after he had resigned his chancellorship, in his hotel in the Place Louis XV.

One evening, however, Mme. de Pastoret was seized with sudden anxiety about a friend, and wanted to go to

her. Her coachman made some opposition, and desired
to speak with her. "I am at your orders, Mme. la Marquise," he said, respectfully; "but I ought to apprise you
that I cannot answer for the consequences. My horses
have never seen lighted lanterns." Others preferred the
afternoon, when they were more secure against interruptions and the advent of numbers.

During the last years of the Restoration, which we
have yet to review, Mme. Swetchine continued occasionally to go out herself, either to hear music, or to visit the
Duchess de Duras or Mme. de Montcalm, who were equally
confined by ill health.

To the lifelong friends we have already enumerated,
must be added, after Mme. Swetchine's return from Italy,
the Duke de Laval, the Countess de Gontaut, sister of
Cardinal de Rohan, Mme. Récamier, and M. Ballanche.
Mme. Récamier had earnestly begged Mme. Swetchine to
adopt, in common with herself, the asylum of the Abbaye-
aux-Bois; and, but for the objections of General Swetchine, this establishment would probably have been the
object of Mme. Swetchine's decided preference.

Count de Sales, the last and worthy representative of
the great name of Saint François de Sales, also became,
along with Mgr. Lambruschini, nuncio of the Holy See, one
of the most constant guests at the hotel in the Rue St.
Dominique. Mgr. de Quélen, also, came as often as the
onerous administration of a diocese like that of Paris
allowed. The King's ministers, and the officers of the
Restoration, could only testify their interest at rare intervals; while she herself was always extremely reserved
about approaching persons in power. Yet this sentiment
never amounted to indifference, in proof of which we will
cite some extracts, selected at hazard, from her correspondence: —

TO MLLE. DE VIRIEU.

Oct. 5, 1824.

While you were writing me, what great events were preparing at Paris[1]! . . . I have but one fear, and that is, that
my favorite opinions will be too much in vogue. That is not
the worst that can happen, certainly; nevertheless, it cannot be
denied that there is always danger. When it is opinions that
are wrong, the evil is only slowly eradicated; but, if authority
makes use of violent remedies, a transient obedience is only
purchased at the expense of future danger. I desire for religion what economists demand for commerce, — that it should be
allowed to take its own course without interference; but, in our
days, people will not call time to their aid, — time which, when
properly employed, weakens all that is pernicious, and consoli-
dates all which is truly desirable.

On the 24th of December, she wrote again to Mlle. de
Virieu : —

"The enthusiasm which the King excites is unparalleled.
One must go back to the days of Henry IV. to get an idea of
his popularity. Parties, one and all, confine themselves to a
flourish of their respective trumpets. Anxieties for the past
and future are alike abjured. The general satisfaction is a
pleasant thing; but one cannot help asking one's self, why
these sudden illuminations come so late; and how a large
proportion of the people can be fickle enough to pass so quickly
from fear and suspicion to the most joyous confidence. The
noble emancipation of the press, and the words uttered by the
Dauphin on the occasion, show better than any thing else
the spirit in which the King proposes to rule. The first page
of the reign of Charles X. is like certain sonnets, — in itself
worth a long poem. I have been a French woman ever since
I knew my own heart. I have never admitted any other
authority in France than that of the Bourbons, and I glory
in their triumphs like their most devoted servants. Ah, what
poor creatures we are! If we could only be just and impartial,
once for all!"

We have seen, by the cares she lavished on the young
Nadine, what a place her adopted daughter held in the

---

[1] The accession of Charles X., and the auspicious measures by which
it was signalized.

interior life of Mme. Swetchine. When Mlle. Staëline became Countess of Segur d'Aguesseau, and undertook, in her turn, the duties of a wife and mother, Mme. Swetchine felt a void which could only be filled by a new attachment.

Mme. de Nesselrode was anxious about the health of one of her daughters, a mere child, whom she could not herself remove from the dangers of the Russian climate. We do not learn from the correspondence of these two friends, how the thought originated of confiding the child of the one to the heart of the other. It is probable that the wish and the consent were the result of one of those spontaneous impulses which reciprocally meet and forestall one another. Little Helen de Nesselrode assumed her share in the maternal solicitude of Mme. Swetchine in the beginning of the year 1829. She was fourteen years old; that is, at the age when the instincts of the heart are all alive, while the reason is as yet undeveloped. From that time, the correspondence of Mme. Swetchine and Mme. de Nesselrode becomes a complete and admirable treatise on education. This precious correspondence, like so many others, deserves some time to be published separately; but meanwhile it may afford us a glimpse of Mme. Swetchine's new cares: —

TO THE COUNTESS DE NESSELRODE.

Dec. 12, 1829.

MY VERY DEAR FRIEND, — Every thing goes well between Helen and me: I have obtained a foothold. It is not words that import: it is their effect; and in her case, at least, my conscience can be entirely absolved by success only. I still pursue, and probably shall for some time to come, my system of temporization. I wish to attack only when I am sure of victory, and this cannot come all at once. I accustom her to think that there are certain things which I do not approve, but which I shall not blame very severely to begin with. What she lacks, in common with all other children, is self-control;

and that is not acquired in a day. I am preparing her for it
gradually. Errors into which she fell two months ago would
be impossible to her to-day, because she herself has condemned
them. Her faith in me increases daily. I court and foster it
with all the skill and strategy at my command; and my strategy
is truth, but truth with the charm of perfect unconstraint.
Thus, to induce her to open her heart to me, I open mine to all
her interests, reminiscences, and feelings. I try to make her
talk of those who are dear to her. I give her a share in the
things which interest me. If she brings me a letter which she
has just received, I make her read one of mine. When I talk
with her, I never condescend to her; I place her apparently
on my own level, and, by means of the habits which I induce
her to form, I acquire necessarily an influence which command
and coercion never would have given me. The right of con-
quest is not equal to the right of birth, say what you will; and
one must make one's self beloved and acknowledged, instead
of imposing one's authority.

January, 1830.

MY DEAR FRIEND, — You seem to feel the need of imparting to me some of the satisfaction which fills your own heart.
Happiness is not enough for you: you want to deserve it;
and I am grateful for your ingenious way of telling me that
you appreciate my affection. Yes, it does not fail; it feeds
upon your cares, is identified with your interests, and makes
me keenly alive to all which affects you. Through those I
love I feel rich, and, as it were, endowed anew with prosperity
and hope. I could never have believed that this dear little
Helen could so have insinuated herself into my affections.
She moves me to the very depths of my being, and I feel all a
mother's deep yet sweet solicitude.

To return to our dear child: she gets on well with her lessons, and I think they will be useful to her. She seizes with
wonderful avidity on all beauties, true or false, which bear the
stamp of elevation and grandeur. When she is moved, she is
transported. Just now we are reading the Greek tragedies.
Each subject, as treated by the ancients, I follow up with the
modern imitations in the languages with which she is familiar;
and so we get a sort of whole, which captivates her attention,
and stimulates her curiosity. You do not yet know, perhaps,
that I have given her an additional master, — M. Saigey, — a
man strongly recommended by M. Cuvier, and who does credit

16

even to that recommendation. I applied to him for a course
of general geography, and he enters into my views admirably.
His knowledge is of the clearest and most entertaining description, and is communicated in so sprightly a manner, that
fatigue is not to be thought of. If Helen develops a taste
for it, they will go on to political geography, which every one
ought to understand, — taking up the different ideas which
attach to our globe under the varying aspects of its structure,
its elements, and the principal phenomena which it presents.
This will amount to nothing else than a history of the earth,
the heavens, and the ocean; but we shall confine ourselves
to the most general facts, and only aim at imparting a knowledge of things which are daily alluded to, even in drawing-room
conversation. I am making the experiment without feeling
confident of its success. We shall widen or contract the course
we wish her to pursue, according to the facilities afforded us by
her natural tastes, and teachableness of disposition.

Dec. 15, 1830.

I leave it to your own heart, my dear friend, to guess the
joy afforded me by your little letter of November 27. The
improvement which struck you in Helen's letter is all the more
real because nothing is urged upon her. I would rather not
see her do well than incur the risk attendant on forcing her to
do so. It is not what she does to-day that I really care for:
it is what she is becoming, — what I may be able to prepare
and develop largely and finely for the future. We are apt to
forget that education is the means, and not the end; that it does
not matter so much what we obtain by immediate influence as
what we may have insured against a time when that influence
shall have ceased. No one, surely, sets a higher value than I
upon a compassionate and charitable spirit; but I avoid every
direct injunction and exhortation thereto. I do not even surprise and take advantage of her generous impulses when I
perceive that they are vague and fugitive. It is thus that
I can best assure myself of the steps she is really taking, and
thoroughly enjoy it where they are progressive. Thus, the
other day, she came to me, with an air of satisfaction which
anticipated my own, and begged to be permitted, out of her
monthly allowance, to pay half the board of a little girl whom
I had just placed in the House of Industry. I asked her if
she had reflected on the matter, and fully made up her mind;
and, after receiving the liveliest assurances on her part, I gave

my consent, and told her.it would increase my pleasure in a good work·to have her share it with me.

Difficulties which, six months ago, used still to come up sometimes, no longer exist. Warned by Helen's own shrewd and correct judgment, I remember that the only genuine superiority is that of reason, and that authority itself must appeal to it.

Mlle. de Nesselrode did not leave Mme. Swetchine till the eve of her marriage with the Count Michel Chreptowitch; and her filial devotion is to this day a living witness to the love of which she was the object.

Mme. Swetchine went in person, and restored Helen to the protection of the Countess de Nesselrode, who was then on a visit to the baths of Brighton, in company with the Grand-duchess Helena. This trip afforded Mme. Swetchine an opportunity for a rapid excursion to London and other parts of England.

These domestic joys, these noble and fruitful years of the Restoration, were saddened for Mme. Swetchine by unremitting anxiety about the health of the Duchess de Duras, and finally by her premature death. After she came back from Italy, Mme. Swetchine felt that she must indemnify herself for the privations of her absence, and had seized every opportunity for passing a few months with her friend at Andilly or St. Germain. "Paris," she said, "is a place where it is more convenient for people to hate than to love each other;" and she wrote to the Countess de Nesselrode, in speaking of some plans for being nearer the Duchess de Duras:—

"Protracted separations are bad things; and a few days spent together remove the most formidable inconveniences of absence. If in our first youth we reckon on the future, and trouble appears only provisional, we do not hold the present so cheap when we get on in life. We want to grasp all, for we feel that all is about to escape us. I feel so old,

that I seem to be only capable of continuing. The sole reason
for doing a thing to-morrow appears to be that I did it to-day.
Most of us have some worldly cares; and, if we would be sure
of accomplishing any thing, the best way is to manage so as to
do a little every day."

This part of Mme. Swetchine's correspondence soon
becomes very sad; and she details fully to Mme. de Nesselrode the symptoms which presage her irrevocable loss:—

October 30.

I told you, in my last, that I hoped to prolong my peaceful
isolation till November; but the news I received of Mme. de
Duras's terrible accident induced a sudden change of plan.
One night, after she had been about as usual through the
day, she saw the light of a lamp near her suddenly disap-
pear, then turned her head and saw it again. The eye and
cheek towards the lamp had been paralyzed; the blindness
of the eye was complete. You can judge of the anxiety and
terror of the moment! The most prompt and efficacious remedies
were employed, and the eye appeared to recover its functions;
but so imperfectly, that even now she can scarcely distinguish
the outlines of objects. As if there were not danger enough
in this appalling menace, we are anxious about her in other
respects. The physicians think that the attack was only a
sympathetic affection, and they seem to apprehend some organic
difficulty. The other day, she suffered excruciatingly for six
or seven hours, after taking a few spoonfuls of chiccory pea-
soup. Add to this, that her nerves are in a state of constant
irritability, that she is extremely depressed, and has fainting
fits, which are very critical, coming at a time when she is so
unable to bear them. The change in her, alone, would give
ground for every apprehension. It is a complete overthrow.
But in the midst of all this, the moment our dear friend feels
a little better, she walks; she makes the tour of her garden;
and I have seen her prolong her walk for a quarter of an hour
without inconvenience.

It is the same with her mind. Her silence and profound
pre-occupation often give place to an overflowing tenderness
of expression when she chats a little, and smiles that kind,
bright smile which imparts such a charm to her countenance.
I am profoundly struck by the affecting religious submission
with which she meets all her sufferings, and the danger which
threatens her. The first thing she said to me was, that she

regarded her present state as incurable, a sort of transition from life to death. She said she felt it to be a warning from God, and her sole wish was to profit by it; in short, it would be impossible to approach the greatest and most solemn thoughts with more courage and actual power of mind. What an immense consolation the goodness of God has vouchsafed us! but it is all the more sorrowful and affecting to turn our thoughts inward, and measure the greatness of the loss with which we are threatened. Those who only knew Mme. de Duras superficially cannot have been prepared for the proof she is affording of genuine greatness of soul; but for me, my dear friend, no emotion of surprise mingles with my sad joy. The world and life may have been too noisy about her; but she was right-minded enough to rise superior to it all, and God is showing forth in her all the triumphs of his grace, by appropriating to himself the capabilities for passionate devotion which constitute the essence of her character. I have met in the world, which, to some extent, ignores these details, people who were persuaded that Mme. de Duras was a prey to all the anguish of an utter revolt against the fear of death, and that she repudiated the idea. They represent her as carried away by an imagination which knows not how to submit; while I and many others can testify, that it would be impossible to understand the truth more fully than does she, or to face it with greater courage and sweetness. Even the natural conflict between the instinct of existence and the fear of the terrible transition, seems to have ceased. Her resignation has surmounted all, and taken away from her sorrow all that was gnawing and destructive. My uneasiness is very great, dear friend; but she herself has intervals of hope. Sometimes I am utterly dejected, and then again I tell myself that I exaggerate her danger, and that there are a good many examples which might re-assure me. No one could be more careful, attentive, and charming than Clara is with her mother. I have found myself doubly attracted to her during my stay at St. Germain. She is one of the best and most thoughtful mothers I know, and the tenderest of wives; but now one would say she was a daughter only, so exclusively does she consecrate herself to her mother. Mme. de Larochejacqueline has been detained, by the sickness of her mother-in-law, at one of her estates in Vendée.

The attack described by Mme. Swetchine with such anxious fidelity, did not cost Mme. de Duras her life; but it shook her health fearfully. An incurable form of liver

complaint soon declared itself, and the mild climate of
Nice was tried in vain. In the month of March, 1829,
Mme. Swetchine, as well as the *élite* of French society
and letters, was called to mourn an irreparable loss. The
Duchess de Duras had barely entered upon her fiftieth
year.

CHAPTER XIII.

Revolution of 1830. — New religious situation. — Correspondence with the Count de Montalembert and the Abbé Lacordaire. — Notes of Father de Ravignan.

THE Revolution of July was a source of grief and terror to Mme. Swetchine. Princes whom she revered, and friends who had long been dear to her, were banished or struck down. Liberal institutions, whose duration she had desired, and which she had fondly believed compatible with order, were suddenly launched upon a new course, and subjected to incalculable tests. Mme. Swetchine had never deceived herself about any of the faults of the friends of royalty. She was no less clear-sighted and no less anxious about the faults of the friends of freedom. Enumerating the alarming symptoms which appeared on every side, she wrote to the Countess Edling : —

"How true was that remark of yours, that we are witnessing the grand judgment of human pride ! When a spiritual element mingles with guilt, it becomes demoniacal."

On the 23d of December, 1830, during the trial of Prince de Polignac, she wrote as follows : —

"You have learned the particulars of the progress of events here during these last days, the issue of the great drama in the Chamber of Peers, and all the agitation and resentment of which it has been the pretext and occasion. Day before yesterday, yesterday even, Paris was like a city with an enemy at the gates. To-day, calmness and even cheerfulness prevail, or so they say ; and death-cries are replaced by *vivats*, which

are not of the sort to prolong the life of any one. Yesterday
you would have supposed that every right had been outraged,
because four victims had escaped the steel of the assassin.
To-day that hideous delirium appears like a dream. I must
say, that, if I am never disturbed in the midst of universal
alarm, no more can I be re-assured by an improvised security.
The men remain the same, the danger very nearly. One must
have been here a good while to be able to grasp or comprehend aught of that complication of emotions, wills, projects,
and especially interests, which is at the bottom of it all.
Those throngs of men, so menacing, so powerful in numbers,
so incensed, were under no apparent direction. If their chance
of success had been greater, those who incited them would
have given them some more definite object; but, instead of
one aim, they seemed to have three or four; and dissension
burst forth with the first advantage they gained. How could it
be otherwise with a sovereign people that recognizes no will
but its own, and in its own only the impulse of the moment.

"The lower classes aim at nothing less than a levelling of
all ranks, and, to succeed in this thing, will renew the conflict
unceasingly. Their power has now been revealed to them,
and they will pursue their aim. They still rely upon legal
methods; but, if these do not insure success, they will undertake to seize it, sword in hand.

"Nothing could be more indeterminate than the results of
this situation. Everywhere we have demi-wrong, demi-usur-
pation, demi-loyalty, and demi-injustice. It is the triumph of
the *quasi*. The foundations are so bad, all is so tainted with
the original vice, that, however good a thing may be in itself,
it requires, first or last, a sacrifice to a wrong principle. Ah,
how careful we ought to be to do *no* evil! for evil always returns by a vicious circle, and re-acts upon itself."

In the midst of the protracted agitations which succeeded the Revolution of July, the possibility of an immediate return of the Duke de Bordeaux occurred to many
minds; and these hopes could not fail to find an echo in
the soul of Mme. Swetchine. She does not omit to mention them in her correspondence: —

"Great re-actions in favor of virtue, even if brought about
by its enemies, not only pave the way for a genuine restoration,
but also of themselves assure its permanence. If there had

not been such, can you imagine the return of the Duke de
Bordeaux in the present condition of people and things? Le-
gitimacy is a fine principle; but it is only one element of
order, and cannot stand alone. I ask of those who hearken
only to their passions, whether the point in question is the
futile triumph of restoring the royal child, the vanity of having won a victory, or rather a rule which shall re-establish and
protect society, and firmly implant those verities which are
useful to states, and conservative of their true prosperity.
No keener regrets than mine follow the unhappy princes into
their exile. I have a tender reverence for the piety and virtue
of the King, the most affectionate and devoted regard for the
Dauphiness; but, while I marvel at the oblivion to which
the most enthusiastic loyalty often consigns them, I do not
think that so many misfortunes can be redeemed by the pueril-
ity of an ephemeral success. I think we must learn to wait;
and leave it to God to take the initiative, and choose the moment which his will generally indicates to man by unequivocal
signs, and which has certainly not yet arrived. So I am quite
of the opinion of Alfred de Damas, and opposed to that of M.
de ——.

"But let us, my friend, give a moment's thought to one
poor destiny, which after many fluctuations, wrongs, and re-
verses, seems to-day to be verging on the last extremity of
distress: I speak of M. de Chateaubriand. There are a
great many people, as Mme. de Staël says, who throw their
friends into the sea that they may have the pleasure of fishing
them out again. But pity men of genius and stormy natures;
for they are weak, and invariably dragged further than they
desire. M. de Chateaubriand has always respected certain
limits: his conduct in this emergency, and his utter abandonment by his party, are the best proofs of it; and, in the age in
which we live, we may well respect men who continue to respect two or three things. M. de Chateaubriand might and
ought to have been at ease to-day. He is almost to blame for
being otherwise; but let us take the fact as it is, cruel, very
cruel. To avoid taking the oath, he has renounced his peerage,
and with the peerage the pension of twelve thousand francs
which it afforded him. Do you know what he has besides? A
capital of from sixteen to twenty thousand francs, still owed
him by his publisher. This sum will be swallowed up by debts
and his journey to Switzerland, or will perhaps be sufficient to
support him for a few months. And afterwards? It is the
insoluble problem of this afterwards which I present to you,
my dear and good friend; and which will surely awaken in
you some concern, and, it may be, give rise to something

more, — an opinion, a piece of advice, an unexpected hope This is the thought which has occurred to me in the midst of my sorrow and perplexity. If the Emperor were informed of the actual and indisputable condition of a man who is a chevalier of his own order, whom the Emperor Alexander greatly distinguished, whose ideas are fundamentally monarchical, and whose conscience has remained faithful to his masters in their misfortunes, — if the Emperor's eyes were to fall on such a man, would it not occur to him to offer assistance? Could the idea be suggested? I must tell you, in the first place, that the thought is entirely my own, and has been imparted to no one. M. de Chateaubriand is so far a stranger to the notion, that, in case you should think it practicable, I should beg you to wait until I had sounded him, and learned whether such a favor at the hands of a foreign prince would be acceptable."

This noble thought did reach the Emperor Nicholas. His reply was, that, if he were to testify any interest in the French Legitimists, he should accord his preference to the Count de La Ferronnays, the last ambassador of Charles X. to his own court. But the overture was without results in either case.

Finally, we have the means of forming an exact idea of the state of Mme. Swetchine's opinions at this epoch; for we can verify it at the very moment when the insurrections were apparently quelled, and the new government found itself confronted by moral difficulties only. The ministry of MM. Dupont (de l'Eure) and Lafitte had given place, on the 11th of March, 1831, to a coalition, in which M. Casimir Périer was President of the Council, and held the portfolio of the Interior. Count Sebastiani was Minister of Foreign Affairs, Baron Louis managed the finances, and the Bureau of Public Instruction was in the hands of Count de Montalivet, who had displayed intrepid courage during the trial of the ministers.

On the 13th of March, 1831, Madame Swetchine wrote: —

" The creation of the new ministry re-assures me somewhat about war, and gives me faith in a respite, at least, if not in the actual re-establishment of security. The fatigue consequent on so much agitation, anxiety for so many interests, and the selection of honorable and strong men, — all these circumstances strengthen the chances of the new order of things. If it is not firmly established, it will be because it is manifestly impossible, in an age when everybody reasons, for a government to sustain itself by methods opposed to the nature of its origin. If this coalition does not succeed, it will be because the evils of the situation are fundamental. I have always thought that if, while everybody here is behaving well, or at least as well as possible under the circumstances, the result should be a political failure, the moral of the fable would appear in the most striking manner. It would have been demonstrated, that the basis of the edifice is at fault, and that the defect is irremediable."

The political situation of France was now radically changed; the religious situation no less so. The relations of the Church with the new government could not be what they had been with the old.

The natural and inevitable result of these rude overturns was a necessity that the clergy should have a *point d'appui* on some more solid ground than the temporary favor or disfavor of the political authorities. Experience seemed decisive. The century was but thirty years old; yet twice in that period had the Church seen compromised all which the world could give or take away from her. When the First Consul had appeared in the character of a restorer and pacificator of society, one of his first cares had been to recall a banished God, and restore to him his temples. But presently, like all men who, in the depth of their hearts, aim less at serving religion than at being served by it, the Consul — now an Emperor — substituted compulsion for respect; and the pomp of the coronation was speedily followed by the captivity of Fontainebleau. This open violence was a revelation to the clergy of that day, who had been under the sway of certain ringleaders, half blinded and half accomplices; and when the Restoration succeeded to the Empire, and restored to the sovereign pontiff the plenitude of his authority, the era of reparation was hailed with chivalrous and spontaneous enthusiasm.

But when political dissensions revived, and parties seized on the weapons at hand, the Church saw herself exposed to the same attacks as the royal power. When the Restoration at last succumbed, the clergy was considered vanquished, and treated accordingly. From that moment, a common anxiety took possession of some eminent members of the clergy, and a few laymen profoundly devoted to the Church. They asked, with one voice, whether the hour had not come for them to adopt a new attitude toward the new times ; and, having early agreed upon a point of departure, they desired to make an appeal to public sentiment, and, for this purpose, established a journal with the title of " L'Avenir."

" L'Avenir" began by boldly claiming full and entire freedom of action for the Church ; no longer requesting it as a favor or a privilege, but on the ground of common right, and the tendencies of the modern mind. In support of this energetic demand, " L'Avenir" professed, with equal frankness, its adhesion to the general principles in force in French society, as they had been sanctioned by the Concordat of 1801, and to the representative *régime* inaugurated by the return of the House of Bourbon. "Destructive force," said the Catholic organ, "is but an additional calamity when there is not a constructive idea behind it." [1] — "Your greatest glory," wrote some one at

---

[1] Reply to M. de Potter, September, 1832.

that time to the founder of "L'Avenir," "will be to have spoken of liberty to the world, with a pure heart, and lips overflowing with the praise of God. It will be to have purified your cause, and shown it to posterity, clothed with a kind of Christian virginity, yet adorned with all the splendor of the priesthood. You have restored to that cause the titles of its divine origin, and reconciled thereto the souls which revolted from the sanguinary worship by which it was profaned."[1]

The enterprise was bold, but favored by all things within and without. The most eloquent of the Christian apologists of that epoch, the Abbé de Lamennais, beheld courageous hearts and eminent minds flocking to his standard, and ranging themselves about him in the character of devoted and ardent disciples.

To deliver the clergy, if possible, from the bonds and the engagements which had become so onerous, and which, twice in so short a time, had been so near proving fatal; to endeavor to release their order, once for all, from the temptation or the danger of falling into the hands of fortune or of chance; to set before it, as the only way of salvation for itself and the souls of men, the exclusive duty of its evangelical mission, — such was the programme unanimously adopted by the contributors to "L'Avenir."

This swift movement was, and remains, one of the most fruitful of our century. The nature of the questions agitated, the grandeur of talent and nobility of character called forth, acquired for it an influence, and have left a memory which is still a battle-ground, whereon must be decided one of the most important problems of human

---

[1] Œuvres Posthumes de M. de Lamennais. Correspondence, vol. i. p. 91.

destiny, the exact definition, namely, of the relations between Church and State.

In the last days of the Restoration, M. de Quélen, who
was residing in the vicinity of Nôtre Dame, in the venerable palace which had been inhabited by the Cardinal
de Noailles, Christopher de Beaumont, and Christian de
Juigné, saw enter his cabinet a young advocate, who had
made no figure at the bar, and had been distinguished only
by the practised and kindly eyes of some of the founders
of the *Société des bonnes Études*, MM. Bailly, Alexis
de Noailles, and Berryer. M. de Quélen approached
the young man, bowed, and said, extending his hand
affectionately, " You are most welcome. You have been
pleading human causes. You shall henceforth plead an
eternal cause." This young man was M. Lacordaire, who
had come for the blessing of the Archbishop before shut-
ting himself up in a cell of St. Sulpice.

He had issued thence an austere and devout priest; and
was offering to the Church the first-fruits of his apostolate,
when M. de Lamennais addressed him in his turn, repeat-
ing, though in different language, the appeal of M. de
Quélen.

A young scion of French aristocracy, of an age to
assume the prerogatives of the peerage, the Count de
Montalembert, had followed, along with M. de Lamennais,
the example of Lacordaire; and these two, so far apart in
origin, so united in ardor and devotion, were bound together by a close and indissoluble friendship. M. de
Montalembert, who was an admirer of Count de Maistre,
had not been unmindful of the residence of Mme. Swetchine in Paris. He had begged for the honor of a pre-
sentation to her; and he it was who, in his turn, had
introduced his friend, the Abbé Lacordaire.

We may imagine the earnest and interesting nature of their interviews, at such a time and under such circumstances. The points in question were vital ones for Christianity; they sought to determine the surest method of preserving her independence, and reconquering or extending her disinterested empire over the nations, who never need her so much as when they aspire to do without her. In Mme. Swetchine's presence youth could interrogate experience, and have no reason to dread timidity or weakness. Her solicitude and apprehension soon became intense. Every thing was tending towards a presumptuous and disorderly liberalism. M. de Lamennais, who should have moderated the excitement of his friends, frequently set the example in exaggeration of language, and gave a handle to his enemies, by the misunderstandings and disturbances which he took no pains to dispel.

"L'Avenir" had been started on the 15th of October, 1830. The opposition it excited in Paris was promptly reproduced at Rome, although under a milder and more temperate form. The Abbé Lacordaire and the Abbé Gerbet were delegated by their coadjutors to seek an interview with the papal nuncio, Mgr. Lambruschini, and present him with a statement of their doctrines. This interview was without result. MM. de Lamennais, Lacordaire, and de Montalembert then resolved to suspend the publication of "L'Avenir," and repair to the sovereign pontiff, Gregory XVI., to obtain a decision from him. They arrived at Rome on the 31st of December, 1831.

The correspondence of Mme. Swetchine with M. de Montalembert began at the time of the publication of "L'Avenir," and was kept up throughout this memorable journey. This correspondence must certainly be considered as one of the most touching models extant of Christian friendship. It assumes, after the first interchange of words of confidence and affection, the most serious character; and we know not which of the two to admire most, — she who sees the right so clearly, and enforces it so authoritatively, or he who is so free to ask advice, and to this rare merit adds the rarer one of permitting the publicity of his request.

The first of the letters here given is dated in the month of September, 1831. At this period, " L'Avenir " was not only awakening religious susceptibilities : it was equally inciting to resistance against the civil power. It had been indicted before a jury, for demanding that the nomination of bishops should be removed from the hands of the King; and, shortly after, M. de Montalembert was arraigned before the Chamber of Peers, for having attempted, in concert with M. de Lamennais, to protest, by the opening of a free school, against the imperial decree which maintained the monopoly of the universities, in defiance of the charter of 1830.

TO COUNT DE MONTALEMBERT.

DIEPPE, Sept. 2, 1831.

. . . Certainly there is occasion for all our lamentations. Within and around us, we have great evils to deplore; but I do not think that faith is either dead or dying. It seems to me that its position to-day is precisely that of science in past times; that is to say, it is withdrawn from the masses, and concentrated with all the more power, sincerity, and splendor upon individuals. The actual increase of light in what are called the ages of ignorance answered instead of its diffusion; and, if the real end of Providence has always been to provide himself in every age with those who will worship him in spirit and in truth, have we any right to doubt the accomplishment of that end to-day, amid such saintly souls, such tried virtue, and such generous efforts?

I loved you for what you were, before I knew you; and since then I have indeed been identified with you by a truly maternal solicitude. You stand between your trial and your examination as licentiate of laws,—two eras of human life which should be far apart. But neither success nor defeat will greatly move you.

In the train of this letter came events of the most serious nature. The arrival of M. de Lamennais at Rome caused evident disturbance. Gregory XVI. was moved, by his clairvoyance as sovereign pontiff, by his natural inclination, and even by the traditions of the Roman court, to wish to save the Abbé de Lamennais. He endeavored to overlook all that was imperious in the interrogations and entreaties addressed to him, and replied, through the medium of Cardinal Pasca, by a letter in which, while he indicated some points of doubtful doctrine, and certain proofs which the Holy See rejected, he aimed at avoiding any more serious measure, and at exorcising public disapprobation. The Abbé Lacordaire, beset by the saddest apprehensions, but moved yet more by his duty to the Church, supplicated M. de Lamennais, in the most earnest manner, to desist and withdraw. M. de Lamennais, however, allowed Lacordaire to depart without him, and persisted in remaining at Rome and demanding an official reply from the head of Christendom. Unable to obtain this, he left Rome, and announced his formal intention of at once resuming the publication of his journal, and the propagation of his religious and political doctrines. This obstinacy rendered it impossible for Gregory XVI. to hesitate longer. He found it necessary to search out, recapitulate, and call attention to, whatever had seemed excessive in "L'Avenir," in the encyclical letter of Aug. 15, 1832. He did so with regret, and in such moderate terms, that a few years later, while Gregory XVI. was still pontiff, and during the long struggle between the French Episcopate and MM. de Montalembert

17

and Lacordaire respecting freedom of instruction, many bishops adopted the general principles of "L'Avenir," modified by experience and a clearer insight into the questions involved. If M. de Lamennais in 1832 had shown himself humble and submissive, he might have stood, without a rival, at the head of the Catholic movement of 1840, greater, stronger, more revered, than ever.

What a different course he did pursue, and how swiftly it led him to ruin, is well known. We shall get glimpses, in the ensuing letters, of the anguish of heart and firmness of faith of his two more illustrious companions.

"L'Avenir" had ceased to exist. Its contributors were dispersed. The Abbé Lacordaire was ripening in retirement his knowledge and his powers. M. de Montalembert left France for Germany, where were awaiting him, at Marburg, those religious experiences which gave rise to the history of St. Elizabeth. Mme. Swetchine's correspondence recommences in 1833.

March 19, 1833.

. . . It does not satisfy me that I am remembered, my dear child. I want some proof of that remembrance; and this is why we do not always agree about the length of the gaps in our intercourse. I know so little of how they are filled for you, and how far your courage has struggled successfully with your sorrows. In such a state of uncertainty, one wants to be re-assured every moment. If you would prefer not to come this evening, I would propose to-morrow evening or to-morrow morning, just as your private mood shall determine. It is because I would combat, that I will not contradict it.

Aug. 26, 1833.

The discouragement of not being able to say what one would as one would, has always made it easy for me to understand that man who, when pressed for an answer to a letter, invariably sent for post-horses, and went to talk with his impatient friend. Unfortunately, it is a method which every one cannot adopt; and he who should attempt it in your case would find himself involved in I know not what vagabond courses. If you only knew how to stay where you are well off, one might be almost sure of making some arrangement; but your internal unrest urges you on, still crying "*Dahin! dahin!*"[1] When you think you are obeying determinate motives, I very much fear that you are only yielding to a vague instinct of change. Ah, my God! it may be needful that this should exhaust itself, but not to the extent of doing you an injury. Every sort of holocaust demands a living being; and such are not those quenched and blighted imaginations, those forceless and unaspirant intellects, which often mistake indifference and inertia for the superiority of reason and the last result of philosophy. Surely, God has impressed a different tendency upon your soul, which would seem to have been formed under the inspiration of that fine word of Plato's, "The beautiful as a means of attaining the true." It is the very course which would have fascinated you, if you had not been thrust, when so young, so weak, and so inexperienced, into the midst of a conflict of passions and interests wholly alien to your nature. You seized only on the disinterested, and, so to speak, poetic side of these questions: but all the same you were in the *mêlée*, giving and receiving blows; and even your utterly pure and upright intentions could not prevent your experiencing the unfortunate effects of a false and rash course. And thus, with a mind perfectly high-toned and honorable, a crystal which is almost a diamond, with faultless manners, with faith and sincere piety, and all the lofty sentiments they involve, you have neither the heart's sweet joy nor its sweet peace: you are dejected, troubled, dissatisfied with yourself. My dear Charles, if you had transgressed no law, your heart might have been sad and desolate; but it would have experienced no such ravages. The reason why you are so ill at ease is, that your conscience lies so near your heart, that their voices and their troubles are confounded. You feel that you have been stópped in your course; but you will not say that you must retrace your steps.

Nov. 17, 1833.[2]

MY DEAR CHARLES, — I know all about your accumulated

---

[1] "Thither! thither!" The first words of the refrain of Mignon's ballad in Goethe's "Wilhelm Meister."

[2] The French newspapers published, at about this time, a letter from Pope Gregory XVI. to Mgr. de Lesquen, Bishop of Rennes, which mentioned, among other symptoms of the impending revolt of M. de Lamennais, the publication of Mickiewitch's "Polish Pilgrim," which had been translated by M. de Montalembert.

troubles; and you may guess how sad and unceasing is my anxiety, understanding as I do that you are deeply hurt. Without having been as sanguine as you, I have followed with solicitude your swift and sudden alternations between hope and fear, anticipation and sorrowful surprise.

But what re-assures me about you, dear Charles, and gives me real confidence in your destiny, is, that your mistakes, your imprudences, and your deviations, have always been followed by trials. You are not yet sentenced, for there is nothing irrevocable about your sorrows or your situation; nor are you abandoned, for faith and all true consolation still remain to you: but you are constantly warned, reproved, and recalled into a straighter and surer way. If you still resisted these solemn admonitions, you would increase the guilt of the struggle in which you have voluntarily engaged. Even if your faith fails not, what can you gain by delay? Under what better auspices could you come back to the truth? What homage and what sacrifice will you bring her? Youth has this advantage: there is indulgence for its weaknesses, and its repentance is welcome. But you must not forget that your youth began so early, and was so prematurely active, that it has fewer years to run than the youth of ordinary men.

I put far from me every fear; but I also check the ardor of my hopes, which would demand for their full justification so generous, so pure, so catholic, an abandonment to the Father's guidance, and which would make so clearly manifest a tender, profound, and unreserved submission. . . .

I fancy that I detect in these Utopian dreams the heresy of the Millenarians, who attempted to naturalize upon the earth a happiness reserved for other spheres. It is the misplacement of a true idea, of our presentiment of a blessed immortality, after sin shall have been destroyed, and mercy, peace, and justice shall have free course. Abandon these vain dreams, dear child. Quit the source of these sudden and violent excitements, which are fatal even to talent. Your own has suffered from the excesses by which your mind has been carried away. It has suffered by the conflict between your intellect and your conscience. These two causes combine to render the present a time of transition for your literary powers. Your intellect is casting its skin. Do whatever appears to you hardest. In your present mood, this will be your best course; and then leave your new wings to grow and strengthen, before you essay a more noble and brilliant flight.

My dear Charles, will you not reward me by being all that my wishes and my prayers would fain have made you? I need not say whether or no you have the power to rejoice or afflict my heart; but, when you awoke in me a mother's emotions, I cannot believe that you condemned me to the sorrow of Rachel.

Dec. 11, 1833.

You might well think, my dear Charles, that your letter would trouble me; and yet it does not rob me of all hope. I can but think that the honesty and purity of your soul will rectify the sophistry of your mind, and that this chimerical compromise between a rash resistance and the submission of a pious and believing heart will yet appear to you an impossibility.

Nothing is so simple, in our weak and imperfect state, as to yield to exaggeration and error. One might say, that nothing is so catholic as error; for nothing is so universal. What really harms us is our obstinacy, our haughty and absurd attachment to our own opinion. My dear child, can it be possible? Will you sacrifice to this idol? No: you do not dream of the burden you are taking on your shoulders, of the self-torture you are preparing, of the sweet, inward joy which you embitter, and perhaps banish for a long season. Until self-renunciation, and a pious, tender, frank repentance, has expanded your heart, it can never know true peace or true comfort.

Doubtless, my dear Charles, it was looking high to take M. de Lamennais for your model: but the Christian can look higher; and, for him, the humblest path is not only the safest, but the most sublime. And how can you tell how great an influence a free, swift, and truly generous impulse, originating in the very depths of your heart, might have on M. de Lamennais? I know that your wishes and your advice have long agreed with the hopes and expectations of the friends of his fame. I do you full justice in this respect; but how much greater might your power over him have been, if you yourself had been what you ought! I believe the great man would have yielded to a pious and tender child; for it seems to me that tenderness alone can conquer M. de Lamennais, and, like Clorinda, his heart is weak, though his arm is strong. And what incalculable sorrows you might have spared him! for it is useless to deny that the displeasure and animadversion which he excites are general. The rare exceptions to this mood are furnished by pious persons, who, in their love of peace, would have liked that less publicity, and especially less precipitation, should have attended the commencement of this deplorable struggle. It is the worldly people who are most severe against him here; first, because they consult only a rigorous logic; and also, because they are not bound to M. de

Lamennais by any gratitude for the services he has rendered them. Neither must you be surprised, dear Charles, if you encounter more harshness yourself than if you had been licentious or impious. This severity is the homage rendered to the estimate which had been made of you, and the hopes you had inspired. It is also a result of the engagements which you seemed to undertake. People are judged in this world according to the stand which they take, and the responsibilities they assume. The world often regulates its demand by the praise it has bestowed; and the purer and loftier your aim is, the greater the tax which it involves. Your conduct, your sentiments, and your talents, make you a conspicuous object; and this is why, my poor, dear St. Sebastian, you are the mark for so many arrows just now. Men are demanding of you, to-day, what they are afraid they awarded you too readily and too easily; but your noble and sacred vocation was not announced and unfolded in human sight alone. This concurrence of painful circumstances, of manifold trials, which causes me to call your sorrow by the name of that multiform demon of the gospel, Legion, — has it not a voice, and does it not say to you, that God is no longer well pleased? My dear child, accept tribulation; or, rather, let us accept it, but let us cease to deserve it.

How can you ask me if I pray for you. My prayer takes on successively the forms of distress, of anxiety, and of a deep sense of weakness and of need. I can do nothing for you, if I cannot render closer and more inviolable the ties which unite you to God and his Church. I have courage to see you suffer; but I feel that I never could bear, I will not say your defection, but the indifference with which you threaten us. What a mood of mind is that of which such thoughts allow us a glimpse! Ah, my dear Charles! if religion should find herself banished from your thoughts, she would soon lose all other power over you; and your faith, not yet sufficiently tested, or sufficiently instructed to be firm, would soon perish in the new world which your intellect would create. M. Lacordaire, faithful to his original duties, has had no wish but to be a priest. Why should you, whose first inspiration ought to regulate your destiny as well, — why should you desire to be aught but a Christian and a Catholic?

Adieu, my dear Charles! may God grant you his blessed light and his precious consolations!

Contemporaneous history has already furnished us with the response of M. de Montalembert to these beautiful exhortations; but, were it otherwise, one could not read them without foreseeing their effect. The man who can inspire such language is already worthy to hear it, and capable of rising to its level.

The Abbé Lacordaire, as we could not have doubted, and as we have just learned from Mme. Swetchine, was not left to hesitate for a moment in his obedience. The difficulties to be removed were not within, but before him. The splendor of his eloquence, and the marvellous effect of his first appearance in the chapel of the College Stanislas, could not fail to awaken the complex emotions which await all success. Even among those who have an interest in talent, and to whom it should be of service, the minds that it disturbs and irritates must be counted along with those to which it gives sincere delight. And, besides these universal conditions, it is necessary, in this case, to take into account the lingering distrust excited by the earlier connection with M. de Lamennais. These different shades of religious opinion were, of course, represented in the council of the Archbishop of Paris, and were all urged with equal vehemence on M. de Quélen. This prelate naturally stood at the exact antipodes of the Abbé Lacordaire. He had been educated in a political and religious clique, with which the young orator had never come in contact. M. de Quélen had only regrets where M. Lacordaire had only hopes. One thing they had in common, — rectitude and true nobility of heart. If M. de Quélen was, by nature, somewhat prejudiced against the brilliant editor of " L'Avenir," he was incapable of cherishing an ungenerous antipathy, of resisting a pledge of sincerity, or of disowning or despising aught which might be of service to his divine Master. And, finally, that which might have escaped his own observation and loyal intentions, was supplied by his profound esteem for Mme. Swetchine, and perfect trust in her.

Mme. Swetchine knew this well; and her double attachment for MM. de Quélen and Lacordaire kept her constant to the one purpose of bringing them together. We confine ourselves to the strict truth, when we count the sermons of Nôtre Dame among the most important services which this true servant of God has done our country and our time, in the silence of her modesty.

It is, then, no matter of surprise, that the first fragment of the Abbé Lacordaire's writing, found among the papers of Mme. Swetchine, should be addressed to M. de Quélen and herself jointly. It is as follows:—

PARIS, Dec. 13, 1833.

MADAME,—I have the honor to send you a copy of my new declaration, since you are so good as to desire it. At the moment of the termination of this serious affair, I feel deeply the need of thanking you for the good and affectionate advice you have given me, though I had not the slightest claim thereto. I shall remember it as long as I live. A portion of my career is now completed; and I enter upon a new situation, where, doubtless, I shall encounter external agitations and varying fortunes; for such is our lot. But I have gained by this experience a wider knowledge of my duty, and a peace which must be lasting; for it is the peace of God. You appeared to me, between two distinct parts of my life, as the angel of the Lord may appear to a soul wavering between life and death, earth and heaven. But, once in heaven, we shall go no more out.

I am, madam, respectfully, your most humble and obedient servant,　　　　　　　　　　　　　　H. LACORDAIRE.

This letter was accompanied by the copy of one addressed to the Archbishop of Paris.

After the Stanislas sermons, some months of suspense shadowed the destiny of the orator. He could not be left in a chapel which had become too small for him; but it was still considered imprudent to open to him a wider career. During the autumn of 1834, M. Lacordaire was walking alone, sad and submissive, in one of the alleys of the Luxembourg, when he was accosted by an ecclesiastic whom he had never seen before. "Why do you live in such idleness?" demanded this unexpected interlocutor. "Why do you not go and see M. de Quélen?" The Abbé Lacordaire responded only by a smile, and continued his solitary walk. But, after a few moments' reflection, he was induced to ask himself the same question, and directed his steps towards the Convent of St. Michel, where, since the sack of the Archbishop's palace, M. de Quélen had occupied a humble cell. He was introduced without difficulty, and found the Archbishop alone. His morning had been spent in reading a memoir of the Abbé Liautard, Curé of Fontainebleau. This memoir had circulated in the diocese of Paris, and contained some severe reflections on the episcopal administration. After some trite conversational preliminaries, there ensued a silence of a few moments, during which M. de Quélen formed a sudden resolution; and, bending on the young friend of Mme. Swetchine a tender, grave, and penetrating gaze, "I give you," said he, "the pulpit of Nôtre Dame; and you will preach your first sermon in six weeks." M. Lacordaire recoiled with a spontaneous movement of alarm. The Archbishop urged him in vain; and the consent of the eloquent apostle, who felt his power, but shrank from its responsibilities, was only obtained after two days of prayer and meditation.

His first discourse at Nôtre Dame at once assured the fame of the Abbé Lacordaire, and renewed the hostility against him. His pride was stirred, and his modesty alarmed, at the same time. After two consecutive *stations*, in the winters of 1835 and 1836, he renounced the most magnificent audience gathered within the memory of the

present generation, and formed the sudden resolution of
seeking once more the glorious solitude and the grand
teachings of the Eternal City.

The friendship of Mme. Swetchine did not fail him in
this time of trial. The first letter of a long correspondence
reached the Abbé Lacordaire in a little town in Burgundy,
whither he had gone to strengthen and bless the last
moments of a beloved brother.

The second letter is directed to Rome. M. de Lamennais had already published the " Paroles d'un Croyant,"
and was at that time preparing a volume entitled " Les
Affaires de Rome."

TO THE ABBÉ LACORDAIRE.

A Rome, via San Nicolo, presso al Gesu.

PARIS, Oct. 31, 1836.

MY DEAR FRIEND, — . . . I have not alluded to the last
threat of M. de Lamennais, because I hoped all the while we
should escape. It has not been so. Nothing can check him.
The publication of his book is at hand; but, saving his genius,
what can he say that has not been already said? and is not evil
from his lips self-limited? Perhaps I am wrong; but I still
hope, in the midst of my sorrow, that this tempest will pass
over our heads without inflicting any serious damage. M. de
Lamennais does especial harm to the wavering and the weak.
He has beguiled none, but more than once he has broken the
bruised reed and quenched the smoking flax. I have just had
a long interview with M. ———, whose book falls far short of
our expectations. The void left by M. de Lamennais in the
circle of superior and pious minds, has deprived him of his support. To think of having one's faith and one's ideas of God
dependent on those of any man! It is idolatry, without its excuse. My dear friend, may you turn to the best possible
account this useful time and precious solitude! There are better days in store for you yet; but, for all that, I am sure you
will look back longingly upon these. Your studies appear to
me excellent. Are there no books which would facilitate your
pursuits? Tell me what you want, — what you want this very
day, without troubling yourself to consider whether you will
want it to-morrow. I like well to be your man of business: it

does not exclude other relations, and a true affection combines many characters in one. It is multiplicity in unity, as my Germans say.

After the appearance of the volume in which M. de Lamennais attempted to gratify his resentment against Rome, the Abbé Lacordaire, who was repeatedly named in that work, felt called upon to refute it. This he did, not by direct polemic, but by a voluntary apology for the Holy See, under whose shelter he then was. In this second volume, and in the "Paroles d'un Croyant," M. de Lamennais made his earliest direct appeal, not merely to liberal ideas, but to those passions and transports which it is the aim of the demagogue to excite. It was at the very epoch when the bleeding wounds of Poland were directing general indignation and entreaty towards the Emperor Nicholas, and when the Archbishop of Cologne was defending the freedom of the Church at the expense of his own personal liberty. The Abbé Lacordaire had thrown his apology into the form of an epistle, with the title of "Lettre sur le Saint Siége." In the preface we read,—

"One of the gravest errors now propagated concerning the Holy See is, that it is in alliance with absolute government, and that it looks with a hostile eye upon all those nations whose institutions attempt to restore the ancient liberties of Catholic Europe. Rome is thus made a partisan,—she who is the mother of all the nations, and who respects all the various forms of government which they have imposed upon themselves, or which may have been created for them by the force of time and circumstance; and this false accusation necessarily renders her obnoxious to a hatred unmerited by the universal impartiality whose tradition she so faithfully preserves. One needs but to live at Rome, with a watchful and unprejudiced mind, to perceive how lofty is the sphere which the Church inhabits, and how far below her feet those earth-born clouds are passing which trouble and divide the individual churches elsewhere."

Before publishing this development of his ideas, the Abbé Lacordaire imparted his design to his friend, and begged her to ask the opinion of M. de Quélen on the subject. Although this tract, devoted exclusively to the defence of the Holy See, was, of all the writings of M. Lacordaire, the one which should have appealed most surely to the sympathies of M. de Quélen, the thought which filled the Abbé's soul, and constantly inspired his speech and his pen, was the reconciliation of Christian authority with freedom; and hence, questions of expediency, propriety, and shades of meaning, kept arising at every page. Mme. Swetchine replied to the Abbé in a first letter, which has not been preserved; and in the ensuing one we read: —

PARIS, Nov. 26, 1836.

. . . If nothing is yet decided, I beg you to wait for the first courier, thus leaving me time in the interval to consult the Archbishop, to whom I shall communicate a portion of your letter to the internuncio, whose opinion I shall also be glad to have.[1] If any greater inconvenience be involved in the initiatory step, which you in your self-devotion are disposed to take, they are most favorably situated for discovering it. When things are once decided, you will go to work in good earnest; and there is no reason to fear that you are too late. Besides, the storm raised by this deplorable volume has not produced any very great or general unsettling of men's minds. Those who have suffered from it might, of course, have been ruined in a great many other ways; and the antecedents of M. de Lamennais, his present attitude, and the astonishing facility with which he maintains successively, and in the most dogmatic and resolute manner, two or three absolutely incompatible assertions, — these things are in themselves a powerful antidote to his book. The first part of it shows us the man whom we had seen before, and who, however censurable his unjust bitterness may have been, reminded one of Dante, in the respect for *things* which mingled with his unjust calumnies against men. So far, M. de Lamen-

---

[1] Mgr. Lambruschini had been promoted to the cardinalship, and his place filled by a simple internuncio, Mgr. Garibaldi, — a man of loyal, mild, and conciliatory spirit. M. Garibaldi afterwards returned to Paris in the quality of nuncio, and there died in the exercise of his high functions, leaving lasting regrets behind him.

nais preserves his identity with the man whom we knew; but the pages which precede and follow the epilogue show him in an extremely disagreeable light; and, if I dared, I should confess that I see in them the hypocrisy which is born of spite. None but an angel or a priest can fall so low. The so-called justificatory parts, on which he relies for the defence of his own course, I found only accusatory. All these encyclical letters are but exponents of the order, the duties, and the virtues which uncreated Wisdom brought down to earth. Nowhere do they express any approbation of tyranny. In them a father reminds his children that it belongs to God to remove the ills that weigh upon them, and that heaven is well worth all the patience and submission exercised upon earth. They give us a sense at once of sorrow and restraint.

Jan. 19, 1837.

. . . I am more than ever convinced that they cannot resist you, if prudence and honesty preside over your determinations. In this case, as in many others, I have seen, my dear friend, that you need but to pause, and that a very few hours suffice to separate impetuous fancies from the calmest and wisest resolve. We never need tremble, except for the *interval*; and, thus far, you have deserved God's unfailing interposition there. I come, then, to your letter, in which, under certain very just and proper restrictions, you placed your manuscript at the Archbishop's disposal. That, of itself, was sufficient precaution and guaranty.

To begin at the beginning, my very dear friend, things have happened on this wise: On the arrival of your manuscript, I read it with delight, fancying that I heard you speak, and yet with trembling and that sort of internal perturbation which makes one reserve one's judgment even when inspired with confidence, which, in this case, I was not. I found in your work admirable fragments, extraordinary beauty, and a charm which is all your own. The point of view which you adopted is mine also. My complete separation from the world renders me really accessible only to the interests of the Church, whither my life has fled for refuge. I think that we owe her all, and that she owes us only eternal bliss.

The policy you unfolded seemed to me that of the common Father of the faithful, as well of all sects as of all nations; and, generally speaking, my assent to a multitude of charming passages was as complete as my admiration of them was lively. But this just and very sincere homage does not prevent me, my dear friend, from perceiving that some parts of your work need revision. Several of the ideas advanced appeared to me

hazardous, and wanting in that rigorous precision, that absolute
soundness, which one always expects of the priesthood.   They
were but slight blemishes, easily removed; and, if you had been
here, you would have perceived them, and at once perfected
your work.   I then determined to consult M. Affre,[1] of all your
advisers the most faithful and devoted to you.   I talked with
him unreservedly about your present position and future prospects, and found him equally interested in both.   M. Affre
took the manuscript with him; and I begged him, after he had
read it, to hand it to the Archbishop, at the same time requesting an audience with Monseigneur the next day.   He unfolded
the objections to the publication of the essay which suggested
themselves to him, — objections which will be stated in full, and
addressed directly to you.   He seemed especially struck with
the fact that there was no real need of your entering the lists;
the moment being unseasonable, and even inconvenient, for renewing the struggle with the malevolence of vulnerable imper-
fections, and exciting fresh clamors, perhaps, while you ran
the risk of compromising what is now secure, — your present
peace, future usefulness, &c.   I replied, that, notwithstanding
the high importance which the approval of Rome would make
you attach to the publication of this effort, your submissiveness
would renounce it without a struggle; that it was very evident,
that, if you had wished to follow your own judgment only, you
would have addressed the manuscript to your publisher, instead
of submitting it through your friends to competent authority.
I said to him, in short, what your own letter has said very much
better, and in a manner calculated to satisfy him fully.   Finally,
I ascertained from M. Affre, that the limits you set to your
compliance had not offended him in the least; that he was
greatly pleased with the sentiments you expressed, and touched
to encounter them under any circumstances.   I have reason to
believe that the Archbishop has given your essay all possible
attention, examining it in the most serious and careful spirit.
He has had it read to him more than once; has taken notes,
and drawn up a reply.   I know that he has read it to M. Affre;
and, when the council met the next Monday, he communicated
it to the assembled members.

   I have had occasion, at this time, to remark M. Affre's devoted adherence to you.   He is most affectionate and tender,

---

[1] M. Affre was at that time grand-vicar of M. de Quélen. It is pleasant to recognize here the same spirit of self-devotion which was to
increase with each new dignity conferred upon M. Affre, till it rose to the
sublime heights of evangelical heroism.

and avails himself of every opportunity to place in a favorable light your rights, and the chances which may favor them. His kindly interest encounters an analogous disposition on the part of the Archbishop, whose silence is very easily interpreted, although he does not say much directly.

The deliberations of Mgr. de Quélen and his council resulted in an adjournment; and there was some reason to fear that the "Lettre sur le Saint Siége" would be entirely suppressed. Mme. Swetchine accompanied the announcement of this sentence by the following letter: —

Jan. 21, 1837.

. . . Time and grace move quicker for you than for other men; and sincere and disinterested affection is always sure to be heard. Last evening, before making the final sacrifice, I reread your manuscript once more; at least, a part of it. The beauties which had struck me each time appeared more remarkable than ever; and I see these pages of your writing going down in book-form to posterity. What a magnificent application you make of the grief of Priam![1]

Nothing could be more happy. And that "heart of man which, incapable of change, makes its deep sorrow eternal in this world"! And that admirable picture of the spiritual power, its conditions and effects! A hundred other ideas and illustrations appeared to me equally new and ingenious. I recur to them constantly with that internal recognition which appropriates all that is revealed to it. My intention, my dearest friend, and, I may add, my consolation, was to retain the manuscript, for it is something to be able to keep watch over one's treasure; but, having been assured that the Archbishop preferred to have it returned, and his right appearing to me the more indefeasible in that you had submitted the fate of the

---

[1] Speaking of a brief address by Pope Gregory XVI. to the Polish bishops, M. Lacordaire says: "Even supposing (which I do not believe), that, in the hope of appeasing a prince who was irritated against a portion of his flock, the pastor expressed himself too strongly, I shall never feel that Priam did any thing unworthy the majesty of a king and the feelings of a father, when he took the hand of Achilles, and uttered these sublime words: 'Judge of the depth of my misery, when I kiss the hand that has slain my son.'" — *Lettre sur le Saint Siége*, p. 527, 8vo. edit.

paper to him, I entered like you, and with you, upon the path of sacrifice, and sent it to him this morning. M. Affre has shown himself very much your friend on this occasion,—a friend who esteems, admires, and loves you. Though he shares certain judgments, and makes certain concessions, and believes some change to be desirable, I see that he is convinced that just now the paper could not fail to have an excellent effect upon a considerable portion of the youthful public, which is eager for your words. Doubtless one of the two camps has been ravaged: but the point is to present an unbroken front to the enemy; and it is needful, not to exorcise, — that is impossible, — but to check and allow no foothold to the malevolence which is ever on the watch.

M. X—— begged me to tell you that a new attack would be made upon you in a fortnight or three weeks. He insisted, and I obey; but it is with great repugnance that I give you this warning. Only God and conscience should come between a man and his idea; and this idea he must develop, and perfect as far as may be, out of a pure love of truth, and with no regard to the attacks of malice, which is always prolific. My poor, dear, amiable friend, how can you excite such a sentiment in the heart, I will not say of any Christian, but of any man? Contradiction has been foretold, and the prophecy is peculiarly applicable at the height at which you stand. Your letter, threatening a long absence, is of course much in my thoughts. You tell me to think and pray over it. I do nothing else; still I am not at all infected by your convictions. I grant that solitude may be good, useful, perhaps necessary, for you, — a solitude which should bring peace, freedom, and self-possession in its train; but I do not approve of isolation, which would take away your supports as well as your barriers, cause you to lose the precious habit of contact with your fellow-men (precious for those who are to live with and for them), and leave your imagination unchecked by the warnings of friendly sympathy, as well as those of severe reason. In all places, and under all circumstances, the divine word, "It is not good for man to be alone," is applicable. You know, in your noble humility, that you can learn much from others; but when you shall have become, once for all, a master yourself, by the addition of age and experience to your rare gifts, even then, my dear friend, it will not be well for you to live apart. Whatever you do, you need disciples under your immediate influence, intrusted to your care by the highest authority, or else to be one of a family of brethren with a common father at their head. My ardent desire for your perfection has assumed no definite shape. Do what you will, only serve God! The world, solitude, preaching, writing, church dignities, or utter renunciation,—all these things appear to me to suit you, and offer you rare chances for usefulness; every thing, in fact, except that retreat, where, though you would be isolated from all others, I should apprehend the greatest danger from the impossibility of your escaping yourself.

Jan. 24, 1837.

. . . I see, my dear child, that you do not yet know me as I am. You may grieve and disquiet me by the precipitation, and possibly the thoughtlessness, of your first movements; but I shall not enfeoff you to anybody. Mistakes, and even faults, would not alienate me from you. The nearer we come to God, the less confidence we feel in the wisdom and utility of our own personal views, while we come to have more and more respect for the very will which we had sought to influence for the good of the individual. I cannot doubt that your soul, so impetuous, so lofty, so pure, so mobile, so simple, so beautiful, is the object of divine love. Providence may subject you to severe trials, but can never abandon you,—never. It would have made me happy always to approve your course, but that is not necessary to my affection; and perhaps the strong shocks to which you subject it, renew with increased intensity my first adoption. And you could think that the ascendency which you allowed me to exercise over you, enhanced for me the pleasure of our connection! My dear friend, nothing could be farther from the truth. If I have sometimes accepted the fact of that influence, it has been without confidence in myself, and only to prevent the ascendency of another. I acted as your ballast, or rather I held you by the skirts of your garment, to slacken your too swift and impetuous movements. Perhaps these are the very attributes with which you would have done well to invest some one at Rome,—some one who might have united the two conditions which I fulfilled so perfectly: first, that of *not being you*, either in natural disposition, antecedents, or age; and second, and more essential, that of loving you better than you could possibly love yourself.

To complete this picture of truly Christian thought and manners, we need the figure of Father de Ravignan. During the interval before the young exile, who soon became a novice in the Convent *de la Minerve*, responded to the wishes of Mme. Swetchine, by the " History of Saint

Dominic," the "Restoration of the Dominicans in France,"
and the renewal of his preaching with ever-increasing
brilliancy and effect, Mgr. de Quélen had been unwilling
to leave vacant the pulpit of Nôtre Dame; and Father de
Ravignan had carried on the work there commenced in a
different manner, but with equal success. This pious and
fervent apostle had also felt the need of intimate communion with Mme. Swetchine, and had obtained an introduction to her through their common friend, Father Rosaven.
Mme. Swetchine hastened to welcome him. The affection
which she felt for Father Lacordaire would have been an
additional reason for her eagerness, even if every impulse
of sympathy and veneration had not tended that way.
Father de Ravignan, on his part, highly valued a hearer
like Mme. Swetchine, and wrote to her as follows:—

Saturday, 11.

MADAME, — I send you a little card, with your name and
mine. Will you be so kind as to take it with you, and show it
when you come to the places reserved for my family, at the right
of the church-warden's pew, facing the pulpit?

Our good Eleuthère [1] says that you are very much afraid of
me. Can it be possible? I would so gladly have you for my
guide and teacher, to check and chide and pray for me!

X. DE RAVIGNAN.

We find the name of Father Lacordaire affectionately
and respectfully mentioned by Father de Ravignan in
several of the billets which Mme. Swetchine has preserved.
In one we read:—

"Father Lacordaire's opinion is precious to me. I believe,
with him, that good will result from this crisis; but will it be
only good?"

---

1 The Abbé Eleuthère de Girardin, grandson of the Marquis de Girardin, of Ermenonville.

And in another: —

"Father Lacordaire has replied by a very friendly letter. You know that I sincerely value his friendship and confidence. I wish I might deserve them."

At about the same date, Mme. Swetchine wrote the following words in one of her own note-books. They revive at one stroke the face, so austere and yet so sweet, of the illustrious *religieux:* —

"'M. Lainé was the orator of the eyes. He moved and convinced by his very silence.' This remark of M. de Lamartine about M. Lainé applies equally to Father Ravignan."

Finally she wrote to M. Lacordaire, —

April 18, 1837.

You will find people here as kindly and affectionately disposed towards you as ever. The Archbishop has always loved you; and the slightest advance on your part will call forth undeniable proofs of his affection. Allow for the passage of time, and leave for God's handwriting that page with its obliterated record, — a true palimpsest, where one may restore at will either one of two texts. I heard Father de Ravignan the last time he spoke, and admired him very much. His discourse struck me as carefully and finely arranged; and the very grandeur of the ideas he reviewed, made his language seem new and rich. His emotion was spontaneous and genuine, and he took his stand on the high ground of authority. One is conscious, indeed, of a slight affectation of manner, and man is never master where he imitates; but still it is a kind of homage rendered you, and a very touching proof, in my opinion, of that love and zeal for the truth, which induces him to try, in the hope of insuring an all-important success, all possible expedients, even those which contradict his nature, and are least flattering to his self-love. A Christian orator is truly a gift of God; but, when Father de Ravignan assumes this beautiful office, does he deprive another of it? Is there not room for two? and, notwithstanding all the suffrages he obtains, are there not many needs unsatisfied, many expectations which, thus far, have been disappointed? One of the most grievous things in this world is the narrowness of absolute praise or blame. "The envious poverty of an exclusive love" is universally applicable; and M. Sainte Beuve spoke the truth even as regards preachers.

CHAPTER XIV.

Death of the Countess de Ségur d'Aguesseau. — Death of Prince Gargarin. — Letter of Mme. Swetchine on the occasion of a severe order of
the Emperor Nicholas. — Mme. Swetchine's last visit to Russia. —
Consecration of her chapel. — Her piety. — Her charity.

" AFTER grace, that which gives most efficacy to pious
words is the holiness of him who utters them."
This idea of Mme. Swetchine's is applicable to herself,
like many more of hers, in which assuredly no thought of
self mingled. We have just seen what language she held
with her friends. The most trifling acts of her life appealed to them no less eloquently; and it is important to
establish this, that the twofold blessing of her teaching and
her example may survive her, and perpetuate that marvellous harmony of goodness, which, when once seen, can
never more be denied or declared unattainable. Mme.
Swetchine lived simultaneously, and with as much simplicity as energy, the most fervent spiritual life and the
most active worldly one ; and worldly people should learn
from her example how much more compatible than they
suppose are the duties of their existence with those of
fervent piety ; while those who are naturally inclined to
consider the life of faith as a mere barren contemplation,
may see how it is possible to reconcile the most perfect
domestic devotion with all the cares of friendship and all
intellectual activity.

A wound, all the more cruel that she would fain have
concealed it, was inflicted upon Mme. Swetchine in the

course of the year 1834. Either as a result of obstinate, and as yet ungratified, malice against General Swetchine, or out of jealousy of the favor which allowed him and his wife to reside in France when the Emperor Nicholas had forbidden Paris to his subjects, Mme. Swetchine was rudely surprised, not merely by the recall of her husband, but by a severe sentence of exile, which confined General Swetchine to any obscure part of Russia he might select, provided it was at a distance from St. Petersburg or Moscow. The order assumed the form of a sentence, and was based upon certain intangible grievances, borrowed, after a lapse of more than thirty years, from his administration under the Emperor Paul. It was in the depth of winter.

Mme. Swetchine did not, for an instant, dream of evading the decree. She had always resisted the advice of friends, who urged her to realize her fortune, and transport it to France beyond the reach of any arbitrary measure. "I shall never consent to this," she would say: "I wish to leave my heritage intact to my sister and her children; but, if there was not one of them left in the world, I could not break the last tie which binds me to my country, — forsake the peasants whom God has confided to my care, and strengthen in the Emperor's mind the fatal prejudice which makes him suppose, that, in becoming a Catholic, one ceases to be a Russian." This sentiment was put to a cruel test. It dictated these words: —

TO MME. . . .

PARIS, Jan. 12.

I feel, my good and dear friend, that you need to be comforted for our misfortunes. Re-assure yourself, I can no longer be unhappy, in the common acceptation of the word, with all this *cortège* of torments, private irritations, and consuming regrets, which the heart's revolt drags in its train. If I could say as much for my poor husband, I should be wretched indeed, but calm, and in a measure comforted. But his suppressed grief, so often betrayed by his sad and heart-rending expression of countenance; the convulsive tears which the suddenness, the difficulties, and the dangers of a long and painful pilgrimage to an unknown goal sometimes wring from him, — actually drive me to despair. I had great difficulty in making myself understood, when I told him the fatal tidings. He persisted in believing there was some mistake. It was not until I assured him that the order was issued two months ago, and that your friendship concealed it with a delusive hope, — not until then, did the truth come home to him. There was one hour, in particular, during the first day, one hour when he was away, that I was a prey to terrors more agonizing than any other earthly torture. Ordinarily, his gentle, amiable nature prevails. He is perfectly patient, only absent-minded, absorbed: you can see that his thought is fixed like his suffering. He had a momentary desire to combat my unalterable determination to follow him everywhere; but then he accepted it, and I may be permitted to say he owed so much to my character and my unfailing devotion to him. I know that both our lives are at stake, and that, at best, this step can hardly fail to shorten our remaining days; but that is no reason why we should not obey implicitly, and perhaps it is not a sufficient reason for great urgency, or the renewal of more earnest petitions. In the age in which we live, the course we are to pursue must be traced by principle; and it must be steady, sure, and invariable. It is by profoundly enjoying all the favors which a good God has bestowed upon me here that I have learned how to relinquish them. I feel that I am prepared for the sacrifice. I have no doubt or uneasiness about the power of Providence to make good to me the blessings he withdraws, or to restore whatever is needful. We are under his eye everywhere, and there is no exile for those who love and trust him.

Thus far, the thing has not been noised abroad, and I earnestly desire that this should be deferred as long as possible. I do not wish, and I never will allow, the interest which may be expressed for me to take the form of those complaints in which surprise at so great severity and indirect blame play almost as large a part as compassion. I will not forget in my wretchedness that I am a Russian, in the midst of France. God knows if I have ever forgotten it, or if a murmur, or a complaint, or even a criticism, of my sovereign has escaped me. I can lift up my head, and say this with a clear conscience. Under present circumstances, I am more than ever desirous that no word or deed of mine should belie my real feelings. In the spirit of my religion I find a double motive for obedience. My submission has no element of servility; it is free, like all that springs from the conscience; it is not even a yoke of necessity; and I say it, dear friend, without presumption, without boasting, and without ill-humor, I would neglect no means which might obtain of the Emperor the favor of remaining here. But, whatever he commands, he shall find in us submissive subjects, faithful, and full of reverence for a will wherein they read the will of Heaven. The letter which my husband has written to the Emperor only ventures to implore a delay until spring. If we do not obtain this, we shall start immediately. The eloquence of this letter consists in the statement of my husband's utter want of fortune, in the mention of his seventy-six years, in the strict truth of what he says about my own greatly disordered and enfeebled health, and in our unalterable resolution to obey.

The order forbidding my husband the two capitals is a strange exception to the identity of the punishment inflicted (I believe) upon him and upon the abettors of the odious conspiracy of 1825; though my husband was animated by sentiments very unlike theirs, and apparently known to be so, since the famous Count ——, in a moment of frankness, went so far as to say that he did not oppose his disgrace with Paul I., for the sole reason that his presence would have thwarted them in the noble end they were pursuing. This is one of those avowals which are balm to the wounds of an honorable man, and whose memory is ennobling in the midst of humiliation. I am sure you will recognize in this letter the accent of truth, unless, indeed, I have neglected some of the little formalities which escape people who have been long away from court.

Mme. Swetchine here enters into some retrospective details without interest for the reader, and then adds, —

Our furniture, my pictures and books, none of these things can be transported eight hundred leagues by people who are travelling at random (so to speak), and feel too old, too sad, and too discouraged, to think of an establishment. After the execution of this sentence, we can no longer hope to do more than live from day to day, and pitch our tent until such time as it shall be folded into a shroud. We may be very destitute, but I feel sure that we shall not want for any thing. When one is unhappy, one needs so little! Adieu, my very dear friend! If your anxiety for me is constant, my prayers for you, while I live, shall also be unceasing. Each one pays his debts as best he can.

The friends of Mme. Swetchine at St. Petersburg did not rest satisfied with their first steps. Using the argument of her beautiful resignation, they obtained, in the first place, a reprieve, of which Mme. Swetchine resolved to avail herself to quit France, cross Europe alone, and go and plead her cause in person with the Emperor himself.

She set out on the 13th of August, 1834, and arrived at St. Petersburg on the 19th of September. Not until the 16th of November was the end of her courageous efforts attained. Her health, which was terribly shaken, did not permit her to leave Russia till the month of February; and she suffered cruelly in her journey across the North in the midst of the most trying weather. She re-entered Paris at six o'clock on the morning of the 4th of March, the first day of Lent, in 1835; ordered her little *calèche* to stop at the door of the Chapel of Saint Vincent de Paul, Rue Montholon, rendered thanks to God, and received the ashes there; and at last regained her beloved asylum in the Rue St. Dominique, to sink down exhausted under an attack of acute disease, which held her for three months suspended between life and death. She had almost a year of inexpressible anguish; but those who approached her saw no ruffling of her serenity, no change in her temper or her mind. To the world at large, she seemed to have undertaken a needless journey; and she let them accuse her in peace of having chosen a romantic method of soliciting a favor which the slightest word would have been sufficient to obtain.

The year 1836 was marked for Mme. Swetchine by two heavy strokes, which fell upon her in rapid succession, — the death of her adopted daughter, the Countess of Ségur d'Aguesseau, and the death of her brother-in-law, Prince Gargarin.

Threatened from her childhood with a cruel malady, Mme. de Ségur had resisted it by dint of courage and the most tender care, only to be cut off in the flower of her youth, after giving birth to two children. In the little southern town of Cahors, General Swetchine, who was hastening to join the Countess de Ségur at the waters of the Pyrenees, was met by the tidings of the irreparable misfortune. Mme. Swetchine made haste to quit Vichy without completing the annual cure which had become, as it were, necessary to her existence. She consecrated herself, as was her custom, to the sorrows by which she was surrounded, without further thought of her personal sufferings.

" We encounter in lingering maladies," she wrote to the Countess Edling, " the very thing which constitutes the poignancy of sudden death : we are taken unprepared. We reckon on time, for the very reason that it has lasted so long ; and getting used to a condition is almost equivalent to being ignorant of it. I shall finish the autumn at Tours with my husband. My constant thought is to soften the sorrow of his grievously tried old age. I see that he grows fonder of my care, and his goodness and perfect sweetness are a part of his great courage."

Prince Gargarin died in the winter of 1837. He had exchanged, in 1834, the embassy of Rome for that of Munich ; but the change of climate soon impaired his health, and he died in the arms of the Princess Gargarin, surrounded by their five sons, the eldest of whom was attached to his father's embassy, and just entering upon his diplomatic career.

" My sister," wrote Mme. Swetchine, " whom a secret presentiment forbade me to detain, and whom I saw depart when the roads were in a fearful condition, arrived only to be mortally shocked by the ravages disease had already made ; and, six weeks later, poor Gargarin, still so full of spirit and of will,

ceased to live. This affliction opens before my sister a great
gulf of perplexities and sorrows. The Emperor has been very
good to her; and her return to Russia, where she is to take her
children, is all arranged, and will soon take place. Various
residences are proposed to her, — Karkof, Moscow, Odessa.
The latter arrangement would take her near you, and that
would be its good side ; but I have objections to it. The point
is to naturalize the children who were born abroad, and I do
not think Odessa sufficiently Russian for the purpose. Moscow
would afford her, at least as far as country and family are concerned, the shelter and protection which were withdrawn with
her husband."

The residence at Moscow was finally chosen by the
Princess Gargarin; and we must henceforth count, among
the sorrows of Mme. Swetchine, the separation of the two
sisters, aggravated by so great a distance and such heavy
responsibilities.

All these trials turned the soul of Mme. Swetchine more
and more toward God. The religious part of her life
assumed a regularity and austerity, which the greater
part, even of those who saw her constantly, never suspected.

She had obtained from the Archbishop of Paris permission to erect a chapel in her house; and, when she
returned from her trying Russian journey, she desired to
decorate this sanctuary in a manner more in keeping with
her sense of gratitude. She therefore consecrated a multitude of precious stones from the mines in Russia. The
cipher of diamonds which she had worn as maid of honor
to the Empress Mary adorned the pedestal of a silver
statue of the Holy Virgin.

These arrangements necessitated a second consecration.
Mgr. de Quélen, who had already blessed the chapel once,
and himself administered the holy-sacrament there, was
quite willing to consecrate for the second time these walls
and this tabernacle, the objects of so pious a worship. He

said mass there for the first time on the 15th of December, 1835, assisted by the Abbé Lacordaire, who was just beginning his sermons at Nôtre Dame.

Notwithstanding this privilege and these indulgences, Mme. Swetchine continued an exemplary parishioner of St. Thomas Aquinas. It was a rare thing for her not to go to early mass. She allowed herself mass in her own chapel, besides, on the days and hours which suited the friends with whom she celebrated their sad or happy anniversaries. Often, too, were gathered there as many as the small space would hold to listen to an appeal in behalf of some good work or new foundation. At the time of the revival at Solesme, and the establishment of the Benedictines, for whom Mme. Swetchine manifested as much solicitude as generosity, Dom Guéranger was heard there repeatedly, as well as Father Lacordaire and Father Ravignan. The Abbé Dupanloup, the Abbé Bautain, the Abbé de La Bouillerie, and Father Gratry considered it an honor to perform service and preach in her chapel. Men who had received in her presence the first inspiration of grace and truth, such as Father Schouvalof and Father Gargarin, testified their gratitude by their partiality for her chapel. Young girls who had grown up under her eyes desired to place under her auspices the celebration of their marriage; and last, but not least, new converts, and those who were returning to Catholicism, but who still dreaded the light of open day, came to this little chapel, which to all the wealth of modern art added almost the mystery of the catacombs, to beg for consecration and secrecy.

None of her sorrows or of her Christian joys found any echo in the salon of Mme. Swetchine, who dreaded above all things any appearance of vanity or ostentation about

her pious practices. Sometimes, in the midst of an animated conversation, an interlocutor rose in silence, and
exchanged an imperceptible sign with Mme. Swetchine,
who drew from her pocket a key, and handed it to her
without pausing. It was the key of the chapel, where
some old friend or some new acquaintance, whose nature
had been revealed to her by a great grief or a great sacrifice, desired to retire for prayer and meditation.

Whenever Mme. Swetchine herself had a moment's rest
and freedom, this was her refuge; and traces are found, here
and there among her remains, of the joys she tasted
there.

MEDITATION.

The concentration of thought upon self, that other tabernacle
of God, implies the weakening of all external influences, if
not entire deliverance from them. The movements of those
who are not weighted by human attachments and servitudes
are all prompt and rapid: our prayers bear the stamp of that
moral freedom which renders us more supple and agile to fly
whither God calls us.

Meditation is at once the greatest aid to faithfulness and its
greatest joy, constantly renewing the cause of it; and through
meditation faithfulness takes possession of its treasure. Meditation is the concentration of all our thoughts and all our
powers on one point. It renders all verities present at once,
and all their consequences plain. Meditate, says the Master
to the Christian disciple, and evil will seem less possible, and
good more easy.

Spiritual drought, when it is not the saint's most fearful trial,
is almost always the result of abandoning mind and soul to
a sort of heedlessness and dulness. The will which is wide-
spread, but not deep, cannot defend itself from attack; but
meditation re-unites all that levity disperses. The microscope
gives us a world, a universe, in a single drop of dew. So also
there is a world in a single instant of simple, profound, earnest
meditation.

PRAYER.

Prayer is the infinite! A single heart that lifts itself to
thee, O Lord! comprehends all hearts. Prayer is eternity, for
it embraces all time; immensity, for it comprehends all space.

All which is, O my God! and all which has been, all men of all climes and ages, their present and future state, their happiness, their love, their virtue, — all this infinity of hearts and souls is reflected in the humble, fervent prayer, as the celestial vault is reflected in the unconscious wave of the tiniest stream.

TO JESUS, GOD AND MAN.

Blessed Jesus! God and man at once! oh, may these two natures of thine, united and yet distinct, render us doubly the objects of thy pity! As God, forget our offences; as man, remember our woes. As God, attract and lift us to thyself unceasingly; as man, retrace with us the rough paths of thy exile, and be the companion of our good and our evil days. O Jesus! pardon as a master, and compassionate as a friend!

There can be no progress in the Christian life without constant self-examination. Doubtless it may enervate and mislead some weak and ill-regulated minds; but there is no simple and upright soul that it will not purify and strengthen. Mme. Swetchine was as remarkable for the delicacy of her scruples, as for the energy of her faith. Searchings of heart occupied as large a space with her as transports of prayer; and so greatly did she dread to see this habitual labor becoming transient and fruitless, that she fixed it in writing, as she did every thing that engaged her serious attention. Here are some fragments which chanced to escape destruction: —

"I said, in writing of some letters that I was quoting, 'a letter which I have this moment received;' whereas I received it two or three days ago. Inaccuracy is never excusable; and this arose from the fact that it seemed to render my quotation more natural. To bend truth to one's caprices or one's necessities is a fault, however limited its range.

"Two painful and seemingly accidental circumstances have led me to new discoveries and reflections about myself. The lamp in my chapel, before the holy sacrament, went out on the Saturday night before Palm Sunday; and that same Palm Sunday I forgot to exchange my Prayer-book for that of the Passion and Easter service, and so, when I went to church, I could not follow the office.

"Now, first for the lamp. If I am ardent and vigilant about any thing in this world, it is the holy sacrament. I have suffered incalculably from apprehension, anxiety, and terror, lest I should offend the majesty of my beloved Guest, the God of love. How many times my feeble heart has well-nigh burst with throbs of love and awe! But here, as ever, it was the victim of its own improvidence. My sentiments are those of a loving heart; my actions, those of an unthinking mind. Thus, I have replenished my lamp a hundred times when it needed it less than then, and on that day the idea that it might go out crossed my mind; but I was in that mood when we are disposed to accuse ourselves of exaggeration. I told myself, what any one would have told me, that the lamp would last over night; and, when I found it extinguished, my heart was wrung with a sorrow not free from remorse. My fault in all this is the vagueness, and oftentimes the sluggishness, of the workings of my mind. There is more here than the mere incident. I have indulged myself too much in a kind of lulling of heart and will very unfavorable to the completion of an action, and its accomplishment while it can be of use. I act thus where I love best. Hinderances and sufferings have helped to form the habit. But it is more than ever necessary that soul should rule my being; and, since the internal strife is over, all my moral force must be concentrated upon prompt obedience.

"The incident of the forgotten book is also a test and a trifling punishment. If I had said on Saturday evening the office for the eve of Palm Sunday, I must needs have had the book; and if, in the morning, my mind had been dwelling upon the special significance of the day, I should have been reminded of my neglect. Ah, how few are innocent! If I studied more carefully in all their consequences the things which I regard as important, I should reap better fruit."

The following fragment, jotted down, like the others, without any date or mark whatever, at the end of a list of commissions, refers undoubtedly to the announcement of the sentence which caused her departure for Russia: —

"On that terrible day, before the hour of the expected visit, I retired into my chapel, and recited among my prayers my little office of the crucifix, praying with unusual fervor and under a very peculiar impression, so much so that I paused on my way out, and, turning back into my tabernacle with an ineffable impulse of love, I said, 'O my God! I never prayed like this before!' One hour later, I was in the depths of despair; but, in the midst of my chaotic anguish, my thoughts recurred to that ravishing prayer; and I said to myself, ' It was the viaticum of sorrow.' "

A feeling like this could not fail to engender charity. Mme. Swetchine considered the two inseparable; and we will hear her explain her views on this subject to a man singularly fitted to understand her, — M. de Melun.

When he first formed the acquaintance of Mme. Swetchine, he was still hesitating between his studies of the past, which he proposed to incorporate into a history of the Council of Trent, and that charitable vocation, of which, fortunately for the world, he soon made choice. In 1836, he was reading, simultaneously, Fra Paolo Sarpi and the life of Saint Vincent de Paul; and Mme. Swetchine wrote thus : —

TO THE VISCOUNT DE MELUN.

PARIS, July 15, 1836.

There is a good deal of talk about specialty. It is highly esteemed in our day, and thought to be of exceeding utility; but I doubt whether God loves it in his saints, and whether virtue of his forming has not universality for its primary characteristic. Thus, in that history of Saint Vincent de Paul which impresses you so much, the world sees only the outward acts, and, in an emergency, would deny the existence of the flame which fed them. It is this very thing which has caused them to find favor in the eyes of so many persons who see only the utilitarian side of charity. Of course, charity ought to be the most natural manifestation of faith; but the effect is not greater than the cause, and certainly cannot dispense with it. To believe intellectually, and to live upon the reasons we have for believing, is to render homage to God. To relieve the poor is to do him personal service. To love him as he would be loved is a very different thing. The swifter the flight of the intelligence, the more powerful the thought, the greater the growth of the mind, the more need there is that the growth of piety should keep pace with and counterbalance it. Why have so many sublime spirits gone astray? It is because, with some degree of integrity and less pride than is commonly supposed, they did not love, and love only could have guided them.

And leaving the realm of intellect, if we come to that of action, useful, charitable, and even holy in its aim, we shall see, that, unless piety lead the way, it will not long preserve the desired perfection.   The function of action is to break up, divide, and as it were materialize the attention.   Read, then, my dear friend, Saint Vincent de Paul, who, with his miraculous conquests, has always appeared to me like a kind of Christian Sesostris.   Read him, that you may make his deeds your own, and conform in all respects to his example.   But read besides some other books about the great masters of spiritual life, which will give you an insight into the adorable mysteries of God's dealings with souls. Among the poor and rich alike you will find this practical instruction very useful.   You have not much of the old man to shake off; it is the new man who must be born and guided aright.

It is but strict justice to say, that the whole life of Mme. Swetchine was inspired by the sentiments she expresses here.   Her charity was not a careless and mechanical practice.   She consecrated to it all her strength and all her skill.

A confidential servant, who was with her all the last thirty years of her life, and whose affecting devotion remains intimately associated with his mistress's memory, penned, after her death, the following artless lines, whose very *naïveté* augments their interest and their charm : —

I should have liked, monsieur, if my health had not been so bad, to furnish you with some notes on the last years of her whom I had the honor to serve.   The more I think of it, the more I am convinced the dear lady shortened her days by her desire to serve her kind in all ranks of life, and by making herself the slave of all.   Here is a proof of it : —

One morning, when I was serving her breakfast after her return from mass, she said to me, "I am in a great hurry.   I have a great deal of writing to do, and am very much behindhand.   I shall close my door to everybody without exception. I beg," she repeated, "that you will admit no one."   But, when she rose from the table, she added, with a smile, "However, if anybody comes who absolutely needs to speak to me, and especially if there are any poor people who have come from a distance and have no time to call again, you must announce them." A moment after she entered the drawing-room, she came back to say, "I had quite forgotten that Mme. such a one wanted to see me alone." Half an hour later came two or three letters soliciting private interviews; then a person from the country, who stopped as she passed, and begged to see her just one minute; but the minute lasted till some one else came. Then, at three or four o'clock, her doors were opened to everybody, and they came in crowds to stay till seven. I saw her seat herself at table, worn out with the fatigues of the day; and people were even then coming to speak with her before her *soirée* commenced. She used often to rise from the table before she had finished her dinner. This would last from six o'clock in the morning till an hour, and sometimes two hours, after midnight. To be sure, she lived in the midst of friends who loved and admired her; but they never could see that her strength was wearing out, especially in the last five or six years. Ah, monsieur, everybody was delighted to see and hear her; for I do not think any one can deny that her conversation was charming. She had a talent which very few people possess, — a different language for every class she met. She knew so well how to console the poor in their misery, — the sick in their domestic trials; to raise the spirits of the sorrowing; and to sustain mothers who came to ask advice about their children. Those who went to her for comfort I used to see come out from her presence with peace in their faces.

If these few lines, monsieur, can be of any service to you, I shall be most happy to have given proof of all my gratitude to my benefactress, so deeply regretted by me and mine.

CLOPPET.

This kindness to the poor, attested by the irrefragable testimony of Mme. Swetchine's most trifling actions, was not confined to waiting for and welcoming them. Her greatest treat was to visit them at their homes. Almsgiving was not, with her, the mere fulfilment of a duty. She liked to give pleasure besides doing good, and her heart always added something to what her hand gave. There is no one who does not need some trifling superfluity. When Mme. Swetchine wanted to plan a diversion or a pleasure for a poor person, it was done with the same

19

care and precision that she displayed in the loftiest efforts of her intelligence. For some she would bring a few pots of flowers; for others, framed engravings, recalling favorite subjects, — battles, for example, if there happened to be an old soldier in the family. For one she selected books; for another, some convenient piece of furniture; for the infirm, a good roomy arm-chair. One New-year's Day she quietly withdrew from all the attention by which she was surrounded, and went to pass several hours with some poor parents who had just lost two sons in rapid succession.

She had adopted, as the principal centre of her charities, the quarter of the Gros Caillou, without explaining to any one why she gave it the preference. The venerable curé of St. Thomas Aquinas, the Abbé Serres, was questioned on this subject, and replied: "I cannot say; but all I know of her inclines me to believe that it was only because she had a better chance of remaining unknown there. In our own faubourg, St. Germain, her name would soon have been known. It would have passed from porters' lodges to antechambers, and from antechambers to drawing-rooms. It would have been matter of common conversation. She would have got a reputation for charity, and that is what she did not want."

Whenever a great joy awoke in the depths of her heart renewed feelings of gratitude to God, Mme. Swetchine used to hasten to the Sisters of the Gros Caillou, and beg for another pauper, receive him from their hands without expressing any preference or personal choice, and often gave him a name which recalled to her the circumstances of the adoption. One day, when, after a protracted season of anxiety, she had received a letter from the Princess Gargarin, she sent Cloppet to the Sisters of the Gros

Caillou; and when he came back, and stated the result of his characteristic mission, Mme. Swetchine exclaimed, joyously, " My dear Cloppet, we will call this one ' Ma Sœur.' " She sent the same message on the day when the French and Russian war closed above the ruins of Sebastopol; and to the poor family which fell to her lot she gave the name of "La Paix." [1]

What Mme. Swetchine could do in the way of private charity did not satisfy her. She felt the need of associating her benevolence with the might of collective work. The Convent of the Madeline, founded by the Abbé Desjardins for the assistance of poor young girls, was in debt during the last years of the holy priest's life. Mme. Swetchine came to his assistance; and, after the death of the Abbé Desjardins, contributed perseveringly for the completion of the foundation. A converted English lady had devoted herself to teaching in the Convent of St. Michel. Mme. Swetchine was intimately associated with her for twenty years, and lavished upon her encouragement and assistance. She engaged in several charitable works set on foot, or prosecuted, under the Restoration. But the vigilance and assiduity which she brought to all undertakings inspired her with the desire of a more exclusive consecration; and Mme. Swetchine devoted herself, with especial affection, to alleviating the condition of the deaf and dumb. Her overflowing heart was keenly sensi-

---

[1] The anecdote of "Ma Sœur" and "La Paix" was published in an eloquent obituary article; and its author will pardon me for pointing out, in this place, a slight error, which is not without interest, as illustrating her character. However unimportant these charitable deeds, they were not made known, as the author of the obituary intimates, by Mme. Swetchine's mentioning them to one of her friends. She admitted no one to this kind of confidence. Facts of this sort were divulged only by servants after her death.

ble of the sadness, and even danger, of the isolation inevitably consequent on this cruel infirmity.

In 1827, the administrative council, which was then intrusted with a general oversight of the institution for deaf mutes, created, on the motion of M. de Gerando, two committees of patronage,—one of men for the boys, the other of women for the girls. To these committees was assigned the care of providing protectors for the pupils, when they came out of the state institution. Mme. Swetchine was the first president of the ladies' committee. Her inquiring mind, so curious about all new methods, could not fail to be kindled, as she beheld that marvellous communication of soul with soul, and the blessed knowledge of God imparted without the hitherto indispensable aid of speech. That miracle of the healing of the deaf mute, constantly renewed and perpetuated, thanks to the charity of a priest of Jesus Christ, touched a heart so profoundly tender towards all the sorrows, and happy in all the consolations, of others. From that day, Mme. Swetchine was won to the cause of the deaf mute. Mlle. Mechin, who deserved the title of mother to these poor children, was employed by Mme. Swetchine; but she liked to refer the honor to Baron Hyde de Neuville, who was no less devoted to the work than herself. The directors had thought it proper to reserve one of the finest rooms in the asylum for the meetings of the committee. Mme. Swetchine, as president, proposed to use this room for an infirmary, and transferred the meetings to the small chamber of the directress. In 1830, she felt it to be her duty to retire from the presidency, that she might not attract attention to her name, at the moment when her compatriots were being recalled to Russia; but she preserved the same tender interest in the numerous family of her adoption.

She was thoughtful of the recreation of these poor children; and being desirous of brightening, for a brief interval, their doubly precluded imaginations, she exhausted the resources of splendid breakfasts, and all the games which could be introduced into the house. One day, she had a fancy to take them herself to the diorama, and the spectacle of their profound astonishment and candid admiration made this one of the brightest fête-days she ever enjoyed.[1] In 1829, she had recommended to Mme. de Montcalm a young deaf mute, who supported a widowed mother by her own unassisted labor. The noble sister of the Duke de Richelieu afforded them abundant aid; but when, in 1832, the cholera marked her as one of its first victims, Mme. Swetchine reclaimed what she called the legacy of Mme. de Montcalm.

A situation was procured for the infirm mother; and the young girl, whose name was Parisse, Mme. Swetchine received into her own house. She adopted the habit of taking the young mute with her on her morning rounds, and found it singularly pleasant. It was not necessary to speak to her, and she did not feel humiliated by silence. "With Parisse, I can fancy myself alone," said Mme. Swetchine, when any one expressed surprise at her singular choice of a companion; "and yet, in case of need, I have an arm to lean upon, and affectionate assistance at hand, which does not interfere with my freedom." Thus,

---

[1] It is needless to describe the gratitude of Mme. Swetchine, when, deferring to a wish repeatedly expressed, Mgr. Sibour instituted a regular religious service for all the deaf mutes scattered about in different parts of Paris. The Church of St. Roque, where the Abbé L'Epée had been buried, was declared their parish; and instruction was given there every Sunday, in the language of signs, to a sadly numerous crowd, whose eyes reflected with singular brightness the vivacity of their impressions. Mme. Swetchine was present at the first inauguratory mass, which was celebrated by Mgr. Sibour in person.

she always tried to make it appear that she was the person obliged rather than the benefactress.

Every one knows the clashing which cannot fail to occur where servants are numerous. The misunderstandings arising from the difficulty of mutual comprehension rendered the jars uncommonly frequent in this case. Mme. Swetchine was often obliged to interfere, and insist upon an indulgence, which her example alone could not enforce. "I love you all," she used to say to her people; "but understand, you would all go before Parisse. She is the most unfortunate, and much must be forgiven her."

And here again Mme. Swetchine furnishes a precious model for us to study. It is a rare thing to know how to keep the mean between cold indifference and the kindness that degenerates into weakness. In Mme. Swetchine, even compassion was invested with that perfect fairness and good sense which seemed inseparable from her nature. Parisse had sterling qualities, which won the esteem and love of her fellow-men; but her very virtue, like her gait and her style of beauty, was a little haughty. When she had deserved severity, when she had assumed what Mme. Swetchine laughingly called her "grand air of an outraged queen," her patient mistress appealed to one of the patrons of Parisse, Mlle. Ferment, a teacher in the institution for deaf mutes, who possessed the secret of making herself loved, as well as the art of making herself understood. This common anxiety for an obscure unfortunate led to a correspondence, of which we present some fragments, — a correspondence insignificant in itself, but which ceases to be so when we realize its moral value, and reflect that these notes were penned at stolen moments, in the midst of all the conflicting thoughts and interests of a life like Mme. Swetchine's.

PARIS.

MY DEAR MLLE. FERMENT, — It was impossible for me to send Parisse to you at the appointed time. I only reached home at half-past eleven, and we are perishing with cold. I beg you to tell Parisse to have confidence in me. Her new room will be at least as pretty as the old, if she will only leave me time to arrange it. What I want is, that she should cease to grieve over the matter, rather than hide her grief. I do assure you, that the bare idea of giving her pain gives me a great deal, and makes me feel very ill at ease.

The trouble I give you does not console me for my own, as you can readily believe; and I should prefer a different sort of interchange.

My dearest, you are my only help. Your goodness will have it so, and I am compelled to impose upon it. I must beg of you, then, to reprove Parisse seriously; for she is beginning quite to forget herself. In consequence of fresh scenes with my chambermaid, and probably from the mistaken idea that I have taken part against her (as if there were any choice between two angry combatants), she has, for three days past, carried her ill-concealed irritation against me to the verge of rudeness. At first, I kept perfect silence; but, on the occasion of a fresh misapprehension on her part, she flew into such a rage that she really deserved to be sent away. Be so good as to inform her of my very decided displeasure. She never offended me so deeply before, and it is but just that she should know it.

Tuesday.

It is Parisse who will take you these lines. If I dared, I should beg you to make her hear reason about her flurry of to-day. Her chimney smokes, or so she says, and it has put her out. But really I cannot help it. The chimney is excellent. It is made after the Swedish fashion, the only one which the room allows. My husband, at one time, ordered it made for himself; and if it smoke occasionally, which happens to all earthly chimneys, it can be only while the wind blows from a particular quarter, or when it has been a long time without a fire. However, I shall have it examined and swept again. I think this a reasonable precaution; but I do not think it desirable to alter a chimney which fulfils every condition of successful operation. A thousand pardons, dearest, for adding my vexations to your own sufferings. If it was words, and not signs, I wanted of you, I would make every other consideration bend to your need of resting your poor dear chest.

Thursday, 6 o'clock.

. . . Alas, my dear! this poor Parisse is doing like all the rest of the world, — spoiling her own happiness. She lets her faults encroach upon a multitude of good qualities. Pardon me for troubling you! If I did not, something else would; for such is life!

Another paroxysm! There have ceased to be either intervals or exceptions to her fits of passion. She has just been to me with some pieces of bread in her hand. I did not know what to understand by this, unless it meant that she could live with nobody. Mlle. Gladie is at least as much the object of her wrath as M. Henri. The two sexes are on a level. Nothing remains but to leave her to make the experiment of freedom. Be so good as to tell her that I will allow her a pension of five hundred francs, which she will continue to receive after my death; and that, since she finds herself so unhappy, she has only to abridge her martyrdom. If you knew a deaf mute with whom she could agree, or a house which would receive her, it would be very kind of you to mention it. Even in that case, it may be only an experiment; but it may be also that she will profit by the lessons of experience.

Here, my dear, is a little word which came to me yesterday, in my retreat, from Cloppet :—

MADAME,— I do not send Parisse to you to-day : Mlle. Ferment wants her to-morrow. She eats almost nothing, is very sad, and I have talked to her a great deal. She appears to understand her position, and is very anxious to submit to you, and be reconciled with everybody. She is disposed to shake hands with whoever will. I think, if they persist, she will fall ill. Your devoted servant,   CLOPPET.

I am the more readily touched, as you may guess, because I am punishing myself as much as her.

This test was final; and poor Parisse finally acquired strength enough to avoid open conflicts, both with others and herself, so that she deserved one day to see her own features engraved by an imperishable burin [1] behind the face of her benefactress.

---

[1] " I saw, while we were watching the sad setting of that beautous star, her beloved mute, following her with her eyes from an adjoining chamber, the vigilant sentinel of a life which had been so lavish of itself, and whose light went out with faithful friendship on the one side and grateful poverty on the other."— *Funeral Oration on Mme. Swetchine*, by Father Lacordaire, " Correspondant " of Oct. 25, 1859.

During Mme. Swetchine's summer sojourns, either at watering-places or in the environs of Paris, one of her greatest pleasures was to make the acquaintance of the Sisters of Charity in the place, and assume the care of some poor family. At St. Germain, she had been a constant visitor at the House of the Ladies of St. Thomas de Villeneuve. A young novice, from a convent of that order in Trinidad, had been forced by unhappy circumstances to cross the sea; and Providence had guided her to Mme. Swetchine, who, not content with placing her in the Convent of St. Germain and paying her board, went frequently to see her, and, after her death, raised a pious monument to her memory.

In 1838, the curé of Chantilly introduced her to a well-educated family, which had fallen into extreme poverty. An aged mother, Mme. Louvos, was supported by the insufficient labor of her daughter, not yet seventeen years old. Mme. Swetchine did not rest satisfied with the assistance she afforded them both during the autumn she passed at Chantilly. In the month of January, she obtained a place for young Eliza Louvos, as assistant directress of a work-room.

"There," writes Mlle. Louvos herself, "what good did she not do my soul by her affectionate counsels! When, sometimes, I had doubts about my vocation, and thought to change my situation, then it was that I perceived how brightly the flame of charity burned in her soul. How kindly she pointed out of what use I could be to the young persons intrusted to me, and exhorted me to patience!"

Mlle. Eliza Louvos is now directress of one of the principal work-rooms in Paris.

At Vichy, where Mme. Swetchine went for ten or twelve successive years, her charitable life was as full as in Paris; and there her memory is still revered.

As soon as she arrived at Vichy, the poor told the news to one another, and gathered about her. Among them, she distinguished a little lame child, disabled in one arm, epileptic, and actually repulsive in appearance. To him she devoted herself. The poor child's intellect was very feeble. His parents lived in a parish at some distance from Vichy, and allowed him to beg from door to door, aimless and solitary, through all the fashionable season. Mme. Swetchine was moved by this sad state of vagabondage, and placed him at the hospice at Vichy, where she paid his board, and took all pains to insure his kindly treatment and Christian instruction. Gilbert's heart was more deeply touched than might have been expected from his condition, which apparently bordered on idiocy. His gratitude to Mme. Swetchine soon became actual worship. They could induce him to do any thing by pronouncing her name, or reminding him of her words. Mme. Swetchine wrote out for him a rule of conduct, adapted to his various needs and sufferings. Gilbert was sometimes unfaithful to it; but, when he found the fashionable season approaching, he would seize his little book, and set about obeying its injunctions in every particular. Nothing could equal his joy at the advent of Mme. Swetchine. Informed of her expected arrival by Mme. Chaloin, the proprietress of the house where Mme. Swetchine stopped, — and who has given us these details herself, — Gilbert was on the spot when she descended from her carriage. And Mme. Swetchine would pat him caressingly on the shoulder, and often said to Mme. Chaloin, " If there was any hope of his cure, I should take him with me to Paris." She gave him some of her husband's clothes, which they fitted to his figure, and which made him so proud that he said one day to the Sisters at the hospice, " My good Sisters, I intend to offer myself to the handsomest and richest girl in Vichy. Nobody will refuse me when they know that I am a *protegé* of Mme. Swetchine." On the day of her departure, Gilbert was the last to take leave of her, and would then stay for hours motionless upon the pavement opposite the Hôtel Chaloin, with his tearful eyes fixed upon the closed blinds. After her return to Paris, Mme. Swetchine kept herself informed about him, by correspondence with the Sisters at the hospice. Instead of improving, Gilbert's health became more and more wretched. Mme. Swetchine, who had never expressed a generous thought without translating it into action, recalled her emotions on witnessing the pious interment of the poor in Italy, and wrote thus to the Superior of the hospice:—

PARIS, Oct. 16, 1849.

MY DEAR SISTER, — Mme. Chaloin has already given you my message; and I desire to confirm and complete the request which she made in my name about Gilbert, in case of an event which, at my age, I should not anticipate were we not constantly outstripped by those who should survive us. If that event occurs, my dear Sister, these are my wishes about poor Gilbert's funeral. I request that the holy sacrament be administered in presence of the body, and his remains taken to a cemetery by four bearers, accompanied by an ecclesiastic. I further request that twelve masses be said on his behalf, and a very simple stone placed over his grave, so that I may know the spot, if, which is very unlikely, I should live longer than he. In case my death precedes his, I beg that the same ceremonies may be observed, and the expense defrayed from the legacy which I shall leave him.

Notwithstanding the care of the physician-in-chief of the Vichy waters, M. Prunelle,[1] who transferred to the poor young man a portion of the attachment which he felt for Mme. Swetchine, Gilbert died at the age of twenty-

---

[1] The old deputy from Lyons.

five, in the month of October, 1841. The Superior hastened to communicate the fact to Mme. Swetchine, who at
once replied by the ensuing letter : —

CHANTILLY, Oct. 28.

MY DEAR AND GOOD SISTER, — I cannot tell you how deeply
I mourn. I was truly attached to that poor child, whose good
and pure heart must, in its simplicity, have been pleasing to our
Lord. I am comforted by the thought that he is released from
his cruel sufferings, and especially by the increased piety which
struck me even last summer. My dear Sister, your indulgence
and commiseration, together with those of your companions,
and, above all, your example, have been the most efficient
means employed by divine pity for his salvation. Thank you
once more for the kindness you have shown the poor dear boy,
on whose intercession I greatly rely. We have changed parts.
Yesterday I was one of his props : to-day he is one of mine.

The little Hôtel de Beaujolais was and is still kept by
Mme. Jarry, who also fulfilled the duties of bathing-woman.
The heart of this humble woman had divined the heart of
Mme. Swetchine, so accessible was she to all. When she
was questioned about her intercourse with Mme. Swetchine, she had not heard of her death, and she burst into
tears. " Ah ! " she cried in a flood of weeping, " Mme.
Swetchine was a holy woman, — a true saint! There are
no more such ! The more unhappy you were, the more
she loved you. She thought more of a poor person than
of a prince. She would not have harmed a fly. If one
fell into her bathing-tub, she would lift it out delicately on
her finger, and say to me, ' My dear friend, put it back in
the sun. It is one of God's little creatures.' I knew that
she suffered a great deal in the bath, though she did not
complain ; and I never hurried her ; and I used to say to
the men of the establishment, ' She is not like other
ladies ! She must be kept alive, and have all the time she
wants. Is she not worth them all ? ' But they did not

feel this at the establishment; and, when I went away, the other bathing-women hurried her, and then she did not go there any more. The moments I passed near her were the happiest of my life."

It may be imagined that Mme. Swetchine's charitable activity stopped here. We have not begun to give an idea of it. She was simultaneously, and as it were doubly, engaged in Russia and in France. Her peasants — guardianship over whom she never would resign — were the objects of her unceasing watchfulness and constant correspondence. Her friends in the interior of Russia kept her informed of all that was done on her estates, and of all obedience and disobedience of her orders; and it is plain from their replies, that she who questioned was much more concerned about what might affect the well-being or moral dignity of her families, than about the increase or diminution of her own income. We see her unceasingly promoting and facilitating manumission, preventing or making amends for the disastrous transportation of serfs from one estate to another, and infecting others with her own perseverance and energy in prosecuting reforms of every kind. We give one short fragment from the countless letters addressed to her on this subject : —

TO MME. SWETCHINE.

I have at last received a confidential letter from one of the fugitives from your estate of Nijni. I gave him an audience on my balcony, under cover of a cloudy, moonless night, that we might not be overheard by the people who were sitting up in the antechamber."

Another passage borrowed from the same correspondent explains the necessity for these precautions : —

" To give you a specimen of the thoughts and hearts of these peasants, whom people are pleased to believe sunk in sensualism,

I will quote a few words from one of your people from Saratov, when they came to my house in a body on my arrival here. After their first outburst of joy at seeing me, they began to re-count their griefs and wrongs, the exactions, the forced labor on the roads, the compulsory marriages; and their eyes filled with tears. I asked if they had complained of these abuses to M. X. 'No: M. X. does not ask us, and we do not dare to open conversation,' was the general reply. A tall young man, with a marked countenance, who had already impressed me by the strong emotion depicted on his face, came out of the group, approached me, and said, with his eyes full, 'Who of us would dare speak the truth? I am the son of Ivan ———, whose life has been one agony. He was twenty-five years in Siberia, sep-arated from all his family and his sons, because, with the best intentions, he revealed certain facts against the surveyor. The same thing will happen to us if we speak the truth.' The un-fortunate young man was right. I myself labored for three years and a half to get poor Ivan back from Siberia. He came four years ago, but he is only the shadow of himself."

The crisis which property in Russia is at this moment going through, and the magnanimous measures decreed by Alexander II. in connection with the nobles of his realm, impose great reserve upon this question. This fragment will suffice to give some idea of what Mme. Swetchine's thoughts and wishes would have been if she had lived.

Along with these sources of sorrow, Russia also fur-nished her consolations to Mme. Swetchine. Almost every year, old friends from St. Petersburg and Moscow came to pass the winter in Paris; and their constant presence in the salon of the Rue St. Dominique bore witness to the charm which allured and held them captive there. Here were seen the aged Count Romanzof, one of the most distinguished courtiers of the Empress Catherine, who undertook the journey after he had entered upon his ninety-sixth year; Count Xavier de Maistre; the Count and Countess Strogonof, son and daughter-in-law of Baron Strogonof; Princess Wittgenstein, daughter of Prince Bariatinsky; Prince Nicholas Troubeskoy, and

Prince Michael Galitzin. Occasionally the Princess Gargarin came to share her sorrow with her sister, and display the progress of her sons. The Countess de Nesselrode never allowed many years to pass without seeing Mme. Swetchine, at least for a few days. When the relations between the court of Tuileries and that of St. Petersburg were such that her presence at Paris might have been productive of inconvenience, Mme. de Nesselrode met Mme. Swetchine at Metz or Nancy, and enjoyed for a few weeks a monopoly of her friend's society, or summoned her across the frontiers of France to Baden or Frankfort. Finally, the Countess Edling consented to suspend for a time her vast agricultural enterprises, and come to Paris; and when her niece, Maria Stourdza, had attained her eighteenth year, Countess Edling secured to her her fortune, and informed Mme. Swetchine that she desired one of her nephews for an adopted son. The marriage of Prince Eugene Gargarin and Mlle. Stourdza set the final seal upon the affection of these two friends; and to this day Mansir holds in veneration those two dear memories, and worships them with the same grateful, filial love.

CHAPTER XV.

Revolution of 1848. — Mme. Swetchine's opinion of the events and personages of this epoch. — M. de Radowitz. — Donoso Cortes. — M. Berryer. — Death of General Swetchine. — Crimean war. — Death of the
Emperor Nicholas.

THE affections of Mme. Swetchine made her so
thoroughly French, that it is natural to mark the
periods of her life by the vicissitudes of our history. No
mind foresaw and judged them more clearly than hers.
No heart did they move more deeply. All the dissensions
and struggles which preceded the Revolution of February
found an immediate echo in the salon of Mme. Swetchine.
Those who yielded to too great a sense of security, and those
who justified their sentiments and their conduct by the
most gloomy predictions, were there in equal force, and
vied with one another. Mme. Swetchine wavered somewhat between the two parties; for she had fewer illusions
than the one, and was less impatient than the other.
When the catastrophe of the 28th of February, 1848,
occurred, it did not greatly astonish Mme. Swetchine,
although, like the authors of the Revolution themselves,
she had foreseen neither its character nor its date. Her
first and greatest consolation in the midst of the universal
anxiety was to commend the efforts, the resources, the
courage and fortitude, of a great people, easily surprised,
but prompt to re-act by a sudden inspiration against its
own imprudence, and triumphing over anarchy without
violating liberty. To the contemplation of this spectacle

she was ever essaying to turn minds over-irritated at their own defeat, or unduly discouraged by the public calamities.

On the 5th of March, she wrote to the Countess de Nesselrode : —

. . . "Two noble decrees have already issued from the nine days' chaos, — the abolition of the penalty of death for political offences, and the suppression of the oath, which means the suppression of perjury. There is supreme good sense in removing this obligation from the French people, which was getting thoroughly used to falsehood. These two decrees evidently emanate from M. de Lamartine, to whom, despite my past and present grievances, I cannot deny lofty views, civil courage, and a generous inspiration. Some one remarked the other day, that, in his ' Girondists,' he had erected the stage on which he himself was to appear. Now, whatever may have been the influence exercised by this work, he spares no pains to remedy the harm he has done; and it would be impossible to show one's self cooler and firmer than did he at the point of the bayonets which touched him the other day at the Hôtel de Ville."

After the revolutionary movement had communicated itself to all parts of Europe, she wrote to the Countess Chreptowitch, then residing at Naples : —

PARIS, April 6, 1848.

MY DEAR HELEN, — When we see what is going on from one end of Europe to the other, does it not seem as if a gigantic and universal design were being accomplished? It is easy to see the mistakes that have been made; but these cannot account for such simultaneousness, such concert, and such rapidity. Do not think for a moment that nothing is needed to arrest these events, save a keener eye and a stronger arm. In the presence of great public acts, men rarely look other than small. To-day all are powerless before the irresistible.

Glancing at the state of England, which was agitated, but not disordered, Mme. Swetchine added : —

"Battles whose issue astonishes the victors no less than the vanquished are less rare than is commonly supposed. What strikes me in the contests of Englishmen is a certain substantial

20

quality about the passions brought into play. You feel, that, be their cause true or false, they venture neck or nothing ; that they throw themselves bodily into public affairs, and make them their own ; and that the interests they are called upon to defend, have been, as a general thing, transmitted through many generations, and have passed, as it were, into their blood. This state of things differs widely from the factitious and superficial character of new constitutionalities, where, when individual interest is not the decisive agent, the vague fancy of the moment plays so great a part. Surely I have no desire to abase France before her rival ; yet one can but feel that habits of political activity have become a second but real nature in England, while in France they are only a conventionalism. The result is, that the witnesses of a national struggle in France follow it with a merely intellectual interest ; while, in England, the general pre-occupation is contagious, and, in lieu of simply observing, one is inevitably involved."

TO THE COUNTESS DE NESSELRODE.

PARIS, March 18, 1848.

It has been said with some justice, that the Republic entered by a door which was accidentally left open ; but it was so left because no one dreamed of such an intrusion. Nothing can be more idle than making distinctions between the republicans of yesterday and the republicans of to-day : for the truth is, that, before the Revolution, there were radicals, communists, and a multitude of generally lawless individuals, but no republicans, properly speaking ; that is, none who advocated a republican form and system of government. The republicans of to-day are perfectly well aware, that the Republic, as a form of government, had not even an imaginary existence. It is therefore unripe, and we cannot but realize it ; for the measures taken to force this fine fruit to maturity are sufficiently harsh. During the first few days, the relief from our fright and astonishment were so great, that we seemed comparatively able to breathe ; but the free air did not long continue to circulate in our lungs, and we speedily entered upon the path of intimidation.

Mme. Swetchine here enumerates the various causes for the decline of the monarchical party, and adds : —

. . . " We must also reckon the handful of men whose numbers may increase, and which lives on the memories of the Empire, personified in Prince Louis and one Prince Murat, who, they say, is crossing the Atlantic in great haste, if he be not swimming. If, then, civil war is possible in this country, it is so only in the very bosom of the Republic, between the elements of '89 and those of '93, between the government of base violence and that of public reason, between the agrarian law and respect for property, &c. It is now some time since the symptoms of this grand division declared themselves. Yesterday, Monday, the 17th, there was a momentary explosion. There is considerable agitation even to-day. The *Garde Mobile*, the National Guard, and that of the Suburbs, composed almost entirely of people who have something to lose, have finally assumed an attitude of resistance. It is much to be feared, that bloody collisions will result, and that we shall no longer be able to say, with M. de Chateaubriand, ' It is marvellous! — fire everywhere, and nothing burning.'

" All violent struggles entail misfortune; but, even if these must come, I can hardly believe that we are in danger of massacres, or even of judicial assassinations, like those of the first Revolution. It is not merely the abolition of the death-penalty which re-assures me. It is that the wind does not blow from that quarter. If there is slaughter, it will only be of purses which are already sick.

" Our protection thus far has been an undefinable instinct of honor and delicacy ; for, with the mass of men, this instinct is not rooted in duty, and has no positive moral sanction. It is a species of good sense, which, thus far, has resisted the most disorganizing doctrines ; but who knows if it will always be in the ascendant? It is only well-grounded principles which can contend against the mind's just apprehensions, and such principles do not exist. It must also be confessed, that the merit of not having interfered with the rights of others is considerably diminished by the mere absence of resistance. All are provided for, and all do as they list ; and, between these two terms, there is no room for discontent. A further distinguishing peculiarity of this time is, that there is no trace, among the people, of that brutality which is so repulsive in the memorials of the Republic of '93. Armed like brigands, and in all the haste of their effervescence, they form a line to let you pass ; they quit the pavement to make room for you ; and, if they address you, it is with the most benevolent politeness. All this implies great national qualities ; but qualities are only natural disposition, which is an insufficient defence. Virtue alone treads firmly in the right way, and inspires us with perfect confidence."

After the terrible days of June, Mme. Swetchine wrote : —

" What a shock, and what an internal palpitation, so profound a commotion leaves behind! This one has lost the character of an *émeute*. It is civil war in its most tragic aspect. Never before were the barricades known to cost the lives of six generals. I fear, my dear friend, that the evil is as deep-rooted as it is striking and salient. It is no longer merely a war between parties, and it may be that the duration of any acquired ascendency has become impossible. Reverence was very weak before; but now the fact that a man seems to deserve some esteem excites implacable hostility. Thus, General Cavaignac, who has come out very nobly in these last conflicts, and whose words and deeds and character are of so lofty an order, already begins to encounter an underhand opposition; and the malevolence which formerly concealed itself in the hearts of his rivals now tinges public sentiment. But thus far — and the fact gives me a little hope — religion, the clergy, and every thing connected with them, have had the singular good fortune to escape this disposition of the great majority. The death of our Archbishop was, of course, a perfectly exceptional case; but never in my life have I seen so vast and general an impression, or one which so united in one service of veneration men of the most radical differences. It is now acknowledged, even by those who are least friendly to Christianity, that, in the midst of disorders which threaten society with dissolution, the Church alone is alive and undisturbed. The theories which oppose her action are not all vanquished; many prejudices still exist; but her representatives have won back the favor they had lost, the opposition to them has no longer the prestige of numbers, and the most indifferent do not repel the priest. He is seen to mingle with all classes of the population, but only with the aim of doing good; and he is scrupulously circumscribed within the limits of his ministry.

TO THE COUNTESS DE VIRIEU.[1]

PARIS, July 7, 1848.

. . . If we have had our terrible battles, you too, they tell me, have been on the alert! It would seem as if now-a-days, there was but one alternative, — either to undergo evil or to dread it. Still I think the situation is improved. The bad passions which have cost so much blood have by no means changed their nature: but they have aroused forces which are conscious of themselves; and confidence on the one hand, and the discourage-

---

[1] The Viscountess de Virieu, *née* de Lostanges.

ment of failure on the other, work together in favor of order. I know, alas! how little reliance is to be placed on this. Nowhere on earth, dear madame, is that poor human race, which St. Augustine once called the great invalid, a unit; but in France it is less so than elsewhere. Here every thing is carried to extremes, and side by side with the most monstrous crimes you see the most sublime acts of self-devotion. What is true of deeds is also true of sentiments, and France often reminds me of that Arabian coast which produces nothing but poisons and healing herbs. Great resources always co-exist with this remarkable vitality; but every thing depends upon the choice of means.

The pre-occupation of the public mind has not prevented us from mourning a death which must have touched you very nearly. The great and growing weakness of M. de Chateaubriand had, to some extent, prepared us for the end; but his death is deeply felt, and a just homage is very generally rendered to his merits. The letter in which the Abbé Deguerry announces the event to the editor of the *Débats*, contains some noble and beautiful sentences, which fairly portray the sentiments by which his life was governed, — sentiments which the whim of the moment was only occasionally able to obscure.

After the election of December 10, Mme. Swetchine wrote: —

TO THE COUNTESS DE ——

Were you not surprised at that Napoleonic recrudescence? at the proofs of a passion which the people had unconsciously borne in its breast for thirty years? It must be acknowledged, that there is a large admixture of hatred in this love, and that horror of the Republic is in a great measure responsible for this re-action toward the memories of the Empire. As a matter of individual preference, the great majority of superior minds would have chosen General Cavaignac: but, while rendering him personal homage, some dreaded what are supposed to be the little weaknesses of his character; others, his avowed preference for the republican form of government; and almost all, his past connections, which he has never been willing to break off. I reject in this connection, as utterly absurd and calumnious, the suspicion lurking in the minds of some, that he was in league with the anarchists. What a strange destiny! General Cavaignac has been rejected by the healthy party in France, out of distrust of his ultra-liberalism; and he is the only man in that same France who is utterly execrated by socialists and communists of every date and description. It is more than probable that he would have fallen under their blows, if he had arrived at the Presidency. But, in the midst of it all, his praise is, with a few exceptions, in every mouth; and, for myself, he is the only man of the time who has appeared to me to be always upright, sincere, loyal, consistent, and perfectly honest. There is something antique about his virtue; and, if his country had been in any sense republican, she would have given him her confidence.

As to his competitor, he is a transparent body, through which every one sees what he wishes, and confounds the image with the medium. The impulse which led to his choice was, perhaps, sufficiently immoral; and he is treated as the cross-eyed man treats the object he wishes to observe, fixing his eyes on quite another point than that which he seems to regard. Whither will this system lead? Are not these combinations which seem to penetrate so far into the future attended by great deceptions? It is the light and wisdom of this world, and it will be curious to watch their effects.

Foreign affairs and diplomatic discussions had always possessed a peculiar charm for Mme. Swetchine. Her personal acquaintance with almost all the statesmen of Europe added another valuable element to the general superiority of her views. The Countess de Meulan, sister of Count Turpin Crissé, sister-in-law of M. Guizot, and thoroughly versed herself in all the politics of the time, rarely allowed a day to pass without calling at the Rue St. Dominique. The Princess Lieven, although a less frequent guest of Mme. Swetchine's, set an equal value upon the moments passed by her side; and we find proof, in a little informal billet, that she would sometimes have preferred her society to that of an English diplomat.

FRIDAY, June 29.

MY DEAR MME. SWETCHINE, — I am in consternation. I hear that you were up yesterday! If I had known it, I would have sent away my Englishman, an old friend of mine, and an interesting and valuable man. Will you forgive me? I shall come and ask pardon in person to-day or to-morrow. Permit me to embrace you. THE PRINCESS LIEVEN.

Among the representatives of foreign diplomacy at the epoch at which we are now arrived, two men in particular arrested the attention of Mme. Swetchine, and testified a sincere enthusiasm for her. They were M. de Radowitz, who was on a temporary mission to the French Government; and Donoso Cortes, the Spanish ambassador at Paris. M. de Radowitz, a Westphalian by birth, had served under Napoleon, and distinguished himself in the French ranks at the battle of Leipzig. On the fall of the Empire, he entered the Hessian service as tutor to the young electoral Prince. But this soon became too narrow a theatre for his energies, and he returned to his native land. Berlin tendered him a brilliant welcome; and Frederic William nominated him general of the staff. His native talents, strengthened by experience gained in foreign lands, soon attracted the attention of the Prince-royal, who was more imaginative in politics than his father, and who, without precisely assuming an attitude of opposition, gave some hint of the tendencies, half mystical and half constitutional, half feudal and half revolutionary, which were to distract his reign. General de Radowitz, banished from the court without being utterly disgraced, for having sided with the Catholics and the courageous Archbishop of Cologne, Droste de Vischering, became more and more the representative of the principles of liberty and conscience in the conservative and monarchical party. This position, which he maintained with prudence and dignity, assigned him an eminent place, when the Prince-royal, who had ascended the throne in 1840 under the name of Frederic William IV., granted to his subjects the rudiments of a representative government.

The troubles in Switzerland and the Sunderbund war, precursors of the Revolution of February, had disturbed and divided the statesmen of Germany, France, and England. General de Radowitz was sent to Paris, in 1847, to arrange a plan of concerted action between Prussia, Austria, and France. He had fully succeeded; and, at his farewell audience, these words were spoken : " Be assured, and assure the King, your master, that two things are impossible, either in France or through her influence, — revolution and war." On his part, General de Radowitz wrote to Berlin, " The throne of France now rests on foundations of adamant."

We can understand, therefore, how bitterly the Prussian envoy was undeceived when the Revolution of February burst forth and triumphed under his very eyes. He yielded to a few hours of despondency; then, one of the Westphalian colleges having chosen him its representative at the Parliament of Frankfort, General de Radowitz reappeared in the front rank of politicians; and his word became law among them.

While the glow of generous ideas, and a search for a possible reconciliation between old *régimes* and modern aspirations, still prevailed, the eyes of all Germany were fixed on General de Radowitz. There was in his political course, as well as in his noble countenance, stamped with an air at once soldierly and meditative, much to remind one of the career, the influence in Italy, and the talents, of Count Balbo. Both acted rather on ideas than on facts. Both saw themselves shipwrecked by the sudden irruption of disorderly elements in 1848. Both died saddened in their ardent and sincere patriotism; despairing, . not of the future of which they had dreamed, but of the generation in which they had prematurely demanded the realization of their dream.

Mme. Swetchine has described as follows the lively impression which she received from the presence of M. de Radowitz in Paris : —

TO THE COUNTESS DE NESSELRODE.

PARIS, January, 1848.

. . . I must tell you, my dear friend, that I have renewed the experience of a well-nigh forgotten pleasure in meeting a person of your acquaintance, M. de Radowitz, whose mind and views have re-awakened all the enthusiasm of my youth. I may employ here the word *sympathy*, which indicates a communion of natures without defining its degree. As I listened to him, I seemed to re-ascend the stream of time, and revisit that world of inquiry, so little to the taste of Frenchmen, where my thought served her first campaign. Yet I have never seen a stranger produce more effect than M. de Radowitz outside political circles. I saw that all the distinguished men who heard him were as much impressed by his personal superiority as by the new turn he gave their minds. They say that M. Guizot and M. Molé were particularly struck by it. The reason is, that, beneath all that intellectual force, we feel, we discern the moral authority, without which, however lofty the range of ideas, human nature has no dignity.

When General Radowitz had left Paris, the regrets of Mme. Swetchine followed him to Berlin, where the Count de Circourt was then residing in the quality of minister plenipotentiary : —

TO THE COUNTESS DE CIRCOURT.

PARIS, March 25, 1848.

. . . You may guess, my dearest, whether I think of you! The trouble of one day is only held in check by the menace of the next. I ought to have profited by the departure of M. de Savigny;[1] but he was in such melancholy haste, that I had no means of so doing. There is one person whom I shall never forget, and that is M. Radowitz. How far he was from foreseeing the rapid succession of events which is bearing us on in the same old way! But in these times it is the good minds and the pure hearts which do not divine the future.

---

[1] M. de Savigny, a Frenchman by birth, and one of the most learned men in Berlin.

It was more than sympathy — it was profound attach-ment — with which Donoso Cortes inspired Mme. Swet-chine ; and he was never more fully and freely eloquent than in her presence.

Donoso Cortes was in his fiftieth year when he was ex-changed from the embassy of Berlin to that of Paris, under the title of Marquis of Valdegamas. The salon of Mme. Swetchine was one of the first in which he took on that grand French naturalization, attested by so many re-grets at the fatal, and, alas ! rapidly approaching hour of his death. Type of the ardor of the South, quick in his impressions, impetuous in his gestures, Donoso Cortes glided easily from the freedom and *naïveté* of the most in-timate conversation to the loftiest flights of philosophic thought. It was in Mme. Swetchine's drawing-room that he was pleased to describe the circumstances of his return to the Catholic faith ; and this story, verified by the mov-ing accents of his voice, left so deep an impression on the mind of his hearers, that one of them conceived the desire of preserving the confession in writing ; and this souvenir will constitute one of the most affecting pages of the biog-raphy of Donoso Cortes :[1]—

"I had arrived at middle life," said Donoso Cortes, one even-ing, at the salon of Mme. Swetchine ; "and the reading of French works, following on that of Latin authors, had destroyed my belief in Christianity : still I considered myself one of the most honest of men. I accompanied the Queen Christina to Paris, and there became acquainted with a Spaniard, Don Manuel ———. He was a simple-minded man ; upright, not at all brilliant, very religious, and devoted to good works. I watched him, and said to myself, ' It is strange ! I am certainly an honest man ; Don Manuel is an honest man : but his honesty

---

[1] It is Count de Bois-le-Comte to whom we owe the editing of this document, from which I borrow only the principal circumstances.

is different from mine. There is something in his honesty which I cannot account for, and which, I think, renders it superior to mine. Whence comes it?' I mentioned it to Don Manuel himself. He replied, with simplicity, 'I am a Christian, and you are not.' The remark struck me: I often thought of it; but I had not quite made it out, when my brother fell ill at Madrid. I hurried to Spain; and, when I arrived, I found his situation very dangerous. Once, when I was nursing him, I repeated my conversation with Don Manuel. 'Yes,' said he, 'he gave you the true reason.' He then explained the remark; and what he said touched me so deeply, that, when he died, a few days later, I thought more of his confessor, whom he bequeathed to me, than of his fortune." One of those present remarked, "Certainly, M. l'Ambassadeur, it was by God's great mercy that you were so suddenly enlightened when you had not thought to seek for light. Was there any peculiar circumstance in your life through which you might be said to have deserved such a favor?" — "I do not recall any," replied Donoso Cortes : "my life has been very commonplace. Yet perhaps one feeling of mine has been pleasing to God. I have never regarded the poor man who sat at my gate as any other than my brother."

The death of Donoso Cortes caused a sad sensation throughout Paris; and the edifying details of his illness will not soon fade from the memory of Christians. Sister Rosalie and Mme. Swetchine lavished their care upon him ; and the latter, excusing herself to a friend for having delayed to write, thus alluded to this irreparable loss: "Forgive me! my eyes are out of practice. At my age, they can only weep."

Meanwhile political events in France were advancing toward a new crisis. On the one hand, attempts were being made to club together all the monarchical forces, under the auspices of the conciliated House of Bourbon ; on the other, there were preparations to escape the dangers of a renewal of republican sway, by a Napoleonic dictatorship, the precursor of a second Empire. The situation was fully revealed during the grave debates which followed a proposition for the uniform revision of the republican Constitu-

tion.   These last accents of the tribune deeply moved the
soul of Mme. Swetchine.

TO THE DUCHESS DE ROUCHEFOUCAULD.

PARIS, 1851.

. . . As for Berryer, it seems to me impossible to deny that
he surpassed himself. There was a concentrated splendor in his
words ; a summing-up of all the elements which constitute the
orator.   It was that might of genius which all obeyed in the
ages of antiquity.   The speech of Berryer might have created
a people, as Amphion built cities.

At the very time when silence was about to fall upon
the realm of politics, private sorrow invaded the heart of
Mme. Swetchine on every hand.   She had recently lost
the Countess Edling.   The Countess de Nesselrode was
suddenly removed in the summer of 1849.   In the midst
of the most overwhelming grief, Countess Chreptowitch
thought at once of her second mother ; and, by her tender
forethought, a friend was despatched with the tidings to
Vichy, where Mme. Swetchine was at that time taking the
waters.   On the very evening previous, she had received
a letter from her friend, who, when she wrote, was in perfect health.   She therefore made light of all the anxiety
which the messenger endeavored to awaken in her mind,
and was crushed by the truth when it was at length made
known.   She let fall only these words, in a low voice, interrupted by sobs: " Taken away suddenly ! like my
father ! like my father !"   Paroxysms of heart-rending
grief continued to recur at brief intervals.   A blow no less
sudden struck down General Swetchine, before the very
eyes of his wife, on the 23d of November, 1850.

General Swetchine was ninety-two years old when he
was smitten by an attack of apoplexy, at eight o'clock in
the morning.   There had been no premonitory symptoms,

and Mme. Swetchine had just commenced reading aloud to him the contents of the morning paper.

The General was a venerable old man. His face wore a serene and constant expression of perfect goodness. He loved his wife devotedly, and spoke of her always with the most tender veneration. Mme. Swetchine responded by an affection full of respect, and by unwearying care. If their minds were not on a level, their hearts were equal in delicacy and generosity. The General was finely educated. He read much, and told a story well; and, in his unpretending conversation, *bonhommie* was pointed by keen good sense. During the last fifteen years of his life, excessive deafness kept him from his wife's drawing-room at the hours when it was invaded by the world. It was painful to him not to hear conversations, which he would not have consented to interrupt by calling the attention of the interlocutors to his own infirmity. Mme. Swetchine would then have closed her doors: but to this he opposed the most strenuous resistance; and, for several years, he compelled himself to pass an hour or two in the drawing-room each evening, taking no part in whatever passed there, but showing extreme politeness to every guest, that he might dissipate, by this apparent community of interests, the scruples of Mme. Swetchine.

The General walked a great deal, inspecting minutely all the monuments and public works of Paris, and liked to witness the experiments and exhibitions of every new branch of industry. He received the most assiduous care from one of his old aides-de-camp, M. de Tiran, who thus testified his gratitude for hospitality long ago shown him at St. Petersburg; and, finally, he had a hired reader, who kept him informed in all recent publications, and whose place Mme. Swetchine herself took for two or three hours each day, however ill and weary she might be. The General shared his wife's sentiments toward all the friends with whom she was really intimate, and was particularly attached to Father Ravignan and Father Lacordaire; but he never manifested the slightest doubt of Russian Orthodoxy, or intention of going over to the Latin Church. His sudden death was a thunderbolt to Mme. Swetchine. The first outburst of her grief was heart-rending. She refused to believe in her misfortune; and the physician feigned efforts, which he knew to be useless, in order to give her time to recover her self-command. The first of her friends who hastened to the spot found her upon her knees beside the lifeless body of the General, her frame rent by convulsive sobs. It was only by kneeling beside her, and by repeated supplications, that they succeeded in winning her attention, and leading her away to her own room. The difficulties in the way of burying the General in the little cemetery of Montmartre were surmounted; and scarcely a month elapsed without her visiting her husband's tomb, accompanied only by Parisse. She would remain there for a long time in prayer; and more than once, when she arose, she indicated, by a gesture to her mute companion, the place where she desired one day to rest beside him. It was a great comfort to her to pronounce his name, and dwell on his memory. A touching example of her devotion is contained in the following words, written from Vichy, to the Duchess de Rouchefoucauld, on the summer after the General's death: —

August, 1851.

... Thanks, my dearest, for your kind letter, which came in place of the farewell visit you should have paid me before you left Paris, and did me a great deal of good. Every thing sounds better in solitude when all are preparing to depart. There is indeed something solemn in every adieu; and the same may be said of *returns*, — of those at least which place you between two dates, as in a frame which incloses all sorrow. Two years ago, I learned in this place the death of Mme. de Nesselrode; and this year I come alone. Some poignant and heart-rending memory is awakened at every step. I dwell within the same walls; but I cannot leave my chamber without pausing before a door which opens for me no more. It is just the same as at Paris. I have escaped nothing. A deep-seated grief defies all external influences.

Many now comprehended, for the first time, the place which General Swetchine had occupied in the life of his wife. For herself, she more and more earnestly besought of God himself to fill the cruel void left by that departure. Until now, she had suppressed her longing for retirement, because she would not leave her husband. From this time, she systematically encouraged it. She curtailed year by year her hours for reception, prolonged her residence in the country, and consecrated the months of October and November to an almost absolute seclusion in one of the convents of Paris. She preferred, above all others, a house of the Augustine nuns, where the view from her modest chamber recalled some of the wide prospects, crowded with religious associations, which she had enjoyed so much at Rome.

A last and unlooked-for sorrow still awaited Mme. Swetchine, in the brief collision between France and Russia. "For the rest of the world," she often said, "it is war: for me, it is civil war." Her grief was keenest when military operations appeared to menace both Sebastopol and St. Petersburg: —

"This entrance of the squadron into the Baltic," she wrote to the Countess Chreptowitch, "produces an extraordinary effect upon me. I trust the country is no more vulnerable there than elsewhere: but there is the sky under which I have lived; those are our rivers; it is the point with which my idea of my country is most thoroughly identified; and I feel as if they were aiming at my heart."

Mme. Swetchine's mourning for the Emperor Nicholas was real, and not conventional. On the 31st of March, 1855, she wrote to the Princess Mary of Baden, Duchess of Hamilton : —

"I had scarcely taken breath when there fell the thunderbolt of the Emperor's death, — crushing in its suddenness, in the solemnity of the moment, and in the magnitude of the loss which his country sustains. No presentiment of the end of that great reign had crossed my mind; and I certainly never should have supposed that I was destined to see, after an interval of forty years, a second Emperor Alexander in conflict with a second Emperor Napoleon. Every day new details of a more solemn and affecting character reach us from that death-bed which has furnished so grand an example. The Emperor Nicholas's elevation of soul has been revealed to the world in death, as it was revealed to himself on the day of his accession."

CHAPTER XVI.

M. de Lamartine and Count de Maistre. — Correspondence with Prince de Broglie and Alexis de Tocqueville. — Mme. Swetchine's failing health. — Her last visit to Fleury.

SOME echo of the old discussions yet lingered in the salon of Mme. Swetchine, where faith and independent thought still loved to meet. The fate of our country still appeared to her the premonitory symptom of the fate of Europe; and the dearest interests of France were almost always discussed along with the dearest interests of Christianity. That unity and general harmony of views, which began with M. de Maistre and M. de Bonald, and was continued in M. de Montalembert and Father Lacordaire, was found in different degrees, and under varying conditions, but controlled by common principles, which served as a connecting link, in almost all her constant visitors, — MM. d'Eckstein, Auguste Nicolas, de Carné, de Cazalès, Frantz de Champagny, de Corcelles, d'Esgrigny, Louis Moreau,[1] Bonetti, Rio, and Turquety. One of those who were most widely separated from Mme. Swetchine in intellectual tendency, never failed to render her a sincere and respectful homage ; and that was M. de Lamartine. They saw little of one another, but they often came into indirect contact. Mme. Swetchine, who never

---

[1] M. Moreau, the translator of Augustine's Confessions and the City of God, was very much in the confidence of Mme. Swetchine; and we owe him many precious communications.

could disguise her thought, did not conceal from M. de Lamartine the points of difference, which it would be needless to dwell on here; nevertheless, she had the art of giving such an intonation to reproach and complaint, that the friends of M. de Lamartine, and even his wife, who was intimate with Mme. Swetchine, were always able to hear her.

"Although I am one of those who are most on their guard against the idolatry of genius," wrote Mme. Swetchine to Mme. de Lamartine, "I must needs recognize in M. de Lamartine an immense power to do me good or harm."

One of these wounds at least will be regretted by none; for to its infliction we owe the ensuing pages, where Count de Maistre, suddenly evoked by avenging friendship, reappears among the last emotions of Mme. Swetchine, — as vivid a presence as on the day when he first sat by her fireside.

M. de Lamartine had traced in his " Confidences " a sketch of the writings and character of Count de Maistre. Mme. Swetchine transcribes some passages, and refutes them thus: —

M. de Lamartine says, that he saw much of M. de Maistre. The number of the sittings makes it the more surprising that the portrait should be such an utter failure. No separate feature is faithfully exact, or even recognizable; still less the countenance as a whole.

"The brothers of Count de Maistre — and the same might be said of himself — were in earnest only where God's honor was concerned."

Count de Maistre was in earnest about every thing which touched his own honor, or even seemed to do so. Devoted as he was to the honor of the Church, which the divine promise has made *par excellence* the honor of God, he was so thoroughly a gentleman, that, in any given case, it would have gone hard with him not to satisfy the demands of that fantastic human honor which has been so aptly called the superstition of virtue.

"Count de Maistre was a man of great height and a handsome, manly countenance."

Count de Maistre was of medium height, and his features were very irregular. There was nothing piercing about his eye, and extreme short-sightedness rendered its glance somewhat meaningless. Yet that irregular and by no means handsome face was full of majesty. The *ensemble*, the carriage of the head, was striking, and stamped with a character of antique wisdom.

"He knew nothing save from books, and of these he had read few."

Where did M. de Lamartine learn that M. de Maistre was a small reader? I knew him well long before M. de Lamartine did so; and I have seen him for years habitually devoting to study twelve and fifteen hours in the day; and, of these, reading had its full share. M. de Maistre was an immense reader. His table was loaded and piled with books. From his earliest years, he had been preparing himself thus to employ the leisure of his age by studying the classics as they were studied by the great minds of the seventeenth century; an education singularly adapted to the formation of strong and sound minds. The career of a magistrate, for which M. de Maistre was destined, imposed upon him equally serious labors; and the invincible bent of his genius made it a duty for him, not merely to study religion in its origin, but to sound the depths of theology, and to add to his acquisitions the most arduous results of ecclesiastical science. Placed in the doorway between two countries, his ear was familiar with both their languages; and two literatures were national for M. de Maistre. The Italian, which was not his preference, was defrauded of none of its rights. Long experience of its beauties kept them fresh in the mind of M. de Maistre; and side by side with what all the world reads and admires, and which he, better than any other, knew how to read and admire, his memory hoarded a thousand unsuspected treasures, — pearls discovered or rescued from oblivion by himself. As for French literature, it shared to the full his predilection for every thing French, — a predilection more decided than he acknowledged, and which betrayed itself in severe criticism, no less than in passionate eulogium. Racine, Montaigne, Molière, La Fontaine, and Corneille were ever on his lips. He had read and retained every thing of Voltaire's, not excepting those productions which are seldom acknowledged. Talent to some extent modified, or at least disarmed him. There was about him something of that savant whom the world has come to tolerate under cover of Horace. He could not quite resist the prestige of Rousseau's eloquence.

"His was a brutish soul, but a mighty one; an intellect uncultured, but vast; a style rude, but strong."

What means the expression "brutish soul," as applied to M. de Maistre? A soul nourished in Christianity, devoted to family affections, displaying in the domestic circle a charming grace and sweetness, sensitive to all the refinements of friendship, elevating the duties of the subject to the height of the most noble and loyal sentiments, — this, then, is "a brutish soul"! Doubtless M. de Maistre resisted the ideas and impulses of his time. It was the courage of sincerity, as M. de Lamartine says, which gave and preserved to him that marvellous originality of style, which, though formed by antiquity, his first master, and the grand models which he ever followed, yet owed nothing to imitation.

"Thus, absorbed in self, all his philosophy was but the theory of his religious instincts."

I would sooner admit that recognized truth gave the law to his instincts and tendencies, and that he appealed first of all to his intellect. Obedience and reverence from childhood up had impressed upon his mind the grand outlines of God's law. Arrived at an age to appreciate the divine wisdom, all its splendors burst at once upon his view. Answering all the demands of his reason, satisfying all the needs of his genius, the Catholic religion was, for him, in a constant state of living demonstration; and never perhaps has Catholicism exercised a more grand and absolute sway. Faith had so far become the second nature of his mind, that he could not conscientiously admit any thing in scepticism, except ignorance, narrowness, ill-will, or a mysterious chastisement. With him the *idea* was supreme; and it brought into subjection a heart more honorable and upright than naturally pious.

"He made dogmas of his prejudices."

If we would leave a shadow of truth to the words of M. de Lamartine, we must reverse them, and say that he was so profoundly convinced of the truth of the dogmas which his conscience obeyed, that he was not perhaps sufficiently free from certain prejudices, but extended his submission to principles which were pushed to their utmost consequences by virtue of a logic whose extreme rigor was not of this world.

¹ VICHY, June 3, 1851.

---

¹ M. de Lamartine will certainly be the first to applaud this chivalrous protest. Perhaps he has learned the fact of its existence, or at least suspected it. Two of the recent numbers of the " Cours de Littérature " are devoted to M. de Maistre. Many of the features of his portrait are there softened or modified. These modifications have decided me to

Unlike in their ages, their careers, and their habits, but drawn together by a common tendency of mind and genius, Alexis de Tocqueville and Prince Albert de Broglie became the friends of Mme. Swetchine in her last hour. Their letters have been preserved with equal care, and, so to speak, in the same envelope. They will attest, better than any other argument, what were the thoughts and wishes which allured this great soul, even to the end. Addressing to Mme. Swetchine an article which he had just published under the title of " Le Moyen Age et l'Eglise Catholique," [1] Prince de Broglie wrote in November, 1852 : —

BROGLIE, Nov. 9, 1852.

MADAME, — I have tried to confess my faith without slandering my time. Can it be done ? I believe it can ; and, moreover, I believe that this is, in the end, the only rational thing to do. All other expedients appear to me only fleeting flashes of re-action, which, if we do not take care, will soon leave us in an intellectual night more profound than that from which we have emerged. Donoso Cortes, who kindly wrote me a letter on his article, concludes that the difference between us is, that I believe in a possible marriage between modern society and the Catholic Church, and that he does not believe in it. I accept this definition of our difference ; and I said to him in reply, that, without overrating modern society, I believed our Lord could sit at its table as well as at that of the publican's, or the marriage in Cana.   BROGLIE.

TO PRINCE ALBERT DE BROGLIE.

Nov. 11, 1852.

MY DEAR PRINCE, — The disposition to see nothing but

---

suppress the last paragraph of Mme. Swetchine's work. She protests with great vehemence against the expressions, " Bossuet sauvage," " Tertullian illettré." M. de Lamartine has substituted the epithet, " Bossuet laïc."

[1] Le Moyen Age et l'Eglise Catholique. I. Sermons preached in 1851, by Father Ventura. II. Catholicism, Liberalism, and Socialism, by Donoso Cortes. III. The Undying Worm of Modern Education, and Letters to Mgr. d'Orleans, by the Abbé Gaume. — *Revue des Deux Mondes*, Nov. 1, 1852.

evil in the present, without looking at its uppermost and providential aspect, is especially faulty, as I think, in pushing its conclusions too far. It is logic carried to extremes, and, in consequence, is often our best ally. What surprises me is, that it seems to cost us so little to pronounce an irrevocable sentence of condemnation, and to see ourselves irresistibly drawn into an abyss. It reminds one of Fontenelle. "My mother," said he " was a quietist. She used to say to me, ' My son, you will be damned;' but it did not trouble her." I must acknowledge, that, if I could see our terrible judges a little unhappy over our misfortunes, I should be better pleased. However, I suspect that these hypotheses are not entirely serious in their nature, and that possibly we re-assure ourselves from time to time, by an unexpressed disavowal. Doubtless there are many exceptions; and, if I could make but one, it would be in favor of Donoso Cortes. I have never known a man whose moral disposition appeared to me more utterly at variance with the movement of his thought; so that, when you dissent from his opinion, the effect is singular: you seem in some sort to be approaching him as fast as you recede.   S. SWETCHINE.

TO PRINCE ALBERT DE BROGLIE.

PARIS, Nov. 16, 1852.

MY DEAR PRINCE, — . . . If too many of the books of to-day are made up of the ideas of yesterday, your article on the contrary, my dear Prince, is evidently the *résumé* of protracted studies. On every page you are seen to have assimilated your convictions; and the thorough familiarity with the question, which arises from your having allowed your thought to examine all sides of it, brings every faculty of your mind into play. I have here given you my own estimate merely; but, apart from all this, you may rely on the absolute justice of the impression left on my mind, by so many utterances of deep and living faith, in the secret moral power of the Church, in her supernatural action, and in her incomparable ability to transform rather than destroy. Never have the accents of your faith seemed to me so penetrating, so irresistibly persuasive. This, my dear prince, is what gives an inestimable value to your moderation, and constitutes its corrective in the eyes of those who are slightly scared by its unaccustomed flavor. The unanimous vote, even of one's own party, is no longer a thing to be obtained: but, parties aside, I have no doubt that you have acted on many scattered intellects, whom you have put in tune with themselves and silently reclaimed; a species of success which seems to me to await an order of ideas without interests to uphold or positive ends to gain, and whose great advantage, especially in our day, is to soften in many ways the re-action which it is only reasonable to dread.   S. SWETCHINE.

TO MME. SWETCHINE.

BROGLIE, Nov. 22, 1852.

. . . If I may trust the letters I receive, I have this time had the good fortune to be better understood. I attribute the change to our successive revolutions, which have taught me a better mode of expression, and, it may be also, my audience a better mode of hearing. The friction of great events inevitably wears away the angles of opinion. I see people everywhere, who, to their own great astonishment, do not take as great a delight as formerly in mutual recrimination. I have forgotten who it is that says, we must take care not to become acquainted with our enemies, or we shall have no more comfort in hating them! The truth in my own case is, that, naturally headstrong, I have acquired the moderation which you over-rate in me, only through the happy accident which early led me to examine opposing ideas, each under its most favorable aspect. As to Protestantism and Liberalism, I have never been able to consider the Protestants and Liberals whom I have known, in any other light than that of truants, who have made the mistake of wanting to fly from the paternal home; the one from fundamental Christian doctrine, the other from its social consequences. I have always aspired, and, for my own part, have always been able, to find in Catholicism all that struck me as true and good in other opinions. This character of universal truth, comprising all the fragments of truth which exist elsewhere, is all that encourages one to enter the arena of discussion in the name of the Catholic Church. There is no end possible to human debates, because each man holds a fragment of truth, and stabs his adversary with its keen point. But Catholicism contains all the virtues which men would fain employ against her. All that concerns her in polemics is to show to every man the aspect of truth most striking to him, and not that with which he is least in sympathy. Why has modern controversy habitually taken the opposite course?

BROGLIE.

TO MME. SWETCHINE.

TROUVILLE, Aug. 9, 1854.

DEAR MADAME,—. . . Men are for ever trying to make peace between philosophy and religion; but it is always a

peace patched up with equivocations. Every one withholds
half his thought, for fear of contradicting the other. I am not
very partial to this arrangement, because I do not believe it
can be very durable. It seems to me possible to go deeper,
and succeed better. The question I would put to philosophy
is this: "Do you believe yourself sufficient? Speak out plainly
for once, yes or no! If yes, we cannot agree; for, if philosophy
is sufficient, revelation is useless. In the words of Dante, —

> "Le potessi capir tutto
> Non fu mestier di partorir Maria."[1]

But, if no, then a peace is possible. As soon as humanity
doubts its own self-sufficiency, the door is open to religion. I
should have liked to say something on this head.

BROGLIE.

TO PRINCE DE BROGLIE.

FLEURY, Sept. 30, 1856.

. . . It would indeed be pleasant to see united in one consistent whole all that deserves our partial approbation, and to
behold the concentration of so much unutilized force; but let
us say for our own consolation, that, when a thing does not
waste, it gathers, and that there is one thing more important
than action, and that is growth.

I have long delayed to tell you of the perfect satisfaction I
derived from your reply to M. Simon. It ranges you among
those defenders of the truth who have learned to love her more
by fighting her battles. You grow better by success. Thank
God for it! This effort of yours, which might have been so
barren, is rendered, by its spirit and its affecting language, —
at once firm and tender, — a sign of sensible progress in the
Christian faith.

S. SWETCHINE.

The correspondence with M. de Tocqueville commences
at about the same date.

---

[1] The complete text is as follows: —

> "Stati contenti, umana gente, al quia,
> Che, se potuto sueste veder tutto,
> Mestier non era partorir Maria."
>
> DANTE: *Purgatorio*, Canto III.

TOCQUEVILLE, July 28, 1855.

. . . Although I left Paris two months ago, it is only about three weeks since I arrived here. It is very sweet, after a long exile, to find myself once more in this place. This little nook, apart from its intrinsic charms, is crowded for me with reminiscences of many of the best years of my life. That invisible part of myself which pervades all surrounding objects gives them a peculiarly touching aspect which no other would perceive. These trees, these fields, this ocean view, are wholly unlike aught that I see elsewhere.

We have thought much of you, Mme. de Tocqueville and I, during the varying fortunes of the war. We could understand the conflicting emotions which such a spectacle must excite in a soul like yours, so apt to admit all loving sentiments, so utterly a stranger to the enmities which distract mankind. Alas! there seems no reason to believe that these public and private sorrows are near their end. I rather fear that the scourge of famine is soon to be added to that of war. In any event, the winter must be very hard for the poor; and those who have means must resolve to make extraordinary sacrifices this year for the relief of others. I must confess that I do not expect all to do this. The succession of bad years, instead of stimulating charity to greater activity, seems to have worn her out. (We so soon become used to the thought of want which we do not feel, that an evil which grows greater to the sufferer the longer it lasts, becomes less to the observer by the very fact of its duration.) And then the ties which should bind the different classes together are strangely loosened by revolutions.)

Were you not, like me, madame, astonished to see that a nation apparently so devoid of public virtue could produce an army so replete with it? So much selfishness here, so much self-devotion there! It is amazing! I see a peasant set forth to join his regiment. He is desponding. Often he weeps. The thought that he is going to defend his native land hardly moves him. He thinks only of his field, his little affairs, the petty interests he is to leave behind. He rails at the duty which snatches him away against his own will. A year later, they bring me letters written by the same man to his family. He is ready to bear all in the line of military duty. He knows that that duty is constantly and freely to sacrifice his comfort and his life in the interest of the army. He found these maxims and these customs established. He adopted them with his uniform; and with that he will put them off, and return the same poor devil whom we knew. He will not import into his social life any of the sentiments which he displayed in the army. Until I reflected upon what takes place in modern armies, I believed that there was a good deal of exaggeration about what we read of the public virtues of some of the nations of antiquity. I was positively unable to comprehend how man could have been capable of such things in those days; for man is always the same. What we daily see in our own armies elucidates the matter. They only did for civil society what we do for military society. The citizens of those days were perhaps no better individually than we, and in private life they may have been worse; but, in public life, they encountered an organization, a discipline, a custom, a revered opinion, and deep-rooted tradition, which forced them to act as we do not.

I am ashamed, madame, to see how the current of my thought has carried me away. Let the reflection that you allow me to write to you as I would talk, induce you to pardon this inopportune dissertation.

TOCQUEVILLE, Jan. 7, 1856.

. . . I will not delay to thank you for your last interesting and affecting letter. It was an image of yourself. I wish I might deserve the kindness you show me; for the friendship of a person like yourself imposes an obligation. It calls on us, not merely to be grateful, but to show ourselves worthy.

As I progress in the work in which you are so kind as to feel an interest, I see more and more plainly that I am being involved in a current of thought and feeling, precisely contrary to that by which many of my contemporaries are carried away. I continue to love passionately things for which they have ceased to care. I regard, as I have ever done, liberty as the first of blessings. I continue to see in it one of the most fruitful sources of manly virtues and mighty deeds. There is no degree of comfort or tranquillity which could console me for its loss. But, on the other hand, I see men of my own time, and, I may add, honest men, — for I should care little for the opinion of others, — who seem only to think how they can best accommodate themselves to a new regime, and (what troubles and alarms me more than all) who appear to make a taste for servitude a kind of ingredient in their virtue. I would not think and feel as they do, if I could. My nature, even more than my will, would revolt from it.

However, madame, you must not think that the object of my book[1] has any connection, near or remote, with the events

---

[1] "L'ancien Régime et la Revolution." Only one volume has been published.

or the men of our time. Still, you know as well as I do, that, however foreign the subject of a work may be to the actual circumstances of a particular epoch, it is everywhere marked by a certain spirit, which is either in sympathy or otherwise with the spirit of the time. The soul of the book lies here, whatever the book may be; and this it is which attracts or repels the reader. I have been talking of myself a great while, madame; but it was you who tempted me to this, and, I assure you, it is not habitual.

TOCQUEVILLE, July 22, 1856.

. . . I have delayed writing, madame, hoping that I should be able to give you a good account of myself; but I see that is not likely.

And, first, let me thank you for your last letter. It contained, as all your letters do, proofs of an affection which consoles and strengthens me. I never received a line of your writing without being sensible of this twofold impression. The reason is, I think, that one finds in you a heart easily moved, in connection with a mind firmly fixed upon abiding principles. Here is the secret of your charm and your sway. I want to profit more than I do by your precious friendship. It distresses me that I succeed so ill.

Yet I have recovered, since I wrote you, some portion of the calmness which was wanting during the last of my stay in Paris, and the first moments of my return here.[1] I have not yet been able, however, to feel a keen interest in any thing. No work, no occupation even, has any charm for me: and this leaves the depths of my being in a state of constant agitation; for I have never found repose in immobility, but rather in a rapid and continuous movement of the mind toward a given point.

I hope this letter will find you in the country. Your life in Paris, so crowded with the interests of others, though it may sometimes afford you the heartfelt satisfaction of doing much good, must yet, in the end, try your health; and I rejoice in your solitude. Consult your own pleasure, while this lasts, madame, and think of others only to recall the affection you inspire in some, and the respect you awaken in others. I know of no more noble plan of life than yours.

[1] M. de Tocqueville had just lost his father, and several of the letters which express his filial grief are omitted here.

I have just read a book which interested me deeply, —
Albert de Broglie's "L'Église et l'Empire Romain, au 14ᵐᵉ
Siècle." There is a great deal of talent in the work; and,
along with a sincere faith, a liberal spirit, which enables the
author to judge of men as the instruments of God. The general composition of the book struck me as exceedingly happy.
I have always experienced a strong disgust for the period of
the decadence of Rome; and Prince de Broglie's work is the
only one which has actually interested me in the subject.

TOCQUEVILLE, Sept. 10, 1856.

. . . I have always been, madame, the most irregular and
fitful of correspondents. I would gladly do like a compatriot
whom I met in America, and who, when he had any thing of
importance to say to a friend, would travel a hundred leagues
sooner than write a letter; very unlike one of my neighbors,
who was so ill at ease in conversation, and so accustomed to
the pen, that, if hard pushed in an argument, he quitted you
at once, mounted his little horse, which he had left at the gate,
and galloped off to his castle to write out his reply. I am the
very opposite of this last individual; but I would willingly do
like the other.

I love to hear you speak so nobly of every thing approaching slavery. I perfectly agree with you, that a new and fair
division of goods and rights in this world should be the main
object of those who conduct human affairs. I only wish that
political equality meant equal freedom, and not, as it is too
often understood in our day, equal subjection to a common
master. I strongly suspected, I must confess, that what I said
about the clergy of the old régime, and the advantage to be
derived from binding them to their country by the ties of
worldly interest, would not win your entire assent. I do not
want merely to touch on this great subject with you by letter;
but I earnestly desire that one of those rare and precious
hours may be near at hand when it is given me to converse
with you freely.

With your permission, I will speak to-day only of the
feeling under whose influence I wrote. There are, as it seems
to me, two distinct divisions in ethics, equally important in the
eyes of God, but which, in our day, his ministers teach with
very unequal zeal. The one belongs to the private life. It
comprises the relative duties of the human being, as father or
child, wife or husband. The other concerns public life, and

consists of the duties of the citizen to his country, and to that special division of human society of which he is a part. Am I mistaken in the belief, that the clergy of our time are very much concerned about the first-mentioned branch of morality, and very little about the second? The fact appears to me everywhere patent, especially in the style of thought and feeling prevalent among our mothers and wives. I see multitudes of these who have a thousand private virtues, in which the direct and beneficent action of religion is manifest, who, thanks to religion, are faithful wives, just and indulgent mistresses, and full of charity to the poor; but of that portion of their duty which concerns public life, they have not the dimmest idea. Not only do they fail to practise it themselves, but they do not seem to dream of enjoining such practice on those who come under their influence. This phase of education is to them, as it were, invisible. It was not so under the old régime, which, among many vices, included proud and manly virtues. I have often heard them tell, that my grandmother, who was a very religious woman, after enjoining on her little son the performance of every private duty, never failed to add, "And then, my child, never forget that a man belongs first of all to his country, and that he must hesitate at no sacrifice for her sake; that he must never be indifferent to her fate; and that God requires him to be always ready to consecrate his time, his fortune, and even his life, to the service of the state and the king."

But I see, madame, that I am insensibly getting deeper into the subject than I meant. I want to talk with you about this thing. I cannot say all I would in writing. I will not close, however, without thanking you for the quotation from Bossuet. I find in that single sentence all that can elevate man, and at the same time restrain him to his proper place. It gives one a sense at once of one's own greatness and that of God. It is proud, and it is humble. Where did you find it, madame? I did not know this admirable fragment.

TOCQUEVILLE, Oct. 20, 1856.

    . . . I assure you, madame, that I am not tempted to make use of the permission you accorded me, to leave your letters unanswered. The simple desire to hear from you would be enough to induce me to write. In short, the pleasure of receiving one of your letters is so great, that only laziness could interfere with the wish to deserve it.

You say some things in your last, which are as true as they are finely expressed, on the inevitable vagueness of our ideas of political duty in troublous, unsettled, revolutionary times like our own, and on the difficulties we encounter in attempting to indicate to mankind the law of conscience in this respect. You would assuredly be right, if it were a question of enforcing or defending any special doctrines of government; but I do not so understand it. I believe that in this matter, as in all that concerns human action, there are, besides the special rules applicable to each individual case, general principles to incul- cate, sentiments to cherish, a certain direction to be given to the ideas and the will. Assuredly, I do not ask of the priests to enforce upon the men whose education is intrusted to them, and over whom they exercise an influence, the duty of favoring a republic or a monarchy. But I must confess, that I wish they oftener addressed them, not as Christians merely, but as mem- bers of one of the great human societies which God has doubtless established to strengthen the ties which bind individuals to- gether, — societies which are called nations, and whose territory is the fatherland. I wish they could make each man feel more deeply that he has a duty to this collective entity prior to the duty which he owes himself; that he must never become indif- ferent to its interests, still less exalt that indifference into a sort of effeminate virtue, enervating to some of our noblest instincts; that all are responsible for the fate of the country ; and that all, according to their several lights, are bound to labor unceas- ingly for her prosperity, and to take care that she submit to none but beneficent, worthy, and legitimate rulers. I know that the inference has been drawn from the gospel of the Sunday before last, that the Christian's duty in political matters is con- fined to obeying the established authority, whatever it may be. Permit me to believe that this is an inference from the com- ment rather than from the text, and that political virtue is not thus circumscribed for the Christian. Of course, Christianity may exist under any government, and may find, even in cus- toms which bad governments impose upon men, the material for noble virtues. But it does not follow, unless I am greatly mistaken, that men should become insensible or indifferent to these customs, or that any one is relieved of the duty of bravely contending for the legitimate methods revealed by the light of conscience.

This is what I would fain see taught to men, and, I would add, to women. Nothing has struck me more, in a tolerably long experience of public affairs, than the influence exerted by women in these matters, — an influence all the greater for being indirect. I do not doubt that it is they who impart to a nation that moral temperament which is subsequently revealed by its policy. I could cite a multitude of names which would illustrate what I say. A hundred times, in the course of my life, I have seen weak men displaying actual public virtues, because there were women beside them who supported them in such a course, — not by advising such and such particular acts, but by exercising a tonic influence on their manner of regarding duty, or even ambition in general. Oftener still, it must be confessed, I have seen the secret influence of the fireside transforming the man to whom nature had given generosity, disinterestedness, and greatness of soul, into a mean, vulgar, egotistical office-seeker, who came to see in the affairs of his country only the means of rendering his own situation more easy and comfortable. And how came this about? Through daily contact with a virtuous woman, a faithful wife, a good mother, by whom the great idea of political duty, in its loftiest and most energetic sense, had ever been, I will not say combated, but ignored!

TOCQUEVILLE, Dec. 29, 1856.

. . . I belong sufficiently to that old régime, which they accuse me of slandering so, to be unwilling to finish a year without telling my best friends of the love I bear them. Allow me, then, madame, to follow with you this old custom of the good old time, and to assure you, with all the earnestness it is possible to put into words written and sent from afar, that there is no one whose fate interests me more than yours, and that I desire for you, with all my heart, the blessings meet for such a soul, — blessings which so far transcend the faculties and even the desires of most; and many occasions of benefiting, consoling, aiding, and elevating all who approach you. You enjoy, and you know the value of, this noble employment of one's time. God has granted you the greatest boon a mortal can obtain; and all one can wish for you is, that you may long have the use of it.

It was very good of you, madame, to remember that M. de Rosambo was my uncle. His death, which we have too long foreseen, was yet a deep affliction. He always held in our family a place apart; he was less than a father to us, but more than an uncle. The last tie which united the remnants of my family breaks with his death. With him vanished the last of that generation of noble parents who gave us such rare examples of virtue. He united to all the most affecting evidences

336   LIFE OF MADAME SWETCHINE.

This man, whose kindness and sweetness of nature bordered
on weakness, became energetic even to heroism, where his
dignity or his duty was concerned. This noble and excellent
man was very unfortunate in the world. He was smitten by
many sorrows. Surely, the justice of God will compensate
him for these; and he alone, in the absence of every other
argument, would prove to me, that such justice exists, and that
the order which has been disturbed in this world will be restored in another. . . .

"It is impossible for two souls to meet in sweet communion, without religion's sooner or later crossing the
threshold of their discourse."[1]   This beautiful remark by
Father Lacordaire was soon verified in the intercourse of
M. de Tocqueville and Mme. Swetchine. He revealed to
her the state of his mind with much feeling and utter un-
reserve. After receiving her reply, he wrote as follows:—

TOCQUEVILLE, March 21, 1857.
Your last letter, madame, has given me a deep and lasting
sense of gratitude. You are not one to stand secure upon the
shore, and feel a cruel joy in watching the tempest-tossed
sailor. Thanks, madame, for the hopes which you entertain,
and bid me cherish. May God hear your prayers! I *have*
sought the truth of which we have spoken, if not always with
the single eye which is worthy to discover it, at least zealously,
and with a sincere desire to find and grasp the blessing. If
trouble led to peace, how long ago would peace have been
mine!

That truth and that peace the noble heart of M. de
Tocqueville could not fail to attain and enjoy. He was
touching it at the very moment when he spoke with such
humble self-distrust, and the consolations of his death
have already shed light and comfort upon his life.

The health of Mme. Swetchine was now growing feebler

---

[1] Funeral Oration of Mme. Swetchine, by Father Lacordaire, "Correspondant" of Oct. 25, 1857, p. 197.

every day. Her unparalleled courage and heroism still kept up the illusion of strength; but those who watched narrowly the progress of her malady saw that the danger was imminent. For thirty years, it may be said, she had not been free from suffering for a day; and her nights, in particular, had been seasons of cruel trial. A liver complaint, the commencement of heart-disease, and premonitory symptoms of dropsy, had long ago induced swelling and oppression. She only resisted their progress by sitting habitually in a high, hard chair, or walking about her rooms. Some of the interviews most deeply engraved upon the memory of her friends were chiefly passed in traversing by her side the length and breadth of her drawing-room, sometimes with hurried steps. We must not, therefore, omit to mention, among the efforts of patience which she imposed on herself for the sake of her friends, the obligation to remain seated when her drawing-room was full, and did not admit of her seeking relief in motion. She said sometimes, with a smile, to the few who knew what she suffered from this inconvenience, "The politeness of the world consists in rising for visitors; mine, in keeping my seat."

During the night, this tendency caused her actual torture. Before midnight she slept quite soundly, but seldom did she hear from her little camp-bed the clock strike one, or at most two, before a sense of suffocation obliged her to rise, and resume her walk. Sometimes a mechanical instinct made her start from her bed before she was fully awake; and, in that case, she would often run with such violence against the angles of the furniture, that she would show visible traces of the blow. More frequently, she mastered her drowsiness; and, in the midst of her feverish agitation, her mind resumed its steady, tranquil

22

workings. And then, pausing at intervals before her desk, she would trace those detached fragments, those almost illegible pencil lines, which she did not always remember to destroy, and which have providentially survived to reveal to us the treasures of her humility.

During the two last years of her life, Mme. Swetchine sought in the summer a country residence more solitary and remote from Paris than had been her wont. Her physicians enjoined in the most peremptory manner this isolation for a few months. The ingenuity of affection opened to her an asylum, which added to its intrinsic charms that of renewing the memory of an affection always present to the heart of Mme. Swetchine. The Countess de la Rochejacquelin, daughter of the Duchess de Duras, placed at her disposal the old chateau of Fleury, on the borders of the forest of Fontainebleau. Here she found a vast ground-floor, where she could take exercise at any time, deep moats beneath the windows, full of limpid water; in the park, the silent shadow of trees a century old; long, battlemented walls, which could still shelter solitude, though they no longer defended power, and all the charms and blessings of the rarest hospitality. The noble aspect of this fine old place, its grand memories, even the shade of the Princess de Tarente, which Mme. Swetchine, as we have already seen, saluted with emotion,—all these contributed to produce a salutary effect, which her friends rejoiced exceedingly to see, and on which they built their latest hopes.

The parish church, which almost adjoined the chateau, received each day a morning visit. "I proposed to her," writes the curé of Fleury, "to say her week-day mass at an hour better suited to the exigencies of her health; but she was seldom willing to consent to this, for fear of

wounding the good Sisters of Charity, who heard the
service with her." On Sundays, all the people of the
parish loved to see and gather round her, when she came
out from high mass. She was very lively with them, and
had kind and cheery words for all. The poor and afflicted, who had experienced her vast charity, waited
patiently till the crowd had passed, and then approached
her; nor did they ever turn away without having felt the
effects of her liberality. Often, when unable to go out,
she sent for them to come to her.

Her friends were careful to respect her retirement.
Not one of them would have consented to intrude on her,
unless in answer to a direct appeal. Among those whom
she thus summoned were the Baroness Seebach, second
daughter of the Countess de Nesselrode, and Mme. Craven,
who, as the daughter of Count de la Ferronnays, was
the representative to Mme. Swetchine at once of a living
affection and a dear and pious memory.

"It was a blessed day," wrote Mme. Craven, on leaving
Fleury. "Mme. Swetchine urged me strongly to reserve to
myself each day some hours of entire freedom in the morning.
'The quality of the time,' said she, is better then.' And it
was not merely for the sake of consecrating the first hours of
the day to God that she began it so early, but also that she
might always have a considerable time to devote to study.
She told me, that day, that her pleasure in study had grown
with her years; 'so much so,' said she, 'that, when I approach
that table to resume my beloved labor, my heart throbs with
joy.'—'Ah!' said she that same day, 'old age is not *the* lovely
age; but be sure, my dear, it is *a* lovely age.'"[1]

---

[1] To form a just idea of that passion for study which possessed Mme.
Swetchine to her latest day, one should read her correspondence with
M. Bonetti, editor of the "Annales de Philosophie Chretienne,"—a cor-
respondence which he has published in a very interesting sketch in the
"Annales" for December, 1857.

340

LIFE OF MADAME SWETCHINE.

Among all the studies recommended by Mme. Swetchine to her friends, the study of self always occupied a prominent place. She herself kept up the practice of self-examination to her dying hour; but no exertions in this line could quiet her anxiety or satisfy her thirst for perfection. Fragments of her scrupulous and unwearied analysis of the most trifling movements of her heart and conscience may still be read upon the worn leaves of two pocket diaries.

"I have no further desire to be pointed out to the children of men, save as a woman who believes and prays and loves."

"Saturday, March 29, 1856.

"Always to begin by doing that which costs me most, unless the easier duty is a pressing one.

"To examine, classify, and determine at night the work of the morrow; to arrange things in the order of their importance, and act accordingly.

"To dread, above all things, bitterness and irritation. To shun display in all things. Never to say, or indirectly to recall any thing to my own advantage. Never to be pleased with any thing that I say myself, nor to press my point. To withhold striking remarks.

"God blesses man, not for finding, but for seeking.

"To choose to have less rather than more."

Some lines of a similar character were traced at Fleury, at the close of the year 1857. Her handwriting was already betraying the progress of the malady which so alarmed her friends. But the employment and direction of her thoughts were always the same.

"Not to have struggled earnestly enough with evil; to have let it gain the advantage. To have allowed every thing about me to grow torpid from my limbs to my mind. To face the danger which threatens me, and which increases every day. I have offered to God my full, entire, and voluntary acceptance of the decree which will cut me off from this world. The hour and manner of its execution I leave with him.

"Blessed death of Mme. de Saint-Clair, the grandmother

of Mme. de la Ferrière,[1] who informed me of it thus: 'She received all the sacraments with great meekness, and then she said, "Ah, how sweet it is to die! No one can know how sweet it is to die."'"

"FLEURY.

"To pay too much attention to the number and variety of my sufferings,—this is a servile weakness, a softening of the will."

"Friday, July 19.

"The dullest and emptiest day possible. A perfect blank. Nothing accomplished. Utter prostration of strength. Good only in that I have suffered in silence."

Thus did Mme. Swetchine, her eyes fixed on the eternal goal, draw rapidly near the end. Her intention had been to remain at Fleury through the autumn of 1857, when she received intelligence that two of her nephews — Princes Gregory and Eugene Gargarin — were coming with their families to pass some weeks with her. They begged her to receive them in her peaceful retreat.

With her customary unselfishness, Mme. Swetchine refused. Although she knew her two nieces to be high-minded women, and tenderly attached to her, she would not consent, merely for her own convenience, to confine in the country these young ladies with their children. She resolved, in spite of all remonstrances, to return to Paris, for the time which her dear visitors had devoted to her. She left Fleury, hoping to return,—a last grace which God did not vouchsafe us.

---

[1] Mme. de Saint-Clair, *née* Egerton, married in England one of the *emigrés*, M. de Cheux, formerly a page of Count d'Artois, who afterwards bore the name of Saint-Clair, to distinguish himself from the numerous branches of his family in Normandy. She became a Catholic after her marriage, and lived and died in France, leaving an example of the most exalted piety. Her grand-daughter, the Countess de la Ferrière Percy, was tenderly beloved by Mme. Swetchine.

LETTER

COUNT DE MONTALEMBERT.

THE last days of Mme. Swetchine were the crown, the illustration, the consummation, of her life. A faithful picture of these not only concerns the honor of her memory, but the influence which that memory is to exercise over the minds of others. I believe I may be pardoned for bringing before the eyes of the public, after long hesitation, a letter destined only for a friend. A more studied narrative would have been less reliable. My heart is full of the last words of Mme. Swetchine herself; and it has seemed to me as if the simple truth ought to take precedence of any premeditated statement. On the same ground, I hope to be forgiven my frequent personal intrusion into the story. The world cannot fail to understand, that it does not depend on me to abdicate my sad privilege of eye-witness.

TO THE COUNT DE MONTALEMBERT.

MY DEAR FRIEND, — Your grief needs all the consolation I can give. Your soul must share in the indelible lesson that I have received. I send you, therefore, a minute and faithful journal of the last days on earth of the friend whom we can now invoke in heaven.

I reached Paris on the 21st of August, at five o'clock, A.M., summoned by a letter from Cloppet of so alarming a nature, that I hardly dared hope to find her alive. I went straight to her door, without stopping at my own. The servants were already up, and their first word re-assured me. The accidental crisis had passed. The chronic malady remained, but Mme. Swetchine, they assured me, was utterly ignorant of the danger of her situation; and I must, they said, take care to assign some motive for my sudden return, which would not excite her apprehensions. I was surprised to hear of this delusion, it was so different from the ordinary courage and acuteness of our sainted friend; still I must needs believe the unanimous assertion of four very zealous and intelligent domestics. It was settled, that they should announce my arrival as the result of a hasty excursion, and that I should not come back till the afternoon, that she might imagine I had come by the night train.

I entered her drawing-room at the hour when it was ordinarily thrown open. Nothing there was altered or out of place. She sat in her own chair near her writing-desk, and there was only one visible symptom of her malady: her head was bowed, and rested on her breast. She raised it only by what seemed a very painful effort, and immediately dropped it again. If one sat low enough to catch the play of her features, her smile was the same as ever, and her voice retained all its delicate shades of inflection. She quietly accepted the reason I assigned for my arrival, and inquired about all my affairs with her own unfailing solicitude. She spoke little of herself, and asked me to stay and dine. I refused; assigning as a reason, that it would be hard for her to walk as far as the dining-room. She replied, " Perhaps I shall not go to the table myself; but I shall know that you are there close by, and that will give me pleasure." I still refused, and said that I would dine at the Quai d'Orsay, which is very near, and come back immediately. "Yes," said she; "but, if you stay, I shall gain all the time it would take you to go and come." So I stayed.

Until half-past eight we were alone. Pressure for breath rendered her speech slow and difficult, and often interrupted it. She would sign to me with her hand to wait till the feeling of suffocation had passed; and, when silence had relieved it, she would resume her train of thought with no loss of clearness and beauty of expression. I asked her a thousand questions about politics and our common friends; and she replied with interest, animation, and even gayety. Speaking of the difficulties and dangers which beset all political relations, both foreign and domestic, she said, "Nothing can be turned to immediate advantage. All is reserved for the winning number. But what will that winning number be?" I asked her if the question of peasant emancipation were not beginning to circulate actively in Russia. "It does not circulate," was her reply: "it boils." At half-past eight, her two nephews came, with their wives and children. The Princess Gregory Gargarin was, by birth, a Princess Dashkof. She belonged to the same family as the celebrated favorite of the Empress Catherine. The Princess Eugene Gargarin, *née* Stourdza, was the niece and the faithful representative there of the Countess Edling. This was Russia's share in that supreme re-union. She invited us all to dine with her on the next day, and took leave of us at nine o'clock, the hour fixed by her physician. I retired, convinced, like all the rest, that she felt no immediate anxiety about herself.

On the next morning, I saw Dr. Rayer. The substance of his opinion, so soon to be completely justified, was as follows : " The incomparable moral force of Mme. Swetchine is at present her principal and well-nigh her sole element of life. Great care must be taken not to impair this. For myself, I· do not visit her as often as I should like, that I may not enlighten her on her situation, which is now beyond the reach of science." He then detailed the nature and character of her various complaints. " Her sufferings of all sorts must," said he, " be inexpressible." The application of repeated blisters had made her body, so to speak, one single sore. As to the dropsy, it was already about the heart, and beginning to affect the head, causing the sense of weight there, which kept it constantly bowed. Dr. Rayer did not apprehend any sudden accident ; but when I asked him, in so many words, whether I could rejoin my family in Anjou, he replied, " I will not answer for more than a fortnight, and I cannot authorize the faintest hope that she will live beyond three weeks." Stricken by these mournful words, I returned to her side, resolved not to lose another of those moments which the mercy of God still accorded me. I did not see her alone that afternoon. At dinner there were eight guests. Mme. Swetchine was led into the dining-room, supported on either side ; and, once seated at the table, she did the honors, and cared for us all with the vigilance of the most attentive hostess. After dinner, she said to her eldest nephew, Prince Gregory Gargarin, " My friend, go smoke your cigar on my terrace." — " Dear aunt," replied Prince Gargarin, " I care so little for my cigar when I am with you, that I have not even brought any." Mme. Swetchine smiled her thanks. Five minutes after, Cloppet entered the drawing-room with a half-dozen cigars on a plate ; and, when Prince Gregory exclaimed at this attention, she said,

"Perhaps you think I put myself to expense for you. Not at all! I borrowed them." Conversation maintained this cheerful tone throughout the evening, which we were very careful not to prolong beyond nine o'clock, though she insisted on our staying.

On the morrow, she asked me if I had fixed the day for my return to Anjou; and, when I told her no, she paused, and from that moment never mentioned the Bourg-d'Iré, or any thing which might call me away. She understood why I was there. In the evening, when I left her, she said in a very low voice, "Come at noon, to-morrow: I want to talk with you alone."

The next day, I was punctual to her appointment; and without preparation, or any especial solemnity or emotion, just as if it came in the ordinary course of conversation, she said, "My dear Alfred, we must now attend to winding up my worldly affairs, and I must tell you just how I am situated. I have, properly speaking, no will to leave. The bulk of my fortune will go directly to my sister and her children; but there are some special bequests about which I am anxious, and I want to be sure that they are executed. You must advise me about some of them, and help me to give them a clear and legal wording."

I would not urge her to delay this sorrowful business. It would have been an attempt at deception which could only have done her harm; but I did try to dissuade her from writing out her requests with her own hand, for she had told me beforehand, that they were somewhat complicated. "Let me write from your notes and your dictation," I said: "then you will only have to sign the paper, and deliver it to a notary before witnesses." — "Do not suggest a notary," said she with animation: "I always had an antipathy for them; and, besides, it would be a gratuitous insult to my sister and my nephews. If I have strength to recopy what you write, I will do it. If that is impossible, whatever you write, or whatever you say on my behalf, will be enough. Let us begin with my burial. Do you think it would be considered singular or affected for me to express the following wishes?" She then handed me these lines, written on an old sheet of letter-paper, and dated Nov. 27, 1851 : "As soon as my eyes are closed, I beg that I may be laid in my beloved chapel. Let the body be kept there two days, and afterwards carried to St. Thomas d'Aquinas, where I would like to have low mass said on my behalf. I want it then to be deposited in the vault, and the next day removed to the Church of Montmartre, where I desire a mass said for the repose of my soul ; and, after that, let them bury me in the little cemetery, in the place already prepared by the side of my husband. I would like my grave covered with a stone similar to his, and a cross engraved on it, with my name and the date of my birth and my death, and, underneath, these words of the Psalmist: 'Domine, dilexi decorem domus tuæ et locum habitationis gloriæ tuæ.' I beg that the hearse may be as simple as possible; and I distinctly forbid any sort of decoration, particularly draping the carriage entrance or the fronts of the two churches, as well as notes of invitation to my funeral, or to announce my death, or the mass at the end of the year."

When I had assured her that no one could misunderstand the spirit of these arrangements, she seemed very much relieved. "Well, then," she said, "take that bit of paper with you, and begin your labors there. And come to me each noon, and so we shall make some progress every day. Now I am quite out of breath," she continued, smiling. "A tête-à-tête is the only thing which I am almost unable to bear. Activity about me is very far from tiring me, if I take no part in it. Conversation still interests me, if I am not directly appealed to, and only join in it so far as my chest allows me. There, I have told you my secret! so now I beg you will act as my shield. Instead of your coming less frequently than usual, I want you to be here all the time. I cannot do without a dragoman." I then left her to take a little rest, and promised to come back at three o'clock, the hour when her drawing-room was ordinarily opened. When I went out, I said to Cloppet, " We need not trouble ourselves any longer about deceiving her. She knew this, as she has always known every thing, long before the rest of us." I did not explain myself further; but it was a kind of satis- faction to me to find, that even to the last, and under so cruel a revelation, our friend was equal to herself.

Five or six days passed in this way. Every day, she spoke to me in detail of her death, of its approach, and what was to follow it; and intrusted to me little notes relative to her intentions with regard to her servants and her charities. When the suffocation became too intolera- ble, she would break off the interview, and send me away. After discharging her debt of gratitude to those who had taken care of her, the subject nearest her heart was the perpetuity of her little sanctuary, which had been worthily intrusted to the Duchess de Chevreuse. At three o'clock, her drawing-room was thrown open. Every trace of the morning's employment had disappeared; and every one continued to believe in her illusion, and strove himself to keep it up. When I endeavored to represent to her the anxiety which this arrangement occasioned me, she said, " You must not suppose that I find all this fatiguing. It rather rests me. I can no longer read or write, and isolation would wear me out quicker than any thing else. Nothing is so painful to me as vacuity."

She spoke the truth, and any one who realized her intellectual force would have ceased to contest the point; yet to one who knew her heart, the suspicion could but occur, that tenderness and consideration for those she loved had some share in her decision. She confessed as much to me a few days later. It had been her wish once more to assemble at her table her nephews and nieces, with the children and their instructors. She was excessively fatigued by the effort, and that night her mind wandered a good deal. I took the liberty to remonstrate with her for the dinner-party, in the name of her nephews themselves. "You are quite right," said she; "but I did so want them to write to my sister that they had all dined with me. That simple fact will be more re-assuring to her than any thing else. Poor sister! ill herself at Moscow. I know how distressed she will be; and I dread it so much. And then my nieces, who have all Paris to visit! Why should I make them anticipate their mourning for an old aunt whom they scarcely know?"

In expressing my anxiety about her bad night, I had not dared to utter the word *delirium*, sure that the thought of losing the full possession of her faculties would be most unpleasant to her. Neither did she allude to it. During the day, she received as usual the few friends who were then in Paris, — M. de Langsdorf, M. de Bois-le-Comte, Mme. de Meyendorf, Mme. Craven, M. Eugène de Ségur, Augustin Galitzin, M. de Berton, M. Marcellin de Fresne. Several times she joined warmly in the conversation, despite her constantly increasing sufferings. There was a good deal said about the trial, then pending, of Captain Doisneau in Algiers. "What disturbs me most," said

Mme. Swetchine, "is the grief of the army, and the conclusions which might thence be drawn unfavorable to France. There are so many people who forget that a nation is a moral agent, and make light of insulting her to the last degree. But a nation is, at least, a neighbor, and ought to be the first of neighbors." And she continued in this strain, with an eloquence which produced all the more impression, that it seemed forced by a kind of supernatural effort from her panting chest. They also spoke of the projected interview between the Emperor of Russia and the Emperor Napoleon. " Of course," she said, " nothing can be nearer my heart than a reconciliation between France and Russia ; yet there is an instinct within me that almost always rebels when two such dignitaries arrive at too good an understanding. I think of the little people who must pay the expenses of these interviews; and I cannot forget that I belong naturally to the majority."

You know, my dear friend, how unwilling she was to have her salon assume the aspect of an academy, and how rare were literary exhibitions there. The desire to remain in her presence, and yet to fatigue her as little as possible, suggested the idea of calling on the prodigious memory of Mme. Meyendorf, who came every evening. Mme. Swetchine showed herself very sensible of the rare talent for recitation which Mme. Meyendorf developed. The latter recited some fragments from St. Chrysostom, translated by Villemain, and some from Father Bridaine. Mme. Swetchine even then brought out, by a few brief but luminous words, their very dissimilar beauties. She dwelt at some length on the peculiar merit of M. Villemain's translation, and every word she spoke created increased surprise ; for, during the declamation, her head had sunk lower and lower, her elbow slipped along the table on which it rested, and one might have thought her asleep at the very moment, when, as she proved most conclusively, she was paying the strictest attention. Mme. de Meyendorf one evening recited, in the most piquant and ingenious manner, the fable of the Grasshopper and the Ant. When she thanked her, Mme. Swetchine remarked, "One has certainly only a child's knowledge of Fontaine till one hears him from you."

The delirium now returned every night, and redoubled the alarm of the attendants who watched with her. She spoke to me about it first. "I have most extraordinary nights now," said she. "Thirty or forty persons come into my chamber; and I try to make them leave, but cannot. I then resolve to talk quietly with them. I say, 'I know very well that you are phantoms. I shall outlast you.'" She related this in such a calm and natural tone of voice, that I asked myself if there were not still a little hallucination in her mind at the moment of speaking; but she dispelled the suspicion as she went on. "This disposition is only aggravated in me. It has always existed. When I was young, and used to travel post several nights in succession, by the second or third night I always saw three or four persons on the seat, and one or two running beside the carriage-door."

Having said this, she went back to the subject of our noonday interviews; that is to say, her testamentary bequests. On the morrow, when I inquired about her night, she replied, "The same delirium. This time I made a great effort to study its nature, and, if possible, penetrate its mystery. I asked myself if my visions might not be an effect of light or of conjunction of colors. I made the watchers change places. I had myself carried to different parts of the room; but the phantoms followed me everywhere. I then said to myself, Enough: it is a symptom of my condition." During the day, she still continued to take an active and sprightly part in conversation. Somebody asked her if she had had no news from the Marquis de Brignole. She leaned toward me, and said, in an under-tone, "He is one of my nightly visitors." Mme. Le Tissier remarked, that, when one came back to Paris, it was difficult at once to recover the concert pitch. "Yes," replied Mme. Swetchine, "one has to polish up one's music a little, and spend a few days in practising scales." One of those present added, that it was true there was a lack of mental stimulus in the provinces and the country, but that Paris had another kind of disadvantage, — confusion. Mme. Swetchine laughed a free and hearty laugh. "Yes," said she, "there ought to be seasons of mental prohibition established at Paris, and a kind of hunting license imposed, so as to leave every one time for his partridges to hatch." When I arrived at Paris, I found her very anxious about Father Lacordaire. "Do you comprehend," said she to me, "this absolute silence on the part of everybody, when the centennial celebration has taken place at Sorèze, and all the bishops and archbishops have been there; and Father Lacordaire must certainly have spoken several times?" She had depended, my dear friend, on hearing an account of these days from your brother-in-law, Werner de Mérode, who had been present along with M. de Mirepoix. She counted the days and the chances, with that affectionate ardor which nothing could ever damp. I was fortunate enough to find in a reading-room an extract from a southern journal, describing in enthusiastic terms the whole celebration at Sorèze, the presence of Marshal Pélissier, the speeches, the toasts, and the repeated applause of the audience. I procured the journal, and carried it to her; and she seemed to derive a kind of new life from it, and enjoyed the most trifling details. "The presence of Marshal Pélissier gives me infinite pleasure," she repeated. "It is enough, and not too much, to satisfy everybody."

A further pleasure was in store for her the next day. Father Lacordaire himself arrived. She questioned him minutely; and never was he himself so winning, so tender, so full of filial devotion. Both felt that it was the last time, and testified the feeling, though not in words.

The general debility was all the while increasing. For a long time she had taken no nourishment, except a few raw peaches without sugar, strawberry-sirup and eau de Saint-Galmier. But nothing interrupted her morning meditations of several hours in her chapel, her daily mass, or her frequent communion. Father Lacordaire had the consolation of several times administering to her the holy sacrament. No entreaties could dissuade her from remaining on her knees almost all the time that she passed in her chapel; and, after she had received the body of our Lord, she knelt for at least half or three-quarters of an hour in prayer that bordered on ecstasy. It was thus that she derived strength, serenity, and freedom of mind for the rest of the day.

On Monday, the 31st of August, she was very sleepy, and received scarcely any one. Tuesday, the 1st of September, she revived. I left her at six o'clock to go to my dinner; and, on coming back, I found her in animated conversation with Father Lacordaire and M. Fresneau. She made us read to her the whole of an article prepared for the "Correspondant" on Sister Rosalie and M. de Melun. It was the last reading she ever heard.

All that evening, her unexpected interest in the reading,

23

and the presence of mind with which she followed it, inspired Father Lacordaire with a confidence which he had
been far from feeling until then. He had quitted Sorèze
in haste, on the first alarm about Mme. Swetchine, leaving
grave interests at stake. He now resolved to go back the
next morning with the expressed intention of returning at
an early day. On Wednesday, the 2d of September, he
came very early to say mass in the little chapel of the
Rue St. Dominique, had one more long and confidential
interview with Mme. Swetchine, and left by the train at
nine o'clock. She made no effort to detain him. She had
expressed no wish to have any one sent for. She blessed
the Lord for what he granted her; but that which he did
not send in the natural order of things, she did not allow
herself to desire.

I knew how fondly she loved Mme. de Sainte-Aulaire;
and I repeatedly mentioned her name in order to give
occasion for the utterance of a wish which I should immediately have transmitted. The affection was always expressed; the wish, never. One day, when M. de Langsdorf
was going into the country to see his mother-in-law, I was
more explicit than usual. Her reply was, "I hope that
she and I are both borne in the bosom of our God. There
we shall meet, and love for ever."

The Marquise de Lillers, who was eighty-nine years
old, came twice a day to inquire for her; sometimes she
went in, and sometimes, for fear of disturbing her, she
stopped in the little dining-room and shed tears, — very
affecting in one of her age. "Do you know," said
Mme. de Lillers to me on that day, "what was the last
word our dear and sainted friend addressed to me yesterday? I embraced her, and said I was going away to
pray for her. 'Thank you, my good friend,' said she,

' thank you ; but do not ask God for one day more or one pang less.' "

The nights of Wednesday the 2d and Thursday the 3d of September were more restless than any previous ones. The confusion of mind continued for a part of the morning, and was followed by utter prostration. For the first time, she spoke to me without entire possession of herself, and thought she saw some one sitting between us when we were quite alone. This alarmed me more than any other symptom. I sent for Dr. Rayer at six o'clock in the morning. Another physician came instead. Mme. Rayer had been taken suddenly and seriously ill. The physician ordered very painful remedies. They procured her some rest that night; but, on Friday morning, the suffocation increased, and drowsiness alternated with a species of delirium. She recognized those who approached her, with a smile, caressed affectionately with hand and eye her nephews and her niece, who lavished on her the most assiduous care ; but, beyond this, there was no precision or connection about her thoughts. Each hour we hoped to see Dr. Rayer return ; but it was his substitute who came at last, and told us Mme. Rayer was dead. We decided to conceal her death from Mme. Swetchine. It was very evident that the slightest emotion aggravated her condition in the most dangerous manner; and there could be no doubt as to how this would affect her. Only the day before, at our noonday interview, which she had never relinquished, she had given me a list of her friends' names, and said, "We must think of something special for each one : I want them all to feel that they have been the objects of no commonplace remembrance, but of a thoughtful and watchful gratitude." She was particularly anxious about Dr. Rayer. " I want a regular plot laid in his behalf," said she ; and this affectionate conspiracy was to have had Mme. Rayer for its chief accomplice. It is easy to see, therefore, how this death, in itself a great affliction, would have interfered with the carrying-out of one of her cherished thoughts.

Dissimulation was easy on that Friday of cruel memory. As the day wore on, her sufferings became greater and more apparent. Towards four o'clock, the suffocation assumed the form of actual convulsions. Our dear sufferer for the first time allowed us to place her in an arm-chair; but presently started up, with an agonized face, throwing aside all the clothing which weighed upon her chest, and uttering hoarse, distressing sounds, which seemed like the final struggle. M. de Melun, who had just arrived in Paris, saw her for the first time in this dreadful state. His despair augmented ours; and he did not hesitate to advise us to call in the curé of St. Thomas without a moment's delay. We sent for him at once, and also summoned the nearest physician. The Abbé Serres arrived first, and undertook the duty of administering extreme unction. He spoke to the agonized saint in the most affecting manner as a priest and a friend. At the sound of his voice, Mme. Swetchine seemed in some sort to triumph over death. She could no longer articulate distinctly, but her hand continued to give responsive signs. As the prayers continued, the effort of her soul's fervent piety became more and more evident. At the close of the litanies, she succeeded in pronouncing almost distinctly the " Ora pro nobis ;" and the sobs, kept back till now by respect, burst forth involuntarily, when, the venerable curé having pronounced the words " for all eternity," the dying lady, collecting by a sensible effort all her strength and all her faith, added, in a voice hollow, stifled, yet full of courage, " Yes, for all eternity." Her servants and the porters had followed the Abbé Serres when he entered the apartment with the holy viaticum. The doors were left open; it was precisely the hour when she used to receive ; friends came in one by one, dropped on their knees, and burst into tears. Albert de Broglie had arrived almost simultaneously with M. de Melun, and quite as unexpectedly. They were soon followed by Mme. Frédro, Mme. Craven, Mme. de Meyendorf, Mlle. Rostopchin, M. de Bois-le-Comte, M. Yermolof, Father Gargarin, and, finally, Father Chocarn, Superior of the Dominicans at Paris. When the administration of the last sacrament was concluded, the Abbé Serres begged Mme. Swetchine to bless the assistants and their families. She made a sign that she blessed and prayed for them with all her heart. The Abbé then beckoned Father Chocarn, named him to her, and said, " Will you not bless, in his person, his house, and Father Lacordaire, and all the children of Saint Dominic ? " They then admitted the physician, who had been summoned at hazard. He made deep incisions in her legs, and drew off a great quantity of water.

The evening was one of the utmost prostration. Still, the suffocation sensibly diminished, and the effusion of water on the brain was arrested. She let them lay her on her little camp-bed, which was brought into the drawing-room ; and the night was comparatively quiet. On Saturday the improvement progressed. M. Andral came twice. At each visit, she begged earnestly for news of M. Rayer, Mme. Rayer, and their daughter. " Those three are so happy together," said she ; " they are inseparable." For the first time, M. Andral perceived evident symptoms of mortification about her legs; but her intellect was clear again, and had all its own peculiar characteristics. Saturday morning, she said to me, " Yesterday is a blank tablet

for me. I can recall nothing of those twenty-four hours.
Even this morning, I have only fractions of ideas." In
the afternoon, she admitted M. Yermolof, who said to her,
" Do you know that you received extreme unction yesterday ? " She replied very calmly, " I did not know it: why
did they not tell me sooner ? "

M. de Melun had come early, and she had begged him
to bring his wife, whom she did not know. She received
her with the simplest and warmest marks of affection.
But we soon began to dread the suffering which protracted interviews always induced ; and I offered to give to
Mme. de Melun the details which she had asked of the
invalid herself. Mme. de Melun was astonished to perceive no trace of illness, and to hear not a single complaint. She was told that it was always so ; and that
those who had been with the dear sufferer, day and night,
had not yet detected a groan. One of us added, " When
we realize all she endures, we cannot understand how
she does it."—"It is because I am content: that is
the extent of my cunning," replied Mme. Swetchine,
with an accent of the most simple and unaffected gayety.
M. de Melun said to her, "I shall come back alone
presently." Mme. Swetchine turned to Mme. de Melun,
and said, " How like a husband he already talks ! But,
you see, it is no arrangement of mine." Mme. de Melun
answered, that she thought her husband was quite right,
and that two people would fatigue her more than one.
" Ah, well!" said Mme. Swetchine, "if I have any thing
sad to say, I shall take him alone; but, if it is any thing
affectionate, you shall both share it."

That evening, towards seven o'clock, she had her easy-
chair moved near the open window. She appeared to
enjoy the beauty of the evening, the purity of the air, and

the smiling view of terrace and garden. "If," she said to me, "it were God's will, I should still enjoy life; but, if he deigns to call me to himself, how can I have any other feeling but gratitude?"—"Yes," said I: "I remember to have heard you say, that resignation is not enough."—"Resignation," she answered, "is still something distinct from God's will. It differs from it, as union differs from unity. Union implies two; unity, only one: and this is the way it ought to be with our will and God's." And then she spoke of herself, a thing of very rare occurrence. "For many years," said she, "my real, and, I might almost say, my only trouble, has been when I have not known or have failed to comprehend God's will in regard to me. However, I have all trust in his mercy; and, in my present state, trust seems my only means of glorifying him." Then, recurring to the death of her nephew, Theophilus, over which I had seen her weep bitterly some years before, she once more burst into tears, as if the blow had just fallen upon her. "My grief was inconsolable," said she, "because I thought God had forsaken me."

Just then, the Prince and Princess Eugene Gargarin came in with their children. Their two little boys, the one aged about twelve or thirteen, the other ten or eleven, were always great favorites with her. On their arrival at Paris, they had spoken of two young Greeks, with whom they had made friends on the voyage; but the Greek family had stopped at Marseilles. "When your young friends come to Paris," Mme. Swetchine said to her grandnephews, "tell me, and I will have you all come and play on my terrace." The little Greeks came; the children told their aunt; but it happened to be one of her most distressed days, and she made no reply. This evening, when she saw them come in, she said, "You think, perhaps, that I have forgotten about your party on the terrace. Not at all. I have thought of it, though I said nothing. It shall be Monday,—the day after to-morrow,—if you wish it: the only question is, whether I myself shall be in Paris on Monday."

Father de Pontlevoi, her usual confessor, was absent, and his place was supplied by Father Soimier. She made arrangements to receive the communion on Sunday morning. M. and Mme. Cochin, and Mme. de la Ferrière, whom she had not yet seen, were present at the service; and she welcomed them warmly. In the afternoon, the Duchess de la Rouchefoucauld arrived from Roche-Guyon. She saw her for a moment, and then made her go away, while they bathed her legs, where she noted the progress of the mortification calmly, as she did every other symptom. At four o'clock, she was carried to her sofa, and then recalled the Duchess de la Rouchefoucauld and Mlle. de Pomaret. I went out for a few moments; and, when I came back, Mme. de la Rouchefoucauld and Mlle. de Pomaret were chatting near her sofa. The name of St. Andral had recalled that of M. Royer-Collard. Mme. Swetchine, who had a great affection for M. Royer-Collard, kept up the conversation. They had just been speaking of the Revolution of July, and of the address of the two hundred and twenty-one. Mlle. de Pomaret related, that when M. Royer-Collard voted for the address, and assisted in drawing it up, he only intended to give Charles X., whom he professed to love and respect, an opportunity to draw back with honor, and re-enter the path of possible prosperity for France and Europe generally. "That reminds me," said the Duchess de la Rouchefoucauld, "of the gentleman who once promised you that he would study the happiness of his wife. Your reply was, ' Content yourself with not preventing it.'" They also conversed with interest and animation about Mme. de Goutaut, and the marriage of her grand-daughter with M. de Cossé.

Shortly after dinner, M. Andral came, and proceeded, as usual, to examine her legs. He came out better pleased. The gangrene seemed to have disappeared. " There is," said he, " a rallying of the vital forces which amazes me." At these words, we could not repress an emotion of un-hoped-for joy. The evening did not belie these happy prognostics. Mme. Swetchine spoke less freely than during the day, but continued to testify the same affectionate interest in all who approached her. She still preserved her gentle gayety, and those happy turns of expression, even about common things, for which she was remarkable. She said to Mme. de Craven, speaking of the more com-fortable arm-chair which she had accepted a day or two before, and which belonged to her maid, " You must know, my dear Pauline, that I am just beginning to appreciate an easy-chair, and that I have lived to this hour without suspecting what comfort really is. How much involuntary maceration," she added, with a smile, " I have imposed upon those who have been coming to see me for so many years, and sitting on hard chairs, with wooden arms!" M. Andral had advised her to eat as much as possible; and, when he went out, she said to Mme. Craven, " Now, I must rack my memory, and summon all my gastronomic science, in order to compose a bill of fare which will please the doctor."

Evening came, and she continued better. She received M. and Mme. Cochin, and detained them after they would have left; and, for the first time, we separated, and went to rest with something like hope. In the morning, when

I returned to her house, my first impression was one of sorrowful surprise. She had had her bed taken into the drawing-room, and received me lying down. I asked her if she had had a bad night. "No," she said; "but I assure you, that better or worse signifies nothing. It is all one to me. I have a vague feeling, that there is perhaps more life in me than people imagine; but, on the other hand, I feel as if I might be in the presence of God in a very few hours." These words, coming directly upon the hopes of the evening, filled me with inexpressible sadness. The accent of her voice, the pressure of her hand, her attitude, all assured me that the encouraging word was spoken for our support, but that she herself was perfectly convinced that her end was very near. I had great difficulty in controlling my emotion. I could not quite conceal it; but I told her, that, at least, I could thank God for having allowed me to be with her at this season. " I was going to say what may sound a little strange," she replied; "but, my friend, I believe you; and I may add that you are right. We must always be grateful when God shows us the truth; and, believe me, the truth is here." She uttered these words with a kind of gentle solemnity, that was full of unction, indicating her bed at the same time with a gesture which said plainly, " It is the bed of death." She then resumed calmly: " We must now make the most of these few moments. You may think it incredible, that any shadow of human regard should cross my soul in this hour; but I am anxious to speak my husband's name to you once more. It may be that he never had justice done him. He was always good to me, and God knows that I have never been consoled for his loss."

It was then that she spoke of her papers. I dared not

question her directly about her intentions, for fear of her imposing upon me some prohibition or absolute condition. She did not, however, appear very anxious on the subject, but passed rapidly from what concerned her personally to the correspondence of Father Lacordaire. I had often heard her say, " Father Lacordaire will never be known aright till after the publication of these letters." She re-affirmed this opinion with the greatest distinctness, and insisted on it strongly. Her little bed was hardly raised a foot above the floor. I was on my knees on the carpet, bending over, that I might hear her better. " Go," said she, " and open the *étagère* in the corner of the room, and bring me a bound volume, which you will find in a box." I found and brought it. It was the life of Saint Dominic, all in the handwriting of Father Lacordaire. Her eyes rested on it with evident affection, but without emotion or tears. She then replaced the manuscript in my hands, and said, " Please read me the letter on the first page." I read that dedication, so full of filial attachment. When I came to this sentence, " I wish that some one of your descendants may one day know that his ancestress was a woman whom St. Jerome would have loved as he loved Paul and Marcellus, — one who needed only a pen illustrious and saintly enough to do her justice," — she interrupted me, and said, " That sentence is disagreeable and absurd as applied to me ; " then, after a short pause, she added, " but, where I am going, praise and blame will be alike."

When I had finished reading Father Lacordaire's letter, and we had exchanged a few more words, she made me ring for Cloppet, told him where to find all her corre-spondence with Father Lacordaire, had it brought her, and placed it in my hands, together with the manuscript,

begging me to take them home with me that very day.
It was easy to see that this was her most cherished care,
and that she would not expose this deposit to the chances
or the misunderstandings which she accepted so readily for
herself. She had designed for the Duchess of Hamilton
a little portable silver basin for holy-water. " Let me
show you," said she, " how to use it ; and then, after my
death, you can explain it to the Princess Mary." And
she gave me the most minute instructions, with unutterable
serenity, holding the little font in her hand. She spoke
with the same affection of the Princess Wittgenstein,
daughter of Prince Bariatinsky, whose name was linked
with the studies and resolves which issued in her conversion. At last she said, " There, I am very tired. We
will not talk of business any more to-day, but to-morrow
we will begin here."

I went into the library ; and there I found several friends,
who, like me, had come in full of hope, and to whom I
communicated my alarm. Still no apparent aggravation
had supervened ; and we tried to re-assure one another,
until the hour for M. Andral's visit. I stood behind the
curtain while he examined her legs. Large blue spots
had re-appeared, and there was erysipelas about the knee.
M. Andral's face was very grave. I was meaning to
follow him when he went out ; but Mme. Swetchine caught
sight of me, and said, in a beseeching tone, " Alfred, I beg
of you to follow M. Andral : I see that they are deceiving
me about Mme. Rayer. Ascertain the truth, and tell me,
I conjure you." Alas ! I did not need to ask M. Andral.

However, I had confidently expected her to say something of the kind. The two first times M. Andral came,
she inquired, first of all, for Mme. Rayer. Sunday evening, she did not mention her ; and I said to Cloppet,

"Depend upon it, she has not forgotten her. She only wants to spare us the equivocations which she detects. How many times I have seen her do so!" On Monday, she would still have concealed her anxiety; but our prolonged silence was more than she could bear. My first impulse was to go at once for Dr. Rayer himself. M. de Melun dissuaded me. We knew the despairing grief into which the doctor and his only daughter were plunged by their sudden loss, and M. de Melun thought my direct appeal would be indiscreet. I confined myself to sending a verbal message by a third person; and M. Rayer replied, that he would come to-morrow (Tuesday), at nine o'clock.

I waited for him in the dining-room. He was choked by sobs. He opened the window, and hid his face for some time without speaking. At last he said, "This morning, I had no courage to keep my word; but my daughter said to me, 'If my mother were alive, she would entreat you to go:' so I came." I could but respect and admire the devotion of the physician and friend, and the deep attachment which our dear sufferer inspired in all who approached her. I hastened, as soon as possible, to interest science, and call it to our aid. I described to Dr. Rayer the symptoms of the preceding night, which had been very serious. Ordinarily she had her windows kept open till late in the evening; but this night she had complained of cold. At one o'clock, a chill had seized her. She made them light a large fire, and keep her wrapped in heated coverings till four o'clock in the morning. The doctor had told me, that he, too, wished to spare Mme. Swetchine the shock of Mme. Rayer's death. He entered, and extended his hand to her with a smile. "How is Mme. Rayer?" was Mme. Swetchine's first word. "Madame, it was she who sent me here," he said, in a tone which those who heard it will never forget. "You need not have left her," replied Mme. Swetchine, with an affection worthy of her friend's sacrifice; "you ought not to have quitted one whom you may yet save, for me, who am past help." M. Rayer continued for about twenty minutes to make the most minute inquiries about the measures which had been adopted in his absence; but, when he came out, he did not conceal from the Princess Gargarin that all hope was gone.

That Tuesday was a painful day; but we had no immediate alarm. The drowsiness and prostration were continual. People came into her room, and sat down by her bed; but she did not seem to notice them. Yet the voice of her niece, and her nephews' kissing her hand, called forth a few words of unfailing affection. She said to Mme. Craven, "The suffocation makes my voice so harsh, that I seem to be grumbling in spite of myself." And to her maid she said, "When I strain my voice, you must not think that I am impatient; but I find they cannot hear me." Indeed, it became more and more difficult to catch her words. She did not leave her bed after Monday, but remained there in a sitting posture, with her head either bent forward, or resting against an upright pillow, on the left side of the bed.

Yet there was no disorder in her drawing-room; not an article of furniture out of place, no apparatus of sickness, not even a table, with a glass or a phial. When she wanted to drink, she either had us ring for Cloppet or Mme. Henri, or made sign to Parisse, who, far or near, kept her eyes constantly fixed on her mistress. Her little bed, in the middle of the drawing-room, seemed as if it had been placed there for her repose during a trifling and temporary indisposition. She would not permit the betrayal of grief by any external paraphernalia, any more than by a murmur or a sigh.

Sunday and Monday, they had carried her in an easy-chair into the chapel, and she had partaken of the communion there. On one of those days, she went, long before the usual hour; and Mme. d'Esgrigny entered, and took her station in the doorway, without Mme. Swetchine's noticing her. She thought she was alone, and prayed aloud, often interrupting her prayer by words and gestures of gratitude to God, full of the most ardent love. On Monday, she remained for some minutes alone with Father Soimier. Every evening, the curé of St. Thomas came to see her, and made arrangements about the next morning's mass. On Tuesday evening, Sept. 8, she requested mass for Wednesday, at half-past seven. The curé promised her; but we were convinced that she could not bear being carried in her easy-chair to the chapel. We remained later than usual in the library,—coming and going between that and the drawing-room,—exchanging our mutual comments and observations. But as the hours wore away quietly, and the chill of the night before did not come on, we separated.

On the morrow, judge of my surprise at receiving, when I awoke, the following little note, in handwriting that trembled slightly in the three first lines, but was otherwise perfectly steady :—

My very dear Alfred, — I beg you to finish the paper you have in hand. I have strong hopes that we can at least continue it to-day. Between eleven and twelve o'clock, I hope to have a moment when I can summon you. How I have taxed you! but it will all be reckoned. It will help to win you heaven, heaven, heaven! I can answer for it.

Wednesday, 9th.

At first, I could not believe my eyes. I flattered myself

for a moment with the belief in a new miracle of her vital energy, or, rather, of divine mercy; but I soon began to fear that it was but the last and crowning pledge of her maternal tenderness. Alas! my fears were only too well grounded.

I hastened to her. She was dressed, and sitting in her own chair, near her writing-desk. She had asked for M. des Essarts, her man of business, and was counting the moments with a kind of impatience. He was later than she expected. When I announced him, she said, "It is too late now. The right moment is passed; perhaps it will not return. But beg him to wait." She then repeated, that the generosity and delicacy of her nephews relieved her of all anxiety, and asked to be carried back to bed. When she had lain down, I returned to her bedside. Her mind wandered a little. At the end of a quarter of an hour, she told me to bring in M. des Essarts. I obeyed; but, when she attempted to talk with him, she could not collect her ideas. She thought people were coming to take away her papers and furniture. We vainly tried to convince her of the contrary. I then said, pressing both her hands, "You know me, surely; you do not think I would deceive you. I give you my word, that this is all the effect of a little access of fever." She replied steadily, "You will not deceive me: you will only spare me. But I do not need to be spared: I only need the truth." She raised her voice, and added, with great energy, "Yes, the truth! I would rather have a hospital-bed with that, than all the luxury in the world without it!" So you see, my friend, that even her delirium had a grandeur of accent which many a sage has never attained.

The agitation and fever continued all the afternoon; yet

she still recognized Dr. Rayer. Towards night, she became suddenly calm. At nine o'clock, she asked for Father Soimier. We suggested, that it was very late to send for him, and proposed to bring in the Abbé Serres, who was in the library. She assented. She could no longer raise her head: but, when she heard him approach her bed, she asked him to grant her absolution once more; and, when she had received it, with the most unmistakable signs of piety and faith she asked if she could partake of the communion the next morning, and fixed on seven o'clock as the hour for mass. At ten o'clock, all was still about her. From time to time, we heard, "My God, have mercy on me!" or some other broken words of prayer. At midnight, she counted the strokes of the clock. After that, she several times asked the hour. At half-past five, she said, "It will soon be time for mass. They must raise me." A few moments later, without another word, or sign of suffering, she was in the bosom of her God. A. DE FALLOUX.

CARADEUC, Sept. 22, 1857.

THE END.

24

No. 143 Washington Street, *Boston,*
Autumn of 1867.

MESSRS. ROBERTS BROTHERS'
List of Publications.

———◆———

SUPERBLY ILLUSTRATED EDITIONS.

A ROUND OF DAYS. Described in Forty Original Poems by some of our most celebrated poets, and in Seventy Pictures by eminent artists.

One volume, quarto. Cloth, elegant	$10.00.
" " Morocco	15.00.

THE PARABLES OF OUR LORD. With illustrations from designs by J. E. MILLAIS, R. A.

One volume, quarto. Cloth, elegant	$10.00.
" " Morocco	15.00.

THE ADVENTURES OF DON QUIXOTE DE LA MANCHA. With one hundred illustrations by A. B. HOUGHTON.

One volume, small quarto. Cloth, elegant . . .	$8.00.
" " Morocco	12.00.

This is a most beautiful edition, equally well adapted for the library or the drawing-room table.

SCHILLER'S LAY OF THE BELL. Translated by BULWER. The designs by MORITZ RETZSCH.

One volume, oblong quarto. Cloth, elegant. . .	$7.50.
" " Morocco. . . .	12.00.

GUSTAVE DORÉ. Two Hundred Sketches, Humorous and Grotesque. By GUSTAVE DORÉ.

One volume, quarto. Half cloth . . . Price,	$3.75.

"As a grotesque designer he has no living rival."— *London Athenæum.*

GRISET'S GROTESQUES; or, Jokes Drawn on Wood. With Rhymes by TOM HOOD. One hundred quaint designs by ERNEST GRISET.

One volume, small quarto. Cloth, bevelled and illuminated. Price, $3.75.

AN OLD FAIRY TALE TOLD ANEW. By RICHARD DOYLE and J. R. PLANCHÉ.

One volume, small quarto. Cloth, elegant. Price, $3.00.

1

Jean Ingelow's Writings.

"Except Mrs. Browning, Jean Ingelow is first among the women whom the world calls poets." — *The Independent.*

"Miss Ingelow's new volume exhibits abundant evidence that time, study, and devotion to her vocation have both elevated and mellowed the powers of the most gifted poetess we possess, now that Elizabeth Barrett Browning and Adelaide Procter sing no more on earth. Lincolnshire has claims to be considered the Arcadia of England at present, having given birth both to Mr. Tennyson and our present Lady Laureate." — *London Morning Star.*

"We have read and reread, always with a better and softer heart. . . . . We wish everybody loved Jean Ingelow's writings, or, rather, that everybody would read them, for their admiration would follow." — *Providence Post.*

POEMS. Illustrated Edition, with One Hundred Pictures from Drawings by the first Artists in England. In one quarto volume, bound in cloth, bevelled and gilt, price, $ 12.00 ; or in Morocco, price, $ 18.00.

"The book is certainly among the most beautiful of the holiday offerings The lovers of the poet will not tolerate even this slightly qualified praise, but pronounce it the *most* beautiful."

SONGS OF SEVEN. Illustrated Edition, small quarto, bound in cloth, gilt, price $5.00 ; or in Morocco, price $ 8.00.

"This work is an acknowledged triumph of typographic art, with its delicate creamy page and red-line border."

POEMS. The first volume.

A STORY OF DOOM, and Other Poems.

Both volumes, 16mo, cloth, gilt top, price $ 3.50 ; or separately, price $ 1.75 each.

Both volumes, 32mo, Blue and Gold Edition, price $ 3.00 ; or separately, price $ 1.50 each.

☞ *Mailed to any address, post-paid, on receipt of price, by the Publishers.*

STUDIES FOR STORIES. Comprising Five Stories, with an Illustration to each Story. In one vol. 16mo. Price, $ 1.50.

"Simple in style, warm with human affection, and written in faultless English, these five stories are studies for the artist, sermons for the thoughtful, and . rare source of delight for all who can find pleasure in really good works of ırose fiction. . . . They are prose poems, carefully meditated, and exquisitely ouched in by a teacher ready to sympathize with every joy and sorrow." — *Athenæum.*

STORIES TOLD TO A CHILD. Comprising Fourteen Stories, with an Illustration to each Story. In one vol. 16mo. Price, $ 1.75.

A cheaper edition, with Five Illustrations. Price, $ 1.25.

"This is one of the most charming juvenile books ever laid on our table. It is beautifully printed and bound, and profusely illustrated. The stories are very interesting, and breathe a sweet, pure, happy Christian spirit. Jean In‌gelow, the noble English poet, second only to Mrs. Browning, bends easily and gracefully from the heights of thought and fine imagination to commune with the minds and hearts of children; to sympathize with their little joys and sorrows; to feel for their temptations. She is a safe guide for the little pilgrims; for her paths, though 'paths of pleasantness,' lead straight upward." — *Grace Greenwood in " The Little Pilgrim."*

POOR MATT; OR, THE CLOUDED INTELLECT. With an Illustration. One vol. 18mo. Price, 60 cents.

"A lovely story, told in most sweet and simple language. There is a deep spiritual significance in the character of the poor half-idiot boy, which should touch the hearts of 'children of a larger growth.'" — *Grace Greenwood in " The Little Pilgrim."*

Mailed to any address, post-paid, on receipt of the price, by the Publishers,

ROBERTS BROTHERS, Boston.

ECCE HOMO. A Survey of the Life and Work of Jesus Christ. In one volume, 16mo. Price, $1.50.

" It will do a service among a very large class of readers, such as are assigned to hardly more than two or three volumes in a century." — *Rev. George E. Ellis.*

"This remarkable book is one of those which permanently influence public opinion. The author has a right to claim deference from those who think deepest and know most, when he pleads before them that not Philosophy can save and reclaim the world, but Faith in a Divine Person who is worthy of it, allegiance to a Divine Society which He founded, and union of hearts in the object for which He created it." — *The Guardian.*

ECCE DEUS : Essays on the Life and Doctrine of Jesus Christ. With Controversial Notes on Ecce Homo. In one volume, to match Ecce Homo. Price, $1.50.

" We believe that many of the most grateful and consenting readers of ' Ecce Homo' will also be the most admiring readers of ' Ecce Deus.' In the main tenor of both the volumes there is nothing to our minds inconsistent. . . . . There are large numbers of liberal minds to which the new book will be a most welcome and helpful volume." — *Boston Transcript.*

" ' Ecce Deus ' leaves ' Ecce Homo ' far behind, and casts a shade over it, as it rises to the higher and grander theme of the Incarnation. We are sorry we cannot enter into the merits of this work, but we advise our readers to peruse it along with ' Ecce Homo,' and they will be satisfied of the important part its author plays as a vindicator of ' the Truth as it is in Jesus.' " — *Scottish American Journal.*

THE SEER; or, Common Places Refreshed. By LEIGH HUNT. In two volumes, 16mo. Price, $3.00.

" A collection of delicious essays, thoroughly imbued with the characteristics of the writer's genius and manner, and on topics especially calculated to bring out all the charms of his genial spirit and develop all the niceties of his fluent diction, and worthy of being domesticated among those choice family books which while away leisure hours with agreeable thoughts and fancies." — *Boston Transcript.*

" The ' Seer ' is one of the best specimens of the modern essayist's dealing with the minor pleasures and domestic philosophy of life, and is a capital antidote for the too exciting books of the hour ; it lures us to musing, and what Hazlitt calls ' reposing on our sensations.' " — *H. T. Tuckerman.*

THE LIFE AND DEATH OF JASON. A Poem. By WILLIAM MORRIS. One volume, 16mo. Price, $1.50.

" In all the noble roll of our poets there has been since Chaucer no second teller of tales, no second rhapsode comparable to the first, till the advent of this one." — *A. C. Swinburne.*

" A poem remarkable for originality, freshness, and vividness of description, and beauty and force of narration." — *London Review.*

" In his style he exercises upon us the spells of the accomplished story-teller." — *Pall Mall Gazette.*

Mailed, post-paid, to any address, on receipt of the price, by the Publishers.

CHRISTINA ROSSETTI'S POEMS. With Four Designs by D. G. ROSSETTI. One elegant 16mo volume. Price, $1.75.

"Two of the best of the younger poets of this generation are women — Jean Ingelow and Christina Rossetti. . . . The woman who could write the 'Songs of Seven,' and 'The High Tide on the Coast of Lincolnshire,' need not look to future successes for applause; and there are many poems in this beautiful volume by Miss Rossetti which entitle her to a high place among the poets of the day." — *John G. Saxe.*

THE BOOK OF THE SONNET. By LEIGH HUNT and S. ADAMS LEE. A Posthumous Work by Hunt, *now first published from the original MSS.* In two beautiful post 8vo volumes. Price, $5.00.

"The genuine aroma of literature abounds in every page of Leigh Hunt's delicious Essay on the Sonnet. His mind shows itself imbued with a rich knowledge of his subject, and this, illumined by the evidence of a thorough and unaffected liking for it, makes him irresistible." — *London Saturday Review.*

ROBERT BUCHANAN'S POEMS. In one volume. 16mo. Cloth, gilt top. Price, $1.75.

"The volume is the work of a born poet. Let any one read the first and last poems in the collection, and he will not fail to read every line which intervenes between them. 'Langley Lane' is one of the tenderest, sweetest, most musical, and most original love-poems in the language." — *Boston Transcript.*

CHARLES LAMB. A Memoir. By BARRY CORNWALL. One volume, 16mo, with Profile Portrait of Lamb. Price, $1.75.

"We advise all young readers to approach Elia and Lamb's Life and Letters through this soft and exquisite prelude of Barry Cornwall's. . . . . Closing the book, and remembering that its writer is seventy-seven years old, and the sole survivor of those evenings which are as familiar to the lovers of Elia as if they had been themselves present, it lingers in the memory like a strain of the saddest and sweetest music." — *Harper's Monthly.*

THE GENIUS OF SOLITUDE. By REV. WM. R. ALGER, Author of "The Doctrine of a Future Life." One volume, 12mo. Price, $2.00.

"Mr. Alger's *Genius of Solitude* is the work of a scholar, of a man who has written critically and comprehensively on Oriental poetry, and on a branch of speculative psychology. It is, moreover, a book intended to have a practical effect — to teach men to dislike what is bad, and to admire and love what is good." — *London Chronicle.*

☞ *Mailed, post-paid, to any address, on receipt of the price, by the Publishers.*

MEMOIRS AND CORRESPONDENCE OF MADAME RECAMIER. Translated and Edited by MISS LUYSTER. One Volume, 12mo, with a finely engraved Portrait. Price, $2.00.

"The diversified contents of this volume can hardly fail to gain for it a wide perusal. It has the interest, in a greater or less degree, of history and romance ; of truth stranger than fiction ; of personal sketches ; of the curious phases of an exceptional social life ; of singular admixtures of piety and folly, of greatness and profligacy, fidelity and intrigue, all mingling or revealed in connection with the prolonged career of one who was, in certain respects, the most remarkable woman of her time." — *Boston Transcript.*

A PAINTER'S CAMP. Book I.: In England. Book II.: In Scotland. Book III.: In France. By PHILIP GILBERT HAMERTON. In one volume. 16mo. Pictorial title. Price, $1.50.

"In the pursuit of his profession as a landscape-painter, the author has not hesitated to plunge into the remote and unattractive nooks and corners of nature, gathering a rich store of materials for his pencil, and describing his whimsical experiences with a gayety and unction in perfect keeping with the subject. His account of the practical methods by which he conquered the difficulties of the position is instructive in the extreme, while the anecdotes and adventures which he relates with such exuberant fun make his book one of the most entertaining of the season." — *New York Tribune.*

CURIOUS MYTHS OF THE MIDDLE AGES. By S. BARING-GOULD. In one volume, 16mo. With Illustrations. Price, $1.50.

"A singular book, and a very interesting one to those who are fond of exploring the dark corners of literature and life, is ' Curious Myths of The Middle Ages,' by S. Baring-Gould, M. A. It treats of The Wandering Jew ; Prester John ; The Divining Rod ; The Seven Sleepers of Ephesus ; William Tell ; The Dog Gellert ; Tailed Men ; Antichrist and Pope Joan ; The Man in the Moon ; The Mountain of Venus ; Fatality of Numbers ; The Terrestrial Paradise ; bringing together many quaint and fanciful legends, exposing the fallacy of some popular beliefs, and suggesting topics for thought and investigation as to various psychological problems." — *Springfield Republican.*

SUNSHINE AND SHOWERS : Their Influences throughout Creation. A Compendium of Popular Meteorology. By ANDREW STEINMITZ, ESQ. The English Edition. One volume, post 8vo. With Illustrations. Price, $3.00.

"We have received from Roberts Brothers a delightful volume, published by Reeve & Co., London, entitled ' Sunshine and Showers : their Influences throughout Creation : by Andrew Steinmitz.' It is a compendium of popular meteorology. As a large portion of the conversation of human beings relates to the weather, we should judge that a book which enables one to talk intelligently about it would have an extensive circulation. It treats, in an intelligible way, of the arrangement of the atmosphere, the moisture in the air, the characteristics and meteorology of the seasons, the method of interpreting the barometer and the thermometer, the prediction of the weather and the explanation of popular weather prognostics, the curiosities of lightning, artificial rain, &c. ; and it answers the questions, ' What Becomes of the Sunshine?' and ' What Becomes of the Showers?' The science relating to all topics connected with the weather seems to have been mastered by the writer, and his volume is therefore full of surprising facts and ingenious theories." — *Boston Transcript.*

☞ *Mailed, post-paid, to any address, on receipt of the price, by the Publishers.*

SHAKESPEARE. The Globe Edition. With all the Poems and a Glossary. In one volume, 16mo. Price, $2.00.

For a one-volume edition, this is the most attractive now before the public. The typography is beautifully clear, the paper fine and good, and the whole well calculated to suit the student or the general reader

SHAKESPEARE. The Handy-Volume Edition. With all the Poems and a Glossary. In 13 volumes, 32mo. Bound in limp cloth, red edges, with a neat cloth case. Price, $12.00.

The present edition is intended, in respect to its appearance and size, — a clear, beautiful type, and a page free from notes, — to form a handy, readable series of volumes, equally adapted for the Pocket, the Knapsack, and the Railway.

THE POETRY OF THE ORIENT. By WILLIAM ROUNSEVILLE ALGER. In one volume, 16mo. Price, $1.75.

This is a complete Introduction to Oriental Poetry in all its families and departments; from the great epics of India, Persia, and Arabia, to their innumerable varieties of lyrical, descriptive, and aphoristic verse. It gives a critical account of the chief Eastern authors and their works, and illustrates them by hundreds of specimens. It is the only work of the kind in our language; and as such, no less than from its intrinsic merits, it possesses a unique value and charm.

POEMS. By DAVID GRAY. With an Introductory Notice by Lord Houghton, Memoir of the Author, and Final Memorials. One volume, 16mo. Price, $1 50.

"His heart and life are mirrored in these poems, and how pathetic is the picture! How the ardent soul, yearning for fame and life, shrinks and shudders as it sees death steadily approaching; how it clings to the dear dreams of youth; how earnestly it strives for resignation and faith, and seeks to make the life beyond the grave as real and tangible as this, which the falling frame feels in its veins! To this identity of the poems with the poet, to this clear showing of the inner man, the book before us owes, perhaps, its deepest and most touching charms." — *Boston Daily Advertiser.*

Mailed, post-paid, to any address, on receipt of the price, by the Publishers.

7

A THOUSAND MILES IN THE ROB ROY
CANOE, or Rivers and Lakes of Europe. By JOHN MAC-
GREGOR, M. A. Fifth Edition. With a Map and numerous
Illustrations. One volume, 16mo. Price, $ 2.50.

THE ROB ROY ON THE BALTIC; The Narra-
tive of the Rob Roy Canoe, on Lakes and Rivers of Sweden,
Denmark, Norway, and on the Baltic and North Seas. By
JOHN MACGREGOR, Trin. Coll., Cambridge; Author of " A
Thousand Miles in the Rob Roy Canoe." With numerous
Illustrations. One volume, 16mo. Price, $ 2.50.

"We recommend Mr. Macgregor's book as a pleasant record of a very remarkable feat in the annals of travelling." — *Athenæum.*

DRAMAS AND POEMS. By BULWER LYTTON. Con-
taining " The Lady of Lyons," " Richelieu," and " Money,"
and Minor Poems. With a fine Portrait on Steel. One volume, 32mo. Blue and Gold. Price, $ 1.25.

" No living English writer is more read on the continent of Europe than Bulwer. His works have been translated into nearly all the living languages of
Europe." — *New American Cyclopædia.*

POEMS. By CHARLES SWAIN. With a fine Portrait from a
recent photograph. One volume, 32mo. Blue and Gold.
Price, $ 1.25.

" Many of his songs have been wafted by their own aerial sweetness across the
sea ; and his felicitous description of Scott's funeral (Dryburgh Abbey), attended
by a procession of the romancer's immortal characters, is too graphic a tribute
to genius not to be recalled with delight." — *H. T. Tuckerman.*

HUDIBRAS. A Poem. By SAMUEL BUTLER. With
Notes, a Life of the Author, and Illustrations. In one volume, 32mo. Price, $ 1.25.

" The choicest of all editions for the reader or student."

☞ *Mailed, post-paid, to any address, on receipt of the price, by the
Publishers.*

8

MELANCHOLY ANATOMIZED; showing its Causes, Consequences, and Cure. With Anecdotic Illustrations. Chiefly founded on Burton's Anatomy of Melancholy. In one volume, 16mo. Price, $1.75.

THE PRACTICAL COOK-BOOK, and Economical Housekeeper's Guide. By Mrs. E. A. Howland. In one volume. 16mo. Price, 63 cts.

THE MODEL LETTER-WRITER, Containing Letters on Business, Friendship, Love, etc., to which are added Legal Forms, useful to every one. In one volume, 32mo. Price, 50 cents.

A POCKET ENGLISH DICTIONARY. By Dr. Johnson. One volume, 32mo. Price, 30 cents.

LIFE AND LETTERS OF MADAME SWET-CHINE. By Count de Falloux, of the French Academy. Translated by H. W. Preston, with an Introduction. In one volume. 12mo. Price, $2.00. (*In Press.*)

Madame Swetchine was a friend and cotemporary of Madame Récamier, and this is intended as a companion volume to that delightful book, being the second volume of Messrs. Roberts Brothers' Library of Exemplary Women.

THE LAYMAN'S BREVIARY. A Selection for every Day in the Year. Translated from the German of Leopold Schefer, by C. T. Brooks. In one square 16mo volume. (*In Press.*)

MY PRISONS. By Silvio Pellico. A new edition, with many beautiful Illustrations. One volume, 16mo. (*In Press.*)

THE FRIENDSHIPS OF WOMEN. By William Rounseville Alger, Author of "The Genius of Solitude." (*In Press.*)

☞ *Mailed, post-paid, to any address, on receipt of the price, by the Publishers.*

JUVENILES.

SWEET COUNSEL. A Book for Girls. By SARAH
TYTLER. 16mo. $2.25.

THE PIGEON PIE. A Tale of Roundhead Times. By
MISS YONGE. Illustrated. 16mo. $1.25.

HELEN AND HER COUSINS; or, Two Months at
Ashfield Rectory. Illustrated. 18mo. 50 cents.

THE TANNER BOY. A Life of General Grant. Illustrated. 16mo. $1.50.

GASCOYNE; The Sandal-Wood Trader. By BALLANTYNE.
Illustrated. 16mo. $ .50.

THE TIGER PRINCE: or, Adventures in the Wilds of
Abyssinia. By DALTON. Illustrated. 16mo. $1.50.

THE PRIVATEERSMAN. Adventures by Sea and
Land. By CAPTAIN MARRYATT. Illustrated. 16mo. $1.50.

SANDFORD AND MERTON. By THOMAS DAY.
Illustrated. Square 16mo. $1.25.

POPULAR FAIRY TALES. Containing the choicest
and best known Fairy Stories. Illustrated. 2 vols., square
16mo. Each, $1.25.

PAUL PRESTON'S VOYAGES, Travels, and Remarkable Adventures. Illustrated. Square 16mo. $1.25.

FIRESIDE TALES. In Prose and Verse. By MARY
HOWITT. Illustrated. 16mo. 75 cents.

THE SCOTTISH ORPHANS; and Arthur Monteith.
By MRS. BLACKFORD. Illustrated. 16mo. 75 cents.

☞ Mailed, post-paid, to any address, on receipt of the price, by the Publishers.

ALPHABETICAL LIST

OF

Messrs. Roberts Brothers' Publications.

Alger (Rev. W. R.). Poetry of the Orient. Page 7.
"   "   The Genius of Solitude. Page 6.
"   "   The Friendships of Women. Page 9.
A Round of Days. Page 1.
Buchanan (Robert). Poems. Page 6.
Butler (Samuel). Hudibras. Page 8.
Baring-Gould (S.). Curious Myths of the Middle Ages. Page 5.
Cornwall (Barry). Charles Lamb. A Memoir. Page 6.
Cervantes. The Adventures of Don Quixote. Page 1.
Doré (Gustave). Two Hundred Humorous Sketches. Page 1.
Doyle (Richard) and Planché. An Old Fairy Tale. Page 1.
Ecce Homo. Page 4.
Ecce Deus. Page 4.
Griset (Ernest). Grotesques. Page 1.
Gray (David). Poems. Page 7.
Hamerton (Philip G.). A Painter's Camp. Page 5.
Hunt (Leigh). The Seer. Page 4.
Hunt (Leigh and S. Adams Lee). The Book of the Sonnet. Page 6.
Heaven (The) Series. Page 10.
Howland (Mrs.). The Practical Cook Book. Page 9.
Ingelow's (Jean) Poetical Writings. Page 2.
Ingelow's (Jean) Prose Writings. Page 3.
Ingraham's (Rev. J. H.) Religious Writings. Page 10.
Johnson's (Dr.) Pocket English Dictionary. Page 9.
Juvenile Works. Page 11.
Lytton (E. Bulwer). Poems and Dramas. Page 8.
Morris (William). The Life and Death of Jason. Page 4.
Macgregor (John). A Thousand Miles in the Rob Roy Canoe. Page 3.
"   "   The Rob Roy on the Baltic. Page 8.
Melancholy Anatomized. Page 9.
Model (The) Letter Writer. Page 9.
Pellico (Silvio). My Prisons. Page 9.
Parables (The) of our Lord. Page 1.
Récamier (Madame). Memoirs and Correspondence. Page 5.
Rossetti (Christina G.). Poems. Page 6.
Shakespeare. The Globe Edit. The Handy-Volume Edit. Page 7.
Swain (Charles). Poems. Page 8.
Schefer (Leopold). The Layman's Breviary. Page 9.
Swetchine (Madame). Life and Letters. Page 9.
Steinmetz (Andrew). Sunshine and Showers. Page 5.
Schiller's Lay of the Bell, translated by Bulwer. Page 1.